WICKED AND FOREVER

SHAYLA BLACK

WICKED AND
FOREVER

TREES & LAILA: PART TWO
WICKED & DEVOTED

New York Times
Shayla
BLACK
Bestselling Author

SHAYLA BLACK
Steamy. Emotional. Forever.

WICKED AND FOREVER
Written by Shayla Black

This book is an original publication by Shayla Black.

Cover Design by: Rachel Connolly
Photographer: Wander Pedro Aguiar, WANDER AGUIAR :: PHOTOGRAPHY
Edited by: Amy Knupp of Blue Otter
Proofread by: Fedora Chen

ISBN: 978-1-936596-94-2

ABOUT WICKED AND FOREVER

He'll make her his again...even if he has to seduce her

When the woman he loves is taken, Forest "Trees" Scott abandons a mission to save her from the enemy. Fearing the worst, he moves heaven and earth to find her—until he realizes Laila Torres left him of her own free will for the man who used her for six years. He's stunned and wrecked. She played him—and he fell for it. One thing he's not doing? Giving up. He'll find her and he'll make her pay...in his bed.

Laila is devastated by her tormentor's return, but when he threatens the bodyguard she's so foolishly fallen for, she risks everything—including her life—to protect Trees. As a mere pawn in a deadly game played by factions of a cartel, she and Trees have no future unless she can somehow destroy them. But she doesn't count on Trees hunting her down, stripping her soul bare, and insisting in the sexiest way possible that she belongs to him and always will.

But danger awaits around every corner, and secrets abound. As Trees and Laila fight for their future, their enemies close in. Will they let go of their hurts and trust in their love before it's too late?

AUTHOR'S NOTE

Dear Reader,

If you have not read Wicked as Seduction, please STOP.

Wicked and Forever is the second half of a duet in the Wicked & Devoted series about tech expert Forest "Trees" Scott and gutsy Laila Torres. In order to fully understand and enjoy this book, you should first read part one of this duet, Wicked as Seduction.

I sincerely hope you enjoy the saga of these two characters I've come to love so deeply, which is why they required two full-length books to tell their whole story.

Happy reading!
Shayla

CHAPTER
One

F or Laila Torres, the day started out troubling. It ended in hell.

As dawn rose, her bodyguard and lover, Forest "Trees" Scott, prepared to join the rest of EM Security on a mission with one objective: to rescue his bosses' sister, who was being held captive by dangerous kingpin Geraldo Montilla. As he headed for the door, Trees lifted her against his tall, hard-muscled body and held her close. Reflexively, she wrapped her arms around his neck, her heart beating fast.

Last night, they had fought. Trees's bosses had proposed she act as bait to lure the narcotics king out of hiding and into a trap. She'd said yes. After all, her sister and her nephew—the only family she had—would never be safe until Montilla was gone. When Trees had refused to let her go, she'd tried to escape. He'd quickly caught her and dragged her back to his house. Then they had skipped sleep and spent the rest of the night electronically hunting their enemy. With the information he'd gleaned, Trees had devised a plan for him and his fellow operatives to nab the kingpin, one that didn't require her to be involved in Montilla's takedown at all.

Now, as he left to put himself in danger so she would be safe, she felt the desperation in his touch. It matched her own as she clung to him. "What are you doing?"

"Telling you I love you, Laila."

She froze. That shouldn't be possible. Yet…how many things had he done to help her, soothe her, and save her? Trees had always been fair and patient, kind yet gruff, but intensely protective. Would he have tried so hard if she didn't mean *something* to him?

Laila wasn't sure and didn't know what to say…but her first reaction was resounding joy. Her heart filled with it and threatened to overflow.

But could she give the words back to him? Had she searched her soul enough to be certain of her feelings?

"I know it's one-sided. I don't expect you to say anything. I just—" He shook his head, let out a curse, then seized her lips in a hard press as if he was determined to imprint himself on her. And he stole her breath.

Just as suddenly, he wrenched away, set her on her feet, and slammed out the door, leaving her gaping and already regretting the things she'd left unsaid.

With a final glance back at her through the living room window, he punched a few buttons on his phone. She heard the house alarms engage—his way of keeping her safe during the twelve hours he would be gone.

After he drove off, Laila roamed his place listlessly. She picked at breakfast. She turned on a telenovela…then turned the silly thing off. She paced, praying Trees would finish this mission unscathed. She showered, hoping the soothing water would help her decide what to say when he returned.

What was love? Did she really know? She felt something for him— a lot, actually. But love?

If that isn't what you feel, why do you have such angst?

It was a fair question. Was she capable of the kind of love Trees had given her? Or had she endured too much to love him the way he deserved? After all, if she allowed another person to be tattooed onto her heart, that gave her tormentor, Victor Ramos, another weapon to use against her, the way he had her family.

After wriggling into her pink tank and short shorts—and wishing for the hundredth time that she'd packed something warmer when she'd fled Florida—she towel-dried her curls, her thoughts turning.

Until an electronic peal shattered the silence.

The perimeter alarm.

She froze. Her heart started chugging. Was someone on the property? In the house?

Days ago, she'd told Trees safety was an illusion. Unfortunately, she'd been right.

Laila tossed her damp towel into the sink, then rushed down the hall to Trees's home office to scan his bank of security cameras. Her heart stuttered when she saw a sleek black truck with unreadable plates lunging up the road. That wasn't Trees. It wasn't his friend Zy. It wasn't one of their three bosses, either. She didn't know for sure who was barreling onto Trees's property uninvited, but he wasn't coming to borrow a cup of sugar or say hello.

Had she been discovered again? By the Tierra Caliente cartel or by Victor Ramos himself?

Either possibility sent panic burning through her. From her bedroom, she heard the ringing of her phone. Trees. He would already know that someone had broken past his security. Did she dare run back to grab the device?

She peeked out the living room window, to the front of the house. The black truck was rolling to a stop in front. She didn't have time to retrieve her phone.

She had to hide—now.

The ringing stopped, only to start again. Trees was panicked. She could practically feel him worrying as he pressed buttons, looked at his cameras, remotely tried to assess the situation and figure out how to save her when he was probably hundreds of miles away. She hated to worry him, but she had to shove regret aside for survival.

As she dashed through the kitchen, she caught sight of the intruder —a man in a ski mask stomping toward the door, gun in hand. Terror iced her veins. As she feared, this wasn't a simple burglar looking for jewelry or cool electronics he could fence. He was armed and furious.

Laila managed to crouch down before he caught sight of her, but the sudden blast of a gunshot, followed by the shattering of glass, had her shrieking involuntarily and clinging to whatever shadows she could find in the morning light.

As the man stepped through the wide-open window, Laila raced to Trees's bedroom, praying she hadn't been spotted, and eased the door shut behind her. She only had one possible hope of staying unharmed now.

Shaking from head to toe, she fought to catch her breath as she crept into Trees's closet and shoved aside his clothes. The keypad to his panic room and dungeon gleamed in the semi-dark. The code. She'd seen him punch it in. And she'd committed it to memory, just in case.

Since the safe house she'd shared with her sister and her nephew in St. Louis had been breached months ago, she'd plotted escape routes everywhere she went. The grocery store. The mall. The movies. And especially anywhere she slept.

But she'd felt so safe with Trees. Oh, he'd terrified her since he could make her body crave things that unsettled her and make her heart ache in ways that unraveled her. But he'd given her a sense of security—one she hadn't had for nearly a decade. She'd rationalized that no one would think to look for her in the middle of Nowhere, Louisiana, out on property that had every security precaution imaginable. So she had gotten complacent. She hadn't planned an escape route. Laila hadn't thought she would need one.

What a horrible time to realize she'd been wrong.

She stared at the keypad, dragging in ragged breaths that sounded way too loud in her ears, as her thoughts raced. She knew the damn code. Why couldn't she remember it?

Taking a minute—and a risk—Laila closed her eyes, forced her respiration to slow, and pictured Trees in front of his panel, punching in the numbers to his underground lair.

The digits swam though her head as another gunshot, this one inside the house, disturbed the air. She bit her lip to hold in a scream. Then she heard footsteps tromping through the place. She had to reach the panic room before the intruder found her.

Finally, she recalled the numbers and lifted her fingers to the buttons, but the whine of electronic devices signaled that the prowler had cut the power.

Oh, god. How would she access the panic room when the panel she needed to open the door was dead?

The worry had barely crossed her mind when electronic devices all over the house began to clink and chime on again. The panel in front of her lit up once more, and she almost cried with relief. Of course Trees would have a generator. In his hidden room, the man kept years' worth of freeze-dried and canned food. It stood to reason he was prepared for any eventuality, including power loss.

As the intruder's footsteps approached the bedroom, she quickly punched in the code with trembling fingers. A low, humming buzz warned her that her first fumbled attempt was wrong. Panic ratcheted up. She almost started hyperventilating. She forced herself to be calm and tried again.

Her finger pressed the last number as she heard the squeak of Trees's bedroom door open. Footsteps paused inside. The opening to the panic room appeared with a whisper. Relief swept over Laila as she squeezed through the crack, moved Trees's clothes to cover the panel again, and eased the door shut—just as the closet door jerked open.

Her hammering heart chugged as fast as her runaway thoughts. What if the intruder had heard her? Or saw Trees's clothes swinging on their hangers or...any of the other hundred things she could think that would tell him he wasn't alone in the house?

Seconds ticked by. With her hand pressed against her rattling chest, she stood frozen, not even daring to creep down the stairs. Since she couldn't risk turning on a light, she closed her eyes and tried to breathe through the suffocating darkness.

Finally, she heard a door slam and his stomping footsteps retreat to the kitchen, where he banged cabinets and broke glass. With every sound, Laila felt this man's rage, and she felt horrible for Trees. He wasn't here to defend his house. He'd likely moved away from the city to avoid crime and people, for privacy and peace.

That was all being defiled and defaced now, because of her.

The sounds crossed the house, getting fainter as he moved farther away, but no less violent. Then she heard more gunfire—multiple blasts. Whoever was above her clearly had an agenda. Destroying Trees's house wasn't enough for him. He wanted blood.

She couldn't let him have it.

Laila turned on the light in the bunker and crept to the bottom of the stairs. She looked past Trees's dungeon equipment—implements she didn't understand that had filled her with both trepidation and fear the first time she'd seen them. Today, she looked around for a way to call for help. But she'd had to abandon her phone across the house, and Trees had taken his iPad, so if there was any way to communicate with the outside world, she didn't know it.

Deep breaths. She could handle this. All she had to do for now was hide. Once whoever was out there had finished what he'd come for and left, she would emerge, call Trees, then stay to help him right his house. It was the very least she owed him.

She wished she could do more.

"Where are you, you motherfucking *cabrón?*"

Laila stopped—breathing, thinking, living. Abject terror gripped her throat. That voice… She couldn't mistake it for anyone else's.

Victor Ramos.

And he hadn't come for her. He'd come for Trees, to get revenge— the eye-for-an-eye kind.

"Are you hiding like a pussy? That won't stop me from avenging my brother. Come out and die like a man." Victor paused in the silence, then let loose a cutting laugh. "I'm not surprised you're hiding like a coward. You couldn't even face my brother to kill him. You shot him from the back. And you pulled the trigger for Laila. I heard you. Where have you stashed that *puta?*"

Her jaw dropped. Laila wasn't surprised that Victor had called her a whore, but how had he heard Trees say that he'd killed Hector for her? If he had been there, he would have saved his brother.

Only Hector's house having surveillance made sense.

As soon as that realization hit her, another truth swept in behind it. Victor didn't know she was here.

"Too afraid to face me, *cabrón?* Then I will burn down your house, and you better start looking over your shoulder, because I'm going to find you and put a bullet in your back, too."

Laila's heart stopped. One thing she knew about Victor? His follow-through skills weren't a problem. He meant what he said.

She had to stop him—now. Somehow. Find a way to protect Trees and his house while keeping Valeria and Jorge's location secret. If it kept her safe, too, even better. But that wasn't important. She had survived Victor once. She could do it again for the people she loved.

Laila froze. That was the second time she'd wondered if she was in love with Trees. Logic said it was too soon. She admired him. She respected him. She'd come to trust him. She melted against him when he gave her pleasure no other man had. She simply couldn't repay all his kindness by letting Victor destroy everything he'd worked for. But that wasn't love.

Or was it?

She didn't have time to figure that out now. The seconds were ticking down, and she had to stop the maniac pacing Trees's home, bent on torching it. Trees had put her first so many times. She needed to do the same for him. Laila knew just how. She simply had to find the right words—and the guts.

On shaking legs, she crossed the room and plucked a semiautomatic off the wall, then jerked down its mate, just in case. She rummaged through some nearby drawers and found the magazines and a box of nine-millimeter ammunition. Of course Trees was prepared.

Thank God.

Then she loaded the guns—grateful she'd paid attention during the years she'd been a captive of her brother-in-law's cartel—took a deep breath, and let herself out of Trees's panic room, ensuring the lights were off and the door closed behind her. Once she'd shrouded the keypad with his clothes again, she did her best to steady her shaking hands and went in search of Victor.

She didn't have to go far. As soon as she rounded the corner out of Trees's bedroom, she spotted Victor striding through the front door, gas can in hand. He held a lighter in the other.

Her heart leapt to her throat, but she forced herself to stay steady. She was going to stop Victor...or die trying. She owed Trees at least that much.

When he spotted her, he ripped off his mask and flashed her a wide smile. "*Chiquita*, there you are. Put down the guns and greet me the way I taught you."

On her knees. She wouldn't do it. She wouldn't betray Trees like that. And the distraction would only delay the inevitable destruction of all he held dear. Nor could she simply shoot Victor. As much as she would love to, there was a way to make the most of this situation, one that wouldn't simply end her rapist. One that would also make her family safe from everyone in the Tierra Caliente cartel so Valeria and Jorge could finally live.

Time to start swaying Victor to a different way of thinking.

"Is that what you really want in life?" she challenged. "All you want? A blow job?"

"You're right. It will wait until I set this bastard's house on fire. You can suck me off while I watch it burn."

Never. "Victor, he is not a man to cross."

Ramos dropped the gas can and stormed in her direction, thunder rolling across his face. "Neither am I. He killed my brother, and for that, he will pay."

Skittering back a step, Laila raised the guns to him, her trigger finger itching. "He told me. But stop. Think about what you are doing."

"Has Hector's killer been keeping you here?"

That question led to dangerous answers. "Does it really matter to you? Does he?"

Victor looked at her as if she'd gone insane. "Of course. Because of him, my brother is dead."

"Your brother is dead because he behaved stupidly and he got lazy. Because he decided to chase pussy and petty nonsense, instead of embracing what he truly wanted—to take over the Tierra Caliente cartel. I respect that he would never have crossed Emilo, but now..." Laila shrugged, then took a deep breath and went for broke. "I have always thought you were too smart to let yourself fall into his trap. Was I wrong? Are you more interested in paltry vengeance when the goal you both sought, the power you both coveted, is right in front of you? You could oust Geraldo Montilla and be king, sit on his throne and rule an empire richer than most governments—if you focused."

Victor scoffed. "Montilla has surrounded himself with an army, and Emilo's remaining men are too few. They are demoralized. Too many have left because the money no longer flows."

"Excuses. Fix it and do what you should to achieve the dream on your brother's behalf. Reign in his memory. Or are you afraid?" she baited him.

His face shouted, but his voice was a quiet hiss. "I am afraid of nothing."

"Good. Then do what is important."

"Why do you care if I take down Montilla and rule his empire?" Victor's eyes narrowed as he had the audacity to grip her chin and force her gaze to his. "You hate me."

"I do." If she lied about that, he would never listen. And she refused to invite or stomach his advances again. "But I can help you take down Geraldo Montilla."

He narrowed his dark eyes. "You lie, *puta*."

"It is true. Since I have slept under the enemy's roof, I have learned things that will help you." Not a lot, but she would make things up if she had to. Whatever it took to divert Victor's attention from Trees and keep her family safe. "Things you cannot possibly know. Things that will turn the tables. But if you are too weak to pursue your dream..."

"I am too weak for nothing," he spat, gripping her chin harder. "I can rule. I *will* rule." His eyes burned with resolve. "And you will help me."

"You will need me."

A smile crept across his face. "Yes. Start on your knees."

She rolled her eyes. "So quickly you revert, giving up your goals for petty pleasures. It seems you are not ready to become the next head of the cartel, after all."

"I am. You know that, or you would never have suggested I take over."

She'd suggested it because she could manipulate him into weakening Geraldo Montilla, perhaps even taking the kingpin down, which would ensure her family's safety. But it would probably mean Victor's death, too.

The perfect end.

"True," she lied with a smile. "But if you want the empire and you want my help claiming the throne, there must be changes."

His eyes narrowed. "Such as?"

"First, get your hands off me." She jerked her chin out of his grasp. "I am your partner, not your whore. Not your punching bag. Do not ever touch me again. Are we clear? If you cannot manage that, I will tell you nothing."

"You think I care? Your pussy, while sweet, is hardly the only one. Since you left, I have been relieving myself with girls in a nearby village. They are happy to slake my lust."

Laila would bet anything that when Victor said girls, he meant that literally. He liked them young...

Swallowing down her distaste, she flashed him a smile. If he expected her to care who he fucked, he was sorely mistaken. "So you agree? You will not touch me."

"Of course." He waved a dismissive hand. "You are hardly irreplaceable."

Then why had he chased her across Orlando just last week, intent on recapturing her so she could warm his bed again? But Laila didn't point that out. She just thanked the heavens that his vanity and ambition outweighed his desire for her.

"Then we are in agreement. We are partners with one goal. You will not touch me. If you forget our agreement, I will pull the trigger."

"Don't threaten me, *chiquita*."

When he made to grab her face again, she pressed the gun to his forehead. "Do not threaten *me*, Victor."

He scoffed. "You think I could not wrest that gun from you? Are you still that naive?"

"You could," she acknowledged. "But then you will never know what I know. You will never be king. And you will never give your brother the tribute he deserves."

Victor hesitated, then backed away with a grunt. "All right. Keep your guns. I don't care. Now tell me everything."

"Not so fast. I have more demands. Not only will you not touch me, you will leave my sister and Jorge alone."

He shook his head. "The old man wants them. If I seize them first, I have a bargaining chip—"

"You will not need them. There is another one, a better one," she insisted, making things up as she went.

But then she realized it wasn't untrue. She could use the Edgingtons' sister, Kimber, to her advantage—all while helping to win the woman's freedom. If she finessed Victor just right, it would work.

"You lie."

"I do not. But before I tell you more, you must agree that my family is off-limits."

"If you're not lying to me, if you know of more effective leverage, then I agree. I have no use for Emilo's shrew or his snot-nosed boy."

Laila tried to hold down her giddiness. She almost had Victor where she wanted him. So, so close... He just had to accept one more condition. "Excellent. You must also abandon this pointless revenge against the man who has been keeping me here. He is simply a paid operative doing his job."

Victor raised a brow. "Pointless? He killed my brother. But I am curious, *chiquita*. Why do you care what happens to this man? Is it because he killed for you? Because he means something to you?"

When her heart started pounding and she had to resist the urge to fidget, she worried he could see right through her. "He means nothing. I merely prevent you from making a stupid mistake. I told you he is not a man to cross. If you do not want to fight him while doing the far more important work of deposing Geraldo Montilla, forget this man."

"He fucked you."

Oh, he did much more than that.

Heat rushed to Laila's face and she hoped Victor didn't notice. "Of course he did. He is a man—a very large one. I had no way to stop him from taking what he wanted."

Never mind that, last time, she had ached to give herself to him.

He shrugged, as if the possibility that someone else had raped her meant nothing to him. "Why do you care whether I seize Geraldo Montilla's throne? Are you hoping for money?"

Dipped in rivers of innocent blood? "No. I want peace. If you rule the cartel, the threat to my family is gone. You become rich and powerful beyond your dreams while Valeria, Jorge, and I are finally free. Our paths will not cross again. I believe it is, as the Americans say, a win-win. Do you not agree?"

Victor stared so long she felt dissected. Could he see through her, down to her half-truths and lies? The urge to squirm rode her, but Laila tamped it down and waited, preparing arguments in case she needed them.

"You are right," Victor conceded.

Somehow, she kept in her giant sigh of relief. "As soon as you leave, I will call you with the first piece of information you need. Every few days, I will deliver more until—"

"You negotiated your terms. Now I will negotiate mine. I have only one." The way he smiled told Laila she would hate it. "You come with me."

Horror gripped her until she couldn't breathe. "No. Impossible. This man—"

"Forest Scott?" She must have looked surprised because he slanted her a superior glance. "Did you think I wouldn't learn about my adversary before I came to kill him?"

Of course he would. Victor wasn't lazy, just half-witted. "He is very dangerous. He will come for me."

"Because you mean something to him?" Victor sauntered closer, his stare speculative.

I love you, Laila.

The memory of Trees's sweet words made her heart ache. Would she ever hear them again?

Probably not, and she couldn't let her anguish about that make her decision. Survival didn't care about her feelings. Or his. Saving her family, Kimber Trenton, and Trees was more important. Someday, Trees would move on. Since he was a good man, he would find someone worthy of his love. Her heart would be a casualty, but for his safety and his future, that was a small sacrifice.

"Pay attention. I told you he is merely paid to keep me here, but he values his job. He is a professional. He will not admit defeat."

"So we'll make him."

"Are you listening? He will be a thorn in your side you do not need while you must concentrate on taking down Montilla."

"If Mr. Scott is a problem, I will dispatch him quickly." Victor shot her a speculative glance. "Unless you can think of some other way to keep him at bay? As you pointed out, it would be better for my focus. I know it would be better for his health."

A chill shot through Laila. How could she prevent Trees from doing what he would inevitably do and rescuing her?

"Another reason you should leave me here, so no one is wise to our plan. I can continue to extract more information from him you can use to your benefit and—"

"You coming with me is a nonnegotiable term. It is the only way I can hold you accountable if your information is, shall we say, ineffectual. If you refuse, I will set this house on fire with you inside, turn all my attention to killing your sister while holding your nephew hostage. After I've dispatched with Mr. Scott, of course."

With her thoughts racing and her panic climbing, Laila tried to think of a way around Victor's demand. But there wasn't one. As much as she wanted to cry about that, it would do her no good. She would rather protect Trees than herself. "You understand that if I come with you, I will not be able to overhear any more valuable information."

It was a last-ditch effort. She prayed it would succeed.

Once again, the world was against her.

"You are resourceful, Laila. Much smarter than your sister. If I need more information, you will find a way—spreading your legs again for Mr. Scott, perhaps—to procure it. But for now, you will come with me."

Laila held back the insane and detrimental urge to sob. She would probably never see Trees again, much less have the chance to tell him she had feelings for him, too. Maybe that was for the best.

She swallowed everything back but her determination. "All right. I will go with you."

The two hours since the alarm had alerted Trees that someone had infiltrated his property had been among the worst of his life. He'd tried a hundred times to call Laila. Nothing. And he had no idea what the fuck was going on. The intruder had shot out every surveillance camera inside the house. So all Trees knew? An asshole wearing a ski mask had shattered his living room window, then climbed in through the gaping hole. Twenty minutes later, he'd walked out with Laila at his side—no struggle, no gun, no coercion necessary. She'd merely climbed into the passenger's seat of the bastard's black truck with its hidden plates. Then the vehicle had screeched away, taking Laila—and his heart—with it.

Who the fuck had abducted her? How had he coerced her compliance? What was she enduring now?

The intruder had to be someone she knew. Trees was convinced of that.

Since she'd tried to escape two nights ago for a clandestine meet-up with Hunter Edgington to help save the man's sister, as well as her own, Trees would have suspected his boss. But all of the douche buckets he worked for, Hunter included, had been thirty thousand feet in the air with him when Laila had been taken.

So whoever had her captive wasn't a friendly, which made the fact that she'd left without being forced even more baffling. Worse, he suspected it was someone from either Geraldo Montilla's or Victor Ramos's orbit.

One thing he knew for sure? Laila would never comply merely to ensure her own safety. But for Valeria's? For Jorge's? They were her weakness. Whoever had taken her probably knew it.

Fuck.

"Anything, buddy?" Zy burst in through the back door, stopping short in the portal, staring at the shards of glass everywhere.

Trees didn't understand the destruction. Had Laila fought in the kitchen but given up by the time she'd been dragged to the front door? "Nothing. I've looked all over the house for clues to understand what happened and who took her."

Laila hadn't taken a single one of her possessions. Not her clothes or her phone. Not even a nightlight. But two SIGs were missing off his wall in his underground panic room, along with a box of ammo. That scared the shit out of him.

"Are you sure Laila walked out of her own free will?"

"It fucking looks that way." Trees tried to stifle both his alarm and impatience and tossed Zy his phone, screen open to the feed from the front porch camera. "Here. Watch. This is all I've got."

As Zy did, Trees paced to Laila's room. He couldn't watch the video again, not without wanting to tear something apart and kill a motherfucker.

Inside her room, he found far fewer signs of struggle. In fact, her bed wasn't even rumpled. The only hint he had that she'd been here? The towel wadded up in the bathroom sink, as if she'd dumped it there in a hurry. The middle was still damp.

He lifted the terry cloth and inhaled. It smelled like Laila. As her scent filled his nose, he tried not to lose his shit or start tearing down the world to find her.

Somehow, someone had swooped in and taken her from him. He was going to fucking get her back—no matter what.

"I don't understand." Zy frowned from the doorway of Laila's bathroom. "But you've got to hold it together, buddy."

Reluctantly, Trees dropped the towel. "How would you be doing right now if someone had taken Tessa?"

"I'd be somewhere between falling apart and wanting to rip a motherfucker into pieces, too. Point taken. So where do we go from here? Do you have any theories about who has her?"

"My best guess? Victor Ramos, mostly because Geraldo Montilla should have been in Florida for that classic car race."

"Unless it was a ruse."

It was possible, but Trees's gut said no. "If Montilla had done this, he would have sent more than one person to abduct Laila. Victor, on the other hand… Now that I've offed his brother, maybe he's alone? I'm not sure how the fuck he found me. And how did whoever this son of a bitch was make it ten feet across the yard without Barney ripping out his entrails?" Trees said of his big-ass Rottweiler.

"Fucker came prepared. He tossed your four-legged mooch a raw steak slathered in something I suspect put Barney out for a while. I found the steak bone and a loopy dog."

That pissed Trees off. "Is Barney okay?"

"Yeah. He's up and walking. A little sideways, but walking."

At least that was one less worry. "Maybe I should call the bosses."

But what could they do when all their resources were stretched thin, trying to bring Kimber home?

"To confirm that Laila is long gone? I think they know, buddy. But

I'll advise them. Why don't you grab your computer, see if you can catch her trail?"

Probably his best course of action, but the last damn thing he wanted to do was sit on his ass when someone had their filthy fucking hands all over his woman. Was she screaming? Crying? Terrified? Begging? Being forced? Violated? Tortured? Was she even alive anymore?

God, he couldn't stand not knowing.

Suddenly, Zy dropped a hand to his shoulder. "You've got to do something constructive. Gnashing your teeth and wishing death on whoever took her isn't it."

Trees had no idea what his friend meant until he realized he'd gripped the pedestal sink and, in impotent fury, pulled it from the wall. With a curse, he released the fixture, leaving it balanced precariously, and zipped past Zy, stomping his way to his home office. There, he grabbed a computer, stalked to the kitchen, and shoved all the broken glassware and china from the table with a sweep of his arm. He lifted the chair and emptied the shards from his seat, then plopped down and pried the machine open.

Where the fuck should he start? What scan could he possibly run that might lead him to Laila?

Apprehension gnawed at his gut as he stared at the blank screen with its blinking cursor. Traffic cams. Police communications. Maybe that would turn up something. Or maybe he should work backward, follow his hunch, and see if he could track Geraldo Montilla's and Victor Ramos's last known locations.

Trees launched multiple searches, then spoke to Zy without even looking his friend's way. "Call the colonel for me. Ask him if he knows anyone on the Lafayette PD who'd be willing to put out a BOLO for Laila. Or better yet, report her kidnapping."

"I don't think that's a good idea. First, I'm not sure they'll take you seriously since it looks like she walked out. Second—and more important—she's someone the Tierra Caliente cartel would love to get their hands on. So if Geraldo Montilla doesn't already have her, he soon will."

Trees snapped an angry glare at his best friend. "Not because he wants *her*. Only because she's a direct line to Valeria and Jorge."

"I know, but if you want to attract all the wrong kinds of attention, go ahead and advertise that Laila is flapping in the wind. I don't think it will help her."

Zy was fucking right.

Trees pounded a fist on the table. "Goddamn it!"

"I know. It sucks. It's fucking awful. But let's talk about what we should do. How can I help?"

Trying not to lose his shit while he waited for his computer to finish, he shook his head at Zy. Hell, Trees barely knew how to help locate Laila. What useful task could he tell his friend to handle? Zy was a demolitions guy. There was nothing to blow up.

Trees's heart was already doing that on its own.

"I don't know. I don't…" He tried not to give in to panic. "Something. I don't fucking know what."

"Okay."

Zy's tone was placating, and it rubbed Trees wrong. Irrationally, he knew that. Zy wasn't the one he should be pissed off at. "Just do…anything."

"After I check in with the bosses, I'll have a conversation with Valeria. She might have some idea where Victor would hole up or take Laila."

Actually, that was a great idea, and Trees was kicking himself for not thinking of it. "Yeah. Good. Thanks."

"I'll be back. Call me if you find anything. In the meantime, keep it together. We're going to find her."

Trees sure as hell hoped so. After less than a week with Laila, he had no idea how he'd ever live without her again.

Yeah, he was so in love he was fucked.

In the distance, he heard Zy drive off. Trees clung to hope—that his buddy would get Valeria to cough up something helpful, that one of his scans would turn up a needle in a haystack, that they would uncover anything that led them back to Laila.

Six hours later, he still had nothing because that's what Valeria knew. That's what his scans showed. That's the communications he'd received from Laila's abductor. That's how much hope he had left.

CHAPTER
Two

Florida

"Laila, your scheme isn't going to work," Victor snarled as they approached the garage on the outskirts of the racetrack shortly before dawn the following day.

Her heart stopped. Had Victor already figured out she was playing him? "I do not know what you mean."

He huffed. "This scam to take Geraldo Montilla's Ferrari… If I want to unseat him, stealing his car does nothing except piss him off."

She let out a silent sigh of relief that Victor hadn't caught on to her ploy. "My plan will achieve everything you want while making him come to you—if you do not mismanage this. But in order to take down Montilla, you must first send him—and everyone—a signal that you are a force to be reckoned with. Stealing his most prized possession will do that. After all, he paid fifty million dollars for it."

"Fucking insane." Victor shook his head, as if he could not fathom spending that kind of cash on a mere car.

"The money for such toys will soon be yours." *If Montilla does not kill you first.* "You simply have to find the *cojones* to take it."

"You already know how big my balls are." He glared her way. "But poking the bear will only make Montilla angrier and more difficult to overthrow."

She pretended to heave a long-suffering sigh, but for once, Victor's logic wasn't totally wrong. Very little else he'd said since they'd left Trees's house and driven all night down the highway before finally reaching this Florida racetrack had. At least he'd lived up to his word and kept his hands to himself. She could probably thank the guns she kept constantly at hand for that.

"Montilla will not recognize the threat until it is far too late. He will fixate on the loss of his precious car. He will devote his resources to recovering it. While he is distracted, you will make your next moves to dominating the cartel."

"Using that bargaining chip you keep talking about?"

"Exactly." Either Victor would kill Montilla while rescuing Kimber or the Edgingtons would follow him in and handle them both. Either way, her family would be safer.

Victor merely grunted as if he wasn't convinced. "I need to know more about it."

"After you have stolen the car. The bargaining chip I speak of will be of no use until Montilla's attention is diverted. Then... Well, you are more ruthless." That might be true. "And smarter." But that wasn't. "You will succeed."

In trying to fabricate a supposed plan for Victor to take over Tierra Caliente, she'd read online that the driver Montilla hired for this classic car race yesterday had fallen hours before the start and broken his arm. Montilla had been forced to withdraw his 1962 Ferrari 250 GTO from yesterday's competition. It seemed likely the drug lord would transport his ridiculously expensive car and fly back to Mexico today, so she and Victor had only this small window of opportunity.

They tiptoed closer to the garage that housed the prized vehicle. When Victor peeked around the corner of the storage unit, he quickly reared back, plastering himself against the side of the building. "Fuck. There are two armed guards standing outside. We did not plan for that."

A problem she hadn't foreseen...and probably should have. "Are they male?"

"Yes. And big. I will have to kill them." He reached for his gun.

That horrified Laila. The last thing she wanted was for anyone else to be hurt.

She grabbed Victor's arm and held him back. "We cannot leave bodies. That will alert the local authorities and bring attention we do not need. Let me handle them. Once they are distracted, you take the car and drive it to the U-Haul. Then it will be yours."

He scowled. "You will distract both of them? At once?"

"How many times did I handle you and Hector together?" she snapped, then wished she'd held her tongue. She didn't want to remind him of all the times he had violated her. She also didn't want to remind him of his dead brother. Being careful and strategic was key.

He leered her way. "Many. You were our favorite toy."

"Now I am your partner," she reminded him, reaching under her tank top to unfasten her bra. After some finagling, she pulled the undergarment free through the side and shoved it at Victor. "Hold this and watch for your opportunity."

With a deep breath, she wriggled her shorts down to her hip bones and folded the legs up to her coochie. Most of her midriff was bare, and the cool breeze had stiffened her nipples. Hopefully, distracting the two sentries wouldn't require revealing more skin than that. She really didn't want to get naked with either of them…but she'd been desperate enough to do worse in the past.

Shoving the thought aside, she swayed around the side of the building. On the alert, both men zipped their gazes in her direction. Security lights from above illuminated their faces. They were under thirty and strapping. On the left, the blond man with an unkempt beard drew his weapon as he looked her up and down. On the right, a black man with arms bulging from his wifebeater followed suit.

"*Hola*, gentlemen. Do not shoot. I am lost. I could find no one else to ask for directions at this hour." She pressed a hand to her chest to draw attention to her nipples as she approached the garage. "But perhaps you can help me? I am driving to Miami. I have no GPS, and I cannot find the freeway. You will help me, yes?"

The blond man gulped and nodded, his stare glued to her breasts.

The other one smiled as if he fully intended to help her—out of her clothes. Then he holstered his weapon and slipped an arm around her middle. "Sure, baby. There's a guard shack around the corner and—"

"But your friend. We cannot leave him alone." She looked back at the blond guy to find him staring at her ass. "Come closer. I am cold. Will you help keep me warm?"

Immediately, he tucked his gun away and zipped to her side, plastering himself against her body. Laila shoved down a shudder, wondering why so many men were foolish enough to fall for such tactics. They were transparent. Obvious. Ridiculous.

Because too many men thought with their *chiles*, rather than their brains.

"That is better." She sent them both inviting smiles. "What are you guarding? If you have been assigned to protect it, I am sure it is very important."

"It's a car," the bearded man answered. "The most expensive one ever registered for this race."

"Oh? Is it yours?"

The black man snorted. "He wishes."

"I do. It's the prettiest thing I've ever seen." He eyed her up and down again. "Except you."

Laila pretended to blush and flirt. "Can you show me?"

The blond guy shook his head. "The doors are supposed to stay locked."

"Of course. And you are responsible men. But I am simply a lost woman, who is all alone and now very curious. Certainly there would be no harm in letting me peek? And it will…what is the word? Arouse me to see it."

The two men exchanged a glance. Then they grinned at one another.

"All right, baby. Just a peek. You'll reward us for it?"

She smiled their way. "Of course."

The dark man punched numbers into the keypad, releasing the lock on the temperature-controlled unit. The other guy helped him push the door up. The lights flashed on. And there sat Geraldo Montilla's prized possession, shiny, pristine, and candy-apple red.

Laila gasped and touched her chest again. "*Que carro más lindo.*"

"Huh?" The blond guy frowned.

"What a beautiful car," she supplied as she sauntered closer. "The more I look at it, the more I become"—she licked her lips, then bit the bottom one as if she held in a secret she could keep no more—"wet. Who will help me with that?"

"I will," the bearded man volunteered a split second later.

The bigger man elbowed him. "Don't you have a girlfriend? Besides, she's too much woman for you. I got her."

She laid her fingers on his brown chest with a sultry smile. When he started preening, she did the same to the blond man. "I am feel-ing...adventurous. There is enough of me to go around."

The blue-eyed man swallowed hard. "You think you can take us both?"

"I want to try." She ran her hand along the side of the sleek red car, silently marveling at how truly stunning the vehicle was. Then she bent over the hood and stuck her ass in the air. "I think I would like it."

If they crowded around her, they'd both be distracted. They would also have their backs to Victor, who now had an open path to sneak in and knock them out. That would do nicely.

"Hmm, baby." The big one gripped her hips and notched his erec-tion against her backside.

Laila held in a tremor of distaste. She did not want anyone's hands on her except Trees's.

"Not here, dude." The other guy bobbed his pale head toward the corner of the garage.

She followed the gesture and tried not to wince. Cameras. *Carajo!* Hopefully, when Montilla saw this footage, he would not recognize her. After all, the last time they met she had barely been more than a child, and he'd treated her as if she was beneath his notice, thank God.

The bigger man stepped back and grabbed her arm. "He's right. Damn it."

Laila turned and buried her face in the man's neck and pretended to breathe him in. He smelled like sweat and testosterone. Then she repeated the gesture with the bearded man, who also smelled of cigarettes.

She tried not to choke. "Let us go to the guard shack, then. I am impatient."

"Good call. Follow me." The big one dragged her out of the garage, around the corner, then down a narrow alley before the darkened guard shack came into view.

"Wait!" the blond guy protested, lagging behind. "We're not supposed to leave the garage open. Anyone could come in and steal the car."

Mr. Wifebeater rolled his eyes. "Who do you think is around to do that? It's not even five o'clock in the morning. The partiers left a few hours ago, and the business heads won't be here until after sunup. It'll be fine for a few minutes."

"But—"

"She's wet," he reminded through gritted teeth. "I'm not giving up good pussy for this shitty-paying temp job. But you feel free to stay."

"I need you both," she whined. "Please."

With a long sigh, the blond guy shook his head and grumbled. "I'm probably going to hell, but fuck it."

Then he stomped after them.

Victor better move quickly, because Laila doubted she could put these two off for long, and she refused to get naked and spread her legs.

When they reached the guard shack, she held back, pursing her lips and batting her lashes. "Turn on the lights first. I am afraid of the dark."

At least that much was true.

The big man hustled in and felt around for the switch.

The blond guy looked shocked. "You want the lights on while we fuck you?"

She dragged a finger over the curve of her breast. "Do you not wish to see all of me? I want to see you."

Despite the fact she nearly choked on the lie, he gave her a bug-eyed head bob and raced into the guard shack, right behind his partner.

She gave them a come-hither smile—then slammed the door, grabbing the flag that proclaimed this the sector twelve security station from its nearby holder. With shaking hands, she shoved the fat pole between the long pull and the door itself, jamming it tight. This wouldn't hold for more than a minute or two.

Laila hoped that would be enough.

At once, they began beating on the door while glaring out the windows at her.

"What the fuck?"

"Let us out, bitch!"

She didn't waste time responding, simply hustled away. When they broke the glass and started shooting, she tried to push back her panic, zigzagging to avoid their bullets.

Pings whizzed past her. Laila gasped, her heart racing with fear. The big guy cursed. A glance back proved he'd reached through the open window to dislodge the metal pole. She didn't stay around to see how long it took them to wriggle it free. She had to find Victor.

Thankfully, when she rounded the corner, she heard the purr of the classic car's engine. Then the vehicle rolled through the double doors, Victor behind the wheel.

He shot her a triumphant glance, stroking the dashboard. "Get in. Montilla is going to miss the hell out of this car. Too bad for that fucking bastard."

Yes, and in less than five minutes, the drug lord would know his car had been stolen and by whom—exactly as she'd planned. But she couldn't attract more of Montilla's attention herself. She had to hope that the kingpin would write her off as a whore who had merely diverted his security for a good time or a buck.

Suddenly, she heard shouting and the pounding of footsteps. The guards—with their guns—were free.

"Go! I will meet you by the rental truck in five minutes." Since the guards would undoubtedly chase the car, she stood a better chance of disappearing on foot.

Laila darted into the maze of side buildings, skulking in the shadows until she lost them. Then she found the broken fence she'd entered through and slinked away from the racetrack, sprinting toward the nearby side street where they'd left the rented truck.

And if Victor decided he didn't need her and left her behind? Well, she would hardly mourn his departure. She had already planted the seed of ambition in his mind. He would go after Montilla until one or both of them were dead.

But when she reached the U-Haul, Victor was there, frantically opening the back. "Get the ramp."

She raced to help him anchor it in place, then he drove the Ferrari into the cargo container. Heart slamming against her ribs, she looked over her shoulders for the guards. Thankfully, no sign of them—yet.

Laila dispensed with the ramp, plucked up a ball cap she'd planted nearby just as Victor cut the engine and hopped to the street and yanked down the door. She charged toward the driver's side, tucking her hair beneath the cap. Once she slid behind the wheel and Victor settled into the passenger's seat, she pulled away from the curb with a sigh of relief.

They'd done it. She was still shaking like a leaf, and the coming adrenaline crash would probably have her vomiting soon, but they had succeeded. Victor was now on Montilla's radar. The kingpin would definitely divert resources to finding his expensive toy. Hopefully, he'd be enraged—and sloppy. That's when Laila would make her next move.

"Where am I driving?" She glanced over her shoulder as she headed toward the freeway, wishing more than anything that she could turn around and head straight back to Trees.

Victor pocketed the keys. "Mexico. I know where we can hide this thing until I'm ready to make my move."

Lafayette

Barely twenty-four hours after he'd last seen Laila, Trees parked in front of a light industrial building on the east side of Lafayette that had seen better decades. At twenty minutes before dawn, he choked back the last of his black coffee and exited his Hummer, slamming the door behind him.

Strung out on caffeine and restless energy, he approached the seemingly deserted place and shouldered his way through the door. Inside, he scanned the busy domain. It could best be described as a war room, complete with wall-to-wall warriors. Unlike the exterior, this space looked up-do-date, tricked out, and high-tech. On any other day, he'd be eager to dig in and check everything out. Today, he was too fucking worried about Laila.

"Trees." Hunter Edgington stood and approached, obviously exhausted and on edge.

He headed in his boss's direction, passing a handful of familiar faces, along with some he'd never seen. "Hey, I got your text. What's going on?"

Hunter didn't look as if he had the patience for explanations, or maybe the apprehension rolling off him worried his father, because the older man stood. Caleb, the team's former leader, stopped him in the middle of the room. If possible, he looked even more grim. "Let me get you up to speed. Then we need your help."

Since the colonel was both OG and the best, Trees nodded. "I'll do my best, sir."

"Thank you." The older man pointed to the head of the table. "That's Jack Cole, my son-in-law's business partner."

"Welcome," the hard-looking Cajun with the badass reputation said before turning his attention back to his computer screen.

"You remember Deke?" The colonel gestured to a big blond hulk of a man. Everything about him, all the way down to his red-rimmed eyes and sunken cheeks, said he was like the proverbial lion with a thorn in his paw. He might be wounded since his wife was missing, but he'd absolutely kill any motherfucker who got in his way of rescuing Kimber.

Trees understood that sentiment. Laila was out there...somewhere. She was clever and tenacious but no match for ruthless drug lords and their violence-happy thugs. Worst-case scenarios kept dive-bombing his brain, and he didn't know how the fuck he'd dig for the patience to give his bosses whatever they needed. All he could think about was finding her.

"Yeah. Hey," Trees said to Kimber's husband.

The man didn't acknowledge him, just turned to Caleb. "This is the computer whiz? He looks better suited to the NBA."

"I'm not into basketball." He turned to the colonel. "Just tell me how I can help."

"I'm getting to it." The older man beat feet to another big blond guy, this one with movie-star looks—except for his nose, which had seemingly been broken more than once. "This is Tyler Murphy, former LAPD homicide detective turned PI."

"A.k.a. Cockzilla," quipped a man with long, inky hair on the far side of the room, setting up hot trays of food.

Holy shit. That was famous TV chef Luc Traverson. How did the colonel know these guys?

"Stop busting my balls," Tyler groused.

"I'm not doing anything to your balls. Unless you want me to roast them." Luc's tone was pure teasing...but Trees sensed history here.

"Pass," Tyler said, then gave Trees his outstretched hand. "Hey, new guy."

"His name is Forest Scott," Caleb supplied. "One of the best tech guys I've ever worked with. Hired him myself."

He shook with Tyler. "Call me Trees."

"Will do, as long as you *don't* call me Cockzilla." He raised a brow at Traverson.

"Wouldn't dream of it," Trees promised.

"I'll bet Delaney still calls you that," Logan shot Tyler's way. "How else could you possibly have three boys with another baby on the way so quickly?"

Tyler laughed. "Need a lecture on the birds and the bees, junior?"

"Fuck you," Logan grumbled.

"Get back to work. We don't have a minute to spare," the colonel growled, then made his way down the long table, pausing beside a guy who, though casually dressed, dripped money. When he turned Trees's way, his gaze looked shrewd as hell. "Sean Mackenzie, former FBI. Thankfully, he still has a lot of contacts."

"Good to meet you," Sean supplied. "I wish it was under better circumstances."

Than Kimber's abduction? Yeah, it sucked. But every minute he spent here on these introductions was another minute he wasn't finding Laila. Or saving her...if she needed to be saved.

"Same."

"And this is Stone Sutter. He's your counterpart over at Oracle," Caleb said, referring to the security firm Jack and Deke co-owned.

Trees had heard of the guy. Ex-con turned straight. The tatted-up operator looked dangerous, a lot more like a thug than a computer nerd, but his smile was friendly. "I've heard about you. Good to finally put a face with a name."

"For sure." Since he wasn't in the mood for chitchat, he turned back to the colonel. "Do you need me to work with Stone on something?"

Caleb sighed. "I wanted to introduce you to everyone since we're pulling you onto Kimber's rescue team indefinitely."

The words had barely cleared the older man's mouth before Trees opened his to balk. "With all due respect—"

"Before you finish that speech, your first order of business will be to retrieve Laila. We think she knows something about Montilla's whereabouts. Or someone who does."

It sounded like they were grasping at straws. Trees scowled. "What makes you think that, sir?"

"Follow me."

Before Caleb could lead him away from the group, the front door opened again. A pair of suits—brothers?—both looking more like hot Latin models than operatives, strolled in. The older one lugged a baby girl in a carrier who sported downy pale hair, shocking hazel eyes, and a frilly pink dress.

Who the hell were they?

"We meant to be here earlier," said the younger one, straightening his tie. "Sorry. Our daughter was a little cranky this morning."

The older one snorted. "More like you were cranky that I pulled you out of bed and away from our wife."

Their wife?

Sean Mackenzie laughed. "You know how it is, Javier. There's always one horny husband. Usually I blame Thorpe whenever we're late for something since it's usually his fault. But this morning, it was all me. Since baby Asher slept through the night, I took advantage of a well-rested Callie."

Sean shared a wife, too? Apparently so, and the fact they were having this deeply personal conversation in front of everyone told him that was common knowledge.

The older brother groaned. "Xander did the same with London."

"Why not? She's sleeping better now that Dulce isn't waking up every three hours. Besides, all our wife's panting and screaming told me she was perfectly happy with the extra attention." Xander grinned as he took the carrier.

Javier gave his brother a sly-dog smile. "Why do you think I sent you to that last-minute meeting yesterday afternoon?"

"Asshole," Xander griped.

Logan stood and scowled. "You dipshits brought a baby to a war room?"

Xander shrugged. "If she grows up like her daddies, she'll want to be involved in everything anyway."

"She's not staying. Dulce has a playdate with Lacey. Morgan agreed to watch the girls today," Javier informed, nodding when Jack Cole smiled at the mention of his wife and daughter. Then Javier glanced across the room at the catering setup. "Ah, glad the food arrived. Xander said none of you has had a good meal in days."

"I'll take care of everyone," Luc promised. "I would have done it sooner if Cousin Deke had called me…"

Kimber's husband scowled like food was the last thing on his mind, so the colonel filled the dead air. "Thank you for feeding us."

Trees wondered how much would actually get eaten by this highly stressed crowd.

"You're welcome. We'll be back to see how else we can help after we drop Dulce off and have a fun-filled meeting with the Joint Chiefs. The work of a military contractor is never done," Xander bantered. "The offer of a plane stands, by the way. We're more than happy to lend our jet to the cause if you need it."

With that, Trees realized exactly who these two were.

Caleb nodded the brothers' way. "We might need to take you up on that."

Did that mean he'd be bugging out to find Laila shortly? Trees hoped so, but the colonel didn't elaborate.

After the brothers waved and headed out the door, Caleb turned to him. "That was Javier and Xander—"

"Santiago. S.I. Industries, right?"

"Yes."

Trees knew of the military contractors. Nearly everyone in this line of work did. After some recent bumps in their corporate road, they had rectified their problems and were now on their way to being the best out there. And they were wealthy as fuck. "How do you know them?"

"Logan and Xander have been friends forever."

That explained how his bosses had gotten their hands on some awesome toys security companies usually couldn't. It helped to have friends in high places. But that wasn't Trees's first concern. "Am I taking a trip on their jet to find Laila?"

"Possibly. Follow me."

Trees trailed the colonel down a hallway before ducking into the lone office filled with an old iron desk and a fuck-ton of surveillance equipment. In the room's only chair, Joaquin sat, furiously scanning a screen. Whatever he'd been watching ended. The guy sighed and plucked out a pair of earbuds, sat back, then gave the two of them his attention.

"If none of us know, why would he?" Muñoz pointed a thumb in his direction.

"He's talked to Laila more than anyone else. Maybe she told him something…"

Joaquin shrugged and stood. "Unlikely, but worth a shot. That's why you brought him here?"

"Yeah. Set up the clip again," Caleb insisted of his stepson, then turned to him. "Sit."

As Trees settled in the office chair and fixed his gaze on the blank computer screen, the door to the office burst open. A guy he'd seen around EM's office, One-Mile Walker's buddy Matt Montgomery, burst in. "There's a new development to all this. A couple of them, actually. If you want to come see…"

Joaquin dashed out immediately. The colonel looked torn, then finally sighed. "We just got our hands on this footage. It happened less than two hours ago. Barring whatever new developments Matt has, this is all we know. Maybe you can fill in some blanks, mostly why."

Whatever it was didn't sound good. Apprehension gripped Trees. Had something happened to Laila? The colonel was gone before he could ask, and Trees figured it was better this way. Whatever was on this video—which must have something to do with the woman he loved—he wanted to see it alone.

As if the earbuds were a snake, he reached for them carefully, blowing out a breath and bracing himself. It was possible she was being harmed. Tortured or raped. Frowning, he shoved the buds in his ears, started the video, and gripped the computer, every muscle in his body taut.

Montilla's classic fifty-million-dollar Ferrari, parked in a garage, immediately filled the screen. If Laila had something to do with this vehicle, did that mean the drug lord had taken her? Though Trees had known that was possible, it still filled him with a whole pile of *oh, fuck.* But he refused to lose his shit—or his hope. No matter what it took, he would save Laila. Because in the last twenty-four hours he'd come to one conclusion: she might have walked out of his house without a fight, but that didn't mean she had actually been willing. If she had been, why had she taken a pair of his guns? She would do anything for her family, and almost everyone knew it.

Ten more seconds of footage later, the garage door opened to reveal night. The light inside the garage flashed on. A pair of armed men walked in, one a scruffy punk with dirty blond hair and a chin-pube beard, the other a beefy black dude in a wifebeater. He scowled. Who the hell were they?

A moment later, Laila entered the garage behind them. No, she swayed, swinging her hips in those goddamn short denim shorts that somehow looked even shorter. Her tank covered less skin than he remembered, and she wasn't wearing a goddamn bra. What she was doing? Flirting her ass off.

What the actual fuck?

"*Que carro más lindo,*" she said, all but feeling up her tits to draw attention to them.

The dirty blond guy certainly stared there—and seemed to get lost. "Huh?"

"What a beautiful car," she translated as she sashayed closer to him. "The more I look at it, the more I become"—she licked her lips, then bit the bottom one provocatively—"wet. Who will help me with that?"

She was *inviting* them to touch her? To fuck her? Why?

But he knew the answer. She was manipulating them. It was the same reason she'd awakened him once upon a time with her mouth around his dick. Because her life was in danger? Because she'd been threatened? Or was there something else going on here?

"I will." The slouchy delinquent was embarrassingly eager.

The bigger man elbowed him. "Don't you have a girlfriend? Besides, she's too much woman for you. I got her."

Laila laid her fingers on the guy's wifebeater and flashed him an inviting smile. Then she did the same to the blond man. "I am feeling...adventurous. There is enough of me to go around."

She couldn't be fucking serious. She was dangling her body in front of them and blinding them with lust for a reason, right?

The exact reason she did the same to you?

The punk's eyes bugged out. "You think you can take us both?"

"I want to try." She ran her graceful fingers along the side of Montilla's car, caressing it like a lover. Then she bent over the hood and stuck her ass in the air, wriggling suggestively. "I think I would like it."

"Hmm, baby." The big one sidled up behind her, gripped her hips, and began dry-humping her backside.

Then Trees saw it. Laila grimaced before she blanked her expression.

"Not here, dude." The blond guy bobbed his pale head up to the corner of the garage.

Her stare followed the gesture, and she blanched when she caught sight of the cameras. Yeah, she was worried. No, afraid. What the hell was going on?

The guy in the wifebeater stepped back and seized her arm. "He's right. Damn it."

Laila turned to nuzzle her face in the man's neck. Then she repeated the gesture with the puny putz. Ruse or not, she was laying it on thick, and it was goddamn hard to watch.

"Let us go to the guard shack, then," she murmured. "I am impatient."

To get tag-teamed by these two losers? They seemed to think so, but Trees wasn't buying it. Or maybe he didn't want to. But he'd seen her face in passion. This was all bullshit.

For what cause?

"Good call. Follow me." The big one dragged Laila out of the garage.

When the two of them disappeared, the scrawny one tried to grow a brain. "Wait! We're not supposed to leave the garage open. Anyone could come in and steal the car."

"Who do you think is around to do that?" the other guy asked off camera.

After some arguing back and forth, the blond guy finally caved and stomped after them, leaving the garage door open.

Thirty seconds later, the light in the garage clicked off. Must be on a motion sensor, he thought vaguely. But what really worried the hell out of him was Laila. What was she doing during this timeframe, fucking frick and frack in the guard shack?

Why?

Not ten seconds later, another man sneaked into the garage. The light flashed on again, and he tried skulking in the shadows, but he was wearing the same clothes, right down to the ski mask, as the asshole who had taken Laila.

Trees's heart rate surged as he watched the man slink around the garage, find the keys to the car hanging on a hook at the back, then slide into the classic automobile. The engine turned over with a purr, and since someone had clearly backed the car in, the stranger in the ski mask merely had to ease it out.

The timing was too coincidental for Laila's "seduction" not to be premeditated. She had cooperated with the man who'd taken her from his house to steal Montilla's coveted car. For money? For revenge? Nothing made sense.

Suddenly, the man ripped off his ski mask. From the back, Trees saw only the man's shoulders and his dark head. Who the fuck was this guy? Why had he taken Laila and coerced her into this mess?

Just as the driver was exiting the garage, he stopped abruptly and stroked the dashboard. "Get in. Montilla is going to miss the hell out of this car. Too bad for that fucking bastard."

"Go!" That was Laila. She sounded panicked. "I will meet you by the rental truck in five minutes."

The man merely nodded, offering no argument at all. *What the fuck?* Was she his captive…or his partner in crime?

As the sounds of frantic footfalls faded away, the guy behind the wheel turned to watch her go. Trees glimpsed the bastard's profile. His blood went cold.

Victor fucking Ramos.

That changed everything.

The bastard disappeared from his view and the clip ended.

Trees ripped the buds from his ears. Since her family was safe, the asswipe must be holding something over Laila's head.

Trees stood, determined to get to her. Laila had been in Florida a couple of hours ago. That was a place to start. With or without his bosses' consent, he was going.

Halfway down the hall, Matt met him, adjusting the cowboy hat he always wore. "You done watching the video?"

"Yeah." He tried to sidestep the guy and reach the colonel.

Matt stepped in his path again. "They're busy working other angles of Kimber's whereabouts, so you and I will be following the lead from that video. What are you thinking?"

"That we need to get the fuck to Florida, and that every second I waste explaining myself is another second this bastard has to use Laila before he hurts her—"

"Why would he do that when she helped him? She's obviously in on it."

"Laila would never voluntarily help that asshole."

"You know who he is?" That clearly surprised Matt.

"Victor Ramos."

"We figured out that he was an 'associate' of Emilo Montilla, like we guessed he and Laila had met in her brother-in-law's compound. What we couldn't figure out was why they would steal Geraldo Montilla's car."

Valid question, but not the one Trees wanted answered most.

"I need to get on the fucking road now. If you want to hear what I think, follow me while I walk, but I'm not standing around jawing about this when Laila is in danger." He stalked down the hall.

"Don't you get it?" Matt asked in small words, as if he thought

Trees was too slow to grasp the situation. "Laila was an accomplice to that theft and—"

"Don't *you* get it?" Trees whirled and growled. "Ramos was Laila's rapist for six years. So no. If she 'helped' the asshole, it's because he forced her. I need to figure out how and save her."

"I'm coming with you."

"Fuck off."

Matt's face hardened. "That's not going to fly with the Edgingtons."

Trees pushed down his volcanic rage. First his bosses thought he was the mole, and now they thought he needed a babysitter? Yep, and since they were sending Matt, who had been brought on expressly to find Kimber, then saving Laila was further down their priority list. "This is bullshit."

He didn't wait to see if Matt replied, just stomped into the war room. Most everyone had grabbed a plate and was now sitting in front of their computers, eating while downing fresh coffee. Luc stood in the corner, quietly on the phone. They all looked up when he walked in.

"Well?" the colonel prompted.

"I won't know anything until I get to Laila."

The older man nodded. "Matt will fill you in on the newest developments."

"Take him with you, and remember that your first priority is to figure out where my sister is," Logan reminded. "If you get any chance to bring her back safely—"

"He knows," Hunter interrupted.

"Yep," Trees assured because Kimber was the glue that held the Edgingtons' lives together. But he needed Laila back to stop his heart from shattering. "Laila is your client. Shouldn't retrieving her be pretty fucking important, too?"

The Edgington brothers glanced at one another, then Hunter sighed. "Yes, and Valeria is beside herself with worry. If you can bring Laila back, do it. But if Montilla is pursuing her, and she can lead us to him…"

He should use Laila as bait. That's what Hunter was suggesting. No one else in the room was refuting him.

Son of a bitch.

Trees gave them a terse nod because if he said anything, he'd speak his mind and be out of a job. The way shit had gone lately, that might not be so bad...except this was his best opportunity to find Laila. This crew knew more about her whereabouts, so he couldn't afford to balk.

"Got it." When he stomped toward the door, Hunter blocked his path. "One more thing before you go. Zy pointed out recently that, as bosses, Logan, Joaquin, and I have been complete assholes."

Trees wasn't about to pull his punches. "You have."

Hunter's tight smile was a silent *mea culpa*. "We've apologized to Zy for keeping him and Tessa apart. We're trying to do better. We owe you an apology, too, for assuming you were our mole."

"Your assumption was logical, but it sucked. Maybe next time, investigate more and assume less before you start throwing accusations around?"

"Yeah. The fact you stayed with us and did a damn great job when we suspected the worst of you..." Hunter stuck out his hand. "Thanks. It won't happen again."

"It fucking better not."

Hunter paused like he was choosing his next words carefully. "Zy says you have feelings for Laila."

"I'm in love with her, and before you give me the speech about not falling for a client—"

"You can't help who you fall for. To be honest, it's fucking inconvenient. Valeria is pissed, and it's not good for our reputation if word gets out that you seduced a client—"

"Fuck you. It's not like I wanted to have feelings for her—"

"But"—Hunter held up his hands to stop his tirade—"it happens. We understand you're worried about Laila. You're motivated to find her and get her to safety."

"Yep. And I want it on record that I think you using her as bait is both wrong and reckless. But I know you're worried about your sister."

"It's been ten days. We're desperate." Hunter sounded choked up.

"I'll do my best to find her."

"Thanks." Logan approached and stuck out his hand. "We're sorry for everything."

Trees shook it and nodded.

Joaquin repeated the gesture, then bobbed his head toward the door. "Go ahead. I know you're anxious to get on Laila's trail. I'll text you the location of the Santiagos' private jet. How soon can you get a bag and get out of here?"

"I have one in my Hummer."

"Of course the prepper is prepped." He smiled wryly. "You and Matt will fly to Florida with one of Oracle's operators, Trevor Forsythe. He's former FBI and a great investigator. You'll also be joined by a friend of Jack Cole's. He goes by the handle Ghost. I don't know much about him."

"You don't need to," Jack piped up from across the room. "Except you shouldn't fuck with him. That's my advice."

Trees didn't want to dick around with any of these guys. "Roger that."

"Report in often, stay safe, and do your best."

Trees didn't want more babysitters. He liked to work alone, particularly since he was usually hacking his way into other people's tech, but he wanted to waste time arguing about his company-sponsored daddies even less. "Any parameters?"

The trio of bosses looked at one another, then shook their head. "Just do what needs to be done."

CHAPTER
Three

"If we want to hit the ground running, we should game plan before we land," Matt suggested in the seat beside him, cowboy hat perched on his knee.

Trees didn't disagree, but it was fucking hard to plan when they had no idea what they'd find once they hit the ground. "I'm going straight to the racetrack to talk to the two"—*horny assholes*—"security guards who last saw Laila."

Matt nodded. "We don't know what she might have said to them once they walked off camera. I'll go with you. The other two can grab a car and start trailing the truck Victor Ramos rented in his late brother's name."

If the cowboy stayed out of his way… "Works for me."

Trevor seemed like a stand-up guy. Coincidentally enough, he and One-Mile Walker had gone to high school together. Neither had been a big fan of the other. Trevor had nicknamed Walker Serial Killer, which proved that Forsythe had decent instincts. Jack Cole's friend Ghost, on the other hand? Trees was more than cool keeping distance between them. If someone had put a gun to his head and forced him to describe the guy in one line, tatted-up, antisocial badass motherfucker would be about right. Apparently, his name was Grayson. Trees didn't know if that was first or last, and he didn't feel like asking since he was pretty sure Ghost would look through him with those dead, silvery eyes—before he tried gouging out his heart with a screwdriver.

Montgomery's phone dinged. "I just got an update from Stone in the war room. Looks like the U-Haul is still traveling north, on approach to Tallahassee."

"They won't be stopping there."

"How do you know?"

Trees scowled at Matt. "They're taking that Ferrari someplace where Victor can either sell it or hide it. Since I don't think he took the car for the money, I'm betting on the latter. And Tallahassee isn't a great place to stash something that flashy. Besides, if Victor is smart, he'll want to get far away from the scene of the crime."

The big blond cowboy nodded in seeming agreement. "True. They don't know when the cops might be onto them."

"Or Geraldo Montilla." But neither was Victor Ramos's biggest issue. Trees was on a mission to separate the asshole from Laila. Whatever he'd done to hurt and coerce her was coming to a violent and very final end.

"If he catches them, I'm sure Ramos would beg for the cops. Where do you think he's taking Laila?"

That question had been bugging Trees. "I don't know. If they aren't going to unload the car for cash, then…my best guess is they're using it as leverage, to hold something over Montilla's head."

"Like?"

"Maybe her family's safety." After all, that was probably what Victor had threatened, too. But what was in it for Ramos?

"Laila is in a rough spot, trapped with someone ruthless who's hurt her before. But from what I understand, she's a tough woman. Smart. She'll—"

"Be fine?" He raised a brow at the cowboy. The son of a bitch better not let those words come out of his mouth.

"Survive. At least until we find her. Sometimes that's all we can hope for." Matt sounded like he spoke from experience, and Trees wondered what that was about. But the cowboy ended the conversation and looked out the window with a somber stare.

Trees glanced across the plush cabin. Trevor and Ghost both hunkered down in their enormous leather seats. Trevor looked like a bureaucrat—nondescript haircut, tailored suit, and nice manners. But there was something brutally shrewd and aware about the guy, even when he seemingly closed his eyes and relaxed. Ghost didn't bother with the pretense of a nap. He focused his unblinking stare straight ahead, exercising the kind of still and patience that told Trees the guy would be a deadly fucking professional in action.

Trees tried to kick back and drift off, but images of Laila pelted his brain. He needed to figure out what she was up against and what she might be planning. He wanted to be fully prepared to help her when he found her.

The rest of the plane ride was silent. After a smooth landing, each of them grabbed their bags and promised to check in with news. Then they hit the ground running, splitting up as soon as their feet touched terra firma.

The ride to the racetrack south of Orlando was both a frustrating snarl of traffic and a total waste of time. The big guard in the wifebeater showed up with nothing but bad attitude and a seeming case of amnesia, because he claimed he couldn't remember anything. A few hundred bucks loosened his tongue but didn't help him impart any new light. According to him, the minute Laila had followed him and his no-show counterpart to the guard shack, she'd trapped them inside and fled.

The interview lasted less than ten minutes.

Matt drove away from the racetrack, navigating his way into a turn lane with a scowl. "What did you think?"

If he was going to have to deal with the albatross of Walker's bestie, he might as well use the guy as a sounding board. "Not much more than I thought before. Laila is helping Ramos for a reason. At first I thought it was because he threatened her."

"That's still possible."

"Likely, even. But I keep replaying things she said to me... She's fucking done with her family being hunted. She wants her sister to be happy and her nephew to have a normal childhood."

"What does she want for herself?"

Trees shook his head. "Laila doesn't think about that. I doubt it's even crossed her mind. But there's a chance she's cooperating with Ramos because she thinks something will change."

"Like?"

Elbow resting on the car door, he tapped his thumb against the hard plastic beneath. "Like helping Ramos will somehow get Montilla —and maybe even Ramos, too—out of the picture."

Matt snorted. "Eliminating them both would be ballsy, but maybe she's onto something. It's not far-fetched to think that Montilla will hunt Ramos down and squash him like a bug for stealing his classic

Ferrari. After all, if we got our hands on the footage of the theft in a couple of hours, what are the odds the owner of the stolen vehicle hasn't seen it?"

Trees had thought of that. "He has, way before us. It also stands to reason that if we could figure out who Ramos was from the clip, so could Montilla—if he didn't already guess."

"You don't get where Montilla is without knowing shit."

"You don't. You also don't get where Montilla is by turning the other cheek or ruling with anything less than an iron fist. He'll come after Ramos—hard."

"If he can find the weasel. Do you know where he might hole up?"

"Since EM Security raided Emilo Montilla's Mexican compound and One-Mile killed the bastard?" Trees shook his head. "But I've done a round with him before. If I can find him, I can take him."

"If you were Ramos, would you stay in the States?"

"Knowing Geraldo Montilla had a long enough reach to get me in either country? I'd go where I have home-turf advantage. Someplace I know better than my adversary ever will and can rely on the locals not to out me for a buck."

"Same." Matt pulled onto the freeway. "Any idea where this fucker is from?"

Trees wished he had a place to hunker down with his computer and dig into this son of a bitch's life, but he could make do with his phone. After a few searches, some cross-checking, and tapping into a couple of hush-hush resources, he found what he needed. "On the Gulf coast in Mexico, in the state of Tamaulipas. It's a little fishing village. La Pesca. I think we go there."

Matt hesitated. "Check in with Trevor and Ghost. See if Ramos is still headed with the U-Haul in the same direction."

Trees texted Trevor and got an instant reply. "Given the truck's most recent sighting by a traffic cam, yep. But they're a good three hours behind Victor and Laila. They're trying to catch up, but…"

"It'll be a while before Trevor and Ghost lay eyes on them. Still, I think you're right. We fly to Ramos's turf, keep a low fucking profile, and wait a day or two. See if he shows up."

"And if he does"—Trees flashed a smile full of teeth and malevolence—"I'll be waiting."

———— •◦•◦• ————

Mexico

Victor's loud demands over the gentle ocean breeze jerked Laila awake from her nap the following afternoon. She jackknifed up and stared around the unfamiliar bedroom blankly, trying to remember how she got here.

After driving all night and half of yesterday, Victor had finally pulled his truck beside a bright green villa, sandwiched between the turquoise water of the Gulf and a similar unit in sunny yellow. Other than food and bathroom breaks, their only other stop had been in Brownsville, just before they'd left the US. There, they had transferred the Ferrari from the U-Haul and into a truck some of his henchmen had brought. They'd abandoned the rental in a retail parking lot and pressed into Mexico after a drive-thru breakfast Laila had declined. She refused to owe Victor for anything.

Around noon, they'd driven through a town so small it could barely be called a village. Ten minutes after that, they'd stopped here. Laila hadn't asked questions when he'd shown her into what looked like a vacation rental. She had simply locked the door, propped a chair under the knob, made sure her guns were loaded and within reach, then showered and collapsed into the fluffy white bed. Sleep had come slowly. She'd tried not to miss Trees while she'd tossed and turned. Despite her exhaustion, she ached for his strong arms, his woodsy scent, his understanding, his kiss. What must he be thinking? Feeling?

The next thing she knew, Victor's raised voice outside her door awakened her. She sat up with a gasp and glanced out the window. The late afternoon sun dipped toward the horizon. Sighing, Laila rolled out of bed, tossed on the robe the resort had provided, then yanked the door open with a scowl. "Why are you yelling?"

He ended the call with a curse and dropped his phone on the kitchen table. "I'm tired of dealing with incompetent fools. I told

Miguel to call me the minute he heard Montilla started looking for me."

"And?" Laila eyed his device, wishing she could grab it and assure her sister that she was safe...at least for now. And she would love to hear Trees's voice. But he must know she'd walked out of his house with Victor of her own free will. Why would he ever want her again after she had betrayed his trust?

"The *cabrón* waited nearly twenty-four hours to tell me anything."

Laila wasn't surprised. Miguel had always been more interested in looking tough than being useful. He'd happily sampled both the cartel's product and whores daily. "Montilla knows you took the car, yes?"

"Of course. They have sicced their *sicarios* on me."

Hitmen. Laila wasn't surprised. Surely, Victor wasn't, either. "That is good. You have *el jefe*'s attention. It is the perfect time to strike. Do you know who they sent to kill you?"

Off the top of her head, Laila could think of more than one killer Montilla employed. Most weren't well paid—except in drugs. No one expected them to live long, so cartels viewed them as expendable. But knowing who Montilla had tasked with ending Victor would tell her a lot about the drug lord's reaction.

Victor looked grim. "He sent them all. The first one to bring me to him—preferably alive—will be rewarded."

Laila's blood ran cold. Montilla was even more furious than she'd imagined. He would demand retribution of the worst kind. She needed to put distance between her and Victor, lie low somewhere else. And she had to come up with a good reason for leaving here. If she didn't... when Montilla's hitmen came, she would be a casualty, too. Or worse, a prisoner tortured repeatedly to within an inch of her life until she gladly begged for death.

"We must act quickly and—"

"And what? This fucking plan of yours is likely to get me killed." His eyes narrowed with rage as he stalked closer. "Was that your plan all along?"

Laila's heart rate surged. Since she'd been startled out of sleep, she'd forgotten her guns on her nightstand. Casually, she eased back into her bedroom and eyed the weapons—but she was still too far to reach them. "No. I simply want to protect my family. And do you truly want to work for that *pendejo*? The way he treats people as if they are beneath him, especially Emilo, who was your friend…"

Not that Victor would win any humanitarian awards. But he was egomaniac enough not to see the very flaws he hated in others reflected in himself.

"I cannot be under Geraldo's thumb. And I would run the business better. Under my leadership, Tierra Caliente would be more powerful than ever."

Laila tried not to scoff at his big dreams. "Exactly. So this is the path you must follow. Does Miguel know where to find Montilla?"

"No, but he has a contact, someone inside. He won't say who, but this person claims to be unhappy with the way Montilla runs the organization. If we pay him well, he will tell us what he knows."

Likely so, but in Laila's experience, information that had to be bought was often full of half-truths at best.

"Once we learn where Montilla is holed up, tell Miguel to have his contact pass along our terms for the car's return. This is where the bargaining chip I told you about comes in. If I explain now, it will not make sense. But information is power and once you know the hole where the fox is hiding—"

"No." He charged her way again. "I'm tired of your games. Explain this bargaining chip now."

Laila scrambled back, plucking the guns from the nightstand and aiming at him. She had known she wouldn't be able to put Victor off for long. Her time was running out. "Think, Victor. Would I really mislead you?"

He stopped coming at her. "I'm beginning to wonder."

"What would you do if I have?"

"I would hunt down your sister, and I would show her no mercy."

"Precisely." So she would have to kill him if he stopped believing her. "You know I would never want that. So I am positive my plan will put you on Montilla's throne."

Victor grumbled. "You promised me information."

"And you will get it as soon as you learn where Montilla is. In the meantime, I will walk to the village, blend in, and see if any of his men have come looking for you."

Victor tried to dissect her intentions with his stare. "And what then?"

"If it is not safe here, we leave and take the car with us. But I do not think it wise to keep it in the truck, sitting in plain sight. It looks out of place among vacationers and attracts attention you do not need."

A grudging grunt told her that he hadn't thought of that, but he didn't disagree. "When you reach town, go see Gustavo Pastrana. He is a mechanic. Tell him I need a favor and to make me space in his warehouse."

As much as Laila didn't want to associate with others on Victor's behalf, she had to appear like his ally, and it gave her an excuse to put miles between her and Victor. "All right."

"While you are in town, pick up food from the market. I am starving."

Laila wanted to remind him that she was his partner, not his slave. But that argument would be lost on him. Instead, she lowered her guns and chose a tactic he would understand. "I cannot be your eyes and ears in town if I return here."

He mulled that over, then pulled out some bills from his pocket. "True. Besides, others who were once loyal to Emilo will be arriving soon. You go buy some clothes. A hat, too. Disguise yourself. Find a place to stay. Blend with the locals and listen in on them. No one will see you as a threat."

As long as Montilla's hitmen couldn't tell at a glance that she was the woman who had distracted the security guards so Victor could steal the car, she should be safe. Not only would the *sicarios* never see her as a threat, they wouldn't even look at her twice if she seemed like just one of the townsfolk. "That will be best. With this money, I will also buy a phone so I can call you if I hear anything important."

Victor glared at her in warning. "Remember... If you betray me, your sister will pay dearly. You know I am well versed in causing pain."

He was, along with degradation, humiliation, and terror. "I will do anything to spare Valeria."

The smile that stretched across Victor's face was nothing short of superior. "Go."

Laila didn't give him time to change his mind. Despite the fact the sun would set in less than two hours, she went in search of her clothes and the flip-flops she'd found abandoned at a park on their way to Orlando, then hustled out the door.

The February afternoon was temperate, much warmer than Louisiana. She'd missed Mexico's warmth and the tropical vegetation where Trees lived.

But if you had a choice between the sun and the man, which would you choose?

Trees, always.

The sun sank lower as she reached the sleepy little village. Laila found a woman selling clothes from a table leaning against the side of a run-down building. She negotiated the purchase of a flowing, lace-trimmed skirt and a matching blouse, both in white. On the next street over, she picked up more underwear, some toiletries, a floppy hat, sunglasses, and a burner phone. After she donned her new things in the store's restroom, she spent a little more money on a street taco that tasted like heaven and pocketed the rest of the cash. It bothered her to take anything from Victor, but she was doing a job for him—watching his ass. That should pay well. As far as she was concerned, they were even.

As she ate, Laila set up the phone, then stared at the plastic device longingly, but she didn't dare reach out to her sister until she secured a location for the stolen car and found a place to lay her head for the night. And she couldn't tell Valeria where she'd gone. The less her sister knew, the less danger she would be in.

What about Trees? Will you call him later, too?

As much as she ached to, no. What would she say? How could she possibly apologize? Or atone?

With the final rays of sunlight, she finished eating and sauntered up one of the town's narrow streets, looking for both Gustavo Pastrana and a place to stay. The mechanic was easy to find. He looked close to her age with tattoos that covered him from his neck to his fingertips.

He eyed her with blatant appreciation that made her uncomfortable—until she dropped Victor's name. Then he was suddenly all business.

"Is he in town?" Gustavo asked.

Laila had no idea how much Victor trusted this mechanic. His ink suggested he'd been more than a little involved with a cartel or two in the past. She didn't remember him from Emilo's compound, but that meant nothing. Her late brother-in-law had employed men all over his territory. And if Victor intended to let this man hide a rival's fifty-million-dollar car, didn't that suggest he trusted Gustavo on some level?

"Soon," she hedged just in case, offering a smile to an older man who passed them, eyeing her suspiciously.

"Papá, finish cleaning inside. I will take care of everything out here," Gustavo told his father in rapid-fire Spanish.

The older man merely scowled and nodded before disappearing inside.

Through a window, Laila watched the old man wipe down a counter and reach for the ringing phone as Gustavo went on. "Don't mind him. He is getting grumpy with old age. So what does Victor need?"

"Do you have a space in your warehouse to store a car?"

Gustavo lit a cigarette and took a long drag. "What can you tell me about the vehicle?"

Why did he want to know? "Nothing. He simply sent me ahead to ask if you had room."

The mechanic looked her up and down. "He is fucking you, I presume. You're a pretty, tasty treat, after all."

Everything inside Laila urged her to step back. Hell, to turn and leave. But since she'd been Victor's possession once, she knew his expectations. So would this man, most likely. Cowering from any of his friends would only earn her ridicule and punishment, even allowing this man access to her body. She would be better off playing along.

"Naturally. Can you help him?"

He took a drag of his cigarette and blew out his smoke. "Yeah, tell him to bring it."

She nodded, hoping the car would be secure here. "I will let him know."

Laila thanked him, then quickly called Victor with the news.

"Good. I'll bring the truck," he told her. "Are Montilla's thugs looking for me around town?"

"I have heard nothing yet." Though she hadn't exactly asked, and it was entirely likely there were eyes and ears everywhere. "But I am still gathering information."

Victor grunted, then hung up.

Grateful that was over, she wandered down the street, toward what looked like a local hotel. The pastel building was a bright, two-story structure, surrounded by lazily swaying palms. A series of tiki huts outside added to the resort-like feel. The one beside the pool seemed to double as the bar. The other, just beside it, had been set aside for relaxation and games.

She bypassed them and went in search of the office. Hopefully, it wouldn't be too expensive to stay here, since it was the closest hotel to town. The others were near the beach.

As she approached the little office with the loud air conditioner humming from the wall, she passed under an awning. Out of the corner of her eye, she saw a pair of men emerge from one of the rooms. One looked well-built and athletic as he settled a hat on his head. But it was the other who caught her attention, broad and startlingly tall and achingly familiar.

Trees.

Shock sucked the air from her lungs. He was here? How had he found her? And how would she muster the strength to walk away when all she wanted to do was run into his arms?

For his sake, she had to.

As if he was attuned to her, Trees suddenly turned. His stare zeroed in on her, swallowing her whole in a glance.

Her heart, her breaths, her thoughts all stopped. She felt pinned in place, as if he saw right through her disguise.

No, that was her paranoia. Trees couldn't possibly know it was her. She wore different clothes and shoes. She had donned sunglasses and a hat. At most, he would think she was a stranger who looked like her.

But the longer she returned his stare, the more suspicious he would be. She needed to act like a local out for an evening walk.

On shaking legs, she pivoted away and headed back toward Gustavo's garage. Her heart roared in her ears, threatening to beat out of her chest, as she lifted her sunglasses higher onto her nose, then adjusted her hat in the breeze. She prayed she looked as if she didn't have a care, because she could hardly breathe past her apprehension.

Trees couldn't stay in this village. Ugly things would happen. The consequences would be too terrible.

Then she remembered that Victor was heading this way. And if he saw Trees... Well, there was no way Victor had forgotten the man who had blown his brother's head off mere days ago.

Dios mío.

Trembling, Laila glanced over her shoulder, hoping Trees had looked past her. But he was charging straight for her on those ridiculously long legs.

Panic hit her. If she turned back to him, he would know it was her. If she continued forward, she would lead him into danger. On either side of the street, she saw nothing but houses closed up for afternoon *siestas*.

She had nowhere to go—and she had to act fast.

But was there really a choice? Trees had to come first.

She turned around, determined to prevent Victor from spotting him during his drive into town and deciding it was a fabulous time for revenge. Trees was already on her. She ran into his chest with a gasp.

"Laila." He plucked the sunglasses from her face as the wind blew her hat away.

She was too ensnared by his nearness to protest.

He looked more intense and even more manly than she remembered. And more beloved. He cupped her shoulders, fastening his stare on her, his green eyes so sharp and full of concern. Laila froze. Every nerve stood on end. Heat sizzled everywhere he touched her. She'd missed him far more than she wanted to admit and ached to press herself against him, to throw herself into his arms and give herself completely to him.

But that was her emotion talking. She couldn't let her feelings rule her. They weren't real. The coming danger was. "You shouldn't be here. Go. Please. Return to Louisiana. Do not look for me again."

"I'm not leaving without you. Tell me what happened. Why did you take off? You could have stayed in the panic room and been safe."

She couldn't waste time explaining that Victor had threatened to burn his house down. It was more important to persuade him to leave this town and this country—and her—behind.

"I did not want to be safe. I wanted to be free. Let me go."

"Whatever you're doing here, whatever reason you had for walking out, I know it had something to do with keeping your family safe. Ensuring that isn't your job; it's mine. I'm going to make sure you, your sister, and your nephew are protected. All you have to do is tell me what's going on."

No wonder she'd been falling for this man. He was noble and watchful. Kind and heroic. And she hadn't believed in him until it was too late.

You never know what you've got until it's gone…

And like a fool, she'd spent so much of her time with him scheming to escape. She had only ever let herself believe in him for a few moments in the dark, in secret, when he'd made love to her after killing Hector. For that one night, she had closed her eyes, pretended to be a woman without a violent past, and given herself to Trees completely.

Laila shook her head. "There is nothing to tell. I do not want you here. Go and leave me be."

"Trees?" the other man in the cowboy hat called with a bob of his head up the street.

On the corner, Gustavo stood, watching their every move.

Laila tried not to panic, but the mechanic would call Victor, who was likely already on his way. There would be violence, and since not many men were as tall as Trees, Victor would know immediately who had come to town and why.

Before she could wriggle away, Trees plucked her off the ground. As if she weighed nothing, he carried her between the nearest two houses, ignoring her struggles, until they were out of Gustavo's sight.

He pushed her against the wall, palms beside her head, caging her in. "I will never leave you. I will never stop coming for you. So tell me why you went with Victor, let me fix it, then I'll take you home, Laila. And I'll love you for the rest of my life."

His words wrenched her heart. There was nothing she wanted more than to throw herself against him, arms and legs clinging, as she lost herself in him and pretended danger didn't exist.

Impossible.

Tears welled in her eyes. She tried to blink them away, but she wasn't quick enough. As one rolled down her cheek, she bit her lip to hold in a sob and tried to wrench away before he saw her weakness.

Too late.

"Laila." His rough voice caressed her. He cradled her head in his massive hands, fingers thrusting into her hair. "Little one…"

She was powerless to stop him when he surged forward and covered her with his big body, plastering her against the wall. He captured her lips with his and swallowed her whimper as she opened helplessly to him, welcoming the press of his mouth and the drive of his tongue. She clung to him. As she drowned in his kiss, she dug her nails into his shoulders, silently begging for more, as she writhed to get even closer. For one selfish moment, she ignored everything, fearing that now would have to last her for the rest of her life.

Trees groaned as he plunged deeper. The sound reverberated through her body. Time stood still. Everywhere he touched her, he seared her. And she welcomed it. Even if the sun was hotter in Mexico, this was the first time she'd felt warm since Trees had left for his mission two and a half endless days ago. Laila basked in him, breathed with him, welcomed the blistering heat of him.

If she hadn't been sure how she felt about Trees before, now it was clear. She loved him. Granted, she had nothing to compare these feelings to. She'd always loved crisp morning breezes in spring, vanilla in fresh-baked cookies, and sea foam on the sand. But this was so much stronger. She loved him as completely as she loved Valeria or Jorge, but this love came with a passion that was unlike anything she knew. She didn't have words to describe it, but having felt it, having acknowledged it, she knew she would never be the same.

Together, they panted and clung. Trees dragged his hands down her back until he cupped her backside and lifted her. She couldn't stop herself from spreading her legs and welcoming him in between, wrapping her arms around him tighter, and, since she could never speak the words aloud, telling Trees she loved him with her kiss.

He yanked away and stared into her eyes, breaths rough. "Come back with me."

Laila was so tempted. Some part of her wanted to rail that stopping the cartels wasn't her responsibility, that she had already suffered at the hands of Tierra Caliente. Why should she now have to rip out her heart and play the hero? It wasn't fair. Unfortunately, life wasn't. If she wanted safety and justice for her family, there was a price. To protect Valeria and Jorge, the cost would be her heart.

"I cannot." She pushed him away. "You have to go."

"Goddamn it, Laila. Tell me what the fuck is going on. I'll—"

"Buddy, there's a truck coming. It looks like the one Trevor and Ghost said they spotted before it disappeared across the border," the cowboy said, standing less than a dozen feet from them, blocking the view of anyone on the street.

Terror chilled Laila's veins. Victor was here. Gustavo would fill him in. Then all hell would break loose. "Go. Please. Now. Don't let Victor see you."

"Where is that son of a bitch?" Trees craned his head around to scan the street, all while covering her with his body.

If they had more time and if she wasn't convinced that Trees would put himself in danger to save her, she would have spilled everything to him—why she'd left, what her plans were, how she saw this nightmare ending. She might also make promises to return to his life, his arms, and his bed. But if she said any of those things, he would not only risk himself, he would do it full-throttle, holding nothing back, until the cartel put him in the ground. If Victor couldn't find the smarts or the guts to kill Trees, Montilla would. Emilo's ruthless father definitely had the resources and the *cojones* to get it done.

"Do not do this. Please. Leave it alone."

Trees turned back to her with a scowl. He wasn't going to let her go, despite her pleading, despite the cowboy telling him danger was approaching. "Like hell. Why did you help Ramos steal Montilla's Ferrari?"

She would have to make him want to leave.

Laila took a deep breath and forced herself to look him in the eye. "Because he wanted it, and I thought he would look sexy driving it."

"Sexy?"

Something inside her died as she forced herself to lie to him. "Do you always believe every sad story a woman tells you? I have been with Victor for a long time. I am attached to him. When he came for me, I saw the chance to return home and resume my life. Of course I took it."

Trees looked at her, dumbfounded. "You want to be with him?"

"Of course. I always have."

He scowled. "Bullshit. You can't fake the terror you felt for him the night he cornered you in the women's room of that hotel. You were desperate to escape. You screamed for help—until he tried to strangle you. You kicked and scratched and tried to get away."

"It is a game we enjoy. It is our foreplay. I like sex rough." That lie turned her stomach, but to save Trees's life, she told it without flinching.

"I don't believe you."

"You should. If you came here to find me, you have wasted your time." She jerked from his grasp. "Leave. Go back where you belong."

"No." He grabbed her arm again. "If you like the way he fucks you so much, why did you just kiss me with your whole heart?"

"I did not say you lacked skills. Your abilities between the sheets are quite good and kept you happily believing everything I told you." She shrugged. "But Victor does me better."

"That's a lie."

"If that is what you need to tell yourself..." She yanked free again. "But the truth would be better for you. I am leaving. You should do the same. Do not follow me."

Then Laila darted down the narrow path between the houses, skirting the cowboy, before she dashed down the street in time to see Victor barreling toward her, gun in hand. A wave of trepidation threatened to pull her under, but she had to stay strong.

She headed Victor off, hands up to stop him, doing her best to keep him far from Trees. "Victor—"

"Where is that bastard? I'm going to fucking kill him."

"I sent him away. Do not be distracted. We have bigger things to do. The car, did you settle it?"

"Gustavo is handling that now, so I have time to put a bullet between that son of a bitch's eyes for killing Hector." He shoved her out of the way. "Where the fuck are you, Scott?"

God help Trees if he was foolish enough to seek a fight now. It would be his demise. He didn't know how dirty Victor fought. He might not understand no one in this town would help him.

She grabbed Victor by the elbow. "You must stay focused."

With a growl, he shrugged her off. "I am—on revenge. He will pay for all he's done."

"Hector was reckless. He and his wife kidnapped a baby with plans to end her little life."

Victor turned to glare at her as if she was half-witted. "I know. I helped them. Who gives a shit about a baby? Oh, you think Scott is noble for saving the poor, innocent child, don't you? That makes him heroic in your eyes. But he still forced you to his bed, didn't he?"

Laila let the lie stand. If she told Victor the truth, he would only come after Trees harder.

"Your fight now is with Montilla so you can take over the cartel. Ignore your petty tiff with that nobody of a paid mercenary. He can do nothing to stop you once you become the leader of Tierra Caliente. You will be untouchable. But you will fail if you let yourself be distracted."

Victor stopped and looked around the street as if he saw nothing and no one. "I don't see Montilla anywhere. I have plenty of time to end the asshole who killed my brother." He gripped her arm. "Who dared to touch what is mine."

Laila blanched. Normally, she wouldn't risk inciting Victor, but she must keep his attention on her, not Trees, whom she prayed had taken her advice and fled. It was a good sign that he and the cowboy hadn't come out to confront Victor.

She jerked her elbow from his grip. "I have fresh gossip. Montilla's men are in town, watching for you. If you do anything to draw their attention…"

"You are sure?" His eyes narrowed.

"Yes."

His curse told her that if he didn't exactly believe the lie, he at least believed it was possible. Hopefully, that would be enough for now. "Walk back to my villa. I will collect the car and meet you there. We will take it and find someplace more secure, somewhere Montilla and that freakishly tall bastard will never find us."

That would never work. If Trees was anywhere close, he would find her trekking the road alone. He would follow her. And he would take her. "Let me stay with you." She forced herself to hold his hand and squeeze it. "Be your eyes and ears. Who else can you trust?"

Victor glared her way, then glanced down at their joined hands. "I'm not convinced I can trust you, *chiquita.*"

"If I wanted you dead, I would not have told you that Montilla's men are coming, and the longer we argue, the closer they get." She tugged him toward the garage. "Let us reclaim the truck before Gustavo locks it away and get on the road. Or instead of hiding, maybe we simply move forward with our plan and exchange the car for Montilla's bargaining chip."

He scowled. "What do you mean?"

"Once we are out of town, I will explain. All of it." She swallowed nervously, looking for Trees.

What was he doing? Thinking? Or had he gone?

Suddenly, she felt his eyes on her. He was still near. Terror gripped her.

"Always promising me later," he snarled. "I'm done waiting. Tell me now or I will find your tall hero and shoot him."

He would. Laila had no doubt. Her heart stuttered. Once she revealed her plan, she would have little leverage left over Victor. He would no longer see her as a partner, just an expendable nuisance. But his mistreatment or his bullet was better than watching Trees die.

"Montilla is holding a prisoner. The Edgingtons, who own EM Security? Geraldo abducted their sister, Kimber, and is keeping her captive. We can use that against him."

"That's it?" he thundered. "That's your bargaining chip? I already know he has her. That's not useful."

Laila blinked. She hadn't considered the possibility that he knew of Kimber's abduction. But it made sense. If he had a spy on the inside, it was possible he'd already been tipped off. *Carajo!* She had to think fast. The tactic that always worked best was to stroke Victor's ego.

"Of course you are aware of the captive. I merely suggest you use her as leverage, so she goes from being a bargaining chip Montilla would use to force EM Security to give up my sister's location to a liability that could weaken them, perhaps even prove their downfall— all orchestrated by you. If you succeed, there are few who would challenge your right to run the cartel."

Victor stared at her as if he could see through her. Abruptly, he snaked one hand around her nape. The other clamped down on her jaw. He jerked her closer, against his body, until his angry face hovered a mere inch above hers. His threat was clear, but still he spoke it aloud. "If you're full of shit, if you're playing me… I will kill you, Laila. And I won't give you a polite double-tap to the head. I'll rape you. I'll starve you. I'll torture you. I will make you beg for the end, and I will not give it to you. I will let you wonder how long I intend to keep you alive to use for my perverse amusement. The answer will be until I get bored with your suffering. And that may be never."

She didn't want to be afraid of Victor, but he never made idle threats. Once her plan backfired and he realized she'd been using him for her own ends with every intention of feeding him to Montilla, he would do exactly what he warned.

Suddenly, Trees emerged from between the two houses, gun drawn, barreling toward them with ground-eating strides. "Get your fucking hands off her. Now!"

Trees watched Laila and Victor Ramos exchange words. He couldn't hear what they said, but it sure seemed like a fight. And he didn't like how the angry son of a bitch was looking at her.

But when he tried to jump out from between the two houses and intervene, Matt jerked him back, one hand wrapped around his arm, the other fisted in the back of his shirt. He was breathing hard. "Don't do it."

"Let me the fuck go," Trees growled.

"So you can commit suicide? No. I'm supposed to make sure you get back in one piece."

He tugged against Matt's hold again. "We're supposed to bring Laila back, too."

"You heard her. She doesn't want to come back with you. Let her go."

"She's lying. She's trying to protect her family." Then he realized Laila had thrown herself into Victor's path moments ago, and that had nothing to do with saving Valeria. "And me. She means to shield me. She's got some scheme…"

"Fucking listen to yourself, man," Matt growled in his ear. "I know you want to believe she's good and noble, but it's possible that after years with a cartel, she's warped, she's getting what she wants, and she played you."

The words went in Trees's ears…and right back out. "You don't know her."

"Maybe it's time to consider that you don't really, either. You spent a few days with her. And you…what? Spent a few nights with her, too, I guess. None of that makes you an expert."

"You trying to figure out this situation on the fly doesn't make you an expert, either. Why don't you do us both a favor? Shut the fuck up and let me handle this."

"No. You're in too deep. You're not thinking straight."

"You don't know me."

"I know what being compromised looks like. I'm staring at it."

Suddenly, Victor grabbed her neck in one hand, her jaw with the other and yanked her against him, looking furious as hell. Then he snarled something in her face that made her tremble.

Trees was done. Matt and his caution could go fuck themselves.

He elbowed the other operator, then twisted from his grip and shoved him back. "You don't make my decisions. If you're afraid, stay the fuck out of this."

Then he emerged onto the street, gun drawn. "Get your fucking hands off her. Now!"

Victor sent him a nasty smile, like he had something horrible planned he would thoroughly enjoy. Suddenly, he whirled Laila around, flattening her back against his chest to use her as a human shield. Then he raised his gun to her temple. "Or what, Scott? Whatever you're planning, I'll shoot her, and her death will be on your hands."

Trees risked a glance at her. Her body went tense. For a moment, she looked terrified. Then she breathed, and the expression disappeared.

Like she wasn't afraid of him anymore? Or as if she enjoyed the way the danger made her heart race? Did Laila actually get some sexual thrill from the adrenaline rush?

He couldn't address that now. He had to defuse this standoff first, make sure the motherfucker didn't hurt her.

"I don't care about Laila, except that I've been hired to bring her back. Hand her over and I'll let you live," Trees told Victor.

The thug scoffed, then gave him a condescending laugh—right before he jerked the gun from Laila's temple and aimed it directly at him. "Fuck off and die."

Then he pulled the trigger.

CHAPTER
Four

T rees recoiled as if he'd suffered a mortal body blow. Laila screamed, watching helplessly as blood sprayed from his right side. Then warm wetness splashed across her cheek. A splatter of red stained her pristine white blouse. He stumbled back. Horror filled her as he tripped on his huge feet and toppled back, falling, falling...like a giant redwood felled by an ax.

As he hit the ground, his head smacked the asphalt with a sickening thud. His eyes slid shut. His body went limp. His gun fell from his lax grip.

He didn't move.

"Trees!" she screeched, wildly elbowing Victor.

As soon as Laila got free, she skidded to her knees and crawled the remaining distance between them. Her heart raced. She trembled, tears stinging her eyes as she felt her way up his body. On his right, she encountered something warm and wet. When she lifted her hand, blood coated her fingers. Panic surged. "Trees!"

He didn't answer. He didn't even twitch.

That terrified Laila even more. His chest moved with each breath, and his pulse was seemingly steady, too. She was grateful for that. But he exhibited no other signs of life.

Her head screamed at her to save him, even as she prayed this wasn't happening. But it was, and she needed to act.

Her racing thoughts jumbled, making every thought seem agonizingly slow. Instinctively, she applied direct pressure to his wound, pressing her previously white skirt to his side, just as she caught sight of a movement up the street. Matt hovered in the shadows between the two houses where Trees had kissed her minutes ago. *Dios mío*, she wished she could go back and make him stay there safely. But it was too late, and now she didn't know the extent of his injuries. What if he wasn't merely bleeding? What if the blow to his head had caused trauma or the bullet had triggered internal damage? Or what if Victor took him prisoner to torture him before finishing him off?

She couldn't let that happen.

Help him, she mouthed at Matt.

But the stranger in the hat turned blurry. Laila hadn't even realized she was crying. It wasn't helpful. It wouldn't solve anything. She needed to stop and do something more productive. But when she blinked away the wetness pouring from her eyes, Matt was gone, melted into the shadows, apparently prepared to let Trees die ignominiously in the middle of a ramshackle Mexican road.

She alone would save him.

Pressing her skirt tighter against Trees's side, Laila tried to stem the bleeding, but red kept oozing from the wound and spreading up the white cotton. It was everywhere, abundant and horrifying. Panic set in. Trees needed medical attention now. But he wouldn't get it here. This little village had no hospital.

Still, Laila refused to give up. She continued pressing her skirt to the wound and started silently pleading with the God she was sure had forsaken her long ago to spare his life. "Please! Trees, no. Do not..." *Die.* She couldn't bring herself to say the word. "Stay with me."

Suddenly, Victor's cruel fingers gripped her hair, tugging her by her scalp. "Get up. Right now! The only man you get on your hands and knees for is me when I fuck you."

Laila opened her mouth to object, but he yanked so viciously she staggered to her feet.

"You lied to me about your feelings for him," he snapped. "So he will stay here and rot in the street. And you can remember him, bleeding out and far from home while he took his last breath. Now we're leaving...unless your claim that Montilla's men are nearby was a lie, too?"

Everything inside her resisted abandoning Trees. She ached to stay and get him help, until he could open his eyes and protect the world again. But if she did, Victor would only put another bullet in him.

As much as it killed her, she could keep him safer by getting Victor far away. Hopefully, Matt or some good Samaritan would render Trees aid once she and Victor were gone.

"I-it was not a lie." She stopped fighting those brutal fingers. "I swear."

"Now that shots have been fired, it's no longer safe here." He yanked even tighter on her hair. "And tonight I will remind you why I was the first man to shove his cock in your tight, dirty pussy and why I will also be the last."

Laila wasn't shocked that Victor had been the one to forcibly take her virginity in that dark, dank bed all those years ago, just as she didn't doubt he would make the next rape even more harsh and painful.

She'd been a fool to believe she could play him. She'd strutted in with her guns, her bravado, and her scheme, doing her best to convince him that she knew how to game the cartel. He'd bested her instead, pretending to be her partner, saying he no longer cared about owning her body. He'd merely placated her for the bargaining chip she'd sworn she had. Once she'd opened her mouth and proven herself an amateur, he'd seized control of the situation—and her. He would use both to his satisfaction.

She had made her bed; now she had to lie in it. But Trees...

He lay sprawled in the street, a puddle of blood forming around his body. She saw no sign of Matt. A few townsfolk stood around with wary eyes, staring at his unmoving form but not daring to help.

Suddenly, Gustavo Pastrana strode from the office and toward the cluster of observers with a cocky swagger. They parted to make a path for him. He passed each by, approaching Trees with purpose.

Then he held up a blowtorch, and his grin turned evil.

Laila tried to scream, hoping someone kind would help the man she loved, but Victor slapped his sweaty palm over her mouth and dragged her inside the warehouse just as the mechanic lit the flame on his device.

She tried to dig in her heels, but it didn't matter. Victor shoved her across the hot, musty interior, toward the truck. He only released his vicious hold on her long enough to hoist her up through the driver's-side door and shove her into the cab. Laila scrambled across the bench seat, reaching for the passenger door so she could flee and help Trees.

Victor merely seized her hair again, his fist at her nape, and yanked her into her seat. "You're not going anywhere. Buckle up. Don't try anything else or there will be a price."

There always was. But maybe she could use his greed for her to Trees's advantage.

"I will give you every part of me without a single protest for as long as you wish if you let me find him medical attention and get him to safety," she offered earnestly, reaching for the buttons of her blouse.

Victor cut her a nasty glance. "Gustavo is tending to him now, so it's too late. Besides, you will give me all of you for as long as I wish, regardless. Now shut up."

Grief sent her tears pooling and plunging down her face. Bartering her body for her bed and her food would be next, no doubt. She hadn't taken her guns into town, and he would soon seize her phone so she would be helpless again. But she no longer cared what happened to her. Trees's death was her fault. If she hadn't recklessly believed she could outsmart Victor, she might still be with him. Now the man she loved had paid with his life.

Victor turned the engine over, then stuck his hand out the window, gesturing to a boy working in the warehouse. The kid opened the door, and Victor gunned the truck, taking a right out of the giant, dilapidated building. Laila tried to peer through the back window for a glimpse of Trees—hoping against all odds that someone had saved him —but she only saw a cadre of well-armed men racing down the street, pointing in their direction, then hopping into a beat-up sedan, gunning their engines in pursuit, and pointing what looked like machine guns out their windows.

Shock swallowed her gasp. Were they Montilla's *sicarios?*

"Victor!" she warned him. "Behind us."

He floored it, glancing in the rearview mirror. "Montilla is on my tail. At least you weren't lying about that, *puta*. Where is your phone?"

She patted her skirt pocket. Empty. "It must have fallen out of my pocket during the commotion."

With a curse, he fumbled in his pocket and thrust his phone at her. "Call Estevan. Tell him we need a new truck and men to cover us right now. Tell him to meet us at..." He scowled, obviously thinking. "Fuck,

I don't know. Tell him to start driving north. We'll head south and meet along the way."

That would never work. The assassins would catch up to them too quickly. But she didn't correct Victor, simply took the phone from him dutifully while shoving back her worry and sorrow. "Passcode?"

Victor scowled.

"I cannot dial anyone without it."

He spit out a six-digit number, focused on rumbling the top-heavy vehicle down twisting dirt roads without toppling over. Behind them, the little blue sedan closed in.

After the fourth ring, voicemail picked up. She relayed Victor's message, then hung up. "Should I try someone else?"

"My brother would have had my back." He turned another sharp corner at insane speeds, and the truck teetered on two wheels. Sweat rolled down his brow.

If Montilla's men didn't kill her, Victor's driving probably would. With Trees gone, she almost didn't care.

There were no such things as miracles. But if there were and Trees had survived, she had to stay alive so she could keep him safe from Victor.

The world was a better place with Trees. He had friends and loved ones who would miss and mourn him. He had refused to see her as expendable, even though everyone else did. Other than Valeria, he was the only other person who would truly care if she was gone.

"Fuck!" Victor growled, correcting his steering as he came out of the turn.

Thankfully, the truck set down on all four wheels again.

"Should I try another number?"

"Call Miguel. He shouldn't be far away, and he owes me for fucking up last time. If he fucks me now, I'll cut out his tongue." He turned and shot her a dark stare. "Which I will do to you if you lie to me again. Do you understand?"

She nodded, trying to make herself as small as possible against the passenger door.

Laila hated falling into these old patterns. When EM Security Management had extracted her from her brother-in-law's compound last September, she'd sworn she would never be Victor's slave again. But here she was, back in his clutches, about to suffer...what? Days, weeks, months, years with him?

No. She would fight. She would get out. She would avenge Trees. She would never give up.

Scrolling through Victor's contacts, she dialed Miguel as Victor swerved at the last minute down a dirt road, fishtailing to kick up dust. But the truck was white and way too massive to hide. The sedan easily followed, now almost directly on their tail.

They opened fire.

Laila shrieked involuntarily, then forced herself to do something more active. "Give me your gun."

"What?" he shot back as if her demand was absurd.

"I will shoot back at them."

Victor hesitated, then snarled just before ripping the weapon from his holster and slapping it in her palm. "Aim carefully. This is all the ammo I have. The rest is back at the villa."

Along with the only other clothes she owned and Trees's semiautomatics.

She handed Victor his phone, disengaged the safety, took a deep breath, then leaned out the window, staring into the faces of Geraldo Montilla's men. Once she pulled the trigger, she would become their enemy, too. They would hunt her as relentlessly. They would not stop until she was dead.

She was tempted to turn the gun on Victor, end his vile existence, along with her torment, then run back to Trees and forget her rapist ever existed. But she would be sacrificing her family for her happiness, because Geraldo Montilla would still be out there, wanting to kill her sister and kidnap her nephew.

As much as she hated it, Laila needed Victor to be her shield against the narcotics king. He might still be her pawn, too, weakening Montilla while engaging in a futile attempt to take him down. Of course, Montilla would kill him. Victor was merely a gnat to such a powerful drug lord. But if she could learn Kimber's location, EM Security could save the poor woman and finish off Montilla. Only then would she and her loved ones have any hope of a future.

Beside her, she heard Victor bark at Miguel. She turned to find more sweat dripping down his brow as he navigated the winding road with both hands, his phone wedged between his shoulder and his ear.

Laila swallowed, clandestinely engaged the safety again, then pretended to struggle with the weapon.

Victor ended the call and scowled her way. "What the fuck are you doing?"

"I cannot fire the gun. I do not know why." She huffed for effect.

"Because you're a stupid whore. Give me that." He yanked the weapon from her grip and flipped the safety off. "Hold the wheel."

Was he crazy? They were driving over a hundred miles an hour, bouncing painfully down something that seemed more like a twisting dirt path than an actual road, and he wanted her to steer with one hand?

Still, what choice did she have?

"All right." She gripped the wheel, hoping this wasn't where and how her life ended.

Victor leaned out the window and started firing. A glance in the rearview mirror told her he hit nothing. He let out an ugly curse.

Up ahead, she saw a river that looked at least a few feet deep. "Victor, I have an idea."

"What the fuck do you want?" he shouted as he took his next potshot at the hitmen.

"What if we drove through that river? The truck is much taller than the sedan. Perhaps we will make it?"

He slammed back into the driver's seat, tossed the gun between them, and jerked the wheel from her grasp as he scanned ahead. "And they will get stuck. It might work. Perhaps you'll eat tonight after all. Hold on to something."

Laila did, clinging to the door with one hand, the dash with another, her teeth jarring as they rumbled down the road, straight toward the river. A bullet pinged off the door inches from her. She bit her lip to hold in a scream.

Finally, they reached the water and plowed into it, sending up a big splash that doused the windshield. Water poured in through the window Victor neglected to close, and he let out another frustrated curse. The gun between them bounced and slid across the seat. She grabbed it.

He ripped it from her hand. "Don't get smart. Sit there and don't move until we lose them."

She would do what he said—until she figured out how to either gain the upper hand or slit his throat.

Beside them the water rose along the sides of the truck, first covering the rims, then the tires, before the tide inched up the doors. Would they be swimming to the shore and abandoning the fifty-million-dollar car—while dodging Montilla's bullets? The engine made noises that weren't encouraging, and the tires wheezed and spun in the silt.

If circumstances forced them to give up the Ferrari and swim, Victor's punishment would be swift and severe.

Panicked, Laila started looking for other ways out of this mess when she realized two things. First, as they inched forward, the water level was beginning to recede. Second, the sedan remained impotently on the other side of the river, its profile too low to travel across. Thankfully, she saw no bridge in sight.

Finally, they made it onto the shore, plodded down a dirt path littered with vegetation, then finally found the remnants of an old road.

They were free—for now.

"That was too fucking close." Victor swiped at his sweating forehead.

Laila seized the opportunity. "I told you Montilla's men were in town."

"But you lied to me about your feelings."

"I simply do not want anyone's death on my hands." She tried to shrug him off. "Besides, you have never cared about them before. And you lied to me about yours as well."

"What do you mean?" he snapped, rattling the truck forward.

He was still obsessed with her, and it would be stupid to remind him that he'd been dishonest about that. "You said you had everything under control and that no one in your hometown would betray you. Someone obviously did."

"Gustavo warned me that his father had been acting oddly all afternoon. For that, I will have him killed."

His cavalier attitude about life and death shouldn't horrify her anymore, but it did. "Gustavo or his father?"

"Both. Neither are of use to me anymore. Now shut up. I need to think."

Laila said nothing for hours, not as they wandered into another town, finally met Miguel with another truck, transferred the car, then made their way to another village, where he found a cheap motel room. From the glove box, he produced a zip tie. Then he grabbed his gun and skipped dinner, buying a bottle of tequila instead.

Now that the adrenaline rush and chaos were over, all she could think about was Trees. Was there any chance Matt or a bystander had helped him? Or had they all simply let him be tortured by Gustavo's blowtorch while he bled out and died?

How would she ever know? Maybe she didn't want the terrible details. The thought of him being tortured and killed filled her with an empty, aching hole. Laila didn't know how she would ever plug up that horrible well of grief.

Inside the roach-infested motel, Victor zip-tied one of her wrists to the headboard attached to the wall. Then he flipped on the TV. "Something for you to watch while I take a shower. Then you'll take yours." He looked her up and down. "And lose those clothes."

"I have nothing else to wear."

His sly smile said that was completely on purpose. "Oh, well."

She shuddered as he disappeared into the bathroom. Then she saw his phone on the nearby table. It was a stretch, but she could reach it.

Laila scraped half the skin off her hand getting to Victor's phone, but she managed. Thankfully, she'd made a mental note of his passcode during their getaway. Though she knew her sister's number by heart, Laila didn't dare call her. Victor would know. And he would have a direct line to reach her. It was too dangerous. Instead, she reached out in the same way she had once used to escape Emilo's compound.

She launched the game Valeria loved to play and found the connect feature. Fingers shaking and tears streaming, she typed out a message.

Hermana, I am with Victor in a motel in Mexico, south of La Pesca, inland from the coast. He killed Trees. Tell EM Security I am sorry. I will touch base again when I can. Know I am trying to escape. Do not worry about me. Protect yourself and Jorge. I love you.

She hit send and stared at the message string. It was foolish to hope Valeria would answer now. Maybe tomorrow. Maybe next week. Her sister didn't play this game every day, and it was late.

To her shock, a bubble with three dots inside appeared next to her sister's screen name. Laila swiped at her tears, her heart racing as she waited.

The water cut off in the shower. Victor stepped out of the enclosure.

Type faster, she silently demanded of her sister.

She had maybe a minute—no more—before he emerged from the bathroom. She needed this message almost more than she needed to breathe. She would mourn Trees for the rest of her life. Avenge him, of course. As soon as she could put a bullet in Victor and get out of the country safely, she would. But right now she needed to know that her family was safe.

I am so relieved you are alive, but I will not let you suffer Victor again. When you pinpoint your location, tell me. I will get word to Trees. He did not die. He is still in Mexico, planning to rescue you tonight.

Laila's eyes nearly popped from her head. Trees was alive? Shock pinged through her veins and her mouth gaped. How was that possible? Who had helped him? It didn't matter; he was alive!

New tears—happy ones—trembled on her lashes. But reason tempered her thrill. Trees must be injured; he had nearly been killed. He shouldn't try to save her now. She couldn't let him. The last time had nearly been his death. This time, Victor would leave nothing to chance.

She had to stop Trees.

Victor jiggled the handle of the doorknob. She wished she had time to reread her sister's message—had she truly read it right?—but the door squeaked as he opened it.

Biting back a gasp, she closed the app, darkened the phone, then settled the device on the table. She nudged it just beyond her reach, hoping that would allay Victor's suspicions.

As she sat on the bed again, he emerged around the corner, looking between her and his phone with narrowed eyes. "What are you up to?"

"Nothing." She fidgeted. "Trying to get comfortable."

As if the notion of her well-being bored him, he shrugged and produced a blade. She flinched as her fear spiked, but he merely cut the zip tie and gestured her toward the bathroom. "Shower now. Then you can get comfortable—on your back with your legs spread. I want that pussy."

Since he had the upper hand—for now—Laila nodded meekly as he opened his bottle of tequila and sat on the bed, watching her with a leer. Best not to infuriate him. It was more important to live another day so she could get revenge and escape.

After she ensured Trees didn't risk his life for her again.

In the bathroom, she peeled off her clothes and climbed into the minuscule cubicle. No wonder Victor hadn't demanded sex here. In this tiny space, violating her would be virtually impossible. But he wouldn't deny his pleasure for long. Laila didn't think she could endure his touch. She could barely stand the sight of him, the smell of him. Even the idea of him made her stomach turn.

She'd have to deal with that, too. Keeping Trees from risking himself to rescue her came first. Since she couldn't call him or contact him through the gaming app, she had to get clever. But even if she could warn him, what were the chances he would heed her?

I will never leave you. I will never stop coming for you.

He meant that. He'd already traveled all the way from Louisiana to rescue her. Why would he stop when he was less than two hours away, especially after Matt had likely told him that Victor had dragged her from him against her will?

Laila sighed. How could she persuade a man determined to save her, who thought he was in love with her, from putting himself in harm's way again?

She couldn't...unless she gave him a reason not to love her anymore.

As she rinsed the blood and grime from her body, Laila turned over ideas in her head. Nothing came to her...until something terrible did.

No. She couldn't. There must be some other way that wouldn't put Trees through hell.

Like what?

She had nothing else, and time was running out. This idea... *Dios,* could she actually find the fortitude to go through with it? Then again, what choice did she have? This was her last resort. The worst part was, after she risked everything to save Trees, he would never speak to her again.

Laila clutched the wall and bowed her head, sobs wracking her as if someone had opened her chest and all the emotions she'd tried so hard to hide were spilling out. She gave herself over to the gaping wound of sorrow and mourned—for the breaking of her heart, for the happiness she and Trees would never share, for the damage she would do to the only man who had ever been good and kind to her. For knowing that he would soon look at her with hate.

Everything she had ever wanted or treasured slipped through her fingers. First, her freedom. Then, her mother. And now Trees. God, would she ever stop losing?

Laila dragged in a ragged breath and forced herself to stop wallowing in self-pity. Trees was more important than heartbreak. More important than pain and humiliation. Even more important than her own existence. No matter how much this plan devastated them both, she consoled herself with the knowledge that at least he would be alive to turn his back on her.

Finally, she dried her tears. Then she forced herself to stop crying and accept what had to be done. Besides, she couldn't go to Victor with puffy eyes and a red nose. He would be able to sniff out her scheme. As always, tears were a luxury she could not afford.

Her first priority was to ensure Victor consumed too much tequila and focused on sex. She would handle the rest.

"Buddy, you've got to lie down." Matt pushed him back to the makeshift bed in the doctor's back room.

Trees resisted, trying to vault to his feet. "Like hell. Laila is out there, under Victor's thumb, and I—"

"Love her. And you're worried about her. I know." Matt shoved him back to the mattress, as if the guy knew he got dizzy and queasy every time he stood. "But you can't help her if you don't heal first."

Trees cursed the limits of his body. "I also can't help her if Victor kills her."

"Given what I saw, he's not going to."

Trees hoped not, but the asshole sure could make Laila wish he had. That's what worried him most. "How much fucking longer am I going to feel like shit?"

"I'm not a doctor and my Spanish sucks, but I'm pretty sure he said twenty-four hours. It's been more like six. You'll have to at least wait until morning."

No. Fuck no. According to Matt, Victor had dragged her away from his prone form by her hair, and Trees could only imagine all the awful things that monster could do to her overnight. "It can't. Get that quack back here and make him give me something for this fucking headache so I can go and—"

"You have a concussion. You need to rest. If I get the 'quack' back here, it will be to give you a sedative so your body has time to heal. Jesus..." He sighed, sliding the cowboy hat back on his head.

Trees wanted to bat the Stetson off and punch the bastard, but Matt had saved his life. And he probably wasn't wrong. Still... "I'm losing my fucking mind worrying about her."

"I know you think she's a tiny thing who's no match for Victor. But she made it six years with him. If he wanted her dead, she'd be dead."

"Is it supposed to be better that he just wants to rape her?"

"No. There's no good answer right now. But if you run to her rescue when you're not up to the fight, then Victor will kill you...and she might be under his thumb forever."

Trees tried to stifle his frustration. He heard Matt's logic. He didn't even disagree. Well, he wouldn't if he wasn't so fucking worried about Laila. Goddamn it. "Has anyone heard anything from her?"

"Let me check in."

Matt disappeared down the hall with his phone, leaving Trees to pant against his pillow, feeling clammy and weak. He stared at the yellowing industrial ceiling, lamenting that the stitches in his ribs where the bullet had grazed him and the others at his crown where he'd fallen back on his head itched like hell. At least Matt had shot the son of a bitch coming at him with a blowtorch between the eyes, then dragged him to safety. Trees was grateful for that. He'd just be a helluva lot less agitated if he was already on the road finding Laila.

As much as he wanted to hop to his feet and track her down, he couldn't even take a shower right now without his head throbbing and his stomach pitching.

Unfortunately, lying here for hours gave him nothing better to do than imagine all the ways she was suffering.

Matt returned a few minutes later, clutching his phone. "Good news. Laila reached out to Valeria via a gaming app."

She must have gotten her hands on Victor's phone. Laila might be a little thing, but she was crafty. She was a survivor. Hope buoyed him. "And?"

"She's in one piece."

"Does Valeria know where she is?" If it wasn't too far, maybe he could muster the energy to jump in their rental and take off after her. After all, if he played this right, his gun would do most of the job. It wasn't as if the world, especially Laila, would miss Victor.

"No."

And there went his fucking hope.

"Even Laila doesn't know where she is, except in a motel southwest of La Pesca." Matt shrugged. "Sorry."

At least he had a clue to start with. Trees grabbed his phone and launched his map app.

Matt yanked the device from his hands. "No electronics for now, remember?"

It took most of his strength, but Trees lurched up and snatched it back. "This is fucking imperative. Life-or-death shit. My head will recover. I don't know if the same can be said of Laila if we don't go after her."

"I'll look for you." He pinched and flared his fingers along the screen, scrolling up, then down, before finally settling on an area. "There are a few villages she could be in. I'd have to do more research to narrow it down. That will take time."

"Hurry. A lot of those villages will be so small they won't even have a motel, so we can rule them out."

"Sure. I'll have something by morning. What do you want to eat?"

"Fuck food. And fuck you. Let's figure out where she is. I have the rest of my life to eat."

"You have to fill your tank."

Trees huffed because Matt clearly wasn't listening. "I won't care if I don't find her soon."

The other guy sighed and plucked off his cowboy hat. "Has anyone ever told you that you're a stubborn motherfucker?"

"Zy mentions that all the time." His mother used to tell him that, too. Said he was a lot like his father. Once, that had made him smile.

Trees shoved the thought away. He couldn't afford this stroll down memory lane while Laila hung in the balance.

"I'm not shocked. I'll get on this and find some food. You're not going to get far in your rescue attempt if you don't eat."

If wolfing down a sandwich would make Matt finally shut the fuck up? "Fine."

"Good." Matt's phone dinged and he glanced down at the device. "Valeria just heard from Laila again. She asked for your email address. Why would she want that?"

Trees wasn't sure. Maybe she'd found a way to send him a map of her location or her surroundings… Whatever it was, he'd take any help finding her.

"Give her this address." He rattled off one that downloaded to his phone. Whatever she sent, he needed to see it as soon as possible.

"Roger that." He texted the address. "Let's focus on food until we hear something."

The audible swoop told Trees the information was on its first leg to reaching Laila. Anticipation gripped him.

An hour passed. Then two. Food came and went. They focused their conversation on the villages southwest of La Pesca. There weren't many, and even fewer with lodgings. They were discussing the merits of two different ones when Matt sighed and stood from the nearby desk. "How do we know any of this is right? It's like looking for a needle in a haystack."

Matt wasn't wrong, but… "I'm not giving up."

"You've made that clear, buddy." Matt sounded exhausted.

Yes, the guy had saved his life, but Trees couldn't let up or stop now. "Ever been in love?"

"You going to give me the speech about how, if I'd ever really given my whole heart to a woman, I would understand why you're so desperate and determined to go after her now, health be damned?"

Trees refused to let the sharp comeback dissuade him. "Yep. Because if you ever had been in love, you'd know all that shit is true."

"Sure, but I also know if you were being rational, you'd understand that jumping in half-cocked to save her would be suicide."

They were at another impasse, and the problem was, neither of them were wrong.

"Look, why don't you try again to shower? Maybe that will make you feel better." Matt peeked out the window at the nearly black sky. "Because I doubt we're finding Laila tonight."

Trees checked his emails again. Nothing. The silence made him antsy. He knew damn well her opportunities to get her hands on Victor's phone would be few and far between. Hell, it was getting late, and she might already be asleep.

And she might also be suffering. Or dead, the seditious voice in his head warned.

As much as he fucking hated it, as much as it fucking chafed, he doubted he was getting any resolution tonight. It would be smarter to clean up and grab a few hours of sleep, then start his search again. But he wasn't leaving this fucking country without her.

"I'll try."

"Good call." Matt gave him a hand.

With a groan and another wave of dizziness, Trees lurched to his feet. He took a deep breath to fight the nausea and headed to the little bathroom, clutching the wall along the way. Fuck, he still felt clammy and weak, but it wasn't as bad. He'd take the small victory.

It took more time and energy to strip than it should. He had to sit to remove everything but his pants. But he finally got naked and stepped under the spray, hissing when the warm water beat down on his stitches. All he could find was a bar of antiseptic soap, but he used it all over, sagging against the wall when his head swam. It sucked to admit that Matt had been right, but if he'd gone out to save Laila like this, he probably would have been more of a hindrance than a help.

Praying like hell that she survived the night and that she forgave him for the delay, he vowed to rescue her come morning. And if Victor had harmed her in any way—hell, if he'd so much as made her cry—he was going to kill the son of a bitch. And not merely with a simple bullet or two. Yeah, he might be the tech guy of the team, but he and Zy had gone through some really shitty black ops training. They'd endured stuff that had killed lesser men in the same program. They'd learned things that would make the average psyche—and stomach—curdle. Despite everything he'd seen and the war zones he'd fought in, he'd never once considered unleashing any of that knowledge on an enemy combatant.

Trees would one hundred percent make an exception for Victor.

When he was finally clean, he sighed in exhaustion and stepped out of the stall, groping for a towel with his eyes closed. Halfheartedly, he dried off. After the room, along with his stomach, stopped spinning, he wrapped the towel around himself. A glance at the nearby basin proved Matt had settled his clean clothes and his toothbrush nearby.

So, Walker's bestie actually wasn't a flaming asshole like his pal.

Okay, he was probably being harsh to his teammate. One-Mile had been a lot more pleasant since his engagement to Brea Bell. Normally he'd think it was because the guy was getting regular pussy, which took the snarl out of most beasts. But he'd met the sniper's fiancée. He'd rarely met a sweeter girl, so he kind of hoped that Brea simply balanced Walker. And their wedding was just around the corner. Good for them. And hey, if someone as bad-tempered as One-Mile could find a woman to love him, Trees figured there was hope for him, too.

Which brought him right back to Laila. He'd threatened to marry her once. She hadn't believed him, but he'd been dead fucking serious. He would marry her tomorrow—if she'd say yes. And when he found her again, he would ask. Not in challenge. Not in sarcasm. For real, with roses and a ring and a promise to honor and protect her for the rest of his life.

As soon as he found her, saved her, and brought her home.

When he opened the bathroom door, a plume of steam billowed out. He felt a hundred fucking years old by the time he made it back to the cot. It didn't help that he was nearly a foot too tall for the damn thing.

Matt stood. There was something on his face Trees didn't like.

"What is it?"

"You okay?"

When Matt answered a question with a question, it was obvious the guy was stalling. "Fine. What's going on?"

Worry gripped his gut. Did he have an update about Laila? Had she reached out to her sister again with bad news? Or had Victor Ramos killed her after all?

"Why don't you sit down? You look paler than hell—"

"What the fuck is going on?" If his scowl didn't make it clear he'd lost all patience, his tone should.

Cursing under his breath, Matt paced to the other side of the room, looking reluctant to speak.

"Out with it," he demanded.

"Fine. You set your phone down with your emails still open, and right after you left, Laila sent you something. I opened it, thinking it might be urgent and that I'd tell you—"

"You snooped?"

"Whatever her message was," Matt went on as if Trees hadn't interrupted.

Admittedly, the cowboy's idea hadn't been bad, but obviously he'd found something horrible. "And?"

"Buddy, I don't think you want to see this."

Trees glared at Matt. "The hell I don't."

Matt looked down at the phone, lying on the corner of the desk. As

Trees lunged for it, Matt stepped between him and the device. "I'm serious. This is just going to fuck with your head more."

Trees didn't care. And he was done arguing.

This was another moment where it paid to have really long arms and legs. Trees shoved the cowboy to one side and lunged just close enough to swipe the phone.

Matt stopped fighting after that and merely sighed. "Fine. Be a stupid bastard. I was just trying to save you from having your heart ripped out."

What the hell was he talking about?

Trees launched his emails and found the one from Laila at the top. The subject line read: `Maybe this will convince you...`

What did that mean?

Inside, the body of the email said:

`I tried to tell you that I am happy with Victor, and you did not believe me. Get it through your head, yanqui.`

Their conversation in La Pesca rang through his head.

"You want to be with him?"

"Of course. I always have."

At the memory, cold slithered under his skin.

But there was more, a video. The still frame alone shocked him. A naked Laila smiled up at the camera she was obviously holding. Her eyes were half-lidded and her head tossed back. Victor Ramos was on top of her with one fist gripping her hair and his face buried in her neck.

Suddenly, the last thing he wanted to do was play the video.

"Don't do it," Matt warned.

But didn't he have to? He had to make sure it was real. It was possible Victor had staged this as a way of making him back off. But that's what someone who felt powerless would do, and Trees's gut told him that wasn't Ramos. That asshole had shot the front window out, broken into his house, and walked right inside—something a man with a vendetta did. Was he hurting Laila for revenge? Maybe…but that didn't make sense, either. Laila was holding the camera, and she didn't look at all distressed.

He was probably a stupid bastard, but he ignored Matt and pressed play.

Immediately, he heard Laila panting. The camera was unsteady. He heard sheets rustling, followed by a feminine moan, then Laila looked up and steadied the phone on them.

"*Chiquita*," he growled. "I want that pussy."

"It is here for you. Like I am," she breathed, rolling her head to one side to offer Victor her neck.

"Hmm…yes." The man she claimed had violated her over and over for six years bounced on top of her. "Good little *puta*."

"For you? Always."

Trees had been feeling queasy all night. Now he felt downright sick. "What the fuck?"

"Stop watching now. It doesn't get better," Matt said.

Trees couldn't. "No."

But seconds later, he wished he'd listened. Victor gave a vicious tug on her hair and sank his teeth into her naked shoulder hard enough to leave marks.

Laila cried out. "Yes!"

"Mine."

Laila gave another heavy-lidded glance toward the camera. "Yours."

The video ended.

Trees sank to the cot and stared at his phone, unblinking. The silence was deafening. His head provided another exchange from La Pesca he wished he could forget.

"*You kicked and scratched and tried to get away.*"

"*It is a game we enjoy. It is our foreplay. I like sex rough.*"

"I'm sorry," Matt finally said.

Slowly, Trees set the phone down. His stomach turned as he tried to make sense of what he'd just seen. But it was obvious, wasn't it? She'd used her body to lure him. He'd fallen for her…and she'd played him.

Pain chopped through his chest like an ax, cleaving him in two.

"Son of a bitch."

"If it's any consolation, when we saw her a few hours ago, I would have sworn she cared about you, probably more than a little. But after seeing that video..."

"There's no way she ever cared about me."

Trees had been bullshitting himself. She was too damaged. Too far gone. Too used to giving her body to cutthroats and criminals to have a heart anymore, much less one capable of love and devotion. He'd just been the sucker who wanted to save her.

Matt clapped him on the shoulder in sympathy. "It seems that way."

"God, I'm a stupid son of a bitch." And how would he ever close his eyes tonight without that video replaying in his head over and over, mocking him for his stupidity?

Then again, why should he be surprised? The people who had given birth to him hadn't found him particularly meaningful or memorable. He'd written home a few times during basic, but they'd never written back. He'd invited them to his graduation. They hadn't responded. He'd sent a Christmas card or two in the years after that. Nothing. Maybe he'd been kidding himself that anyone could really love him.

"No, you just trusted the wrong person. We've all done that." Matt sighed. "What do you want to do? Keep searching this village or..."

"Let's get a good night's sleep. We were given a mission to find Laila and bring her back. Come morning, we'll do that. I don't give a shit what she wants."

"Then what?"

Laila thought she could play him? Oh, she hadn't seen his dark side.

He smiled coldly. "She'll deal with me."

CHAPTER
Five

With tears burning her eyes, Laila jerked away from Victor's mouth on her neck and groped for the empty bottle of tequila. Thanking God the glass was thick, she bonked him on the head.

She didn't hit him hard enough. Instead of passing out, he stiffened, lifted his head, and glared, eyes narrow with rage.

Fear flared through Laila as she dropped the phone on the nightstand and prepared to fight for her life. Yes, she knew Victor's tricks. It helped that she was more nimble and clever. But when he was this drunk, he usually passed out. Why hadn't he this time?

Panic gripped her. She'd already made the agonizing choice to hurt Trees—and stab herself in the heart—to save him. She still had to make her sister and her nephew safe. Whatever that took—even if she had to scheme, lie, cheat, steal, or kill—she would do it so that neither Victor nor Montilla threatened her loved ones again.

First, she had to get Victor off of her.

He had other ideas. After he wrapped his fingers around her neck with a growl, he squeezed until he cut off her air. "You want to play rough, bitch?"

She choked, unable to answer—not that he would care if she spoke. He'd often threatened her, but in the past few years, she'd stopped believing he would actually kill her. The way he strangled her now had her changing her mind. Terror soaked her veins. She clawed at his hands and kicked for freedom. Victor didn't budge.

Black spots danced in her vision. Her lungs burned. But she couldn't lie still and hope he found mercy. He had none.

With her head swimming, she smacked his head with the bottle harder, praying it wouldn't shatter. This time, he collapsed on top of her, now deadweight.

As his hands fell away from her throat, Laila coughed and gasped in precious air, despite being trapped under his unmoving body.

Dios, had she killed him? A part of her celebrated that idea, but that was her selfish desire. Victor's death would mean the loss of her pawn. That wouldn't keep her loved ones safe.

A quick touch to Victor's carotid proved his black heart beat on.

With a shudder of disgust, Laila shoved him off of her. He lay unmoving, facedown across the mattress, with his pale backside in the air and his boxers halfway to his knees.

"*Cabrón.*" She spit, then backed away, trying not to hyperventilate. "I hate you. You will never touch me again. Never!"

She forced herself to think. What next? Send the video to Trees?

Yes, but did she need to if she could simply escape and return to the man she loved?

That notion filled Laila with relief as she reached for the phone with shaking hands, stopped recording, then disabled the device's password. Happiness pinged to every corner of her body—until she realized that Victor would only come after her—and he would start by hunting down Trees, who would try to kill Victor on her behalf. After his injuries, she couldn't take a chance Trees would lose that fight. And she had her family to think about, too. They would never be safe as long as Montilla lived, and since Laila could never hope to kill him alone, she still needed Victor to at least weaken him.

So escaping this hellhole and Victor wasn't a possibility.

On the other hand, if she stayed, Victor might actually kill her. Then she'd be unable to help her family at all.

Panic encroached again. Laila tried to breathe and think of some solution. Absently, she groped around for clothes, but her white skirt and blouse were ruined, stiff and stained with Trees's blood. Even if she could leave Victor, those garments would draw too much attention. She would have to make do with something of his.

Wincing, she yanked off his boxers and donned them. Then she grabbed his shirt off the nearby chair, where he'd tossed his discarded clothes. It was musky and it smelled like him. The stench made her want to vomit, but she couldn't waste time recoiling. She had to sort through the jumble of her thoughts and decide what to do.

As Laila slipped on the shirt, her thoughts drifted back to Trees. She didn't want to send him the horrible video of her "passion" with

Victor, but she couldn't risk him coming to rescue her and running head on into this dangerous vendetta when he should be healing. Eventually, he would find a nice girl without baggage and a nightmarish past, like Madison. She would make him happy.

That reality made Laila cry.

She swiped at her tears angrily and retrieved Victor's phone, then forced herself to buck up and ask Valeria for Trees's email address. While she waited for the information, she edited the video to remove all the footage that would prove she'd staged the scene. As she saved that version, her sister sent Trees's email address.

Taking a deep breath, Laila drafted the man she loved a wrenching lie. She sobbed as she bled each word from her heart. Trees had undoubtedly given the address in trust, hoping it would somehow help him rescue her. Certainly, he hadn't imagined she would use it to tear them apart.

When she finished typing, she reread it, tears flowing. She raised her finger above the button to send it...but she hesitated. She would give anything not to press SEND. It was unforgivable. It would murder whatever he felt for her. Yes, she'd been over all the reasons she must. But...maybe there was some other way to keep Trees from coming to her rescue.

What?

Suddenly, she remembered the informant feeding Victor information. What if she worked with him herself and found another way to bring Montilla down? Maybe she could escape Victor and return to Trees after all—without ever hurting him—while still keeping her family safe.

Excitedly, Laila set the phone aside and dug the keys to the truck from Victor's pants pocket. Beside them, a giant wad of cash all but fell into her palm. It was more money than she had ever seen in her life. Drug money, no doubt. Payment he had taken for selling poison chemicals to *gringos* looking to escape the monotony of their boring, "stressful" lives.

In her brother-in-law's compound, they had offered her narcotics regularly. Once, shortly after the first rape, she had accepted. But the drugs had made her feel sick and less in control. She'd hated the high.

It had also made her more of a target for the ruthless men Emilo had employed. Never again.

It bothered her to steal Victor's dirty money, but survival didn't care about her feelings or scruples. She would gladly give those up, along with her soul, not to hurt Trees. To save everyone she loved, she would pay any price.

Hurriedly, she stepped into her flip-flops, then grabbed Victor's phone again and searched his texts. Messages about drug deals, information from cohorts once loyal to Emilo, even conversations with his late brother. Finally, she found the interaction between Victor and his informant inside Montilla's inner circle. She read the string in its entirety. It was clear the double agent was merely toying with Victor, promising him information and telling him what he wanted to hear. Of course, Victor was too arrogant to see that.

Quickly, she wrote Montilla's supposed spy with her heart pounding. Would you like to be a hero?

She didn't expect an immediate reply, but she got one. You've got big cojones, contacting me after stealing Geraldo's Ferrari. That is not what we agreed to.

This is not Victor. She snapped a picture of him sprawled across the yellowing sheets, tequila bottle nearby. But I can tell you where the Ferrari is if you would like to be a hero. I assume your boss wants it. Think of how he will reward you if you retrieve it…

What is your price?

He was willing to play? Laila glanced at Victor again. He still wasn't stirring, so she excitedly tapped out another response. It is steep, and I do not have the patience to negotiate. I also assume your boss would like to know where to find Victor Ramos since he sent sicarios.

If you tell me where to find the car and the rat, I will be most generous.

And once Montilla had his hands on Victor, he would kill the bastard. Trees would be safe.

Hope built as Laila typed back. Montilla has a hostage,

an American woman named Kimber. I want her location and the means into wherever she is being held.

She would pass the information on to EM Security. When they rescued Kimber, they would likely take Montilla down. Then her family would finally have a future—just like she might with Trees.

The informant's reply was immediate. You ask me to betray a man who will kill me for such disloyalty.

But you will be in favor when you give him both the location of his precious car and his worst enemy. If you are smart, and you must be, he will not suspect you of betraying him, she argued.

Who are you?

No one you need to know. What is your answer?

Laila's heart pounded as she waited a long moment for his reply. Why should I trust you?

She had to think about how to answer that. If I tell you where to find the car, you tell me where to find Kimber. Once I have verified that information, I will give you Victor's location.

The reply was a long time coming. Laila bit a ragged nail and double-checked Victor's still form.

Finally, a new message popped up. That is acceptable. The location of the Ferrari?

Laila clutched the phone, her mind racing. Finally, she rattled off the name of a small market she remembered thirty minutes up the road. It should take her informant at least that long to get there, right? Now where is Kimber?

Not so fast. Once I get the car, I will give you the location.

She wanted to argue since she hadn't anticipated taking Victor's phone with her, but she didn't have a choice. Immediately, she turned off not only location services but cellular data, so neither Victor nor Trees could ping the device.

Fine. The car will be there. If you want Victor's location, I will need Kimber's.

She received no reply, so she pocketed Victor's phone and looked back at him, wishing she had another zip tie or some way to secure him. But she didn't and she didn't dare waste time looking for one. She had to get the car to the drop-off point.

Laila let herself out of the motel room without a backward glance, driving north until she reached the little family-owned market just off the highway.

Since it was the middle of the night, the place was closed. Laila didn't see a soul. She breathed a sigh of relief as she backed the classic sports car out of the truck and parked it behind the building, ensuring it wasn't visible to traffic. Then she hid the keys before hopping in the truck again and steering it down a dirt road behind the market. She parked behind some overgrown brush, between some trees, and waited in the dark, fighting the demands of her overtired body for sleep.

She had nearly drifted off when a car with squeaking brakes stopped near the Ferrari. The sedan's interior light came on as a man exited the passenger door and slammed it shut. Another man remained behind the wheel of the idling car.

Quickly, she dashed off a text. **Keys are under the driver's-side floor mat.**

It took a few minutes before the man circling the classic car looked at his phone, then he bent for the keys. That told her that neither of the men sent to retrieve the Ferrari was the informant. That also told her he had some power and position in the organization since he had men of his own.

The lackey started the sports car, then dashed off a text to someone. Three minutes later, Victor's phone lit up with Kimber's location and a schematic of the compound, which the Edgingtons had been desperately seeking for nearly two weeks. Still, she had to be cautious.

She typed out a question. **How do I know Kimber is really where you say she is?**

Moments later, a picture of the woman herself, all matted auburn hair and big, terrified eyes filled the screen. Laila had never met Kimber, but her heart went out to the wife and mother suddenly torn away from her comfort, her family, and her life. Kimber was holding a phone displaying a map that pinpointed the location the man had told her.

As a precaution, she will be moved tomorrow or the next day. Montilla does that often. That is beyond my control.

Laila would do everything she could to ensure Kimber was rescued before then.

Now where is Victor Ramos? the man on the other end demanded.

Since she had the information she needed, Laila answered in kind. She typed out the name of the motel, which she had noted on her way out. Our business is now concluded. I will not answer again.

Yes, you will, Laila. As you pointed out, it is good to be a hero. Montilla saw the video of you helping Ramos steal the car. He wants blood. My boss would definitely think me a hero if I brought you to him.

Laila's blood ran cold. She sat frozen, not daring to reply. When the men who'd come for the Ferrari both started coming toward her, guns in hand, she started the truck and floored it, putting as much distance between her and them as possible.

Blindly, she flew down dark roads, heedless of where she was going, simply relieved she'd been too fast for them to follow. But she needed to ditch this truck, to find safety, and to tell EM Security where to find Kimber before Montilla moved her. She had to return to the villa outside of La Pesca and try to retrieve Trees's guns and her clothes. And as much as it killed her, she would have to send Trees the email meant to break his heart and hope that he hated her too much to ever want to save her.

A few hours later, Trees found himself sitting beside Logan in a rented van, rumbling away from an airstrip northeast of San Luis Potosí in tense silence. The bosses had called fifteen minutes after Laila sent her backstabbing video and told him that his mission to find her was on hold. They needed all hands tonight to rescue Kimber.

Fuck.

Of course the bosses wanted to save their sister. But the timing goddamn chafed. Laila was out there, double-crossing him and EM Security. Hunter, Logan, and Joaquin had to know he'd been the fidiot who allowed that to happen. So he had to be the one to stop her. But Trees itched to hunt her down, tie her up, and extract some fucking answers. After she confessed when and how she'd decided to play him so he wouldn't make the foolish mistake of trusting her again, he would do whatever necessary to exorcise her from his stupid, shattered heart.

While Matt had driven them the 250 miles from the doctor's office to meet Logan, Trees had tried to close his eyes. But the visual of Laila being touched by Victor Ramos—and her obvious pleasure—replayed through his brain in an endless, destructive loop. Fury boiled his blood and jacked up his mood. Sleep wasn't happening. His one consolation? If he couldn't get his pound of flesh from Laila now, he'd at least get to fuck up assholes pushing drugs.

That thought had kept him going until he'd stood to greet Logan at the airstrip. Then he'd puked everywhere.

"You still look green," Logan remarked an hour later, steadying the wheel as he drove down an empty highway just after three a.m. Once their plane had landed, he'd sent the rest of the team ahead. Matt was now sacked out in the back of the van.

"If you're looking to get laid, flattery won't work."

"Ha ha." Logan shot him an acidic stare. "Matt says you have a concussion. You probably shouldn't be turned loose with a gun."

"Matt should keep his mouth shut. I'm fine." Well, good enough.

As long as he didn't think about Laila…which was proving impossible. How had she suckered him so badly? How had she lied and so thoroughly convinced him of her sob story? He would have sworn everything about her was painfully honest, but maybe life with a cartel had carved the need to survive—fuck her scruples—into her psyche.

Maybe she'd decided she could stay alive most easily by mesmerizing schmucks like him with her body. Maybe she'd never felt anything for any man who'd been inside her, except Victor. Maybe her wide-eyed surprise when he'd supposedly given her both her first kiss and her first orgasm had been bullshit designed to make him feel special. And maybe he'd believed it because he'd wanted to.

If he were a forgiving man, he'd reconcile himself to the fact she was damaged and simply let her go. Too bad for her. Laila was about to find out that he was a nice guy…until he wasn't.

"You're full of shit. You seriously look ready to puke again."

Trees shook his head and lied through his teeth. "Nope. I'm solid."

"Stay in the van and be our lookout."

So he could…what? Fixate on how he'd repay Laila and miss his chance to kill some motherfuckers? "Is that an order?"

Logan sighed. "Fine. You're a big boy, and we need all the guns we can get. But you better not be BSing me. I don't want to take anyone back in a pine box."

"If you do, it won't be me." Not when he had a score to settle.

"Hunter is going to kill me."

Trees didn't care. "What's the plan?"

Since most of EM Security, along with Deke Trenton and Caleb Edgington, Oracle agent Trevor Forsythe, and Ghost had flown in together, they'd powwowed on the plane midair. Once everyone had landed, Matt had warned his bosses about Trees's injury, so no one had felt the need to clue him in.

He was going to change that bullshit now.

"Fine. According to our intel, Kimber is being held in one of Montilla's haciendas. It's remote, up in the mountains. Getting up there will be a bitch. Deke, Dad, and Hunter took Ghost and went ahead to do some recon. Once they return, they'll join Joaquin, Matt, Trevor, Zy, Walker, and the two of us. We'll split into two teams."

Trees guessed Kane had stayed behind to guard Valeria and Jorge. "Roger that. Then what?"

"The preliminary plan is that one team will go in from the south, near the stables. The other will go in from the west, between some storage buildings. Supposedly, security is more lax around those sides of the estate. We'll avoid the front altogether. We've got a schematic of the place, so I'm confident that, if the security pattern holds, we have the right approach. But..."

The bosses were meticulous strategists. They could be motherfuckers, but they were smart. He didn't remember a time any of them had sounded less than confident. "What's the catch?"

"We got here as fast as we could, but the information is already a few hours old."

"That's why we're inserting on top of recon?"

"Yeah. We were warned that Montilla moves Kimber frequently as a precaution. But this also might be a trap. Are you sure you want to do this if you're not one hundred percent? It's going to be rough."

Then it would match his mood, but they weren't leaving him behind. "And abandon everyone else when another gun could make the difference between success and failure? No. How reliable is the information?"

Logan hesitated. "We really have no idea. Laila called it in."

Trees scowled. "Tonight?"

"About four hours ago."

Around the same time he'd received the video of Victor fucking her. "Then I hate to burst your bubble, but it's probably bullshit. She's proven she's a really good liar."

"Matt told us what happened."

"Happened?" Like the universe had just shit out that horrible fucking video to rip out his heart. "No, what she did. Let's be clear. And I'm fucking sorry I fell for it."

"This is why you shouldn't touch a client. But that train left the station. I know." And Logan looked pissed. "Did you ever think she sent that video to stop you from coming after her because she didn't want you in danger?"

Logan still believed there was a chance Laila hadn't played him? It was a nice fantasy, and definitely something Laila would do—for Valeria and Jorge. He'd just been an annoyance, a toy she'd been done playing with, so she'd made sure he wouldn't bother her with his protectiveness, his affection, or his heart beating for her anymore.

"No. I learned a while ago that when people show you who they really are, you should pay attention. Let's just say she opened my eyes with a crowbar."

Logan winced. "I know you don't trust her, but my baby sister's life is hanging in the balance. We have to try."

"You do." Trees and his attitude backed down. Laila had stabbed him in the back, but he'd recover...eventually. The Edgingtons and Deke Trenton had a hole in their lives that would never be filled if they didn't recover Kimber alive. She had children who needed her, and she'd done nothing to deserve death at these monsters' hands. "Just... watch your six."

"That's your job tonight." Logan hesitated. "No idea where Laila is now?"

With Victor Ramos, probably celebrating the moment that asshole had shot him and he'd conked his fucking head on the pavement. "No. Don't you? You've talked to her."

"Not me. She reached out to Valeria, but Laila refused to even tell her sister where she'd gone. Valeria said she sounded rattled. She was crying. That's why I thought"—he shrugged—"I don't know, that maybe the video she'd sent was fabricated so you'd keep your distance."

There was a time he would have thought that, too. Now he knew better. "Nope."

Logan must have realized that was a closed subject since he changed it. "We're less than ten away from the meet point. You need anything?"

Like a pep talk? Fuck that. "No. I'll gear up when everyone else does."

"All right. The colonel is supposed to call with—"

The phone rang, interrupting whatever Logan had been about to say. He lunged for it, putting it on speaker. "Talk to me, Dad."

The team's former owner sighed tiredly. "We poked around as much as we dared. We don't know if Kimber is there, but the place is as quiet as it's going to get. We need to go in now. If this security is their version of a skeleton crew, it's heavy duty. It's obvious the Mexican army is rubbing elbows with DEA to protect the cartel."

Trees couldn't say he was surprised. He'd seen plenty of evidence over the years that both were corrupt to the core.

"Money talks," Logan drawled.

"Sadly, it does," the elder Edgington agreed. "But I suspect security will get even more serious after sunrise, so it's now or never."

"South and west still the best ways in?" Logan asked.

"Yeah. There's only a handful of guards by the stables, all armed to the teeth, of course. But something's…off. As far as Hunter and Ghost could tell, there were no horses in the stables, so why bother guarding them?"

"Maybe that's where Montilla is stashing drugs or counting money," Logan surmised.

"Or holding hostages," Trees added.

"I'm wondering that," Caleb Edgington said. "Deke and I got a brief peek inside the main house. It's ostentatious as hell and over the top, like Hugh Hefner and Liberace decorated the place together. Booze was flowing, and there were naked women everywhere."

"So Montilla is there partying?" Logan surmised.

"I caught a glimpse of the son of a bitch, yeah. And since he has others in the house, I doubt he'd keep Kimber where anyone might find her."

"Why not? No one will double-cross him, unless they want to die," Logan pointed out.

"For the right cash incentive, people will risk anything." The colonel smiled tightly. "He knows that."

"True." Logan turned to Trees. "Maybe you're right about what Montilla is really stashing in the stables."

"How far are you from the meet point?" Caleb asked.

"About three. The others there waiting?"

"Yeah. Listen, Hunter is talking to Kata now. I think you ought to—"

"I was already planning to call Tara. I'll see you soon."

The Edgington brothers were both notoriously devoted to their gorgeous, gutsy wives. But missions like this would rattle even the strongest women, despite the fact they'd dealt with their husbands being Navy SEALs once upon a time.

"Tell her you love her." The colonel hesitated. "I'm worried about this."

Since Laila had provided the intel, Trees was, too. If she was playing for Victor Ramos's team, it stood to reason that her lover— fuck, that term made him grind his teeth—wanted them all dead. If Ramos pulled that off, he'd have a nearly open path to Valeria and the means to pull Montilla's strings.

Caleb said goodbye, and Logan immediately dialed his wife. Trees heard a sleepy female voice answer. "Hello?"

"Cherry," Logan murmured.

Trees tuned out their intimate conversation, giving his boss what privacy he could, but the tones of their devotion still seeped into his ears...then stabbed his wounded heart. He'd never have that since he'd been dumb enough to fall for Laila. Yeah, she'd done something shitty, but even knowing that, he couldn't seem to wrest the organ in his chest back from her cold grip.

God, he was a stupid bastard.

He was getting hardcore on his mental flagellation when Logan braked in front of what looked like an abandoned barn in the middle of nowhere.

"I gotta go. I'll call when I can. I love you and the girls, Cherry." Logan clenched his jaw, then hung up.

The doors in front of them opened, then his boss drove in and parked beside a pair of other vehicles. Trees hopped out, fighting off the queasiness again. Wordlessly, he and Logan began to gear up.

The colonel took over. "We're going in with two teams. I'll lead Joaquin, Walker, Trevor, Matt, and you, Ghost."

Trees wasn't surprised when Ghost merely nodded, then looked toward the doors with burning eyes, like he was itching to get into the fight.

"Hunter will lead Deke, Logan, Zy, and Trees." The elder Edgington singled him out. "If you're sure you're up for this."

He wasn't a pussy, and there was no fucking way he would sit around while the others, with so much more to lose, risked their lives so he could mope like one. "Locked and loaded, sir."

The colonel didn't look convinced but carried on, which told Trees how desperate they were. Caleb communicated their plan of attack, places of interest, timeframes, and the extraction point. "Anyone who doesn't reach that helipad by oh-five-hundred..."

Would be left behind. They all understood the risk. They had no permission nor coordination with the government. They hadn't talked to the right people, and they hadn't greased the right palms. If Montilla called for help, Trees had no illusions about what would happen. Every operative caught would be arrested, and Mexican prison wouldn't be kind—if they even lived long enough to see it.

After a thumbs-up all around, they split into teams, then left the barn, trekking through the desert on foot in different directions so they could approach the massive estate from different sides.

Zy fell in beside him as they hiked toward the hacienda. He looked concerned. "You okay?"

"My head doesn't hurt much anymore." Trees did his best to smile.

"Glad to hear it, but that wasn't what I was asking. Talk to me about Laila."

"What is there to say? She fucked me over."

"Trees—"

"Here. You look at this video and tell me what you see." He handed his best friend his phone.

Zy watched it grimly. "I know what it looks like, but—"

"You in Logan's camp? You think she sent me this to protect me? Even if she did, news flash: she fucked him. Last night. Willingly. I took apart that video in the car. I don't have all my software on my phone, but I've got enough to tell when it was filmed." Sure, it was spliced at the beginning and the end, but she'd probably sent him the best parts and discarded the rest.

When the clip was finished, Zy sighed. "I'm not buying it."

"What part? Where she's spreading her legs for Victor Ramos? Despite the sheet over them, I think it's pretty obvious what they're doing."

"I know what it looks like, but you're...tangled up in her, man. I'm not denying that she filmed him on top of her. But I doubt she did it for her pleasure. Or even for his. My impression of Laila was that she would do or say whatever she needs to keep her loved ones safe. If she didn't care about you, why would she bother to warn you away? If you didn't matter to her, why wouldn't she just let Victor take you out?"

Trees scowled. "Because she doesn't want me to kill Victor."

"I doubt that's what she was thinking after she'd watched the son of a bitch shoot you hours earlier."

Zy had a point. Trees mentally weighed it, but he just couldn't get past the fact she'd intentionally gone for his emotional jugular. "It doesn't matter now. We're here for Kimber."

"But you're going to go after Laila as soon as this is over. I know you."

Damn straight. "It's my mission. The bosses want her back. They want to know what she knows. I'm sure her sister wants her safe, too."

"Don't bullshit me. You want her back for you. For revenge." Zy dropped his voice. "I know somewhere deep down you think you're not good enough for love or some crap like that."

Trees sent his best friend a sharp glare. "I never said that."

"Not in so many words, but I know you think it when you talk about your family. I'm telling you, that's not reality, buddy."

Zy didn't understand his childhood. "That has nothing to do with Laila."

"I think it does. Before you go all V is for Vendetta on her ass, make her explain."

"The way you did when you had Tessa in my bunker?" Zy had been fucking furious at her seeming betrayal when he'd gotten her alone and naked...and there hadn't been much talking.

"Different circumstances."

"You're right. Tessa loves you. Laila doesn't give a shit about me. But I won't let her lie. I fell for that shit once. You know the old saying. If it walks like a duck and it quacks like a duck..."

Zy shook his head. "She's not a duck; she's a wounded sparrow. But I'm obviously not going to change your mind. Just...think about it."

Trees sighed. "I haven't been able to focus on much else."

"You better get your head on right for this mission. It's going to be dangerous as hell. I hear we're outnumbered five-to-one—at least."

Fuck. Zy was right. If Trees didn't want to end up dead, he'd better fucking focus. "Yeah."

"How did Tessa take you leaving suddenly?"

"She's all right. Nervous. Hallie cried, and that didn't make anything easier. But my girls are tough."

They were. Tessa had been through a lot while protecting her infant daughter. They would be okay. And Trees would do his best to make sure Zy stayed okay.

It occurred to him that nearly everyone present had a reason to stay frosty and come home alive—a wife, kids, siblings, parents—people who loved them.

Trees would go home alone.

Fuck that, he would find Laila, track her sexy ass down, and make her pay—in his dungeon, in his bed, under his cock. If she wanted to fuck for her survival, he would happily oblige her. After he killed Victor Ramos.

It wasn't much longer before the silhouette of the hacienda came into view. Dawn was a couple of hours away. Night had swallowed up the other team a while ago. Hunter, Deke, and Logan had all trekked ahead of them, heads together, strategizing. Zy jogged to catch up. Trees followed suit.

Hunter turned to them. "The stables are just inside the edge of the property, about three hundred yards ahead. There are five rows of six stables each."

"Who the hell keeps thirty horses?" Zy asked.

"The bigger question is, why would anyone have thirty stables but zero horses?" Hunter drawled. "When we get there, we'll fan out. Zy, you'll come with me on the north side. Logan will take Deke and Trees and wind to the south. Both teams will work their way to the middle. It's heavily fortified, gentlemen. Stay low and stay aware. They aren't fucking around."

"Neither are we," Logan added darkly.

"Let's go get my kitten," Deke growled, his voice gravelly and harsh.

Trees sipped some water out of the pack he'd strapped on in the barn. "Let's do it."

Before Hunter and Zy broke off, they all slipped comm devices in their ears and checked them. Then Trees bumped fists with his best friend, hoping like hell they all came out of this in one piece.

The night was silent as they crept to the stables. The wind whipped up, masking the sounds of their footsteps. They clung to shadows. Since disturbances and loud noises would bring every thug running, the team understood that guns were a last resort. Still, Trees had his handy as he watched Logan and Deke's six while they approached the first line of stables.

For a "retired" guy, Logan was a stealthy motherfucker, taking down the first guard, slumped against the wall, eyes closed. Deke took down his partner, enjoying a smoke out back. After they dragged the bodies into an empty stable, ripped out their comm devices, then zip-tied their hands and taped shut their mouths, they secured the door.

Why did stables where no one kept horses come equipped with doors that locked and windows with bars, like a prison?

The question swirled in his head as they scoured the rest of the stables in that row, avoiding the obvious panning of security cameras above. As one swung back to the interior of the estate, toward the pool in the distance, they filed through the darkness to the next row.

The first guard saw them coming. Before he could alert his cohorts, Logan tossed a blade at the suit, hitting him right in the heart. He fell to the ground, his mouth still open with an unspoken syllable. Deke carried his corpse into the nearest stall and kicked him into the corner, out of sight.

In the back of Trees's head, he heard a ticking clock. They'd been at this less than two minutes, and all was still quiet...but how long before someone called out to a guard who no longer answered? How long before they came to investigate and all hell broke loose?

Another guard stepped out of the john, yanking up his zipper, then stretching like he didn't have a care in the world. Trees crept behind him and twisted his neck. He fell back into Trees's grip with a gasp, deader than dead. Since the can was closest, he shuttled the asshole back on the toilet and locked the door.

When he emerged, he waited behind the door until the security camera turned to scan the opposite direction. Logan and Deke were taking down a pair of thugs. Deke all but carved out a guy's throat, then tossed him in a stable. Logan dragged another guard in next and pointed a gun under his chin. When he gave a head bob and pointed to the guy's comm, Trees quickly divested the thug of his equipment in silence and squashed the earpiece beneath his heel.

"Where is the American woman your boss is keeping hostage?" Logan demanded.

"*No habla.*"

"He's useless," Logan snapped Trees's way. "Cut out his tongue."

Trees withdrew his knife. "On it."

"Wait! She is in the next row, middle stall."

Really? So it was possible lying Laila had actually given them the truth? Maybe she'd done something good. After all, there had been no ambush awaiting them. And it looked as if her intel was panning out…

Logan smiled acidly. "Damn, you learned English fast."

"Fuck you," the man spit.

"Right back at you," Logan snarled, then slit the guy's throat.

Trees had known the colonel was a badass. That's why so many guys had come to EM Security, to learn from a legend. Edgington had sworn his sons were the real deal, but he'd never seen them in action. Trees had to admit, he was fucking impressed. Yeah, they'd been assholes at times…but maybe with good reason. Besides, the job wasn't about their people skills.

Logan pressed on his comm and relayed Kimber's possible location to his dad, then nodded to Trees. "Let's go."

Deke was already barreling in that direction.

The younger Edgington caught up and snagged his brother-in-law by the arm. "Don't get stupid."

He meant Deke couldn't afford to be impatient. Trees agreed.

Jaw clenched like he was working hard to hold his shit together, Kimber's husband nodded. "I know."

But the waiting that came with caution was killing him.

"We're a team," Logan reminded in a low-voiced growl. "We succeed together or we die together."

Deke obviously didn't like it since he looked like he wanted to rip off Logan's face, but he nodded.

No one spoke then. They crept closer to Kimber.

Ahead, Trees caught sight of a skirmish in the shadows. Hunter gutted one guard while Ghost had pinned another against the building and muttered something in the hired gun's ear. The guy pissed himself, and Ghost finished him off with a sharp tug of his blade from belly to throat. After a few additional clashes and more dodging the mechanically panning cameras, Deke and Logan reached the middle stall.

It was locked. And there was a man inside.

Every single operative fell silent. If they remained out here, it wouldn't be long before another random patrol came or the camera swung back and captured them. If they alerted the guard inside the stall, he'd call for reinforcements. They had to make a decision now and it had to be quick.

Fuck.

Trees turned to Hunter in question. This was his sister and his show.

The elder Edgington cursed silently, then crouched in front of the stable and scratched on the wood.

"Do not move," the inside man said in thickly accented English as he approached the door.

From the shadows, Trees caught on, watching the guard close in until he pressed his scowling face against the bars covering the window to look outside. At Trees's nod, Hunter jumped up, thrusting his hand inside the stall, thunking the guard's head against the solid metal bars, and knocking him out cold.

"Kimber?" Hunter whispered.

"Oh, my god. I'm here," her voice trembled.

So Laila hadn't lied about Kimber's location. It stood to reason she hadn't lied to him about her feelings, either.

"Oh, thank fuck, kitten." Her husband rattled the door, sounding ready to tear the whole building down to reach her.

"Deke!" she whispered emphatically.

"The door is fucking locked. Search the guard for keys," her insistent husband said.

"I can't. I'm tied to a chair."

Hunter turned to his father and brother. "We can't shoot this lock."

Logan nodded. "It'll bring attention."

Trees frowned. Had he been the only one with a less-than-glowing youth? "I can pick it."

He retrieved his survival multitool and went to work. The lock was designed to keep thoroughbreds in more than to keep trained operatives out. He'd picked it in thirty seconds.

"Thanks." Deke shoved him aside and dashed into the stable after his wife.

Hunter, Logan, and Caleb all filed around, watching their six as Deke bent to cut Kimber free, then scooped her up in his arms, holding her tight against his chest. "Are you hurt?"

"No. Just get me home."

He turned to the colonel. "Relay to the other team that we're out and tell them to head to the meet point."

Caleb nodded. "I'll go with you and keep your six safe. Hunter, Logan, Zy, and Trees, get us out clean. Make sure we're not followed. Mop up any messes. We've taken out most of the guards around the stables, but when they don't report in…"

More would flood in from other parts of the estate and all hell would break loose. Something kept itching at the back of Trees's neck that their time was running out.

"Roger that," he affirmed.

The others did the same.

By a flash of moonlight, Trees caught the stark emotion in Deke and Kimber's shared glance. Tears spilled down her dirty cheeks. His barely controlled fury said he'd give anything to erase what she'd endured, but he was so fucking grateful to have her back, as if someone had stolen the stars from the sky and finally given them back when he'd lifted her into his embrace.

That gaze was like a kick in the gut. They had each other and the eternal, binding love they shared. Trees had never thought he wanted that—until Laila. But the last twenty-four hours had proven that his heart couldn't be trusted. He'd fallen for a temptress who used him for her own gain. And her lover's. He couldn't forget that.

But Laila had done one decent thing in helping to reunite two people who lived and breathed each other. In returning a loving mother to her young children. Sure, she had probably done that for some selfish reason he could only begin to guess at. But that didn't matter in this moment. Kimber and Deke were back together.

Trees blinked, then the couple was gone, melting into the shadows together, her father right behind them.

"Let's get the fuck out of here," Hunter insisted as he plastered himself to the shadows.

The boss didn't have to tell him twice.

The four men crept through the dark spaces around the buildings until they reached the end of the row of stalls. They were feet away from a clean escape.

Suddenly, a man's shout split the air north of them, something in rapid-fire Spanish he didn't understand. But he'd bet someone had discovered the bodies they'd tucked away. Which meant he and the other three operatives were in a world of shit.

The voices coming from the north started blending with those of the reinforcements pouring in from the main house to the south.

"They're about to cut off our fastest fucking way out," Hunter growled.

He was right. That meant shit was the least of their problems. They were fucked. They had a split second to flee.

Trees scanned his surroundings. He needed perspective. The roof of the stables was accessible to someone of his height. "Stay hidden."

"What are you doing?" Logan hissed.

Trees didn't respond, just jumped up to grab the overhang, hoisted himself up, then slithered onto his belly. Lights flashed on. Two goons were hoofing it from the north end of the stables. A dozen reinforcements were charging from the south.

Geraldo Montilla was in the thick of the pack, gun in hand.

"Run north," he growled into his comm. "Two tangos at three o'clock. A shitload at ten. Take out the pair to the north and keep running. You'll be home free."

"Get off the roof," Hunter barked.

"*Allí!*" a reinforcement from the south shouted, pointing at Trees.

"They've seen me. Get out of here."

"Without you? Fuck that," Logan growled.

Trees pulled his gun from his holster. "Your father just got his daughter back. He doesn't need to lose his two sons. You have wives and children. Go."

Then Trees focused on the assholes surrounding the stables, aiming their guns his way. If he was going down, he was going to take as many motherfuckers with him as he could.

As the first shots rang out, he lifted his SIG, wishing he had Walker's crazy accuracy. There was a reason everyone called him One-Mile. But Trees took out the closest thug. As the criminal's head exploded, he turned his attention to the next guy, giving him the same treatment.

A bullet whizzed past his ear. He rolled to avoid another asshole's line of fire and narrowly missed that shot, too.

Fuck, he was outnumbered and about to get tagged by a dozen different guns. If he bailed, they would come after him—unless he gave them a reason not to.

He gave it one last Hail Mary effort and took a shot at Geraldo Montilla. If the drug lord was going to make himself a target, Trees was going to aim for him.

His first shot missed. His second hit, ripping somewhere into the kingpin's chest. Montilla went down where he stood.

Pandemonium erupted. Shouting ensued. Half the suits rushed to help their *jefe.*

The other half turned their weapons on him.

Trees thanked God for his long fucking legs as he jumped from the roof of one stable to the row north, crouching across shingles and tossing back potshots. If he could get to the last row, he stood a chance of escaping.

Just before he leaped, two guards climbed onto the next roof ahead and stood directly in his path, balancing on the pitched surface with sinister grins.

Trees's gut dropped to his toes. He could take one guy out, no sweat. But the other one would blow his head off before he could fire again. Goddamn it.

But he didn't have any other options.

He feinted and crouched, then zeroed in on the suit on the right, taking him out with a shot to the forehead. He moved as rapidly as he could, but by the time he aimed at the other guard, the goon had already locked him in his sights.

Fuck. He was a dead man.

As the thought zipped through his brain, another shot resounded. The gunman jerked and stumbled back. Blood splattered as he fell off the roof and plummeted to the ground, dead.

Who the fuck had killed him?

Trees didn't waste time figuring it out. He jumped to the final roof. The rest of the guards swarmed in his direction, but the path between the hacienda and the open desert was clear. Moonlight dipped back behind the clouds, giving him some cover. He just might make it…

He leapt to the ground beside the body. Zy appeared out of the shadows and pressed a finger to his lips. Trees was grateful but not surprised that his buddy had bailed him out. He and Zy had kept each other alive in more than one awful scrape.

Zy tipped his head toward what looked like a garage around fifty yards in the distance, then disappeared behind some brush. Trees followed. They looped around the far side of the building, easing away from additional guards now coming in from the east corner of the estate. Pounding footsteps and heated shouts told Trees the guards had lost their trail.

Less than two minutes later, they approached the garage and Zy spoke into his comm. "We're coming in hot."

To his shock, no one was guarding the building. It wasn't even locked.

Zy rushed in, weapon drawn. But Hunter and Logan had already dispensed with a quartet of guards inside and now sat behind the wheel of a souped-up Jeep—with a mounted fifty cal on the back.

It was a sweet fucking sight.

Hunter turned the engine over, and Zy pressed the button on the wall to open the garage door. The second the vehicle was clear, the elder Edgington floored it. Zy got behind the gun, blasting away anyone who gave chase. Then the desert swallowed them up and they headed straight to the meet point—and safety.

But Laila was still out there...somewhere, probably hunkering down with Victor. Warming his bed. Sucking his cock. Giving him her body. Trees wasn't resting until he had her back.

CHAPTER
Six

Trees paced his living room with restless energy. Barney watched from the sofa with confusion. And he probably wanted more food, since he was a typical dog.

It had been ten long, fucking empty days since he'd returned from Mexico. Deke and Kimber were together with their children again. The family remained in hiding until they got some solid intel about whether Montilla had died by his gun.

The colonel had come to visit him at the office more than once to express his gratitude. So had Jack Cole, who co-owned Oracle with Deke. The crafty Cajun had jokingly offered him a job, then insisted he wouldn't dream of poaching from Hunter, Logan, and Joaquin. But he hadn't sounded like he was kidding at all.

Trees wasn't interested in jumping ship.

One-Mile and Brea had tied the knot in a small ceremony this past weekend. Trees hadn't attended. Pictures had been nice, but he hadn't felt like he could watch two people in love tie their lives together without snarling. Apparently, he'd been surly since their return from Mexico and his inability to find Laila had dragged on. Go figure.

Zy and Tessa had moved in together. They were planning a wedding, too. Trees was thrilled for his buddy. Those two had endured a long, hard road to their happily ever after. They were great people with big hearts who deserved happiness. Which was exactly why the same would never happen for him.

Besides, he still hadn't seen or heard a single peep out of Laila since he'd left Mexico. Every attempt to trace her had come up empty. Victor Ramos was missing, too, so that fit. They'd holed up together somewhere, fucking their brains out. As much as Trees told himself that he didn't miss Laila, he'd give anything to be the lucky guy between her legs.

After he found out how and why she'd played him and he paid her back.

Since returning from Mexico, he'd been on a couple of short missions, bodyguarded a TV personality's son during his drunken Mardi Gras weekend, and spent the rest of the time preparing for the moment he got his hands on his pretty backstabbing Latina.

Madison had called more than once. He hadn't responded with more than a vague text to say he was drowning in work and would call when he could. He wasn't fit to keep someone so kind and well-meaning company.

He glanced at the clock. Almost ten. He couldn't take another fucking sleepless night, burning for Laila as much as he seethed to shake her and fuck her so bad he could almost taste it. He didn't want to dream about her again. He didn't want to fixate on her anymore. All the polite ways of locating her weren't working.

Now he was going to get ruthless.

Grabbing his gear and his keys, Trees gave Barney a pet on the head, set the house alarm he'd had painstakingly rebuilt once the plate glass window in his living room had been replaced, then hopped into his Hummer and headed to Lafayette.

When he arrived at Zy's apartment complex, he buzzed himself through the gate, using the guest code his buddy had given him. But he didn't stop in front of Zy's unit. Instead, he rolled two buildings down and parked, then made his way to the second floor, stopping in front of the door of Valeria's safe house.

Trees weighed the possibility that Kane would let him in to see Laila's sister. Since everyone, especially the bosses, had refused to let him even speak to her on the phone, he figured his odds sucked. He'd been nothing short of a growling son of a bitch for the past week and a half. With every day that passed, his temper only got shorter, his mood snarlier. On the one hand, he understood their point. His personal shit wasn't their client's problem. On the other hand, Laila clearly thought they were done.

She was fucking wrong.

He crept up the stairs to the second-floor apartment and hopped onto the railing. Six feet away was a little balcony that led to the main bedroom. He knew the schematic of the unit; he'd looked it up online. He'd also bet that Kane was bunking down on the sofa or in the unit's tiny office. The bedroom would be Valeria's.

Trees used the railing as a springboard and leapt to the balcony. He caught it with his hands, cursing under his breath. The wood needed a good sanding. Then he hoisted himself up and over.

Once on his feet, the balcony groaned in protest. Yeah, it probably wasn't used to anyone hanging out here in the shitty Louisiana humidity, especially someone his size. But with any luck, he wouldn't be stuck outside for long.

He yanked his multitool from his pocket. The lock was a little more difficult than expected. Someone had probably replaced it recently. But a few minutes and a handful of curses later, he peeked in, glimpsing Valeria dressed in black yoga pants and an overlarge T-shirt, leaning over a playpen, patting her son's back.

As he pushed the door open wide, it squeaked. She whirled around, her eyes widening when she caught sight of him.

"What are you doing here?"

"You know exactly why I've come. I want to see your sister."

"She does not want to see you." Valeria crossed her arms as if that was the end of the conversation.

Wrong.

"So you've talked to her?"

The woman didn't answer, but she didn't have to. Trees knew. That meant Laila was alive and well. The relief that filled him pissed him off. He shouldn't give a shit; she'd tossed her lot in with Victor Ramos, who had never wanted to love, honor, and cherish Laila for the rest of her life.

He was even more pissed that she was still able to communicate… and had simply chosen not to contact him.

Too bad. They were going to talk, even if he had to go to the ends of the earth to find her.

First, he had to get through her protective older sister.

"We have unfinished business," he said.

Valeria sniffed. "You merely want to get her into bed, as you always did. From the first moment you saw her, I knew. It was all over your face."

Trees didn't bother denying the truth, merely opted for another tactic. "Aren't you worried about her cozied up with Victor Ramos? He's hardly a nice man."

"Neither are you."

"The difference is, I would never hurt her." Maybe make her beg for orgasm until she screamed her throat raw, then withhold pleasure for the evil thrill of watching her twist and writhe for him, sure. But he would never truly hurt her.

Trees sensed Valeria thinking and pressed his point home. "She's your little sister, and she's playing with big criminals, warming the bed of a cartel bigwig. Aren't you fucking worried about her? About what Victor will do if he decides he's done using her?"

The small brunette crossed her arms over her chest, lifted her cleft chin, and paced to the other side of the room, licking her lips nervously.

Like Laila, Valeria was his "type." Little thing with curves and attitude. But he wasn't remotely attracted to the woman. There was something about her that seemed hard, her exterior shell almost impenetrable. He didn't sense any hint of vulnerability, the way he had in Laila. He didn't see pain or uncertainty in her eyes.

Instead, she sized him up and measured his worth.

"She is…no longer with Victor. She has not been for over a week."

That shocked Trees to the core. He hadn't expected Valeria to answer, much less to tell him anything useful.

"Because?"

"I cannot say."

"Can't or won't?"

Valeria shrugged. "What do you want with my sister?"

Trees got the distinct impression Valeria would smell bullshit. "She owes me answers."

"Do you deny that you want her in your bed again?"

So Laila had told her sister they'd had sex? "No."

The little boy in the playpen grunted and rolled over. The single mother glanced her son's way, watching until he settled again. It was the only hint Trees had that Valeria had feelings at all.

Finally, she faced him. "I overheard Zyron and Kane talking. Your friend seems to think my sister broke your heart."

Fuck.

But her obvious bullshit meter, along with her arched brow, warned him not to be dishonest. "She did."

"Do you still have feelings for her?"

Jesus, she wanted him to open his chest so she could inspect all the cuts her sister left? "Would I be here if I didn't give a shit?"

Valeria shrugged. "Revenge is a powerful motive."

It was, and he wanted it. But he couldn't deny that some part of him wanted to make sure Laila was whole and safe—wanted to see it with his own two eyes—and protect her from the violent drug lords she continued to foolishly bait and taunt. "If you're asking whether I'm in love with your sister, I am. But if you tell her that, I'll deny it with my last breath."

Valeria was quiet another long moment. "All right. I will keep your secret and I will tell you where to find her, *if* you promise me that you will stop her from playing dangerous games with the cutthroats of Tierra Caliente."

There was nothing he wanted more. "Done. You call my bosses and demand that I retrieve her, and I'll have Laila back in twenty-four hours."

Mexico

Dawn painted the beach ethereal shades of pink, orange, and yellow. The water lapped at her toes. The coming Mexican spring had warmed the surf a bit since she'd arrived, but it still felt too cold.

Like her heart.

Day eleven without Trees. She still couldn't decide what to do. Everything inside her wanted to rush back to him and throw herself into his arms, confess the video had been a lie, admit her feelings, and pray he forgave her. But that was impossible. She'd burned that bridge. Now she could only move forward.

After she'd fled Victor's seedy motel room, told Valeria where to find Kimber, and sent that awful email to protect Trees, Laila had used some of Victor's cash to purchase a vehicle from a farmer outside the nearest village and left his truck behind. From there, she'd retrieved her things, including Trees's guns, from the abandoned villa near La Pesca and driven nearly a hundred miles south to Tampico.

As soon as she'd arrived, she braided her hair, shoved it under a cap she'd purchased at a seaside tourist shop, then rented a condo on the water from a woman and her sister with friendly smiles. Not that she trusted them. She didn't trust anyone who hadn't proven them- selves. Thankfully, the sisters had allowed her to pay cash and hadn't asked questions.

From the moment she'd arrived, she had done her best to disappear into the city. So far, it had worked. She felt more invisible than safe. But maybe that was the best she could hope for.

Being here, surrounded by people yet removed from them, had given her time to think—mostly about Trees. But she hadn't managed to make any decisions.

Nor had Victor reared his head again. She still had his phone. She'd powered it down to preserve the battery, but in case she needed it or his contacts, she'd hung on to the device. But his uncharacteristic silence had her hoping that Montilla's men had picked him up and ended his miserable existence.

The few times she'd powered up Victor's mobile, she had poked around his messages and social media for information about his whereabouts or his plans. She'd only found rumors that Geraldo Montilla had been gravely injured when some Americans had broken into his hacienda and rescued the woman they'd been keeping captive.

So Kimber was free. Laila could feel good about that, at least. Everything else? Wretched. She'd abandoned her sister, though Valeria was seemingly safe with Kane Preston. She'd left Victor to die, though he deserved it. But she felt beyond guilty about Trees. He had done nothing but try to protect her and love her, and she had hurt him in the cruelest way possible. Yes, for his safety, but her reason wouldn't matter to him. He'd surely written her off as a mercenary whore. He would never absolve her of her sins. Laila doubted she would ever absolve herself, either.

Gulls cried overhead. The smell of salt filled her nose. It was peaceful in the early hours. Soon, locals would flock here with their significant others or jog with their pets. Then families would show up with sunscreen and beach towels to bask in the golden rays. But right now, she felt like the only person in this corner of the world. She could be alone with her thoughts, her regrets. That should have brought her some level of peace.

It didn't.

What was Trees doing now? Oddly, when she had called her sister a few minutes ago, Valeria had been oddly reserved, almost oblique. Laila didn't know what to make of that. When she'd asked about Trees, Valeria claimed she knew nothing but warned that she likely hadn't seen the last of him. When Laila asked why her sister believed that, Valeria had dodged the question, claiming Jorge needed her before she hung up. Laila had been walking the beach since.

What would she say if she ever saw Trees again? What would she do? The truth was, until she knew Victor was dead, any communication would put him at risk. And given all the years that *cabrón* had tyrannized her life, Laila couldn't just blink or wave her magic wand to make her nemesis disappear. And if Montilla was actually at death's door, did that mean Victor had slipped through the kingpin's fingers? Or had Montilla exercised his version of justice on Victor before being felled by a bullet?

Despite continuing to look through every message and connection on Victor's phone, she hadn't seen an update in over a week.

What did that mean?

On a nearby balcony, a dog barked. A couple jogged by, obviously on vacation and enjoying the Mexican sun. Someone behind her opened their window. A car horn blared in the distance. The world was waking up. Laila wished she could just tune all of it, along with her reality, out. But she needed to make some decisions, then take her next steps.

She didn't dare return to Louisiana. She would endanger her

family, and she would be too tempted to see Trees. But she couldn't stay here much longer. In fact, fleeing Mexico altogether would be wise. If she didn't, someone would eventually find her. It was a matter of time.

Laila pulled the ball cap lower, adjusted her overlarge sunglasses, and headed back to her rental. Her stomach turned. No surprise. She'd barely eaten in days, but the thought of food held no appeal. Maybe she would go back to bed. After all, she felt exhausted. Who wouldn't, though, after almost no sleep?

Was this what a broken heart felt like?

Shaking off the maudlin thought, she eased through her sliding glass door, back into her unit. Then she locked up and drew the drapes. When she whirled around, nothing was out of place, but the air felt…disturbed, as if someone had been here. She smelled something that didn't belong here. No, some*one*. A man.

She smelled Trees.

That wasn't possible. Her imagination must be in overdrive. She'd missed him so much that her psyche had dreamed up his scent. Or maybe she was finally losing her mind.

Laila checked the lock on the front door, just to be sure no one had breached her unit, but it was secure. Then she sighed, divesting herself of her hat and glasses. She left both on the breakfast bar before ambling to the kitchen. Listlessly, she opened the refrigerator, then closed it again before making her way to the sink to wash her mug after pouring out the coffee she hadn't felt like drinking. But once she set down the sponge, she bowed her head. Tears fell. God, she'd been crying for days.

Yes, this must be what a broken heart felt like.

She didn't have time. She didn't have the luxury, either. Not until everyone she loved was safe.

Today was another day. She prayed it would finally provide the information she needed to move on.

Laila prowled back to the sliding glass door, kicked off her flip-flops in preparation for her next walk on the beach, probably at sunset, then pulled off the tank top and shorts she'd been wearing the past few days, which she'd retrieved from the villa. They were the same clothes she'd worn when she'd been with Trees, the ones that had made him look at her with lust and lose his train of thought. Having them against her skin had both made her feel closer to him and tortured her with his absence. But she was being foolish. He would never be hers again.

After dropping her clothes in the washer, she turned the corner and wandered to her room, heading straight for the bed. She could take off her bra and panties and don the huge T-shirt she'd bought in town. But that seemed like a lot of effort since she probably wouldn't be able to sleep.

When she was two steps from the bed of rumpled white sheets and colorful blankets, the door closed behind her with an irrefutable click. Laila whirled at the unexpected sound. She froze when she saw a face she hadn't expected in her bedroom.

"Trees," she gasped.

"Laila." His frigid smile looked anything but happy as he prowled toward her.

Her heart pounded. Instinct told her to back away. "What are you doing here?"

"Did you think you'd seen the last of me?" His stare raked her up and down. His smile turned even more arctic.

Laila swallowed. "We have nothing to say. Get out. You are not welcome."

"You don't want to talk to me? Fine. But I'm not leaving without you."

He meant to take her with him?

She scanned the room for an escape, but Trees had her trapped. Other than the window along the far wall, she had no way out of the condo since he'd blocked the door.

Laila knew better than to believe she could run past him.

"No. I have chosen to stay here."

"Alone?"

He was asking her about Victor. "That is none of your business."

"Oh, you're wrong. Everything about you is my business. So, we can do this the easy way. You can pack your things and come along obediently. We'll board a plane and I'll take you back to Louisiana. You can visit your sister and your nephew, show them that you're okay. And then you'll deal with me."

Fear surged through Laila. She was even more afraid to ask him what would happen if she chose the hard way. "I cannot go back. I would put too many people at risk."

"You *will* go," he contradicted, teeth bared. "Or I'll restrain you right now, transport you back to Louisiana, and toss you into my dungeon for some…corrective discipline. I won't let you go until I'm convinced you're done playing dangerous games with drug lords and cartels. What's it going to be?"

Corrective discipline? Laila thought about all the equipment— restraints, paddles, whips, floggers, and other things she couldn't iden- tify—in his dungeon. She shivered.

But she'd be lying if she said she didn't feel a disconcerting thrill, too.

She studied Trees's face. Those green eyes that used to gaze at her with warmth, that had reassured her as he'd searched her soul to see past her hurts and find the trembling girl underneath? They were glacial now. Raw and cutting. He looked terrifyingly eager to unleash his worst on her. He was so large, so powerful, so determined.

"Trees…" she pleaded.

His expression only turned chillier. "Whimpering won't work anymore, Laila. How do you want this to go, easy or hard? You have ten seconds to decide."

Let herself be led like a lamb to slaughter or fight him with her last breath?

Even five minutes ago, Laila would have sworn she would take any opportunity to throw herself in Trees's protective arms and burrow her way to warmth and love in his embrace. But now? She saw nothing but terrifying wrath on his face.

She slid her nervous gaze around the room again, this time in search of a way to protect herself.

Her stare fastened on the guns she had swiped from his dungeon. She pounced for them, nearly knocking them to the ground in her trembling haste.

Trees was right behind her, one massive arm wrapping tight to crush her. With his free hand, he ripped the weapons from her grip and swept them to the floor. "You want to kill me?"

"I want to defend myself," she panted out.

With his chest pressed to her back, his mirthless laugh shook her body. A shudder went down her spine. "By killing me. But I guess since your lover didn't manage the job, you thought you'd do it for him? Will he fuck you extra hard and raw as a reward for that?"

"Do not do this," she pleaded.

"You did this, *honey*."

The sweet endearment that had once flowed off his tongue was now bitter. She quivered and held in a ridiculous urge to cry. Trees no longer loved her. He didn't even care, not that she was surprised. She'd known that was the likely outcome. But maybe if she explained, it would defuse some of his fury. "I did not leave your house with Victor because I wanted to."

His fingers bit into her arms. His lips slid against her ear. Her heart rate surged—and it had nothing to do with fear. How could she burn for a man who hated her?

"Since you walked out the front door with him, I'm calling bull-shit. But I'm not here for details about your torrid fuckfest with Victor."

"You do not understand. I—"

"Stop. You open your mouth, and lies come out. I don't want to fucking hear them anymore. Easy or hard, Laila? You tell me how it's going to be." He sucked in a hissing breath as he pressed his erection against her backside. "I fucking hope you choose the hard way. My palm is itching. I want you strapped to my table, under my thumb, utterly helpless and unable to stop me until you learn to be a good girl."

Nothing about that should turn her on, but everything did. Even fear gave her desire an edge she didn't understand. Her heart revved harder. She swallowed to moisten her suddenly dry mouth. Her nipples felt hard enough to cut glass. Her womb clenched. She got unbearably wet.

"No," she said more to herself than to him.

"No?" The hand clamped around her waist lifted, caressing up her arm. Then his palm engulfed her breast. His thumb flicked the engorged tip.

Laila sucked in a shocked breath of pleasure, then bit her lip to hold in a moan. "Stop."

He didn't. "Your nipple is hard, Laila. Why is that?"

"I am cold."

"You weren't cold two minutes ago."

She hadn't been, and he was too astute not to know. "I am now."

"You know what I think?" He nipped her lobe with his teeth, sending another wave of sensation crashing through her. "I think you're lying. I think you're aroused as fuck."

"No."

"Yes. I think you're wet for me, too."

Laila pressed her lips together. If she denied it, he would only slide his big fingers into her panties and prove she'd been dishonest. If she admitted it...then what? Would he toss her on the bed, strip her bare, and make her scream with ecstasy? Or would he laugh and ignore her?

She remained mute.

His growl in her ear sounded low, grating, and not remotely amused. "Nothing to say, little one?"

"Let me go."

"Oh, that's never happening, not unless I'm good and ready. You're going to learn to stop lying, misdirecting, and obfuscating with me—and we're going to start now. Are you wet?"

Something in his voice warned against lying. He wouldn't physically hurt her, but there would be consequences if she wasn't honest. She felt too emotionally naked, too vulnerable to relinquish the truth. If he knew how much he aroused her, he would use it to his advantage.

"It is none of your business."

"Tsk, tsk," he murmured in her ear. "You just keep digging yourself a deeper hole. I'm starting to think you want me to punish you."

"I want you to leave me alone."

"If you did, you wouldn't be so"—his hand slid down her ribs, over her abdomen, and inside her panties—"wet. Oh, fuck, Laila. This pussy..."

She tried to steel herself against the desire, but his fingers diving between her folds and trailing through her flowing juices had her gasping, her back arching, her hips writhing. Now that he knew how much she wanted him, there was no hiding. Despite the dread and need clashing in a dizzying thrill, she twisted away from him, pressing her thighs together in an attempt to evict his hand.

"No." Her protest sounded far more like a panting plea.

"Yes." He used his free hand to hoist one leg into the crook of his elbow and spread her wide open. His free hand curled over her mound. "This is mine. You're mine. The sooner you realize it, the easier this will be."

The objection on the tip of her tongue dissipated to silence when his slick fingers grazed her clit. He'd primed her for his touch, and she was beyond sensitive. Tingles erupted, melding with the heat of his skin. The new sensation mowed down her resistance and sent her up on tiptoe with a cry.

"Easy or hard, honey?"

Laila couldn't remember why he was asking that question. All she could focus on was the molasses slide of his fingers over her most nerve-rich spot and the destructive pleasure he was undoing her with. "Trees..."

"Still trying to get away with not answering me? Maybe I can give you a little incentive to speak."

He withdrew his hand. Without his touch, she felt aching and shaking and desperate almost immediately. Then he settled his hand above her mound. Even through her underwear, the heat of his palm enveloped her. Laila tried to restrain her shudder, but it was no use. Her body was hardwired to his. Her head told her to resist, but the rest of her wanted to beg him to lay her down and fill her with every one of his hard, veiny inches.

She hadn't even begun processing the destructive arousal when the hand above her sex swept down, striking her with a short, sharp smack.

The blow against her most female flesh stung. Burned. Reverberated through her entire body. Shock replaced desire for a suspended moment. Then need boomeranged back twice as strong, roaring to hungry life. She couldn't stop a trembling cry from slipping out.

Trees slid his hand back inside her panties. "Oh, so you like your pussy spanked?"

She shouldn't. Laila knew that. She pressed her lips together and shook her head, refusing to validate his effect on her. He already knew it. "No."

"You just keep lying to me. Bad, bad girl..." He strummed her clit again. Then again. Not stopping until her eyes slid shut and another moan, this one loud, escaped.

"You cannot..." Her attempt to scold him ended in a breathy exhalation that almost sounded like begging.

"Touch you? Oh, honey, I can. Anytime I want. Anywhere I want. Any way I want. This? You?" He cupped her pussy again. "All mine— until I say otherwise." He punctuated his edict by plunging a pair of fingers inside her and thrusting deep. As she mewled with sensation, his thumb slid over her sensitive bud again. Laila felt herself melting against him as his lips blazed a path across her shoulder and up her neck, then back to settle against her ear. "Did your pussy sting when I slapped it?"

She didn't dare answer.

"It did, didn't it? And you loved it."

Trees wasn't the gentle lover he'd been when she had last been in his bed. This man made her tremble and fear that she would yield her free will to him for pleasure. Laila shook her head stubbornly, terrified to give him that power over her body.

But it didn't matter. He removed his hand from her panties again, then popped her slick, swollen flesh through the silky fabric with a quick swat of his fingers.

The sensations were even stronger. Her knees nearly gave out. She couldn't stop a warbled, desperate cry from filling the air.

"Your body is being honest," he taunted. "Let's see if we can get your mouth there."

Without warning, he started grinding the heel of his palm over the puffy, sensitive pad of her sex, manipulating her clit in the process. The heat, the friction, the dark hunger of his touch... Laila didn't know how much longer she could fight Trees and the screaming climax he seemed determined to force on her. And if she gave in, what would he do next? How would she ever convince him that she felt nothing for him? That she belonged to Victor?

"Your whole body is trembling. With need. For me." He slid his fingers beneath the elastic of her underwear again and dragged his rough fingers over her clit. "You're getting close to orgasm, aren't you?"

Laila did her best to hold out, panting her way through a rise of pleasure that was lighting up her body and setting her skin on fire.

"Aren't you?" He spanked her pussy again, this time even harder than the last.

Another strangled, shuddering cry slipped out against her will. She dug her nails into his arms and squeezed her eyes shut, trying to focus on holding back her peak, on not giving him the satisfaction of knowing that he could manipulate her body to respond to him so utterly and so easily.

"Come on. I want your fucking honesty," he growled as he skimmed her bare sex again, his big fingers circling her nub once more. "Are you about to come?"

Yes. She ground her teeth together. Stubbornly, she shook her head.

"If you don't want this, stop me. I taught you the word. You know it. All you have to do is say red."

He would stop—everything. She might not know this aggressive, confrontational Trees, but she believed he would honor that safe word.

Laila couldn't bring herself to say it. It was wrong and it was weak, but she needed his touch too much to make him stop. "Shut up."

"Bad girls don't get orgasms. They do without." He ripped his hand free from her underwear again and landed three hard, rapid spanks on her pussy.

The air left her lungs. Her whole body jolted. Pleasure disintegrated her resistance. Her legs collapsed beneath her, leaving her no choice but to give herself over to Trees. Her head lolled back against him, her breaths hot, hard blades cutting through her chest as she went up in flames.

Climax was right there...

Then suddenly, his hands were gone.

Her eyes fluttered open. Disoriented, she blinked and tried to take a steadying breath. Her nipples felt beyond engorged. Her sex throbbed in relentless need. Laila didn't want him to stop. But she didn't want to let him go.

She was terrified.

Laila whirled on him with a frown, shocked when she caught sight of a syringe in his hand. Her eyes went wide. She tried to step back.

He held firm.

"What are you doing?" Her voice shook.

"You picked the hard way, honey. I gave you chances to be honest and you chose to lie. So I'm making sure you can't run. Your sister wants you close, not in Mexico where you're not safe. It's time you stopped playing dangerous games with dangerous people. And I want you in my fucking bed, all to myself."

Her eyes widened, and a protest formed on her lips, but he'd already pressed the needle into her neck. Seconds later, her world went black.

Lafayette, Louisiana

Laila woke groggy and disoriented. Her head felt fuzzy. How long had she been out? She had no idea. She wasn't even sure where she was except in a moving vehicle with the sun beating through the windshield, blinding her sensitive eyes. Every one of her limbs seemed to weigh a thousand pounds.

"You awake?"

That voice…it was familiar. She'd heard it in her sweetest dreams. But it also haunted a nightmare that tugged at the edge of her consciousness.

Instinctively, her heart beat faster. Her breaths came quicker.

It took all her concentration and most of her strength, but she turned her head and found the man who stopped her heart. "Trees."

The last time she'd seen him, at her condo in Mexico… It all rushed back. "Where are you taking me?"

"Right now? To Valeria. We landed in Louisiana about twenty minutes ago. She and Jorge are eager to see you."

Panic filled her. She tried to swim through the thick cotton wrapped around her thoughts and remember why she shouldn't want to see her sister. It was like casting a line into a yawning abyss. "No. I cannot."

His face softened. "You're worried about their safety."

"Yes." That was it.

"We aren't being followed. I'm making sure of that. You'll have an hour with them."

Then what?

Laila's mouth felt dry and sour. A result of the drug he had given her. She swallowed.

As if Trees had read her thoughts, he handed her an unopened bottle of water. His other hand was curled around the wheel. The sunglasses perched on his nose, his head-to-toe black, not to mention his size, all made him intensely intimidating.

She took the cool plastic, screwed off the cap, and downed a few sips. It helped, but she still didn't feel like herself.

Laila shifted in her seat, startled to see that he'd clothed her in a bright sundress and a sweater. Where had these clothes come from? Had he dressed her himself?

That wasn't all she noticed… Despite the fact she'd been out for hours, her sex still felt sensitive, swollen. Memories rushed sensations through her body, as if every nerve ending remembered the pleasure only he seemed capable of giving her.

Again, he read her mind. "We should talk about what happened."

"No. You should return me to Mexico."

"That's not happening. Is your pussy sore?"

She closed her eyes, an unwanted thrill burning her skin. He knew the answer. He must. The way he'd growled the question… She heard the pulse of his excitement. Giving him the truth terrified her. It would make him more feral. More relentless. More possessive. It would embolden him to lay claim to her. Best to come at Trees sideways. "Is Geraldo Montilla dead?"

He pressed his lips together. "We don't know. My gut says no.

Injured, yes. I know that because I shot the bastard myself. Now answer my question."

She didn't. Her heart went to her throat. "You were involved in Kimber's rescue?"

"How did you know about that?"

Carajo, she had said too much, so she gave him the one answer that might shut down conversation. "Victor."

Well, his phone had given her the information. It wasn't a total lie.

"Why weren't you with him when I found you? Last we heard, Montilla sent his hitmen after Ramos at some motel—I guess that's where you filmed him fucking you—but by the time they arrived, Ramos was gone. So were you."

So Victor hadn't been captured and offed by Montilla's men. Then where was he?

"Laila?" Trees prompted impatiently.

Admitting that she'd ditched Victor days ago would only encourage Trees in his insistence that she belonged to him. "I-I...um, have a headache."

From the middle console, he pulled out a bottle of ibuprofen and a granola bar. "I thought you might."

Laila took the items with a frown. She didn't understand Trees. He'd threatened her, he'd unleashed his sexuality on her, he'd withheld orgasm, and he'd abducted her. Why was he caring for her now? Being considerate?

She studied him as she chewed a couple of bites of the bar, then downed a pair of the tablets and drank more of the cool *agua.* His strong profile, his control of the wheel, his focus on the road... Something about all that aroused her. She shifted in her seat. Her sex burned. "Thank you."

As she set the bottle in the cupholder, Trees zipped his gaze her way. "Why, Laila? And before you think of lying to me, I know you hadn't been with Ramos for a while. Your sister told me."

Why would Valeria give up her confidences? Come to think of it, Trees should never have been able to find her...unless her sister helped. Had Valeria divulged her secrets in some misguided attempt to protect her?

Laila's ire rose. Valeria must know she was doing her best to keep her family safe. More than anyone, her sister should understand the consequences of failure. Laila had to be the one to get the cartels off their backs. Jorge needed his mother. Valeria must stay alive to raise her son. While Laila often wondered…if something happened to her, who, besides her sister, would even miss her?

She turned again to look at Trees. He might. This big, dominating bundle of muscle and testosterone seemed determined to have her. To own her. He might mourn her death and yearn for her if she was gone. But why?

If he loved you two weeks ago, could he have truly fallen out of love after you sent him one awful video?

Why did the possibility that he still loved her make her heart flutter? Why should his feelings matter?

Because *he* did. Because she loved him. Lying to herself about that was foolish.

"I tried to give Victor's location to someone in Montilla's organization in exchange for information that might ensure my family's safety."

He raised a brow. "You tried?"

"Victor had an informant. Someone in Montilla's inner circle." She licked her lips. Her next admission would tell Trees so much… "I offered him the location of his boss's car and the man who had stolen it if he told me where to find Kimber."

Trees sent her a weighty stare. "So you sold Ramos out. Then you called Valeria with the information, and she passed it to EM Security."

She nodded. "Now Kimber is safe, yes? How is she?"

"Better than expected. No one raped, beat, tortured, or starved her."

"They would not. She was too valuable a pawn to risk. If they had abducted her to exploit her or to use her as an instrument of revenge, their treatment would have been much different."

"Makes sense that they didn't abuse her. They always intended to exchange her."

"For Valeria and Jorge. That is why I tried to beat them at their own game."

"Gutsy," Trees said with admiration, then his expression became a glower. "But dangerous and absolutely forbidden in the future. You won't do that again."

Laila didn't refute him. It would only start an argument, but she couldn't afford to let him dictate if or how she kept her family safe.

"How long before we reach my sister?" She pulled down the visor and stared in the little mirror, blanching at the mussiness of her curls as she tried finger-combing them into submission.

"Just a few minutes."

That was a relief. Sitting this close to Trees, knowing he was furious, yet remembering how he made her feel when he'd touched her... She fidgeted anxiously.

Who do you think you'll be with once the visit to your sister is over?

Trees. And God only knew what he would do to her next.

"Now answer my earlier question. Is your pussy sore?"

She changed the subject again. "Where are my things?"

Trees clenched his teeth in anger. "In the back seat. I cleared out the condo. There's no trace of you left. If either Ramos or Montilla's men come looking for you, they'll find nothing. I even paid the sisters who own the place to swear you were never there."

He'd thought of everything. Laila supposed she should be grateful. She hadn't wanted to admit that she might be in over her head, but she couldn't afford to stop, not until Montilla and Victor were both dead.

"Thank you for packing up everything."

He cut her a glance as he rolled down the highway. "But not for taking you from Mexico?"

Since she would rather not lie to him, she pressed her lips together, not saying a word.

He sighed. "You know, once we're done here, I'll take you home. Then you'll answer to me."

"You do not own me."

"I don't. But I'm responsible for you." He slid his free hand to her thigh and his fingers tightened. "I'll do whatever I need to keep you safe. And let me be clear. The corrective discipline I mentioned in Mexico? That's still coming to you. Is your pussy sore? I'm not going to ask you again."

Laila remained mute as Trees pulled into the parking lot of an upscale apartment complex, drove straight to a building on the edge of the property, then turned to her, his expression sharp. "Laila?"

"My sister has been staying here?"

He nodded. "Since she and Kane arrived from Florida. Sit there. I'll come around for you."

Did he think she was going to run?

With a sigh, Laila let herself out of the vehicle. When he rounded the back and saw her on her feet, he glowered. "You don't listen well."

"I heard you." She smoothed down her dress.

When she looked up, he was against her, pressing her against his Hummer. He took her chin in his grip. "Then you need to learn to obey."

She raised a challenging brow at him. "You need to learn that I will bow to no man."

"I don't want you to bow, honey. I want you to kneel." He shocked her by leaning in and raking his tongue up the side of her neck. "To learn to trust me to keep you safe." Then he smacked her ass with his big, broad palm. "And to fucking answer my questions."

"You do not—"

"Get to tell you what to do? We'll see about that—after you visit your sister." Trees gripped her arm and led her up a flight of stairs, to a nondescript front door, then knocked. "And you'll be very sorry you refused to answer me."

The fear and thrill that jolted her veins startled Laila.

Before she could think of something to say, Kane Preston answered and ushered them in, scanning the lot before shutting and locking the door.

"We're clear," Trees said.

Kane nodded, then turned to her. "Hi, Laila. Valeria is eager to see you."

Oh, she wanted to speak to her sister, too. "Where is she?"

"Changing Jorge," he added. "She'll be out in a minute."

"Thank you."

Kane offered them a drink, which they both declined. Together, they made their way to the sofa and sat in uncomfortable silence. Thankfully, Valeria emerged with her long hair piled on top of her head and Jorge in her arms, looking adorably fresh from a bath with slicked-down hair and a dimpled smile.

Laila jumped up from the sofa. *"Sobrino!"*

Valeria handed Jorge to her with a soft glance of love. "He missed you."

"I missed him." She clutched the boy close, basking in the hint of his powdery baby smell. "It has only been three weeks since I saw him, but he has grown so much!"

Her sister nodded. "More every day, it seems."

"He is recovered from his illness?"

"Completely."

"Good." Laila swallowed, then looked at her sister with a million questions in her eyes. She didn't dare ask them in front of Trees and Kane. And if she switched to Spanish, Kane would understand. They needed privacy. "Where can we talk?"

Valeria hesitated. Clearly, her sister knew she was displeased.

"The bedroom?" Kane offered.

Laila nodded to her sister. "I will follow you."

Clutching Jorge, she kissed his little head as she and Valeria made their way to the back of the small but comfortable unit. Inside, she sat on the edge of the bed and bounced Jorge on her knee.

Valeria shut the door. "We are alone."

"Why did you betray me? Why did you tell Trees where to find me?"

Apology softened her face. "Because I am worried about you."

"I am doing all I can to keep you and Jorge safe."

"If you had asked me, I would have told you not to risk your life. I pay EM Security to do that."

Laila huffed. She understood her sister's perspective, but as before, they saw this matter differently. "They have yet to succeed. If I do it myself, I know it will be done."

"At what cost?" Valeria took Jorge from her, set him in the playpen, then turned back to her. "You are my only sister. Other than Jorge, you are my only family. You worry about us—"

"Of course I do."

"We worry about you."

"So you sent Trees to stop me?"

"I sent Trees to make sure you stop baiting dangerous men who would make your end terrifying and awful simply for the sport of it and leave me without the sister I love. We have been apart for too long. After I escaped, I felt incredibly guilty that circumstances did not allow me to bring you along. I could not save you for nearly two years. I did not risk everything to get you free so that you could throw yourself back to the wolves in some misguided attempt to save me. Stop sacrificing yourself for everyone else and start living for yourself."

Laila sighed. Of course Valeria saw the situation that way. And she could hardly tell her older sister to care less. "As Emilo's wife, you did not see the worst of his men, of their plans. You do not grasp how they think. You do not understand just how ruthless—"

"They can be?" Valeria laughed bitterly. "My husband did not love me. He did not even like me. To survive, I had to learn his business, hoard information, figure out how to manipulate him and those around him to provide for my own comfort, as well as yours and Mamá's." Then her sister seemed to remember Laila's reality, and her voice grew small. "Or I tried. I had no idea what was happening to you…"

"We have been over this. You could not have known. Emilo made sure of it."

"But I should have guessed." Valeria did not often cry, but she looked close to breaking down.

She had also inadvertently made the point Laila had been trying to. "You did not because you do not understand the criminals and degenerates of that horrible cartel."

Her sister fell silent, gripping the side of the playpen as if she needed the support and strength. "If I could tear the whole thing down, I would. Today. In one fell swoop. I would wipe it off the planet and I would laugh."

"I know." Laila would like that, too. But she understood full well that something more violent would only grow and metastasize into that criminal space. Because she was a realist, she had been happy to settle for eliminating the people who wanted her and her sister dead. "Why did you send Trees after me?"

"I did not. He came to me, desperate to find you."

Laila hadn't expected that. "And you told him where to find me? I trusted you."

"He loves you."

"Did he say that?"

Valeria frowned. "Has he not told you?"

He had…before circumstance had forced her to break his heart. "It does not matter."

"It does," Valeria insisted. "You have the one thing I never will, a man willing to give you his whole heart. Trees stood here less than twenty-four hours ago and promised to bring you back safely if I told him where to find you. So when he admitted that he loves you, I spilled everything."

"That was yesterday?" After she had sent him the video? Apparently, and she shouldn't really be surprised. Hadn't she wondered on their way here if it was possible Trees still loved her?

"You can be angry if you want, but I would do it again. For you, *hermana*."

"What if I did not love him in return?"

Valeria's gaze was softly chiding. "Why ask when you do? I had only to see the way you looked at him just now to know how you feel. But you are afraid. Is that why you fight him?"

Laila considered her sister's question. The truth smacked her in the face. "Except for you and Jorge, everyone I love has been taken from me. It is easier not to love anymore."

"Easier but empty. What sort of life will you have with no one in it? I can tell you. Meaningless. Jorge gives me purpose and a child's love, but what I would not give for a man's strong, protective arms around me. For him to give me more children and stand beside me as we raise them. I threw myself at Mr. Preston." Valeria looked embarrassed. "He would not have me."

Empathy softened Laila. Valeria had never expressed any of these feelings, and she was stunned by her sister's loneliness. "I am sorry."

"If I upset you, I am sorry, too. But I meant well."

Valeria had. She always had. And Laila now had a lot to think about.

"Trees means to take me back to his house for 'corrective discipline' until I learn to stop playing cartel games. Do you not worry what that means?"

Her sister cocked her head. "No. Anything he does to you would be far less than the cartel. He is not a bully, Laila. He is not Victor Ramos. And if he teaches you to value your own safety, why should I balk at his method?"

"So you condone whatever he means to do to me?"

"I suspect he will do it with a loving hand." She sighed. "Has he given you pleasure? When he took you to his bed, did he not show you the good parts of being a woman?"

"Yes." Laila couldn't lie about that.

"Then you have nothing to fear...except your heart surrendering itself to him."

Laila was afraid her sister was right.

CHAPTER
Seven

Laila visited with Valeria and Jorge for far longer than an hour. Trees hadn't minded. She'd needed the opportunity to connect with her sister and cuddle her nephew. And he'd used the time to ask Kane questions about Valeria's habits, actions, and communications. His fellow operative didn't think Valeria was up to anything, much less no good. That told Trees Laila had likely hatched her schemes alone.

Now he intended to find out what she had up her sleeve next and put a stop to it—before it killed her.

They left the apartment as twilight was falling. With his palm lingering on the small of her back, he reviewed his plans. While he'd waited, he'd sorted through possibilities, discarded ideas, and settled on a strategy. He knew exactly what to do when he hit his door.

The forty-five minutes between now and the minute he had her naked and tied down for his punishment were going to chafe.

He drove fast, heading straight toward the setting sun. Silence prevailed.

Laila surprised him by breaking it. "Thank you for taking me to see my family. I have missed them."

She seemed quieter, more thoughtful than earlier. Softer. He liked it. But he didn't expect it to last. As soon as she understood his intent, she would fight back. There would be fireworks.

"Of course. They're important to you. I would never keep you from them." Unlike Victor Ramos.

Trees didn't say that aloud. The dig served no purpose now. He had to stay focused on his objectives. Still, he couldn't stop wondering… When she'd left his place with Ramos, had she really become the thug's whore again, eager to take his cock hard and raw? Did she miss Ramos after selling him out to Montilla for her family's safety?

Laila sent him a faint curl of her lips. "Where are we going?"

"My house."

"How long do you intend to keep me there? I know I cannot stay with my sister; it is too dangerous for her and Jorge. But Victor is still alive, and he knows where you live."

Was she saying in a roundabout way that she was worried about him? Or just her own hide? "Oh, I hope he steps foot on my property again. I will blow his fucking head off." Ghost and Matt had offered to watch his six tonight to ensure Ramos couldn't creep up on him. "Does the possibility that I might kill him upset you, Laila? Or did you stop caring about him and the rough sex he gives you once you sold him out?"

She dodged his question. "You cannot keep me against my will."

"With me is where Valeria wants you. Right now, it's the safest place to be. So you'll stay with me until you learn to stop running headlong into danger and the people hunting you are either dead or behind bars."

She hesitated a long moment, and Trees wished like fuck he knew what she was thinking. "What will you do to me once we reach your house?"

"Take you to my dungeon."

"But—"

"No." He stopped at a red light and turned to her. "You can't be surprised. I told you in Mexico to make a choice, easy or hard. You didn't. The same way you wouldn't admit you were wet. You were stubbornly mute again when you refused to tell me if your pussy is sore. You've run from me. You've lied to me. You've stabbed me in the back. You've put yourself in danger again and again. I gave you every chance to trust me. To open up to me. You didn't. So I'm going to peel you back, layer by layer, until you fucking get honest."

Once he'd stripped away her emotional defenses, she would have nothing and no one to rely on but him. Then he'd find out what she actually felt for him…if anything.

What if she doesn't love you in return?

It would suck, but that wasn't the point of this exercise. He couldn't force her love any more than he could force her trust. What he could compel? Obedience. Honesty. Communication.

He hoped that, somehow, it would be enough.

Beside him, Laila pressed her lips together and said nothing.

Trees swore under his breath. Why did she insist on keeping so many fucking secrets? Why was she trying so hard to hide from him?

The drive passed. Tension vibrated between them. He could have cut it with small talk, but he wanted her to feel it. So he let her drown in the silence. Once he'd stripped away her defenses and had her emotionally naked, then he'd get her talking. At the very least, he would show her that he could both rebuild her and be worthy of her trust.

What she did with that knowledge was up to her.

As they ambled down the road to his place, darkness fell. He disabled his exterior security gate and rumbled down the dirt driveway, then reinstated the perimeter fencing behind him with the press of a button. Barney barked out his greeting, chasing his truck up the side of the fence.

Laila smiled. "He is always so happy to see you."

"I've taught him to trust me."

Her smile fell. "He is lucky. Trust is not a luxury everyone can afford."

She didn't think she could afford to trust him? What the fuck had he done to earn her doubt?

Nothing. He was fighting her past.

Finally, he parked in the garage out back, then repeated the command he'd given her before she'd visited her sister. "Sit there. I'll come around for you." He turned to pin her with a glare. "Do you understand?"

For once, she looked chastened. "Yes."

"Good." He climbed out, gave Barney a scratch between the ears and a few treats from the bin on the nearby shelf. Once the dog trotted away, munching happily, Trees rounded the vehicle.

He opened the door and held out his hand to Laila. As if she finally understood there was hell to pay, she looked from his outstretched palm up to his face. Their gazes connected. She shivered. He felt the answering ping, just like the first time he'd laid eyes on her.

Her fingers shook as she settled them across his own. Then she edged off the seat, sliding toward the ground.

As her body skimmed his, he sucked back a sharp breath at the heady sensations. Fuck, he was supposed to undo her, not the other way around. "Let's go. I'll get your things out of the back seat later."

She nodded. Once he shut the passenger door and closed his detached garage, he led her across the backyard and toward the door, his hand hovering over her delicate spine.

When they stopped, he reached around her to unlock the back door. She stayed him with a hand on his wrist. "Will you hurt me?"

Trees swiveled a stare her way. If she was afraid, it didn't show. "In my dungeon? That's up to you."

"How?"

Her expression softened him. She was worried, and the knowledge in her hazel eyes was far too old for her young face. Laila was so full of fire and resistance and irrepressible purpose, he often forgot that she was a dozen years younger.

"I'll explain everything soon." He opened the door, guided her inside, then locked up behind her and enabled the alarm. Against his better judgment, he turned and cupped her face. "And I promise I'll never intentionally leave you confused. Do you need anything before we head down? Food? Water? And don't think of refusing either just because you don't want to owe me."

Laila nibbled at her bottom lip, then shook her head. "I am fine."

"You've barely eaten all day, and we'll fix that soon. I'll insist you eat something."

"I will be all right until morning."

"You think that, but you'll need to keep up your strength and stamina for what I have in mind."

She swallowed nervously. "Trees—"

"No. I gave you chances. You flung them back in my face, so we're moving on to punishment. How's your headache?"

"Gone."

"Good. Do you need the bathroom?"

She shook her head.

He lifted her chin in his grip. "When we're in my dungeon, nonverbal answers aren't allowed. Yes or no?"

"No." Her voice quivered.

"Anything else you need?"

She hesitated, and Trees suspected she was thinking through her options and deciding how best to combat him. "An explanation."

"You'll get one as soon as we're downstairs. What's your safe word?"

"It's red. Trees—"

"Come with me." He wasn't arguing with her anymore.

He was getting the truth.

Taking ahold of her elbow, he led her forward. She seemed to gather her courage, like a prisoner facing a firing squad, and headed for his closet. As he swept his clothes aside on their hangers, he motioned her to turn around. "Face the wall."

Trees made sure she couldn't see his security code. He'd learned from his past mistakes.

As soon as she obeyed, he tapped in the digits and the door to the dungeon popped open. It wasn't lost on him that Laila would be the first person he played with in the kink paradise he'd built for himself and his eventual missus.

Trees gathered her by the elbow, led her to the opening, then leaned in to flip on the light. "Inside. Watch your step."

She descended with quiet grace. Trees shut the door behind them. It clicked closed with a satisfying thud.

Let the games begin…

"Strip."

Laila choked. "Excuse me?"

"Anytime you're in my dungeon, you're naked. I want you completely bare to me, body and soul."

She blinked up at him, trembling. Trees knew she wasn't as afraid of a beating or torture as she was of him getting under her skin and seeing the real her.

"Tick tock, Laila. You're only making things harder on yourself by procrastinating."

"Why do you demean me?"

The loaded question would only lead to a mind game he wouldn't play. "I'll make everything clear once you comply. But I'm seeing a pattern here. You argue. You refuse to answer. You twist my words.

You try my patience and do your best to wear me down in the hopes that I'll get frustrated or tired of dealing with you and give in. That won't happen. I'm single-mindedly focused on you, Laila. I will get the answers I want. Last time I'm going to tell you. Strip."

She bit that lush lower lip that drove him insane in obvious indecision, then she swallowed, lifted her chin, and kicked off her shoes. "If you wish to beat me into some sort of submission, you will not be the first. You will not be the last."

Nice try. "You can't guilt me into backing down. I'm not going to beat you."

But I'm going to use your body against you.

She slid the little white sweater that clung to her breasts off her narrow shoulders and set it on a nearby table. Her stretchy dress followed as she whipped it overhead and tossed it haphazardly beside her cardigan. Her indifferent stare was meant to goad him, but no matter what her face said, he didn't believe that getting naked for him meant nothing to her. He also didn't buy that it did nothing *for* her. Her pebbled nipples poked her bra like twin nubs begging for his attention. She couldn't blame the cold for that. As he'd waited for Laila to wrap up her conversation with Valeria, he'd used the controls on his phone to pump up the heater in the dungeon to a comfortable seventy-four degrees.

"Shall I keep going?" she asked as if she didn't care how he answered.

He raised a brow at her. "Are you naked yet?"

Laila gritted her teeth, then quickly smoothed her expression, as if she refused to show even the tiniest vulnerability. Instead, she slid her bra straps down her shoulders and reached behind her to unclasp the garment before tossing it away. Then she shot him a challenging glare, as if to say, *I hope you're enjoying gawking at my tits, asshole.*

Trees merely smiled—and felt the blood rush to his cock. "Beautiful. Now the panties."

A part of him hated to lose the transparent lace perched on her lushly curved hips. The silky fabric clung temptingly to what sure looked like her swollen pussy, delineating the engorged curves of her labia and the crease in between. But for what he had in mind, the lacy scrap needed to go.

With a huff, she worked the undergarment down her hips, then bent and stepped out of them, rising in all her naked glory to stand before him, seemingly detached and unafraid.

He knew better.

Her pussy was definitely puffy and rosy from his earlier spankings. Even at a distance, he could see that. He'd bet she was aroused, too. But he'd get to that.

With a nod, Trees acknowledged her. "Next time, I'll reward you if you comply faster and give me less attitude, but some effort is better than none. I've got something for you. Come here."

Laila stiffened, unmoving, as if it had finally occurred to her that he couldn't hurt her simply by looking. But now he intended to touch her. She was afraid of what he might do. That fact was all over her face.

His expression became a warning even as he lowered his voice into a coaxing rumble. "Laila, if I have to ask you twice, your reward is off the table. You won't like what happens then."

Her jaw tightened. Yeah, she hated being coerced. Trees understood.

He softened his tone. "But it's your choice. Everything that happens between us is."

Cajoling seemed to do the trick, because she finally shuffled forward, stopping in front of him. To his shock, she laid her palm over his chest. "What is happening? I do not understand this game."

"I think you do." He covered her hand with his own. "But I promised to explain, so I will."

He led her to a nearby chair and sat, then drew her onto his thighs. She settled stiffly against him...but curled her legs onto his lap, unconsciously giving him more of herself.

She blindsided him by tracing a fingertip across his chest and skimming her pouty lips up his neck as she wriggled on his hard dick. "Can you not simply ask me what you wish to know, then take me to bed?"

Her touch induced tingles that threatened to scramble his brain, despite the fact he knew she'd switched tactics purely to usurp him. That wasn't happening. He grabbed her wrist and stilled her hip to stop the distraction. "Not when you've proven you can't be trusted to tell the truth. Besides, this isn't about sex."

"I am naked."

Too many people confused nudity with sex, so he wasn't surprised. "This is about control. It's about power. You cede it to me, along with your trust, and we grow together."

Trees didn't tell her that he would give things she needed back to her. Attention, affection, praise, reassurance, caring, boundaries. A safety net she'd never had. Those were bonuses she had to figure out for herself, because if he explained, she'd either dismiss him or laugh in his face. Or both.

She scowled. "Why would I cede anything?"

"I'll reward you when you do."

"And you will punish me when I refuse?"

"Yes. But your punishment won't be a beating, Laila. Hurting you against your will is something I'll never do." She still looked as if she didn't quite believe him. No shock there. Too often, words were just BS in syllable form. But he'd get through to her...eventually. "There are rules while you're in this room with me. One is that you're honest to the best of your ability. If you don't know something, tell me you don't know. But if you lie...I'll take that as a sign that you're seeking punishment and act accordingly. Two, you have to try to trust me. I'm not expecting miracles, but this will go a lot easier if you just believe that, when I tell you something, I mean it. And three, you have to let me know if I'm hurting you beyond what you can bear. My goal isn't agony or humiliation. If you need your safe word, use it—with the understanding it isn't for minor pain or mental unease."

"If you have no intention of hurting me, why do I need a safe word?"

"I said nothing about discomfort. There will be lots of that if you choose not to cooperate."

"So I must give in to you or suffer the consequences?"

She was trying to make him feel bad; it wasn't going to work. "Do you have any other questions?"

"No."

"Stand," he commanded.

She got to her feet, then he rose behind her.

"That's a good start," he praised. "I promised you a reward earlier. As a show of good faith, I'll give you two." He reached into the drawer of the desk behind him, withdrew a little foil square, and unwrapped it. "Open your mouth and stick out your tongue."

She didn't right away. They would work on that. But when she glanced at the chocolate square between his fingers, she sent him an unconscious smile of delight and obeyed.

He settled the square on her tongue. She drew it into her mouth with a moan, eyes closed in pleasure.

As she sucked and swallowed it, he skimmed his thumb across her plump lips. "Did you like that?"

She nodded, opening her eyes and looking somewhat puzzled. "I love chocolate. How did you know?"

He gave her a wry smile. "I've met very few women who don't."

"Valeria does not."

Trees was surprised she'd volunteered anything remotely personal. He took it as a good sign. "She's missing out."

"I think so, too. But chocolate has always been a rare treat for me."

If she stopped trying to throw herself into danger at every turn, he would give her plenty more. "Want your next reward?"

She nodded. When he raised a rebuking brow, she corrected herself. "Yes."

"Good." He drew her closer and cupped her face, staring straight into her eyes.

Laila's breath caught. She blinked up at him. The pulse pounded at her neck.

She might be afraid of his intentions, but he aroused her. Trees would bet money on that.

Before he talked himself out of it, he lowered his head and slanted his lips over hers in a soft, lingering press, sinking into the moment. God, he'd been wanting to kiss Laila since he'd set eyes on her again.

After a stiff moment, Laila rose on her tiptoes with a little whimper and clutched his shoulders. Her eyes fluttered shut. Then she kissed him in return.

Clearly, she wasn't immune to him. He could work with that. And with any luck, they would come out on the other end of this punishment with a new understanding, maybe even a new closeness.

Before he lost himself in her sweetness, he straightened and took her hand. "Follow me."

She didn't look convinced that whatever he had in mind was a good idea, but she offered no resistance.

Until he laid her on a padded table with a dangling cuff at each corner.

Her eyes went saucer wide. "What are you doing?"

"Starting your punishment." By the time he'd answered her, he'd secured one of her wrists in the attached cuff above her head. She tried to retract the other, but it was too late. Trees held firm, extending her arm until it stretched to the restraint above. He secured it with a quiet click.

"Why are you tying me down? What are you doing to me?" A note of panic wound through her voice.

"You've spent time in this room. I've told you I'm a Dominant. Nothing that's happening now should be a huge surprise."

Her face told him she screwed up her courage. "You cannot break me. Many times, I have endured the worst at others' hands."

Wouldn't she be surprised to realize she'd never endured anything like this and she had no way to fight him?

He caressed his way down her body slowly—shoulder, breast, abdomen, thigh—letting her feel every touch of his rough fingertips and broad palm. "Then you have nothing to fear, little one."

As she met his stare with defiance, he grabbed her ankle and fastened the cuff around it. Fresh shock spread across her face.

When she bucked and kicked, he merely stepped back, crossed his arms over his chest, and waited until she gave him her full attention. "This isn't how you earn more rewards."

"I will give up chocolate."

"That's not the reward you're going to want, Laila," he promised in a dark, silky voice. "Give me your foot."

"No."

"Give. Me. Your. Foot. Now. Or there won't be rewards of any kind, no matter how much you beg me. If you comply, you'll find I can be very generous. If not..." He let her infer that the result would be deeply unpleasant. "But like I said, what happens is up to you."

She looked so heartbreakingly unsure. Not for the first time, he questioned this tactic, but he'd tried every other fucking way to get her to understand that he was on her side. If he had to be underhanded to make her stop risking herself, he would. It was better than her ending up dead.

"Laila, when have I ever hurt you?" He gave her a moment to work that out in her head.

"Never, but—"

"No buts. Never."

"Then why restrain me?"

"Because you have a nasty habit of running away. This way, I can be sure you're here and focused on the conversation we need to have. I'm going to ask questions and you're going to give me honest answers. Right after you give me your foot." He held out his hand, palm up, inches from her toes. "If you don't, we'll move straight into punishment."

Slowly, Laila slid her last free limb in his direction, looking nervous as hell. He took hold of her ankle and secured her with the padded cuff.

"Good," he praised, brushing a gentle hand up her leg. "Anything feel too tight? Too uncomfortable?"

"No."

He reached under the table to tilt it, angling her feet toward the ground. Then he grabbed the rolling stool behind him and plopped down, parking himself in front of her. Then he adjusted the height until he sat eye level with her pussy. With a smile, he swiped a soft thumb over her cleft.

Her breath caught.

"Your pussy is swollen." He petted her again, trailing kisses up her thigh. "This is the very last time I'm going to ask you. Is your pussy sore from my spankings?"

Her exhalation came out rough. And when he parted her labia with his thumbs, exposing her rosy clit, she squirmed. "What are you doing?"

"Waiting for an answer. If you don't give me one, I'll assume you're not sore at all and spank your pussy again."

"Yes," she finally gasped out. "I am sore."

"See, that wasn't so hard, was it?" He thumbed her clit, pressing down and rubbing a slow circle, smiling at her indrawn breath. "When did you first become aware of it?"

"When I woke up in your truck."

Perfect. "What about while you were visiting your sister?"

"Yes. And when I crossed my legs, it burned."

Even better. "As we drove back here, too?"

"It was stinging."

"And now?"

"It feels as if all my blood has rushed there," she whined. "It...throbs."

Fuck if that didn't light his blood on fire and make him even harder.

Trees swallowed back lust and pressed on. "I appreciate your honesty."

To reward her, he dipped his hand into the desk drawer again, whipped out another square of chocolate, and offered it to her. Laila opened immediately, wrapping her lips around the confection with another moan. He watched her chew it, savor it, swallow it. The second the sugar left her tongue, her resolve returned. "I have answered you. Release me."

He laughed. "Not even close. Let's try the other question I asked you earlier. You know, to get you used to this new concept called honesty, make sure you get some practice with it before I ask you the questions I really need answers to."

She scowled. "I do not owe you all my truths."

"See, I'm going to disagree. As long as you're in my house, under my protection, and in my bed, you do. So you're going to learn to share every single thing. Now, are you wet?"

Trees knew the answer. In the moments he'd been sitting in front of her pussy and petting her, she'd gone slick. He nestled his knuckles between her folds and brushed them directly across her clit. Her breath hitched. His fingers came away more than damp. He held them up under the overhead lights. There was no way she couldn't see the sheen of her own juices.

Laila closed her eyes. "Yes."

"Open your eyes and tell me why."

"I do not know."

"Yes, you do. Try harder."

She pressed her lips together. "My body responds to you. There, are you happy?"

This wasn't about him, but *them*. "No. Did you get wet when I asked you to strip? Or when you got naked for me?"

"I-I do not know."

Maybe she hadn't thought about it consciously, but she must have some idea. "Maybe it was when you sat on my lap and felt my dick hard for you? Or when I kissed you?"

She shrugged. "I did not pay attention."

Sure, she hadn't.

"Or did it take a little more than a kiss? Maybe you gushed for me when I started staring at your pussy. Talking about it. Petting it. Salivating for it."

Laila tensed. Her indrawn breath shuddered. He was getting closer to the truth.

Trees leaned in and gripped her thighs, gratified to see them trembling. "That's it, isn't it? You're aroused by the fact I'm fixated on your pretty pussy."

"No," she breathed.

"Now you're lying to me. Or are you lying to yourself?" Trees didn't wait for a reply. He simply caressed the pad of her pussy, thumbing her clit again.

She hissed. "Trees…"

"Answer the question. And think carefully, because they're going to get more difficult. Punishments will only get harder, too."

"All right. Yes, I like that," she managed.

"Me focusing on your pussy?"

She cast her gaze down, fidgeting against the table self-consciously. "Yes. That is when I started feeling damp and achy."

Trees loved that answer. But something else had her revving, too.

Oh, this line of questioning had just gotten fascinating. "Thank you. Something else must have taken you from wet to throbbing... I don't think it was our back-and-forth banter. That's just an everyday argument for you. I'm not convinced it was me telling you that we're going to play this game, since you didn't even know the rules. That leaves either my threats or my restraints."

"I do not understand." She sounded near tears.

It was possible she didn't comprehend her response and the way her own body worked. Her responses inclined him to believe what she'd told him while they'd traveled back from Florida in the RV a few weeks ago over the words she'd spewed in the alley in La Pesca. Until him, she'd never been kissed, never had an orgasm, never known real pleasure. Given her past, maybe she genuinely couldn't reconcile why either the notion of being punished or restrained aroused her.

"It's all right," he reassured. "We'll figure it out together."

She blinked like his answer surprised her. "You are not angry?"

"Are you being honest with me? This isn't bullshit embarrassment, right?"

"I am telling the truth. I do not understand."

"Okay. I believe you. I'm assuming you'd like another reward?"

She nodded. "But I do not think I could eat more chocolate."

Was she telling him she wanted something else from him?

Trees stood and approached, settling his body against hers, then taking her face in hand. "Open your mouth to me, little one."

Her lips parted instantly, and he was toast. He leaned in, seizing her and sinking into her honeyed depths, stroking against the sweet confection of her tongue.

Hesitantly, she kissed him back, growing progressively bolder with every sweep and each additional inch he claimed as his own. He groaned into her, laving the roof of her mouth before nibbling on her bottom lip, then filling her again with his tongue.

Against the table, she strained to get closer, opening wider, writhing for him, pouring herself into their kiss. Trees spent a timeless moment losing himself in her before he eased back, brushed a kiss across her wet, swollen mouth, then stepped back.

"Will you kiss me again?"

Her request surprised him. He smiled as he sat on the stool. Her pussy was right in front of him, and he swiped a finger through her cleft. Still wet...but not any more than before.

"If you keep being honest, I would love to. If not, expect punishment."

"What kind?"

Trees sent her a wicked smile. "The kind that will make you beg and squirm."

Her hips gave a reflexive jerk, as if his words excited her. Trees settled his fingers between her folds again. She was wetter.

The idea of his sensual punishment turned her on? Maybe she'd also enjoy more restraints. That possibility boggled his mind. The first time he'd done it simply to keep her from escaping him in the RV, she'd flipped her shit. Now?

Time to find out.

Trees strolled to the far wall, behind the table, and found a length of silk rope, then he approached the side of the table and attached it to a hook underneath. He watched her face as he draped the length over her abdomen, attached it underneath again, then crisscrossed it between her breasts and ended by laying the soft length over her throat just tight enough for her to feel.

Her breath turned choppy.

"Does that scare you?"

It took her a long time to answer. "No."

And her tone said she was shocked by her own response. When he tested her pussy again, she was even juicier, the wetness spreading to her inner thighs.

Wasn't that intriguing? No surprise that Laila didn't understand.

But he did. She was wired for him, far more than he'd dared to hope.

He scrubbed a hand down his face. His instincts had led him here, and he'd been questioning his judgment since he'd demanded she strip for him. But now...

Hell yeah.

And if he could finally get some honesty out of her while arousing her out of her damn mind, even better.

"You've done really well so far, Laila." He stroked her pussy again, sailing his lips up one hip before skimming his teeth back down the sensitized flesh. "Let's try some more difficult questions."

"Before another reward?"

Did she want more of his kisses, was she stalling, or simply afraid of her own responses?

"If you answer these next questions well, the reward will definitely be worth the wait. First, why did you leave my house with Victor the morning he broke in? You told me in La Pesca that you'd always wanted to be with Victor because your struggles against him are the foreplay that arouses you before he fucks you rough." When she winced, he pressed on. "Is that true? Do you get excited when he holds you down, pulls your hair, rips off your shirt, shoves your pants down, forces his way between your legs, and—"

"Stop." Laila closed her eyes, obviously fighting tears.

"Are you going to cry?"

"No." She sniffled.

"You want to."

"I don't."

"You're lying. I can see you're upset. It's all over your face. Why?"

Trees half expected her to double down on what he suspected was a whopping lie and tell him that she missed Victor. Instead, she turned away and tried to hide her expression from him.

"Please…"

While begging was better than defiance, it wasn't acceptable, either. Trees swallowed his disappointment. Why did he keep trying to save a woman who didn't want to be saved? But he knew the answer. She had been through all nine circles of hell, and his heart insisted she was worth the effort. "I'm disappointed, Laila. I'm not asking hard questions. Punishment it is."

Trees bent his head, parted the dewy folds of her pussy with his thumbs, and licked her already stiff bud mercilessly, dragging his tongue across the tip, then sucking it into his mouth before adding more stimulation with a gentle scrape of his teeth. He moved closer, settling in for a lingering onslaught and working her up to the edge of pleasure.

She gasped. Her whole body tensed. Her toes curled. She jerked and writhed to get closer to him. As her cheeks flushed and her need ramped up, she grabbed the restraints and cried his name. She was sexy as hell to watch.

When he sucked her clit again, he was thrilled to find it harder.

"Trees…"

"You close?" He knew she was. When he fitted a pair of his big fingers inside her, her pussy tightened in little warning pulses.

"Yes," she gasped out.

"Good. There's some honesty." He licked her again, reveling in her harsh breaths, her tension, her body stretching and straining for that one last touch that would put her over the edge.

He backed away.

"No!" Her voice was sharp, something between a demand and a whine.

"Want that orgasm, honey? I'll bet you do." He licked his lips, moaning at the taste of her. He was gratified when her stare followed his tongue and her eyes darkened. He started petting her mound again, dragging his finger between her folds and over her labia, completely avoiding her needy clit. "I'll bet you're aching for me to put my mouth all over that pretty little pussy and suck you. While I do that, I'll settle my fingers inside you, fill you up, and rub you just right…"

She whimpered, her body quaking from head to toe. "Please…"

"You beg so sweetly." He kissed her inner thigh, teasing and nipping his way close to her clit. "But I can't since you'd rather plead with me than be honest."

She whimpered in response. "Trees…"

He cupped her mound as he stood slowly and kissed his way up her body. He stopped at her turgid nipples stabbing the air, latching on in strong drags. He strummed her clit with his thumb again. Just once. That was all it took before her body ratcheted up, vibrating with undeniable need once more.

Then he kissed the rest of his way up her body, settling his lips just against her ear. "Tell me why you voluntarily left my house with Victor that morning."

"I didn't have a choice," she sobbed. "Please!"

Bullshit. "Why? He didn't force you. My security camera captured you walking to his truck and getting in of your own free will. But you made it down here to my panic room. I know you did because two of my guns are missing off the wall."

"I have them," she vowed.

"I know. I took them back. What I want to know is why the fuck you left with him when you'd made it safely down to the panic room and you were armed?"

"You do not understand Victor."

"Make me understand."

Her exhalation trembled. "He was going to do things…"

Now they were getting somewhere. "Like what?"

"Trees…"

She always implored him in just that tone when he was digging too close to a truth she wanted to bury. Time to show her the real power of this punishment.

"Not going to tell me?"

"You will only get angry, and it changes nothing. Please." Tears clung to the long, upswept curl of her lashes.

With one hand, he tortured her clit in slow, lazy circles. With the other, he took hold of her chin and leaned close, getting right in her face. "You *never* keep things from me because you think you have to protect me or my feelings. I'll deal with the fallout from whatever you say. That's *my* responsibility, not yours."

"It is not that simple," she managed to gasp out between jerks of her hips, her silent, involuntary begging for more of his touch.

"It's exactly that simple." And Trees got the distinct impression that whatever she refused to admit…she'd done it not for her own selfish desires or even to protect her family. She'd done it for him.

Why?

God, he hoped it was because she fucking cared about him. She must, at least a little…right?

Don't get ahead of yourself, buddy.

"Tell me why you left with him," he demanded.

"I-I wasn't thinking."

"Bull-fucking-shit. You're always thinking. From the moment we met, you've proven that you're constantly looking at your situation and finding ways to finagle it to your benefit. You wanted to escape me. You wanted to save your family. You wanted to keep your distance... You always have your reasons. What did you hope to achieve that morning?"

She pressed her lips together. "Do not make me say it."

What the fuck was she trying so desperately to avoid admitting? Trees didn't think it was her feelings for Victor. If falling for the asshole was her big sin, she would have already said it. In fact, she would have flung it in his face, like she'd done in La Pesca. But this was something else...

And he knew how to get it out of her.

"All right. Let me know when you're ready to tell me." He backed away and rolled across the room on the little stool. Bracing his elbow on the desk, he tried to ignore his angry cock throbbing in protest and pulled out his phone. Then he launched a game app and did his fucking best to focus on winning the medieval battle, not staring at the naked beauty with the haunted eyes and pouting pussy less than six feet from him.

"Trees."

"What?"

"Why do you insist on this torture? Why not accept that I am no good for you and turn me loose?"

He'd answered those questions, and he wasn't about to let her change the subject. Besides, he wanted her to understand his frustration. Well, as much as she could. No, she didn't have a cock hard enough to pound nails, but he doubted she'd much like being misdirected and lied to.

"Maybe I like toxic. Maybe this shit amuses me. Maybe I just like to tie women up and hear them beg because I'm cruel." He shrugged.

"No." She frowned. "That is unlike you."

"Is it? Then maybe I just don't want to burden you with the truth, and I decided keeping it to myself would be better than treating you like a rational adult capable of making her own decisions."

"You are being ridiculous."

"So are you. Stop changing the subject. There's only one thing I want to hear from you now, and that's the reason you left with Ramos. Tell me."

Laila bit her lip, looking as if she was searching for the right words. "Starting a vendetta with Victor will only get you killed. He is already furious that you ended his brother's miserable life. If you use whatever I tell you against him in some vengeful retaliation—"

"That's my choice, Laila. My business. And you're still dodging me. You're being a bad, bad girl. I guess it's time for more punishment."

"No. Please. I do not want this."

"Really? Then why do you keep choosing it? All you have to do to make it stop is give me an honest, straightforward answer." She didn't reply, so he darkened his phone and set it aside, then rolled the stool back to her, taking her hips in his hands and forcibly tilting her pelvis to his waiting mouth. "Let's see if I can incentivize you."

He slid his tongue between her engorged folds and licked her from opening to clit, then focused relentlessly on the little bud, laving, nipping, tormenting her until every inhalation was a gasp, until the blood flushing her warm brown skin turned her rosy. Until her nipples poked the air desperately. Her clit had engorged again, now on the verge of bursting. Then he gave her one last slow, seductive swipe and backed away.

Instantly, she whimpered, her eyes closing, her head whipping from side to side in protest.

She looked fucking beautiful, and Trees would give anything to scale the wall she'd put between them, hold her while she clung to him, then take her to his bed and love her so thoroughly she never thought about leaving again.

Good luck with that...

"You motivated to answer me yet, Laila?"

She didn't reply, just sucked in steadying breaths. Every part of her body looked taut, swollen, aching...

"No?" He sighed. "I wish you'd make a different choice. Can't you trust me and believe I'm acting with your safety, happiness, and best interests in mind? I guess not. You keep refusing."

"Why?" she sobbed.

Why was he punishing her? Why did he care? "Because I love you. That hasn't changed. It never will."

Laila gaped at him, tears running down her face. "After everything I have done to you?"

He shook his head. "Until you answer me, Laila, I'm not answering you." He rolled away and grabbed his phone again. "Should I continue with this game, or are we finally going to talk? And before you answer, you should know that I can do this all night. I can get you to the verge of orgasm over and over again, never letting you fall over. I'll enjoy spending hours with my head between your legs, lapping up that sweet pussy and keeping you on the verge of climax. So you can either tell me the truth now or go through the torment—"

"He threatened to burn down your house," she squeaked out.

Of all the things she might have said, Trees hadn't seen that coming. "What?"

She sighed, more tears clinging to her lashes. "I did not want to tell you. You will only get angry and chase revenge. He is underhanded and brutal. He is ruthless and—"

"I can be all of those things, too, honey. Every fucking day until he's dead. But you're saying you left with him because he threatened my *house?*"

Laila nodded miserably. "I can no longer stand this torment you have heaped on me, and I cannot stop you from pursuing Victor. No matter what I say or do, I will lose you forever. So if you want the truth, fine. I was—"

"You won't lose me." He stood and approached her again, cupping her face and delving deep into her hazel eyes. "You can't lose me."

"He will kill you."

"He can try, but I'll see him coming. And I'll keep us both safe. Keep talking." When she looked reluctant to go on, he cupped her mound again, sliding his fingers teasingly across her clit. "If you do, I'll reward you."

Her head slid back. She moaned, a long, high-pitched wail of need. "I locked myself in this room when I heard him shout for you. He threatened to burn the house and kill you, so I—"

"Rushed out to stop him because you were afraid of being burned alive? This room is fireproof. You should have stayed hidden and safe."

"And sacrificed you?" She shook her head feverishly. "No. Not when I could save you."

"You came out of hiding to protect *me*?" Did she comprehend how insane that sounded? Trees was well over a foot taller than her. He outweighed her by at least a hundred pounds. And he'd been trained by the best to be a lethal son of a bitch. But she'd put herself on the line to save him? "How did you think that was going to work?"

"I talked him out of revenge by focusing him on another target for his violent urges. I could not bear him plotting your death or destroying your home."

"Fuck the house. I bought this place for the land and the privacy, not the structure. Did you really think you needed to protect it with your life?" And why would she?

She squirmed, gyrating against his now-still fingers. "I saw an opportunity to accomplish many goals at once."

"Explain that."

Laila hesitated. Apparently, he'd ventured on to something she didn't want to admit. Trees wasn't about to let her hold out. He dipped his head and tormented her clit with his tongue again until it was hard as a stone, until she bucked in silent pleading, until he wrung a loud wail of surrender from her.

"Laila? Explain."

"Okay. I-I ache. I cannot…"

"Think? Yeah, you can." He brushed his thumb over her again, giving her enough friction to tease but not enough to send her over. "Don't filter. Use the first words that come to your head."

She nodded, gasping. "My plan was meant to save you and your house while distracting Geraldo Montilla, who would then focus more on Victor and less on my family."

"And put Ramos on Montilla's radar?"

"Yes. I hoped Victor would fight back and weaken Montilla."

Was she serious? "Did you grasp that it would probably mean Ramos's death?"

She hesitated, licking her lips, squirming again. The answer she was withholding right now was the something she didn't want to admit. Was she afraid he wouldn't give her this orgasm if she said she hadn't meant for Ramos to get hurt?

"Tell me," he demanded, dropping his voice. "Now."

"Yes," she gave in with a cry. "I suspected Montilla would kill Victor. I hoped for that."

She expected him to believe that after the video she'd sent? Trees scowled. "Bullshit. How about the truth this time?"

"It is the truth!" she insisted. "After that, I planned to find Kimber's location to give EM a reason to hunt down Montilla—"

"So we would off him for you and your family would finally be safe?"

"Exactly."

He had to give her credit. If that was the truth, her plan was both ballsy and brilliant. And something he absolutely itched to spank her ass for.

But she'd also given him a lot to unpack in that statement. He started with the things she was most likely to answer without pushing back. "So...the distraction to focus Montilla's attention on Ramos? Is that why you helped him steal the Ferrari?"

She nodded. "It was my idea. I convinced Victor that if he could show the cartel he was clever enough to take the man's prized possession, then perhaps everyone would think the old man incapable of continuing the operation and that he should be replaced by someone as daring and crafty as Victor."

Trees didn't ask if Ramos had been dumb enough to believe it. Obviously he had. Laila had appealed to the man's ambition and vanity and said exactly what he'd wanted to hear. "And you're seriously telling me you wanted Montilla to kill your lover?"

"He is not my lover. He is my rapist."

"That's not what you said in La Pesca. You insisted that you enjoyed everything he did to your body and that you were with him of your own free will."

"I said what I had to so that you would not fight Victor in the street. I knew he would do his best to kill you," she argued passionately. "When he shot you, I died a thousand deaths."

He wanted to believe her, but they were a long way from trust. "Why should I buy that after you criticized me for being suckered by your 'sad story'? Which lies are the genuine lies, Laila? You sent me a video of you two fucking, so it's a little hard to believe you didn't leave me because you have feelings for Ramos and that you weren't helping him for your own greedy ends."

"I swear, I only meant to protect you."

"By spreading your legs for him, filming it, and sending it to me with a kiss-off email?"

The tears that had been trembling on her lashes fell. "Valeria told me you intended to rescue me that night. I knew you were injured. I watched you fall. I held you and you were unmoving. If you had come at Victor, he would have killed you. I could not have borne that."

"Because you have so many feelings for me?" He shot her a dubious stare. "You going to try to tell me next that you didn't mean to hurt me with that video?"

"No. I knew I would hurt you, and I hated that."

"But you sent it anyway. After you let him fuck you, of course."

"He did not! I stopped him."

Did she think he was stupid? "Really? Were you naked in that video?"

"I was, but—"

"Was he on top of you?"

"Yes, but—"

"Was he between your legs? Was his cock hard? Were you smiling for the camera while telling him that your pussy was there for him and that you'd always be his good little whore?"

Her expression reflected both misery and exasperation. "All of that, yes. But it was a calculated risk. He had been imbibing tequila all night. He had finished the bottle—straight. I knew from experience that it was a matter of time before he passed out."

Trees wanted to be convinced, but he needed to get away from her naked flesh, the smell of her creaming pussy, her dilated eyes imploring him to trust her just one more time... "I have two more questions."

"No rewards? I have been honest."

Well, she had answered. He would have to think through every-thing she'd said rationally to decide how much of it was the truth.

"You're right." He reached behind him and dipped into the plastic bag of candy.

"Not chocolate. Kiss me," she panted. "Touch me."

So she could cloud his head again? He should probably see her request as progress, but without knowing her motives, he couldn't. There was more than a passing chance that she'd tangled him up so badly that he couldn't be logical anymore. "You don't get to demand rewards, honey. You get what I give you. Do you want the chocolate?"

"No."

"Then I'll go back to my questions."

But resisting her wasn't easy. Desire plagued him. She was right in front of him, stretched out, tied up in his dungeon, naked and begging. He'd had his hands on her, his mouth on her. He could smell her. He was on fire for her. He'd rather sink inside her than snap more ques-tions at her, goddamn it.

"A-all right."

Trees tried to focus. "You say you staged the video of you and Ramos having sex to protect me, but you didn't let him fuck you? What if you hadn't been able to stop him? Would you have allowed him to have sex with you to 'save me'?"

Laila closed her eyes. "Do not make me answer that."

Oh, so she didn't want to tell him. Too bad.

He slid his hand between her legs again and glided his fingers over her needy flesh. During their argument, she'd come off some of her arousal high. With a few circles around her clit and a drag of his lips across her skin, he fixed that. "Tell me, Laila. Or I'll take you right to the edge and deny you again."

Her fingers curled into fists. Her face screwed up as she tried to resist the pleasure. "Why? Because you wish to torment us both? There is no acceptable answer. If I say no, you think I was not committed to keeping you safe. If I say yes, you decide I am a *puta* who spreads her legs to earn the favor of whichever man I am with."

She wasn't wrong, but that didn't make his question invalid. "Yes or no?"

"If you love me, why do you want to know this? Can you not accept that I did my best to help you? Perhaps I did not do it the way you would have chosen, but—"

"No, I can't accept that." Mostly because he was a stupid bastard who apparently wanted to torture himself with the answer.

"I am sorry." She pressed her lips together mutely.

Did she think she was going to hold out on him? Not happening.

He leaned in and stroked her clit in an achingly slow sweep with his tongue, then growled against the vibrating button. "Answer me."

"Trees..." She sucked in a shocked breath of pleasure, then wailed, "Stop. This is a no-win situation."

She wasn't wrong about that, either. As much as it made him bristle, he had to be fair. "I promise, honesty won't earn you more punishment."

"No, just your anger." She sighed out raggedly. More tears fell as the fight finally left her. "Yes. I would have given my body to Victor, despite the fact I hate him and the thought of him touching me makes me sick. While I filmed that video, it took all my will to hide my revulsion. Even though I would have done anything to keep Victor from hurting you, you will still condemn me."

If he took her reply cynically, she absolutely looked like a whore willing to spread her legs for Ramos's favor. But if he looked it like a man she cared for, she had done everything in her power to protect him—even if it cost her.

"Why?" he blurted. "Why would you sacrifice yourself for me?"

"If I tell you, what will you do with the knowledge?"

He vaulted off the stool and took her face in his hands. "This isn't a negotiation. Answer the goddamn question."

"Or you will toy with my body again until I am on fire, at the edge of bearing this horrible need?"

"If I have to."

She swallowed and looked away.

Trees's heart leapt into his throat as he jerked her stare back to his. "Why, Laila? How do you feel about me?"

"I cannot fight you. I do not know why I tried." Her chin trembled as she fought more tears. "I love you."

Those three words blew him away. He sucked in a shocked breath. His heart turned over. He stepped back and stared at her as he tried to process her admission. Was it true? Or was she merely telling him what she thought he wanted to hear?

Trees didn't know. And he wouldn't until he got distance from her naked body, his desire cooled, and he had the opportunity to think.

Fuck.

Without a word, he rounded the table and laid it flat again.

"What are you doing?" She sounded scared.

He didn't answer. What the hell could he say? Instead, he uncuffed her ankles, then her wrists, and helped her to her feet. Immediately, her trembling legs folded beneath her, and she swayed into him, all but melting against his side. He caught her, wrapping his arms around her for support.

"Trees." She clung to him—with her hands, her eyes, her expression.

It took everything he had not to carry her to his bedroom, lay her reverently across his bed, and make love to her until dawn. She'd proven she could be wily and dangerous. She knew how to work men. The Edgingtons had Kimber back mostly unscathed, but that hardly meant the danger was over. Now both Montilla and Ramos would come after them. He didn't dare let himself be drawn in by a potentially pretty viper until he'd had the opportunity to think this through. Until he figured her out.

"Stay here. There are water bottles in the refrigerator. Drink one. There are protein bars in the basket on the counter. Eat one. Don't argue. Don't touch your pussy or get yourself off. And don't get dressed. If you're cold, there are blankets in the cabinet along the far wall. I'll be back."

When he stepped toward the stairs, she gripped him tighter. "Do not leave me. Please."

She hadn't asked *where are you going?* or *what are you doing?* She'd just spilled a seemingly heartfelt plea at him not to walk away.

Her words broke him. It made him a stupid sucker, but Trees just didn't care right now. He couldn't fucking stand the distance between them anymore.

He picked her up, settled her back against the nearest wall, then crowded her personal space as he bent his head and seized her mouth. For a handful of forbidden seconds, he let hope control him. He let his hunger rage. He let his need for her boil over into a love that scalded his veins and burned away all good sense.

He delved into her mouth, pressing himself against her until there was no air between them. He forced her lips wider and took her tongue. Laila responded unabashedly, opening herself, giving her all to him. She clawed at his shoulders, clung and climbed him, lifting her legs to wrap them around his hips. He helped, taking her ass in his hands and tilting her up. She rocked frantically and feverishly against him.

When he wedged her against the wall with the ridge of his hard cock, rocking against her, she keened. He wanted her. He burned for her. He was sweating for her as he forced himself deeper into her kiss, not giving a fuck if he ever came up for air again.

What if she's playing you, too?

As much as Trees hated that voice, it was rational. He couldn't keep recklessly falling into Laila without self-destructing, so if he had any intention of saving himself and figuring out what the hell was going on, he had to break away from her now.

Tearing his mouth free, he released her and stepped back, his panting breaths harsh. He swiped a hand down his face, pausing to palm her taste from his lips, trying not to give in to his need for Laila's sweetness again. "I won't be long."

Terror crossed her face. "You will not leave me in the dark, will you?"

He softened. "No. I know you're afraid. I would never intentionally scare you."

She stopped him with a hand on his arm. "Thank you. And I am sorry. For everything. Perhaps my plan does not make sense to you, but I only meant to spare you the danger…"

Because she supposedly loved him.

His heart urged him to believe her and take a leap of faith. His head told him she was a bad bet and to back off.

He couldn't address her feelings—or his own—right now, but he could address her scheme. "Actually, your plan made a lot of sense. It was smart and well thought out…right up until you tried to tackle an entire cartel and a splinter faction on your own. You have knowledge of these people. I'll give you that. But you're not fucking trained for this." And had she really needed to throw them under the bus to do it?

"I know." She dropped her head.

Because she genuinely saw the error of her ways? Or because she was playing him?

Fuck, he was going to what-if himself into making a stupid mistake if he didn't get the hell away from her and get a few minutes to think.

He merely nodded, then punched in the digits to open the door. "By the way, I've changed the code in and out of this room, so you won't be leaving here until I say so."

CHAPTER
Eight

Trees climbed the stairs, made sure all the lights were on, then let himself out of the dungeon. He hadn't dared to look at Laila again before he left. He couldn't let himself be swayed. Or suckered by those hazel eyes he kept losing himself in. He had to figure out—once and for all—where her allegiances lay.

How the fuck are you going to do that?

Sighing, he headed for the shower. He needed to clear his head, and he thought better here. If he didn't rid his thoughts of Laila—her scent, her taste, and that look in her eyes when desire overwhelmed her defenses and she finally moaned and spilled secrets from her lush lips —he'd get nowhere.

He turned on the water, undressed, then stepped under the pelting spray. Then he went through the motions—soaping up, then jacking off to a hollow orgasm he hoped would purge Laila from his thoughts. It didn't. He sank to the tiled bench and hung his head with a sigh. He hadn't managed to accomplish much in the last few minutes, except to fixate on Laila more.

God, this need for her had him so fucked up.

With a sigh, he cut off the shower and toweled off. After he yanked on some fresh clothes and padded out of his bedroom, he didn't feel any better. Everything inside him wanted her to be innocent, but he was afraid the truth would crush him. Still, sticking his head in the sand wasn't his speed. Lives were at stake, and he couldn't let emotions cloud him.

Trees knew what he had to do, no matter how much it killed him.

After flipping on the coffeepot, he headed to the garage while his brew dripped and retrieved Laila's belongings, which he'd gathered from her beach bungalow. After planting in the kitchen, he yanked open the duffel he'd shoved everything into, prowling around for anything useful. Unfortunately, there wasn't much except a phone he'd never seen her carry. Since it showed some wear and tear, it obviously wasn't new. The case around it was black and gray and geometric. Definitely masculine. He flipped it over and found initials: VMR.

Holy shit, was this Victor's device? Why would Laila have it? Had she swiped the man's phone…or had he given it to her in the hopes it wouldn't fall into enemy hands?

Somewhere along the way, she'd turned the device off, so he powered it up. To his shock, he got right in, no password required. What the fuck? A man in Victor's line of work should definitely have the protection of a secure password—at a minimum.

Quickly, Trees checked the device to ensure that every means of tracking was disabled. Wifi and cellular off. Ditto with location services. No roaming.

Time to take this bitch apart.

Before he could dive in, his own phone rang in his bedroom. He thought about ignoring it. There wasn't anyone he wanted to talk to now.

Except Laila. You need the truth from her.

No, what he really needed was to get naked with her and avoid talking altogether, except with their bodies.

That was a bad idea.

Muttering a curse, Trees plucked the device off his bathroom counter, surprised to see Zy calling this late. "What's up, buddy?"

"Checking in on you. Kane told me you brought Laila by to visit her family."

"Yeah. She needed it." There was a point to Zy's call, and Trees just wanted to get to it. "What's up?"

"Not much. How's it going with her?"

"It's going about like I expected. Everything with Laila is somewhere between a battle and a riddle. You?"

"Good. Hallie started a swim class tonight. The whole thing was cute as hell, but it wore her out. She went down early, so Tessa and I are just hanging out."

Translation: they had the rest of the evening to themselves. "And you're wasting your time with me?"

"Well, I'm hoping we can make this chat quick." Then Zy's levity died. "Kane said you didn't look like you were in a good place mentally. Want to tell me about it?"

Kane's snitching pissed Trees off, even if the guy had meant well. "I don't know whether Laila is trying to protect me from Ramos or sell me down the river to save herself."

"I hate to give you your own tough love, but the advice you gave me when I wasn't sure about Tessa was spot on. You're going to have to probe her for answers—whether that's with your words or your dick is up to you. But you have to get to the bottom of whatever she's up to. Not only does EM need the info but I know you. The uncertainty is killing you."

Sometimes he hated the way Zy could read his mind. "Yeah."

"Can you do some of your Dom stuff on Laila and make her talk?"

"I tried. Not happening, at least not now. I'm too far gone, and I need answers too bad. So I'm sitting here with Victor Ramos's phone, trying to decide if I really want to open this can of worms."

"You don't have a choice."

"Yeah." He'd come to that conclusion, not only to see if it held any information about Laila's allegiance but to discern Ramos's whereabouts. The fucker was loose and dangerous.

"Zy?" Trees heard Tessa call softly in the background. "Oh, sorry. I didn't know you were on the phone."

"Be right there, baby," his best friend replied.

"Don't worry about me, man. I'll figure this out," Trees assured. "Enjoy your evening with Tessa."

Zy let out a harsh breath. "With her dressed in lingerie like that, I definitely will. I don't know what I did to deserve that woman, but I'm a lucky son of a bitch. Call me if you need me, okay?"

"Sure." But Trees wouldn't. Zy had the love he deserved because he'd listened to his feelings and followed his heart. No matter what wrongdoing he'd suspected Tessa of, he'd led with his gut. And now he was living a happily ever after that made Trees envious as hell.

Would he have the same outcome if he trusted his instincts, too? Or was Laila's *I love you* just messing with his head?

They ended the call, and Trees returned to the kitchen and dived back into Ramos's phone. It took him less than three minutes to realize the asshole had done his best to mitigate the loss of the device. The emails had stopped delivering days ago. Half the social media accounts prompted him for new passwords, which he didn't have. That was fine. It might take a few minutes, but he could hack in. Even without doing that, Trees would still be able to see everything Ramos had downloaded and saved to his cloud. At a glance, it looked like plenty—locations, past operations, future plans for taking over Montilla's "throne."

Just like Laila had told him.

If she'd been honest about Ramos's scheme…maybe she'd been telling him the truth about everything.

Trees wanted to roll with that theory so bad. But his feelings for Laila tangled his logic. If he had a little more evidence—anything to support this two-ton yearning dragging him under—he'd fuck the doubt, grab Laila in his arms, and never let go. But he couldn't, not responsibly. It wasn't just his life at stake. After Kimber's kidnapping, he couldn't discount the safety of the team and their loved ones, not to mention EM's reputation. When it came to that woman, he wasn't objective.

But he knew someone who might be.

Cursing, he set Ramos's phone aside and reached for his own.

Matt answered on the third ring. "Trees?"

"Yeah. Sorry to bother you. How is everything out there?"

"On your perimeter? Quiet. You can relax."

"I don't think so."

"What's up?"

"I need your two cents."

"Sure. About what? I'll do my best."

Matt would. Trees didn't know the other guy well, but he'd been solid while they'd traveled to Mexico. Hell, Matt had saved his damn life. "I'm calling to ask you about Laila. About what you saw and heard between her and Victor in La Pesca."

"You sure you want to do this?"

He had to. If Laila had sacrificed herself for his safety, Trees needed to know. He also needed to know if she was lying to save her hide.

"Yeah. What did you see? And hear? Where do you think she stands? Or I should say with whom?"

Matt blew out a long breath. "When we first saw her, I was convinced she was playing you for Ramos's benefit, but after the son of a bitch shot you, I had doubts."

Trees got that, but it didn't tell him what he really wanted to know. "What do you think her feelings for Ramos are?"

"Are you asking because you want to know what yours should be? Man, I can't tell you how to feel about her."

"I'm not asking you to. I doubt I could stop loving her if I tried. I just don't know if I can trust her." Trees sighed, feeling suddenly exhausted. "Thing is, she gave me this elaborate story to explain her backstab. It fits...but I'm not sure I believe it. I need a more objective perspective."

"I'll be honest, I've gone back and forth a couple of times because Laila's choices don't add up. On the surface, what she told you—that she's always belonged to Victor and loves the rough sex they have— seems like the most obvious scenario. But if that's the case...then a lot of her other behavior makes no sense. I mean, she was emotional when you said you wanted her for life. And she kissed you like you were her everything. But the instant you insisted on rescuing her from Ramos, she turned on you and claimed he was her man and all that shit. If that was true, why did she do everything short of tackle you to keep you hidden from him? And why did she misdirect Ramos and focus his attention away from you and onto Montilla?"

"I've had similar thoughts." Trees squeezed the phone. "What happened after Ramos shot me?"

"And you fell on your head? Dude, Laila sobbed like her world was ending. Then she dropped to her knees and did her best to stem your bleeding."

Also just as Laila had claimed. "Anything else?"

"In retrospect, I gotta give her credit. She begged me silently to help you without giving away my position. She never asked for any help for herself. And when the mechanic came after you with a blow-torch, she nearly lost her shit. But she couldn't help you. She tried. I overheard her offering herself like a sacrifice to Ramos forever if he would get you medical attention."

Trees sucked in a shocked breath. "You don't think it was a ploy?"

"How would that have helped her cause?" Matt challenged. "In the end, it didn't matter because, after Ramos dragged her away by her hair, he accused her of being in love with you. That's when I began to wonder if I'd been looking at the situation all wrong."

Trees understood. He was definitely wondering that now, too.

"But then she sent you that shitty video of them in bed, and...I started questioning everything again."

So Matt couldn't shed any light. Then again, the guy was right. Matt couldn't tell him how to feel about Laila. As much as Trees hated it, he was either going to have to take a leap of faith or cut her out of his heart...somehow.

"Same, but thanks for your opinion," he told Matt. "I owe you, and not just for saving my life."

"You're welcome. The Edgingtons have offered me a full-time gig if I want it. I'm past due to return to Wyoming, but..."

"You're thinking about staying?"

He hesitated. "There's nothing for me back there."

No friends? No family? No women falling all over themselves to be with a hot, hunky cowboy type? "Here ain't a bad place, man."

"Different than where I came from. What about you? Every so often, I hear the South in your voice, but it's not like any accent from these parts."

"I'm from coal mining country in West Virginia. Here's really different. But I like it. The bosses can be tough, but they expect results. They only hire the best. I hope you'll think about it. We've been short-staffed, and it wouldn't suck to have you around. I wouldn't be alive if you weren't."

"Thanks. I'm definitely thinking about it. And I hope you figure this thing out with Laila soon. And I'll stay diligent out here, because Ramos probably knows you're alive by now and he's out for your blood."

Trees figured as much. But what about Laila? That was the million-dollar question, and he didn't have an answer. Either she was keeping him occupied so her lover could sneak up on him and blow his brains out or she'd been telling the truth about her power play to use Ramos as a pawn to weaken Montilla, keep her family safe, and protect the bodyguard who had fallen for her.

He plucked up Ramos's phone again, turning it in his hands. Laila hadn't had this device when he'd run into her in La Pesca. And if she'd had a phone of her own, why would she have stolen Ramos's? For the information on it? Maybe. But the more likely scenario was that she hadn't had one of her own and had needed a way to contact her sister. She'd done that through a gaming app, right? Why choose that method if she had her own phone and could simply call or text? And if she hadn't been carrying a phone then, that probably meant she'd used Ramos's to film their fucking.

With shaking hands, Trees opened Ramos's photos—and immediately hit pay dirt. The last thing saved was the video Laila had sent to convince him that she was Ramos's willing whore.

He pressed the button to launch it. Instantly, the screen filled with a familiar scene—the cheap motel room, the slightly yellowing sheets, the ugly brown and blue bedspread, not to mention a naked Laila. But the footage he was seeing? She hadn't sent this to him when she'd emailed and told him to kiss off.

In this version, Ramos wore his boxers and stumbled onto the bed drunkenly, holding a nearly empty bottle of tequila in one hand. Some sloshed on her neck and shoulder. He laughed, pouncing toward her, the view wobbling as he flattened her against the mattress. "What's with the camera, *chiquita?*"

As he leered toward her neck, Laila called to him, her voice sultry. "I am going to film us, like you used to."

Ramos lifted his head with a loopy, smug leer. "I recorded hours and hours of you screaming for me. I watched them often for my pleasure." He sucked in a hissing breath. "Your fear makes me hard."

"I know," she breathed like she was entranced, like she wanted his degradation and pain.

Trees wanted to hurl.

"Hold the phone out. Make sure you capture all the ways I'm going to fuck you."

Instantly, she complied, positioning the camera arm's length from them, pulling the sheet up to their waists, covering the fact that Ramos was dry humping her thigh.

Then she suddenly smiled for the camera, looking heavy lidded and aroused. Her expression sent an electric ping of recognition through Trees. It was the same come-hither glance he'd seen in the first frame of the video she'd sent.

Screw upchucking the contents of his stomach. He wanted to hurl this phone across the room, beat the ever-loving fuck out of Ramos, then lay into Laila for lying to him yet again. Then he apparently needed to beat his own ass for believing her.

"*Chiquita*," he growled. "I want that pussy."

"It is here for you. Like I am." She rolled her head to one side, eyes closed in ecstasy, offering Ramos her neck.

"Hmm...yes." He bounced on top of her like they were fucking. "Good little *puta*."

Trees froze the video, took it back a few seconds, and replayed the frames. But he hadn't missed anything. The first time he'd watched this footage, he'd been convinced Ramos and Laila were having dirty, raunchy, very consensual sex. But clearly Ramos was still wearing his boxers and treating her thigh like his bitch.

"Damn it," Trees muttered.

Laila had intentionally led him to believe she and Ramos were fucking.

Because she was trying to convince you not to come to her rescue? Because she wanted to protect you?

He wasn't sure, so he continued the torment of watching.

On the video, Laila moaned in answer. "For you? Always."

Victor gave her hair a vicious tug and sank his teeth into her shoulder hard like she was a piece of prime meat he intended to chew up and swallow down.

Laila cried out. "Yes!"

"Mine."

Laila gave another heavy-lidded glance toward the camera. "Yours."

That's where the video she'd sent him ended. But it wasn't ending now. There was almost a minute more.

Starting with Laila groping around on the mattress for Ramos's empty tequila bottle. She lifted it and bonked him over the head.

Trees reared back. He hadn't seen that coming. Why would Laila try to knock him out if she wanted him to fuck her?

In response, Ramos stiffened, lifted his head, and glared at her, his narrowed stare suddenly vowing retribution.

With a gasp, Laila dropped the phone. All Trees could see was the peeling, water-stained ceiling, but he could hear plenty, starting with the sound of her choking.

"You want to play rough, bitch?" Ramos growled.

The sounds of Laila fighting him, grunting and struggling, her screams suppressed by what Trees suspected were the asshole's hands around her throat made him beyond furious. She didn't actually enjoy scum like Ramos damn near choking the life out of her, right?

Seconds later, he heard what sounded like the bottle against someone's skull again. Then Laila coughed and gasped, audibly dragging air into her starved lungs.

"*Cabrón.*" Had that noise been her spitting on Ramos? "I hate you. You will never touch me again. Never!"

Her words rang like a solemn promise.

Suddenly, Laila grabbed the phone, looking shaken and angry. The device wobbled in her hands before he got a flash of Ramos unmoving, face down across the mattress, with his pale backside in the air and his boxers haphazardly halfway to his knees.

The video ended there.

Holy. Motherfucking. Shit.

Trees sat back, his thoughts racing. But they all circled back to one conclusion: Laila had been telling the truth in the dungeon. She had altered the clip she'd emailed him to convince him she was Ramos's willing lover. So he wouldn't try to save her while he was injured.

He was done questioning her and her loyalties because every betrayal he'd believed had clearly been a lie. She really had been trying to protect him.

And what had he done in return? Accused her of deceit, denied her at least half a dozen orgasms, then left her all alone, aroused and shaking.

Fuck.

Now what?

Trees stood and scrubbed a hand down his face. He wasn't exactly sure what he was going to say, but he needed to see Laila right now.

———————

The hissing of the dungeon door's seal decompressing brought Laila's head snapping around. She gathered the blanket tighter around her naked body with one hand and wiped the tears from her eyes with the other. Trees had made his feelings clear. He no longer wanted her. He cared for her now only as the body he had been paid to guard. She had hurt him too much, and she understood. Since she had never once had anything remotely like a boyfriend, what did she know of relationships? Of course she had screwed everything up.

Now she had to face his repudiation. He would separate them in all ways except proximity.

Despite the fact Laila knew his rejection was coming, it was crushing her.

Trees's big feet were surprisingly light on the stairs as he descended. She sipped more of her water as she watched him appear. First, his boots became visible, then his muscled legs, clad in denim. Next, his narrow hips, followed by his lean, corrugated middle, obvious even through his T-shirt.

Laila's heart began to race. As always, being near him thrilled her, but this time she feared the harsh words he would use to dismiss her.

When she caught sight of his massive shoulders and the dark tip of his close-cropped beard, she lost her nerve to meet his gaze and bowed her head.

In the past, she had stared down drug lords, murderers, and rapists without flinching because she hadn't cared what they did. They could hurt her body—and had many times. But they had never touched her heart.

With one sentence, Trees could utterly decimate her.

Suddenly, the half of a protein bar she had choked down earlier churned in her stomach, threatening to come back up. Her heart hammered faster, louder, filling her ears when he loped off the last step and crossed the room toward her.

"Laila?" His gruff whisper twisted her heart.

She bit her bottom lip, trying so hard not to cry. She failed, tasting blood and defeat. God, she'd never felt more fragile in her life. "I am sorry. Please do not say anything. I know you despise me now and—"

"Why the hell would you think that?" He hooked his fingers beneath her chin. She resisted, but he forced her face up.

Laila squeezed her eyes shut tighter, but nothing would hide the fact she was crying. "Do not look at me. I know you are angry, and I bear the responsibility for—"

"Shh." He caressed her face so softly, his thumb brushing over her cheek, wiping away her tears. "Listen to me. I'm the one who's sorry. I didn't believe you. I didn't trust you. I tormented you for answers. I was wrong." He kissed her forehead so softly he made her sob again. "Hey… No more crying. I hate that I hurt you."

She pressed his words into her heart. "Please do not tell me what you think I want to hear. I do not want your pity."

Trees cupped her face, his touch beyond gentle…but a hint of his other side, the one that had mercilessly strummed her body less than an hour ago, rang in his words. "I don't pity you, honey. I'm apologizing to you. Now open your eyes and look at me."

Laila resisted, but everything about Trees compelled her to comply.

Slowly, her lashes fluttered open. He filled her vision, his expression achingly soft, his eyes full of remorse. More tears spilled down her cheeks.

"You believe me?" The question slipped out, and a foolish part of her wished she could take it back. The hopeful, headstrong girl inside her who had faced so much of life alone wanted him forever. But the woman in her—the realist—took over. "Never mind. You do not have to—"

He placed a finger over her lips. "Yes, I do. I'm sorry, Laila. I fucked up. I was an asshole, and I have no problem admitting it. I hope you can forgive me."

"I-I do not understand."

"I saw the full video of you and Victor on his phone, including the parts you cut off, so I know what really happened. I know the lengths you went to in order to save me. I'm just sorry I didn't believe you."

Laila felt her eyes widen—and hope fill her heart...even as it shattered. "I had given you no reason to. I only meant to protect you, but..."

"I know you did." His expression gentled even more. "You risked everything to keep me safe, the way you do for your family. And I love you for that."

"I have seen Victor and his minions kill people horribly for even the smallest slight, so after you killed his brother and risked everything to protect me, I shudder to imagine what he would do to you. I do not want to live in a world without you."

"Oh, honey...you don't have to." Then he scowled at her. "But if you ever sacrifice yourself for me again like that, I will make the orgasm deprivation you suffered tonight seem like an easy-breezy paradise—right before I blister your ass. Are we clear?"

She looked away again, trying to understand her two very different reactions. Her feverish body, desperate for the relief only he could give her, flushed hot and began to throb. Why she should be aroused by his threats of punishment was something she still did not comprehend.

Right behind that response came the opposite reaction. Giving up wasn't in her vocabulary, mostly because she knew they weren't out of danger. They might never be. If cutting out her heart and leaving him now would keep Trees safe and alive, Laila would do it. But he was in too deep. Both Victor and Montilla knew he was involved. She and Trees were safer together. And it was selfish, some part of her was glad.

"You expect me to do nothing because I am female? Because I am smaller?" She shook her head. "If I can save you, I always will."

Trees sighed. "I know you're a fighter. You've had to be. But it's my role to save you." When she opened her mouth to rebut him, he held up a hand. "How about I make you a deal? If I need rescuing and no one else can do it, you can—as long as you don't put yourself in danger, okay? And if you ever concoct another scheme to put down the bad guys, talk to me first. Your plan might have succeeded if you'd had trained operatives, backup, weapons, equipment... But you're *never* my first line of defense. Do you understand?"

It went against her grain to back down, but Laila grasped what he was saying. He had a whole team behind him, and as a well-trained warrior, he wanted to do his job. He was merely asking her to respect that.

"Yes."

His smile transformed his face and brightened up her world. "Good. Now come here to me."

He scooped her up in his arms, blanket and all, and headed for the stairs.

"What are you doing?"

"I'm going to take care of you, honey. The way I should have all along." He nudged the door open wider with his shoulder, ducking to avoid the hanging rack in his closet, and kicked the opening closed behind them. Then he carried her through his bedroom, to the dining room table, where he set her in a chair, wrapped the blanket tighter to ward off the chill, and dropped a soft kiss to her lips. "First, I'm going to feed you."

"That is not necessary."

Trees sent her a quelling stare. "It is. You've barely eaten. What sounds good?"

The fact he wanted to feed her, nurture and take care of her choked her up. No one had done that for her since childhood. The pesky tears stung her eyes again. "Whatever you want."

He came closer, brows a disapproving slash as he crouched beside her. "It's not about me. Right now, I'm here for you, and you deserve to have what you want. Tell me."

Despite the blanket, she was cold to the bone. Tired, too. She wanted something warm and comforting. "Soup?"

"What kind? Everything I have will come out of a can, but..." He poked his head in his pantry and rattled off more than a dozen flavors.

"Gumbo. I have never had that."

Trees smiled. An hour ago, when he had been withholding orgasms and demanding answers, he had looked intimidating, severe...yet so sexy her body ached. Now, the warm welcome on his face sent her heart fluttering.

"Until I moved here, I'd never had it, either," he told her in a conspiratorial murmur. "The stuff out of a can is passable. If you like that, someday I'll take you to a restaurant I've found that makes downright amazing gumbo."

Would they be together that long? Would they even be alive? Would it be safe enough to go on something like a date?

Laila shook the question away. He was merely making small talk, so she nodded and smiled. "I would enjoy that. Where did you live before here? What was your family like?"

He paused, looking reluctant. It was odd that she knew Trees's capabilities, habits, and predilections but nothing about his past.

"I'm from West Virginia. Grew up dirt poor. A coal miner's kid, the oldest of eight. I'm not close to my family."

"Why?"

"We...drifted apart, I guess. My parents were always working to make ends meet and raise my siblings. Not much else to say." He shrugged. "I left when I joined the service at eighteen. That's where I met Zy. We went through some really hairy shit together, both on US soil and overseas. I eventually got out, heard about this private security firm in Lafayette that needed a tech guy, made a few calls...and here I am."

She got the feeling the story was more complicated, but that was another conversation for another day. While they'd been talking, he'd heated up the gumbo in a saucepan and poured it in a bowl, then shaken some chips from a bag onto a side plate. He brought the food to her, along with a spoon, followed by a napkin and another bottle of water.

As the soup steamed, he tossed together a sandwich. "Eat up, little one. Want some roast beef, too?"

"No, thank you." She dipped her spoon in the dark reddish broth and tried a bite full of chicken, rice, and tang. Flavor burst on her tongue. It was spicy, but different than the foods she'd grown up with.

"You like it?"

"Very much."

He carried his sandwich to the table and sat beside her, then he dragged her chair closer. As she yelped, he lifted her onto his lap and maneuvered her food in front of her.

"What are you doing?" She turned to him in confusion.

Trees wrapped his arms around her and pressed a kiss to her bared shoulder. "Holding you and keeping you warm. Eat up."

Laila didn't protest, just dug into her food, wrapped in his warmth and their oddly comfortable silence. Soon, he'd consumed his whole sandwich, along with an orange he grabbed off the nearby counter. She had barely managed half her soup and a few bites of chips before she felt full.

When she pushed her bowl away, he cradled her closer. "Full?"

His voice rumbled in her ear, and she settled her head against him, eyes drifting shut in contentment. "Yes."

"Good." He stood, lifting her with him, then headed for his bedroom.

She froze. "Are you returning me to the dungeon?"

"No. I'm taking care of you tonight. No man ever has. I'd like to be the first."

He was going to make her cry again. Every time she thought he couldn't make her love him more, he did. "What about the dishes?"

"I'll do them later. And don't you dare try that BS of bartering for your food."

Without meaning to, her refusal to owe him had insulted him. Since Laila couldn't take it back, she merely shook her head. "Not a word. Thank you."

Trees carried her into the master bathroom and set her on her feet. "You're welcome."

Then he took her face in his hands and kissed her softly, removing the blanket from around her shoulders and tossing it out the door and across his massive bed. She stood naked, still aware of her cheeks heating, her nipples pebbling, her sex throbbing as Trees consumed her visually. "What are you doing?"

"Taking care of what's mine, Laila." Then he turned on the faucet in the enormous shower and shed his clothes one garment at a time, his eyes never leaving hers, until he wore absolutely nothing but a smile.

Blinking, she drank in his shoulders that were nearly as wide as the doorframe, tapering down to his ridged middle, narrow hips, and strong, tree-trunk legs. The thick stalk of his cock in between stood tall, almost imposing. He was a big man, so it was no surprise he was large everywhere. But he still took her breath away.

"Trees..." She wrapped her fingers around his erection.

He shook his head as he took her wrist and lifted her hand away. "No, I'm taking care of you. Step in."

Steam rose from the giant enclosure as he opened the door. She filed in. For a reason she didn't understand, her obedience made him happy. Knowing she had pleased him made her happy in return.

He cupped her shoulders and settled her under the warm spray. As she tipped her head back, water splashed over her face and sluiced down her body. Her chill receded. A moan slipped from her throat.

Trees leaned in and settled his mouth over hers in a slow slide of a kiss that seemed to last forever. He was in no rush, made no demand for her to take him deeper. Instead, he seemed content simply to be near her, to breathe her in, to share this tick of the clock with her.

The moment felt profound. They didn't exchange words. Yes, they had more to discuss, but it was as if they both realized nothing was more important than connecting.

Laila sighed and gave herself over to him, gladly drowning in the warm water and his hot flesh around her. In his scent, like the forest filled with damp earth. In the desire only he had ever filled her with, bestowing it every time he touched her.

Until Trees, she had hated having a man's hands on her. She had never known what it was to be treasured. He had coaxed her body, teaching her to enjoy his caresses that gave her untold pleasure. Now she felt herself mentally falling to his feet and surrendering to whatever tender demands would please him.

But instead of deepening the kiss, he backed away, brushing wet strands from her upturned face before he grabbed a bottle from a small corner shelf and dumped a dollop of shampoo into his hand. "Come here, little one."

She trembled when he called her that. Instead of a jab about her height, as she'd first thought, the soft way he verbally stroked the syllables told her it was an endearment. Immediately, she complied.

"Good girl," he praised before he kissed the tip of her nose. "Close your eyes."

Obeying took more of her trust. But Laila reminded herself that, not only was there plenty of light in the bathroom but this was Trees. Even when he'd suspected her of conspiring with Victor to kill him, he hadn't hurt her. Set her body on fire with throbbing need for him, yes. But he hadn't raised his hand or his voice. He certainly hadn't punished her in any of the vile, cruel ways Victor and his brother had over the years. She was in good hands.

Laila let her eyes slide shut.

He kissed each lid softly, reverently. "So very good. Now just enjoy."

She had no idea what he meant until he worked his fingers through her hair and began sudsing her scalp with strong, slow circles. She moaned, swaying on her feet as his touch made her pliant and boneless.

Peace seeped into her. It was momentary, she knew. But so welcome.

Though Laila ached to see Trees, drink in his expression while he touched her with such reverence, she didn't want to disappoint him. Instead, she kept her eyes shut and focused herself on him, his touch, his scent, his breathing. And she felt him, not with her eyes but with her senses. She didn't have to see his face to know he was pleased. And his approval was a pleasure all its own.

"God, you're so beautiful, Laila," he murmured against her lips, then dipped to kiss her again, as his long, strong fingers worked at her hairline, cleansed her crown, then lowered to massage her neck.

She pooled into a melted puddle, sighing his name like a benediction. "Trees…"

"I would love to pamper you every day. The world hasn't shown you the kind of love you deserve. But I can. If you let me, honey, I will." He settled her under the spray and rinsed her hair, his fingers gently working their way through the curly mass until it felt clean.

Before she knew what he was about, he squeezed the excess water from her tresses, then doused the ends in something that smelled like coconut. "Let that sit for a few minutes."

"Can I open my eyes?"

"Are you all right? Or nervous? Scared?"

"I am"—she sighed, smiling in the direction of his voice—"happy."

"Good. Keep your eyes closed. I want to show you that I could make you happy every day."

Words like that warmed the corners of her heart, which she'd been sure would be dark forever. It sounded as if he saw a future for them beyond this dangerous life dictated by cartels and plagued by violence. It was a beautiful fantasy. But she couldn't let herself think beyond tonight, beyond the pleasure of his tender touch. Killers and drug lords were still waiting to tear them apart, but they had this moment. Laila basked in it.

"That sounds perfect."

"There's nothing I want more," he vowed, then he fell silent.

Laila did, too, not wanting reality to intrude on their idyll.

Moments later, Trees added to her paradise by spreading a citrus-smelling soap across her skin with his hands, starting with her neck, then working down to her shoulders and her breasts, where he paused to pay special attention to her nipples now hardening as he slid his thumbs across the sensitive peaks. When he wrung a moan out of her, he caressed his way over her ribs, down her stomach, then dropped his hand to cup her mound.

With a single touch, her earlier desire rushed back to tingling life. Her breath caught. She clung to his shoulders, unsteady on her feet as his fingers dipped between her folds and he slid a finger over her nerve-rich nubbin…

"Oh," she moaned out, digging her nails into his solid biceps.

"Your pussy is still so swollen and sensitive. I love the way you respond to me." He tapped her left thigh. "Raise this leg."

Without thought, without hesitation, she did.

"Excellent," he crooned as he positioned it to the side and gently released her, resting her foot on the tiled bench in the corner and giving him unfettered access to her female flesh, growing more and more slick by the minute.

"What should I do now?"

"Feel everything I'm going to do to you, come when I ask you to, and enjoy."

Then he rinsed the soap. The bubbles cascaded down her skin, seeming to tickle every sensitive spot along the way, until every inch of her felt clean and new.

Trees bent his head to her, taking her mouth in a sweeping kiss of tongues and slow passion—except that insistent hand between her legs, circling and thumbing the needy bud now throbbing again. He groaned. His breathing roughened. He inhaled her as he filled her needy sex with his fingers, making her gasp and hold on tighter.

"You are trying to undo me." Her voice sounded scratchy.

"There's no trying about it, honey," he muttered against her lips, then worked his way down her neck, lingering behind her ear to whisper, "I'm going to make you come so many times tonight, you won't be able to feel your legs."

Her heart surged with excitement, but it wasn't just for the pleasure he was promising. It was the way he vowed to send her to the stars, like it was a gift he wanted to give her because he wanted her happiness.

"Please…"

She felt him smile against her skin as he bent to lick one of her nipples. All her focus had been on the ache growing and swelling between her legs and the man bestowing bliss on her. But now…she tossed her head back under the shower spray, her long, pleading cry echoing off the tile.

"That's my girl," he praised as he switched to the other breast and his fingers inside her shifted, moving, pressing on a spot that had her eyes flying wide open, her body lifting on tiptoe, and the pleasurable pressure under his fingertips nearly dissolving her spine.

"Yes. Yes. Yes…" The chant fell from her lips. Laila didn't even know what she was saying, only that she craved everything Trees was doing to her.

Then he swiped his thumb across her hard nub again and growled. "There you are, just about to tip over. Now look at me."

She did. His green eyes glowed with a tender demand that made her heart skip as their stares fused. The electric connection jolted down her spine, spreading to every nerve and far-reaching appendage. Tension strangled her throat, and she barely squeaked out a plea. "Trees?"

"That's it. Stay with me. Don't look away."

"I cannot."

"Good. Come for me now, little one. Fall, and I'll catch you."

Laila didn't know if it was his voice or his permission or the cocoon of safety she felt in his arms, but everything inside her released. She surrendered herself for him, to him, allowing him to wring her inside out. As pleasure surged, firing through her veins and shutting down thought, she shuddered and became a shocked, gasping puddle of satisfied woman.

Seconds later, her legs threatened to give out. But Trees was already there, squatting in front of her to plant his mouth on her still-pulsing flesh.

She was so sensitive and she stiffened, but he was gentle, patient, planting almost chaste kisses for slow minutes on her lower abdomen, her hips, her trembling thighs, then finally her puffy mound. She should have felt overwhelmed and exhausted by the climax that had overtaken her whole body. But the moment he slid an experimental drag of his tongue against her distended clit, she choked in a shocked breath, thrust her fingers in his wet hair, and let out a stunned gasp.

He took that as a sign to attack.

A heartbeat later, he opened his lips over her sex, laved her hard button again, then sucked it into the heat of his mouth, showing absolutely no mercy.

"Trees!"

"Hmm," he hummed into her most sensitive spots.

With that one syllable, her entire body torqued up again. She hadn't quite finished descending from the last peak, and another one was about to replace it—bigger, stronger, threatening to turn her legs to jelly.

"*Trees!*" she gasped even louder.

He didn't bother answering, simply sucked her clit harder and ruthlessly rubbed that spot inside her.

She took off like a rocket, her head seeming to explode as she screamed in pleasure so loudly her ears rang. That seemed to spur Trees on. He kept at her, reading her body perfectly, knowing just where to touch her, when, how hard, how long, how much as he cajoled every last ounce of ecstasy from her.

Then she fell limp against him, her legs all but giving out.

"Oh, little one..." He stood and shut off the water, then gathered her in his arms and left the glass enclosure, heading toward his bed. He didn't bother with a towel, seemingly not caring if his mattress got soaked. He simply lay back, then lifted her over him. With one hand, he held his cock up to her waiting, clutching sex. With the other, he pushed her down and filled her until she hissed at the stretching of her flesh necessary to accommodate his length and girth.

Quickly, he lifted her again, settling for a shallow thrust and a seductive rhythm. But the effort was costing him. She could see that on his face.

She wrapped her fingers around his shoulders, nails burrowing into his skin, and shook her head. "No. No... I want all of you."

When she positioned herself directly over him, wriggled her hips, and pumped down, every last inch of him slid inside her. It burned. She hissed, swearing she could feel his length up half her body. But the pain was its own sort of ecstasy, and she tossed her head back, arching her breasts and losing herself in the sensations.

He gritted his teeth and gripped her thighs so hard it would leave bruises. For reasons she didn't understand, the idea aroused her. Reminders of their passion they could study later with pride? Laila wasn't sure, but when his whole body shuddered under her and he growled her name, she lit up.

"Fuck." His raspy curse filled her ears the way his hard cock filled the rest of her—completely, until she could think of nothing else. "You take every inch of me and squeeze me so goddamn tight. The minute I get inside you, all I want to do is take you in every way possible, make you come, and mark you as mine."

When he said things like that, her brain melted. So did any remaining resistance. Her body should have been sated in the shower. She definitely should have stopped aching for the bliss of his touch after he'd heaped open-mouthed pleasure on her sex. But no. Now that she was stuffed full of this man, Laila wondered if she would ever get enough of him.

"Please," she begged, not even understanding what she was pleading for.

Her breasts felt heavier and achier. Her folds were so engorged and sensitive. Every bit of her body felt electrically alive.

"Come," he demanded.

Again? Was he insane?

"I do not think—"

"Then don't," he ground out. "Just feel—and let go."

He tensed beneath her and lifted her up his heavy stalk. Gravity slid her back down. It was good. So good. The pending orgasm that should have been impossible climbed and gathered quickly, suddenly becoming inevitable. She was sputtering and gaping, dying for him. But he was holding back.

"No! More." Her demand came out like a wail, high-pitched and entreating.

Trees gripped her hips tighter. "I can't. I'll hurt you."

"No. No. I swear. More. Please. Now."

"Fuck. Little one…"

"Trees." She caught his gaze, praying the need on her face would say what her voice seemingly couldn't.

He froze, gripped her lower, fingers digging in tighter. More bruises. They would be delicious. She couldn't wait to see them tomorrow, and she wasn't sure why.

An almost inhuman sound poured from his chest and erupted from his throat. Then he lifted her all the way up his cock before slamming her back down in an unmerciful, implacable pounding that had her silently screaming and digging her nails into him as the need to climax poured through her veins like lava. She gushed out in another feverish peak that left her near limp and boneless.

But Trees still wasn't done.

He rolled her to her back and kissed her feverishly, delving into her mouth with an urgency that left her dizzy and thrilled. He drank as if her tongue held some elixir he would die without. Laila opened totally and gave him her all.

Then he lifted her thighs around his hips and drove deep inside her in one long thrust. She cried out, her head swimming, need rising inside her again. Trees set a hard, hammering rhythm, his whole body moving, his bed shuddering.

Laila grabbed him tighter and held on, arching her breasts up to him, lifting her hips in offering and tilting to take him even deeper.

He groaned out long and low, seizing her wrists in his hand, his fingers biting as he anchored them above her head. "Grab the headboard. Don't let go."

She didn't question him, and she didn't hesitate, merely wrapped her fingers around the metal slats and gripped as if her life depended on it. But she couldn't touch him, and she needed more—of his scent, of his flavor, of his flesh.

Her lips burned a path up his shoulder, stretching to nip at his neck before she reached his jaw. "I love the feel of you inside me. You fill me up, give me both pleasure and pain and"—she bit at his chest as he pummeled her again and hit a spot that nearly sent her soaring for a third time—"oh!"

"I'm never going to stop, Laila." He maintained his wild pace as he reached up and covered her hands with his, gripping the iron rungs of his headboard and using the leverage to work his way harder and deeper. "Do you hear me? I love you. You're it for me. Marry me."

Yes! she shouted silently. There was nothing Laila wanted more than to spend her life with Trees, having a safe home, building a future, having his children, and sharing their love.

She doubted that kind of happiness was in her future. How could she and EM Security ever vanquish their powerful enemies so that she could live out her dream? She couldn't accept. He didn't deserve a lifetime of her danger, but she owed him as much truth as she dared. "I would love that. Because I love you."

As if that flipped some switch inside him, he hardened and swelled inside her even more, slamming her with a force that rattled her body even as he set her on fire. "Oh, fuck. Laila... Fuck! I need you to come with me."

It was incredible and insane, but she wasn't far from another explosion even more incendiary than the last. "Yes."

"And as soon as this shit is over, I'm going to put a ring on your finger and a baby in your belly. You're mine."

She closed her eyes and sank into the fantasy of having Trees by her side each day, inside her every night as she swelled with his sons and daughters. He squeezed her hands tighter and forced her mouth open for his kiss.

Her entire body detonated with an involuntary buck and an ear-piercing cry.

Seconds behind her, his thrusts picked up pace. His breathing turned harsh. He bared his teeth and stared into her eyes. "Mine," he growled again, his heart thundering against hers.

Then he let go with a hoarse cry, filling her with warm jets of fluid and all his love.

Breathing hard, he held her close and punctuated their pleasure with a tender kiss before he brushed a curl from her cheek. "I love you, Laila. I'm going to keep you safe so I can make you mine."

Tears stung her eyes. He'd undone her in every way possible tonight, but his words now stripped her bare all the way to her soul. "Trees…"

"I mean it. I will—no matter what it takes."

She knew he meant it. And that's what worried her most.

CHAPTER
Nine

A few hours later, Laila slept beside Trees, curled into a ball on her side, her back cuddled against his chest, one hand beneath her chin like a contented cat. He dropped his palm to her head, fingers stroking a curl from her cheek, knuckles gliding over her soft skin.

He wanted her here, by his side, forever. He hadn't been kidding when he'd told her that he intended to put a ring on her finger and a baby in her belly ASAP. The urge wasn't logical, which he usually was. Instead, it felt like a biological imperative, and Trees couldn't explain why.

Was he trying to make a family now to replace the one he seemingly no longer had in West Virginia? No, he could pick up the phone and call home if he wanted to. It wasn't as if they weren't speaking to him. More like they didn't have a use for him. Then why was he so consumed with the idea of making Laila Mrs. Scott?

Was this some possessive caveman thing? A bit. Maybe more than it should be. But a big part of him wanted to give her safety, security, comfort, love—all the things she'd never had. And in turn, she would give him something that, Zy excepting, he'd had very little of in life: acceptance.

From the time he'd been little, he'd been freakishly tall. As kids, other boys had avoided him. Girls had feared him. As a teenager, he'd been useful in pickup basketball games but not friendships. He'd been hungry for companionship and love. The opposite sex, now filling out bras and wearing makeup, had been a beautiful lure. They'd buzzed around him aplenty. At first, he'd loved it. He'd wanted a girlfriend. Then he realized they'd merely thought fucking him was something between a curiosity and a challenge.

As high school graduation approached, he'd taken a few college campus tours. He'd had the grades to go. He'd even been offered a basketball scholarship. But matriculating hadn't been for him. Socializing with kids during his weekend campus visits? It had been the same everywhere he went. If his height and quiet nature hadn't turned people away, being a poor miner's kid had.

He'd joined the army instead. Easier. Safer. Less need to fit in. Not too long after that, he'd been blessed with Zy's friendship. It had been great—more than enough, he'd told himself—for years. But since his bestie had paired off with Tessa...Trees had to admit he'd started yearning again for more.

Laila loved him. She'd nearly given her damn life to prove it.

He'd be an idiot to let her go.

But to keep her, he had to make sure she was safe—once and for all. Not for one minute was Trees naive enough to think that Laila was in the clear. Ramos still wanted her. And after she'd outed him to Montilla, the crazy son of a bitch would come after her for vengeance. Montilla had a use for her, too. Everyone knew Laila would do anything for her nephew. If the drug lord took her captive, he'd be one step closer to getting his hands on Jorge, the grandson he'd never met, supposedly to groom the toddler to someday take over his narcotics throne.

Everywhere he looked, Laila was in danger.

He'd also managed to dig himself a grave. Killing Victor's brother, Hector, then taking Laila from the surviving Ramos brother had put a target on his back. Now Montilla had cause to want him dead, too. After all, he'd helped free Kimber from captivity and shot the son of a bitch.

He'd be an idiot not to realize that he had mountains to climb and obstacles to overcome before he and Laila could have any sort of future. But he was determined to do whatever he could to make that possibility a reality.

No more sitting at home, trying to solve this defensively. Time to play offense.

After slipping from bed, Trees donned a clean pair of boxers, then headed out to the kitchen. He didn't bother turning on the lights. He had an uneasy feeling, like they were standing in the calm before a raging storm. If Matt or Ghost had encountered anything that looked like an intrusion, they would have told him...but Trees couldn't shake the feeling that someone—probably multiple someones—was out there, just waiting for an unguarded moment.

With a sigh, he plopped down at the kitchen table and grabbed Victor Ramos's phone. He launched Ramos's Abuzz account without any prompt for a new password. The cartel had been using the social media platform Zy's father had once owned and was now selling as a part of his imminent divorce. The chatter among Ramos's contacts had died down over the past week, but there was still plenty of dirt.

The most recent post made his blood run cold.

As of a few days ago, a spy Ramos had inside Montilla's organization had claimed *el jefe* was in a coma, but when he awoke, he would be out for Ramos's blood. Victor had written back to ask if Montilla would consider their feud settled if he served up the *cabrón* who had shot him.

No reply, at least not one visible in the chat. But the message string gnawed at Trees. Ramos knew exactly where he lived. It was only a matter of time before he showed up. With Laila here, that made her vulnerable, too.

Sure, he could defend his property. He'd updated and equipped it to deal with most any possible apocalypse. But he'd never imagined he'd be fighting off a cartel and their criminal assets while trying to defend the woman he loved.

It was too much to risk. There was too much at stake. He'd examine the rest of the phone later. He had to get Laila to safety now.

Trees retrieved his own phone and flipped through his contacts. Which of his bosses would be the least difficult in this fucked-up situation? None of them, but he hoped Laila providing them Kimber's location so the team could rescue their sister provided her some cred with the trio. Plus, her sister was paying them to keep her safe. That should mean something, too.

Finally, he settled on the brother who seemed most straightforward, least likely to waste time growling about the fact he was emotionally in deep with Laila, and quickest to help him come up with a plan.

He tapped the screen. Hunter Edgington answered on the first ring.

Though he'd probably been asleep, his voice didn't sound scratchy or slurred at all. "What's up, Trees?"

"I think I have a situation. Or I will if Laila and I stay here." He explained the contents of Victor's Abuzz account in a few succinct sentences.

Hunter paused a fraction of a second, then jumped into action. "I agree. Pack up. Get ready to head out. Matt and Ghost still there?"

"Should be. I'll check in with both as soon as we hang up."

"Good. Laila will head out with Matt to another secure location. I'll find one in the next hour."

With Matt? His boss intended to separate him from Laila? "No. Where she goes, I go."

"Stop thinking like a guy who fell for a client and start thinking logically. Ramos will expect you to be together. If he can get two for one, that just makes you a juicier target."

Trees ran that advice around his mental track...and had to admit Hunter was right. Laila was even more at risk if he was with her. He fucking hated that fact. "What do you have in mind?"

"I need to do some legwork. I'll text you when I find a location for Laila."

"Where should I go?"

"The office. My brothers and I will meet you there."

"Who will be watching Laila while we're meeting? Just Matt? He's great, but alone he won't be enough to defend her."

Hunter hesitated, his pause uncharacteristically long. "We've been in talks to have a long-term working relationship with Oracle. They're professional, well trained and managed, and fucking good at what they do. They feel the same about us. EM Security has gone well beyond the original scope of our business—bodyguarding, corporate security, and the like. We never anticipated taking on a motherfucking cartel. But my brothers and I agree with Jack and Deke that there's safety in numbers. Intermingling teams on an as-needed basis makes sense."

Trees concurred. "So you're saying some of theirs will help watch over Laila, too?"

It wasn't his first choice, but until he could protect her himself, this would be safest for her.

"Yeah. I'll call over there as soon as we hang up. He'll give me guys besides Ghost. Trevor would be a good choice since he's up to speed with the situation and a hell of an all-round good operator. Jack Cole also grew up around these parts, so I suspect he'll have a good safe house in mind."

"Fine," Trees grumbled. "I'll pack up. You call with details."

They ended the call, and he checked in with both Matt and Ghost. Apparently, all was quiet.

Too quiet?

Trees couldn't explain the nagging feeling. He didn't like it. Unfortunately, he didn't have time to dissect it.

Vaulting out of his seat, he took ground-eating steps to his bedroom and crouched beside a slumbering Laila. "Little one?"

Her eyes fluttered open. She looked disoriented for a second. Then she blinked again and her wide hazel eyes looked alert. She sat up, holding the sheet to her breasts. "Trees?"

"We have to go." He grabbed his bug-out bag, double-checking its contents as he explained everything.

She scowled. "We will be separated?"

So she'd latched onto that first, too? That reassured him on one level, scared the hell out of him on another.

"Temporarily," he promised, cupping her face. "I'll make my way back to you as soon as it's safe."

But until he and the rest of EM Security managed to take down all their adversaries, how would that even be possible?

Trees shoved the thought away and helped her from the bed, doing his goddamn best to ignore the lush curves of her naked body. He ached to lay her down and escape inside her again. Instead, he retrieved the duffel he'd shoved her stuff in when he'd packed up her Mexican bungalow and set it on the mattress beside her. "Do you need anything else?"

She glanced inside, then shook her head. "No. I do not require much. I will be all right."

He swore under his breath. She didn't require much, but he'd saved nearly every penny he'd ever made. He'd invested wisely. He had money. Someday, he'd shower her with everything he could so she would have a better life. She more than deserved it.

After they finished packing, Trees set plenty of food and water out back so Barney would be fed for the next few days. Zy would check in on him, too. Then he ensured the house was secure, grabbed his keys, and took Laila's hands. Standing by the back door, he peered at her through the shadows. "I don't know how long this will take."

"I am scared."

He cupped her cheek. "You'll be fine. I would put my own life in Hunter Edgington's hands. He'll make sure you're well protected."

She shook her head. "I am not afraid for me. I am afraid for you. What Victor is suggesting…"

Trading Trees for his own freedom? "Are you really surprised?"

"No. But I am angry." She dropped his hands and curled herself against his body. "And I do not have a good feeling about this."

He didn't either, but staying here wasn't wise.

"It will be fine." Trees hoped she believed him as much as he hoped it was true. Then he lifted her face to his for a lingering kiss before reluctantly backing away. "Time to go."

When he reached for the knob, she stayed him. "I am sorry. For everything since we met. I have been difficult. I have run from you. I refused to trust you…"

Coming from Laila, that was huge. He knew how difficult it was for her to trust. It was even harder for her to admit that she should have all along. "Water under the bridge, honey. Just know that I love you and I'm coming back for you."

"But should you?" Tears welled in her eyes. "Because of me, you made enemies you never would have—Victor, Montilla, the whole Tierra Caliente cartel and their hitmen… Simply because you swore to protect me. If you let me go—"

"Ditch you for my safety? Never. Do you love me?"

"Yes," she whispered. "Until you, I never wanted a man. I never wanted entanglements of the heart. But then you touched me and took care of me and tried to heal me. How could I not fall for you?"

He wiped her tears from her cheeks. "You make my life worth

living, my future worth looking forward to. You've given my empty world meaning. I'll be back for you, come hell or high water. Wait for me. And whatever Hunter or EM Security tells you to do to stay safe, do it. Promise me."

Her chin trembled as she held back more tears. "I promise."

As he kissed her one last time, someone knocked on the back door. He shoved aside the back drape and looked out the little square window. Matt and Ghost. Trees wanted to bash their faces in for taking Laila from him, but they were just doing their jobs. He should be grateful.

He wasn't.

"You got the phone you left here last time?" he asked her.

"Yes." She squeezed him again. "You will call me?"

"Every chance I get, little one."

The knock sounded again, this time impatient. Trees cursed. His time alone with Laila was up.

He wrenched the door open to find Matt leaning against the porch railing, cowboy hat shading most of his face from the patio lights. Ghost stood a few feet behind him in darkness, wearing a black ski cap nearly pulled down to his inky brows, which accentuated his other-worldly gray eyes. The shadows clung to the angles of his face, more suited to the runway than undercover work. Dark stubble clung to his aggressive chin and a sharp jaw. His mouth was turned down in an eternally pissed-off smirk.

"You got a problem with me?" Trees challenged the guy.

The look Ghost shot him would have felled any man who didn't make their living by a gun. "I have a problem with you fondling on the client while we should be getting the fuck out of here. It's unprofessional. You mooning over her risks all of us getting killed."

Trees couldn't argue with Ghost's logic; he was right. But the motherfucker didn't understand. "I'm sorry this isn't to your liking, Casper. Laila is upset and afraid."

His dark brow arched up, almost disappearing under the cap. "So you're going to revive her with mouth-to-mouth?"

Trees lunged for him, violence sizzling through his veins. In the back of his head, he knew attacking an ally was stupid, but he didn't need this shit. Neither did Laila. Based on size alone, he could take the guy, but… "I thought we were on the same team. I guess you just want to flap your gums so you can feel superior?"

Ghost, who hadn't moved a muscle, suddenly snapped to life, moving so fast he was a blur.

Before the guy could make good on his furious snarl, Matt stepped between them, glaring at them both. "Let it go. We need to get on the road before we have uninvited company."

Fuck. The cowboy had a valid point. As for Ghost…Trees admitted he probably was out of line. Having to separate from Laila was fucking with his mood. He let out a deep breath and backed down. "Fine."

Ghost stepped away, too. "Fine. But don't ever fucking call me Casper again."

Whatever. Trees didn't have time for this guy's ego. He turned his attention to Matt. "Where are you taking her?"

Apology crossed his face. "Need-to-know basis, man. And you don't need to know."

"Seriously?"

Matt nodded. "Precaution. She won't know where to find you, either."

Clearly, the cowboy didn't understand Trees's role on this team. Otherwise, Walker's bestie would have figured out that he'd already given himself a way to track Laila's phone. He'd also given her a way to track his. She didn't know yet, but all she had to do was look.

Trees forced himself to relax. "Let's go." Then he turned to Laila and pressed a kiss to her forehead. "Soon."

She blinked up at him as if he were her moon and stars. "Soon."

Ghost glared his way. "Looks like you're stuck with me. I'll follow you in my truck."

Trees shook his head. "I can take care of myself. She's suffered six years of rape and abuse. Stay with them." He gestured to Laila and Matt. "Make sure neither Ramos nor Montilla gets their hands on her again."

"Those aren't my orders."

Did this asshole love to argue for the sake of arguing? "In my shoes, what would you suggest?"

Ghost hesitated for the span of a heartbeat, then pulled his keys from his pocket, grumbling. "I'll trail them and stay with her. You leaving first?"

To provide a target if anyone was watching. "Yes."

"Don't get too far from us until we're on the open road."

Where there might be traffic, witnesses, and cameras. "Sure."

Silently, they made their way to Matt's truck. Trees settled Laila's bag in the back seat of the cab, everything inside him hating this idea...yet knowing it was the safest choice. The cowboy settled behind the wheel. Ghost hopped in the back of the bed, gun drawn, looking watchful.

Laila paused beside the open passenger door. "Stay safe."

"You, too. Don't try to run from your bodyguards. Don't balk when they feed you. And no matter what, don't put yourself in danger."

"Will you promise me the same?"

Crafty girl, answering his question with a question he was guaranteed to refute. "Danger is my job."

"Danger has been my life," she countered. "But for you I will do my best to stay safe."

Trees brought her against his chest and held her close, breathed in the spicy floral musk of her scent, and closed his eyes. He was putting off the inevitable, and he knew it. But he didn't want to let her go.

Unfortunately, he didn't have much choice. He was Ramos's number-one target, so she was safer in someone else's capable hands. End of story.

Laila laid her head on his chest and exhaled, melting against him. "I can hear your heart beat."

He dropped his lips to her ear, whispering to her alone. "It beats for you. When I come back, you'll marry me?"

She eased back, a tear perched on her lashes. "I want that more than anything."

Trees believed her...but there was something she wasn't saying.

"Let's go, kids," Ghost growled.

The longer they were here and unmoving, the more they were sitting ducks.

"I love you," he murmured.

"*Te amo.*"

Since he didn't dare delay any longer, he helped her into Matt's back seat, where she would be less visible, gave her hand one last squeeze, and shut the door."

Matt drove away slowly with a jaunty salute in his direction, his truck rumbling toward the end of the lane and pausing at Ghost's. Jack Cole's buddy hopped out of the bed and dived into his Tundra, starting the engine and idling.

Waiting for him.

Trees cursed, then grabbed his own duffel from the house, set the alarm, locked up behind him, gave Barney one last head scratch and a few more treats, then climbed into his Hummer. It wasn't long before he pulled around Matt, settling in for the long miles until they were no longer on a dirt road. Ghost followed them.

Though Trees gripped the wheel tightly, the drive to the edge of town and the hard road was uneventful. He stayed watchful, looking everywhere for Ramos or his violent drug mules to jump out and try to take Laila from him. With every mile that passed, he relaxed.

During the drive, he peered at Laila in his rearview mirror. The sadness on her face was a stab in the heart, and he swore that somehow he'd make this shit up to her and keep her safe for the rest of her life.

Finally, they reached the main drag bisecting the nearest little town. There wasn't much—a dollar store, some churches, a mom-and-pop grocery store, along with a couple of gas stations, a body shop, and a one-window post office.

At the town's last intersection, the light turned yellow just as Trees made it through. Matt followed. It was red by the time Ghost reached the limit line, and he watched the guy shudder to a halt. In his rearview mirror, Ghost's dark blue Tundra got smaller and smaller.

A few feet off Trees's bumper, Matt kept going, probably figuring the other operator would catch up in two minutes or less. Trees scowled. He'd feel better, especially for Laila's sake, if they waited for the tail, but it was stupid to sit around and wait like no one was after them.

As they reached the intersection at the interstate, Trees slipped into the left turn lane to head east on I-10. Traffic was almost nonexistent, so he paused, watching Matt zoom past him and continue heading south. Where was he taking Laila? What had Hunter and the other bosses cooked up? Trees hated not knowing as he watched the beat-up Chevy drive away.

Vowing to put an end to this shit separating them soon, he caught a green light and made a left toward the freeway's on-ramp.

From a dirt corner, a black van lurched forward, tires spinning, kicking up dust. It barreled toward Trees, heading straight for his passenger door. Holy fuck, the driver intended to T-bone him.

Trees stepped on the gas, trying to outrun them and jet onto the freeway. A glance behind proved Ghost still hadn't caught up.

The Hummer didn't move fast enough, and the van clipped his vehicle, sending Trees spinning around on the otherwise deserted road, closer and closer to an embankment wall.

His head reeled as he tried to steer out of the over-rotation. But it was too late. The top-heavy vehicle flipped onto its top, then rolled over twice more before slamming against a guardrail and coming to a shuddering stop.

Pain roared in his head. A trickle of warm blood slid from a gash above his brow. His limbs felt like they weighed a ton as he tried to swipe away the blood and clear his suddenly blurry vision, but darkness ringed the edges—and started closing in.

No. No! He needed air. But he couldn't find the fucking handle. When he did, he couldn't muster the strength to open the door. It was stuck. Crumpled from the accident? He groped around the armrest until he found the button to roll down the window, but even the chilly winter night didn't jolt back his dimming senses.

Shit. He was going to pass out. He must have hit his head harder than he'd thought...

Help. He needed help. Nine one one.

With the last of his strength, he felt in his pockets for his phone but couldn't seem to yank it free.

Suddenly, movement through the passenger window caught his attention. The occupants of the van poured out, illuminated by their headlights—three men shrouded in head-to-toe black. All carried guns pointed straight at him. They spoke rapid-fire Spanish as they wrenched his door open, yanked him from the cab, and dragged him toward the open door of their van as his consciousness gave way.

Laila scrambled to the far side of Matt's back seat, craning her neck as Trees's truck was blindsided before it rolled twice and hit the guardrail. She screamed. Her heart lurched as cold fear washed through her. "Stop! We must help him. Now!"

Matt glanced in his rearview mirror, looking into the night, then gunned the engine. His truck surged forward. "We can't. I have to get you to safety."

"We cannot leave him! I am safe. I am fine. He is injured. He is—" Laila whipped her stare back to the scene of Trees's accident to see if he'd managed by some miracle to get out. Instead, she saw him being dragged away by three men in ski masks who blended in with the dark. Fear became horror. She felt ready to peel off her skin, jump from this moving vehicle—anything to save him. "They are taking him! We must—"

"Keep going. If that's Ramos and his thugs, they probably think you're in the truck. As soon as they figure out you're not, they'll come looking for you. I have to get you far away."

"We cannot simply leave Trees! He will die. They will kill him!"

"He's trained for this and—"

"He is injured!" Couldn't Matt see that? "He cannot fight all three of them by himself. And Victor wants revenge. He will torture and execute Trees. We must go back and save him."

Matt shook his head, scanning his surroundings with a sharply watchful gaze. "Ghost is seconds behind him. He'll pitch in, but Trees would tell me to get you away from the danger. That's what our bosses would say, too. I'm doing what's best."

"You are doing what you have been told. I am doing no such thing." If she had to jump out of a moving vehicle, she would. But she refused to let Trees be taken, tormented, and terminated.

Matt glared at her through the mirror. "Yeah, you are."

She ignored him and reached for the handle to let herself out of the backseat. It was locked. She scrambled to find the button to release it, but flicking it did not disengage the lock. "Let me go!"

"I can't. Never thought I'd use those childproof locks. Good to know they're useful for something." Then he reached for his phone.

Who was he calling? The police? It was too late for that, and fighting with the door was doing her absolutely no good. Trees and the scene of his accident were now several blocks away. Terror that she would be too late to save him threatened to shred her composure.

"I will not let him die!" She pounded on the window, still pulling on the door handle, hoping it would magically give way.

"Let us handle it, Laila. Trees would want you to." Then Matt spoke to whoever he had called. "Hey, we've been ambushed. I'm still rushing Laila to the drop. As far as I can tell, we haven't been followed. We lost Ghost at a light about two miles back, but Trees was broadsided..." He must be talking to one of his bosses because he explained the rest of the incident, including the location.

Laila listened with half an ear, scrambling for the front seat of the cab, where the childproof locks wouldn't stop her from escaping.

"Yeah, that's Laila. She's losing her shit." He paused, one hand on the wheel, the other holding her in the back seat. "I'll have her there in less than ten. Is there anyone who can calm her down?"

"I do not want to be calm. I want to save Trees! He has risked everything for all of us, and you cannot allow Ramos to take him."

Matt went on as if she hadn't just screeched in his ear. "Good thinking. I'll have her there as soon as I can. Then I'll double back and help you if you need." A pause. "Yeah. See you there."

"Double back now and I will help you!" Laila insisted. "Why waste time?"

"We've covered this. Let me focus."

"On a deserted road?"

"On watching our surroundings so that if those assholes in the van come after me to find you, I can get you away safely."

"I do not care about myself." She had escaped before. Sometimes it took biding her time and arranging help, but she could do it again.

Trees had never known the extent of Victor's cruelty. She didn't want him to know it now.

"You will if they take you. Then you'll be in no position to help anyone."

That shut her up. Laila wanted to refute him…but couldn't. Still, she refused to give up on Trees.

Matt's phone rang again. He pressed the device to his ear. "Talk to me." A pause. "Nothing?" Another pause. "No idea where they went? Fuck." Then he looked in the rearview mirror again.

Laila whirled to find the dark blue truck on their tail. Ghost. That must be who he was talking to. "Did he find anything?"

She knew she was being foolish, but she couldn't seem to stop hoping and praying that the other man had found some clue about who had taken Trees. The concern on Matt's face dashed her hope.

"We're working on it," he told her. When she opened her mouth to demand again they return to the scene, he cut her off. "But he's already gone. So is the van."

Laila's terror ratcheted up again. Barely thirty minutes ago, she had been in his arms. Now he was most likely Victor Ramos's prisoner and would probably die for the great sin of trying to save her. *Dios mío*, she had to do something. She had to contact Victor. Yes, and make a deal. Trees's freedom in exchange for hers. Trees would be angry, but it was for the best. The world needed him. He was a hero. Everyone but her sister had given up on her long ago.

No matter what, don't put yourself in danger. Trees's demand rang through her head.

Laila shook her head. She couldn't heed her promise to him now. She couldn't live with herself if she had the means to save him and she selfishly did not. Besides, her misery didn't matter, only Trees staying alive did.

"Any idea which direction the van went?" Matt asked into the phone.

She couldn't hear the answer, and it was killing her. She would do anything to know…

As the inky night rolled past the windows, leading them into a sleepy residential neighborhood with older houses farther apart, her thoughts scrambled with possibilities. Then Matt screeched to a crawl in front of a blue house with white trim and black shutters. He turned down a dirt path that flanked the structure, rolling behind it to sandwich the truck between the back porch and a tall privacy fence. Other vehicles were already parked out back, including one she vaguely recognized riding in when she'd first reached the States last September.

Matt killed the engine but made no move to open his door—or hers. Ghost pulled up beside them, hopped out, then made his way to her. Finally, Matt disengaged the locks and slid out as Ghost wrenched her door open and all but dragged her from the back seat, carrying her as if she presented no challenge at all, despite her squirming protests. He might be on the wiry side, at least compared to Trees, but he was ridiculously strong.

As they approached the rear of the house, Matt sidled up behind them, gun poised for battle, just in case.

The back door opened. Joaquin Muñoz stood waiting, weapon in hand as he scanned their surroundings, too.

As soon as Ghost set her on her feet in what looked like someone's living room, Joaquin shut and locked the door. Matt remained outside. An unfamiliar man sidled up to Joaquin, dressed in an impeccable suit, despite the fact it was well past midnight. She wasn't fooled by his attire. This man was lethal. He made Laila nervous.

"Who is he?" she asked Muñoz.

"Trevor Forsythe. He's with us."

Maybe Muñoz had brought Trees more help. "You are all going to find Trees now, yes?"

Laila knew better than to believe they would let her come along. But she had other ways of helping. She just needed time to think of a crafty approach and some privacy.

Muñoz shook his head. "My brothers have already searched the scene. So has Ghost. These guys were good. We couldn't find anything."

She turned to look at the operative in the ski cap with the unusual eyes, then back to Trees's boss. "So you intend to do nothing? He is your employee. He risked his life because you assigned him to protect me, and now he may die horribly because of it. You cannot—"

"Of course we're doing something. We're working on it now."

Matt crashed inside a moment later, carrying Laila's bag. She ran to the duffel and dragged out her phone, just in case Trees had somehow reached out to her.

Nothing.

She bit her lip to stifle a cry. Tears served no purpose. She had to stay strong and think.

Laila hardly noticed when Matt stepped outside again. But the disturbance when he walked back in, Trees's go-bag in hand, had her head snapping up. The sight of it crushed her all over again, and it was foolish. Of course no one had hit Trees merely to rob him of whatever worldly goods he'd had in his vehicle. Victor wanted Trees under his thumb because he wanted revenge. He wanted to torment her again. He wanted to snuff Trees out as revenge for his brother's death.

She had to stop him.

Matt dropped the duffel on the floor. "Hunter and Logan are coming up the drive. Deke isn't far behind."

"Deke?" Muñoz was clearly puzzled. "Is he coming for support?"

Matt shrugged. "Where should I put Laila?"

"You will not put me anywhere. If you are making plans to rescue Trees, I insist on helping."

"He's our operator, and this is our area of expertise." Muñoz scowled.

Laila assumed he meant that expression to be intimidating. She had neither the time nor patience for his male posturing. "Do you have six years of experience dealing with Tierra Caliente? I do."

The room fell silent.

Ghost raised his brows in a silent signal of agreement. "She's got a point."

"Son of a bitch." Muñoz ground his teeth and pointed to a stool at a breakfast bar overlooking the kitchen, on the far side of the living room. "Sit there."

Laila did, clutching her phone, her mind racing. Every moment she didn't think of a clever plan was another moment Victor had to kill

Trees. She needed to be pulling herself and her thoughts together, crafting a scheme.

Before she could, Hunter and Logan entered through the back door, immediately making eye contact with Muñoz. "We weren't followed. No one's out there. What the fuck is going on?"

Logan looked her way. "Laila?"

"Men in a van. They crashed into Trees's truck. He rolled. He was hurt. They dragged him out—"

"We know," Logan cut in. "Is there anything else we don't that we should?"

She frowned, thinking back over the last few hours. But those were memories she would share with no one. Trees's loving touch, the selfless way he gave her pleasure, the patient way he handled her fears... Then she remembered something else and hopped off the stool. "Let me see his bag."

"What for?"

Laila wasn't sure who had asked the question, and she didn't care. The shock and panic that had seized her brain were finally losing their grip. In their place was pure determination. She would do whatever it took to save Trees.

When she reached Matt, he held the bag again. She didn't want to wrestle him for it. He would win. But surely he could grasp how she might help without putting herself as risk. "Please."

He glanced over her head at Trees's bosses. Someone must have nodded because he handed her the bag.

She took it to the nearby table and unzipped it in a rush. The scent of him clung to his clothes and wafted out, making her knees weak. Making her want to sob again. She only managed to hold on to her emotions through sheer will and plowed through the contents until she finally found what she was looking for and held it up triumphantly. "Victor Ramos's phone. He is probably the one who took Trees. If I reach out to him—"

"Hold up, Laila," Hunter cut in, his eyes so intensely blue, like Logan's, they were almost startling. "We don't know that Ramos took Trees. Remember, he shot Geraldo Montilla twelve days ago. It's possible that's who orchestrated this abduction for revenge."

His assertion took her aback. That possibility made everything a hundred times more dangerous. And it terrified her even more. "You are right."

"We need to do some fact finding and recon, figure out what we're dealing with. Ghost checked the scene. So did Logan and I. No hint of who did this. No witnesses. We talked to the Lafayette PD. There are no traffic cams on that rural stretch of road. So we'll have to figure this out by rattling some cages and seeing who howls. Let me have that phone, Laila. I want to examine it."

She didn't love that idea, but he might be able to find something she couldn't, so she complied. "Trees started to study it…"

Then he had seen the real video of her with Victor at the motel and come to apologize. After that, they had been too busy making love to focus on the danger coming straight for them.

The realization threatened her hard-won facade.

Suddenly, there was a soft knock at the door. Matt, who was closest, scowled, then looked out the little window. "What the hell is Kimber doing here?"

The woman Geraldo Montilla had held captive. Why would she come?

Matt didn't wait for an answer, just yanked the door open. A tall woman with auburn hair and a willowy body, rounded slightly with curves given to her by childbirth, entered and scanned the room. When Kimber's gaze settled on her, a smile lit up her face. "Laila?"

She nodded. "Hello."

What else could she say? She didn't want to be rude, but…

"I couldn't stop her from coming," said an imposing blond man with a buzz cut and a bad attitude who stepped into the room behind her. In one arm, he cradled a baby girl wrapped in a pink blanket and dripping bows. With his other, he held the hand of a little boy who looked somewhere around five.

Suddenly, Kimber stood in front of her, looking hopeful and uncertain. "I know you don't know me. But I've been begging my husband and my brothers to let me meet you in person for days." She surprised Laila by taking her hands. "To thank you. I wouldn't be home and reunited with my children—hell, I probably wouldn't be alive—if not for you. If there's anything I can ever do for you…"

A dozen things crossed her mind. Laila had no plan…but it seemed she finally had an ally. None of these overprotective, testosterone-driven men would let her help, but this woman gripping her fingers tightly just might. "I spent years with those animals. I know how horrible they can be. I could spare you what I endured, so I was happy to do it."

"And I appreciate you from the bottom of my heart. My brothers suggested that you might be missing your nephew, so I brought my children…"

"Against my wishes," Deke called across the room. "You're supposed to be in hiding."

"Those lowlifes don't want *me*," Kimber called back. "They merely wanted someone to use as leverage."

Because Montilla wanted to punish EM Security for rescuing and harboring Valeria. And he wanted Jorge. Always back to that eternal, unavoidable problem that had no solution…unless the drug lord died.

Kimber hustled across the room, lifted her sleeping daughter and took her son by the hand, then returned to Laila. "I wanted you to see the lives you made better with your heroic gesture. I know you risked yourself, and I wanted to show you all the grateful people. This is Cal." She urged the boy closer. "Well, Caleb, but that's my father's name, so we call him Cal. Less confusing. He'll be five in June."

"Hello." Cal stuck out his hand politely, eyeing her as a child does a stranger he's unsure about. "Nice to meet you."

The boy had manners, and he was absolutely adorable with his mop of sandy hair. He had incredibly blue eyes, the same shade as his father's. Someday, he would be a heartbreaker.

"Hi," she said as she shook his hand.

Laila didn't want to seem rude, and Kimber bringing the children was a lovely gesture, but she was impatient to help Trees—before it was too late. The men were now clustered on the other side of the room, clearly plotting without her.

She couldn't let that stand.

"And this is Sierra." Kimber handed the baby to her. "She's almost eight months old."

Laila looked down at the precious face with the bowed lips pursing and smacking in her sleep. A bolt of envy pierced her. How she would love to have a son or daughter with Trees, to know the motherly instinct to protect and devote her heart to… Her eyes watered again. She sniffed the tears away.

"She is lovely. You have been very blessed." Laila handed the baby back to Kimber.

"And I have a future, thanks to you."

"You are welcome."

Kimber looked reluctant to leave. "Can I get you anything? Help you with anything?"

"My…boyfriend has been taken by our enemies. Just now."

The other woman looked stunned. "Oh, I'm so sorry. I overheard that Trees has fallen into enemy hands, but I didn't know… The two of you?" She smiled. "Good for him."

"I need to know what they are plotting." Laila pointed at the men across the room. "I doubt they will tell me, and I am going insane with worry."

"I'll work on that. Let me give the children back to their father. Wait here."

Not as if she had a choice. "Thank you."

Kimber took the kids and crossed the room. When she did, Laila longed for the bit of comfort the woman, despite being a stranger, had given her. She mostly wanted Trees, but since she couldn't have him— was worried to death about him—she intended to reach out to the only other person she could.

Slipping from the room, Laila headed through the rest of the unfamiliar house, finding a hallway and a bathroom.

When she turned to shut the door, she found Matt in her face. "You okay?"

"Fine. I need a few minutes to myself."

"Take your time."

So they could make a plan without her? Like hell.

Still, she shut the door and locked it, then pulled out her phone and dialed her sister.

Despite the late hour, Valeria answered right away. "What is happening?"

So her sister knew something was up. "Trees was helping to transport me to a new safe location and he was taken by three men in a van. I am scared, Val. Someone took him. I am worried they will kill him. It will be my fault. I should have killed Victor the first time I had the chance. And now—"

"Slow down. I know you are worried, but take a deep breath. You love him?"

"Yes. He is…everything to me. EM Security must save him—now."

"Do they know who has taken Trees?"

"Not yet. But are they not supposed to be good at these things? Can they not figure it out?"

"Laila…" her sister chided gently. "You must believe that if they had the power to save Trees this minute, they would. Your worry and impatience are driving your panic, but they kept you alive for years. Me, too. Kimber Trenton made it out, yes? There is a chance—"

"We survived because we served a purpose to them. You as a wife, me as a whore, Kimber as a bargaining chip. Trees means nothing to them…" Then Laila realized she might be wrong. "Unless whoever abducted him means to trade him for you."

Her sister let loose a long, exhausted sigh. "That may very well be, and I hope that is enough to keep him alive for your sake."

"Hope is not enough for me. If EM Security will do nothing, I must."

"No."

Did Valeria think she would value her safety over the man she loved? That she would not lift a finger to save him? "You cannot stop me."

"You are right; I cannot. But I can *help* you."

"Help me?" Laila gaped. "You have Jorge to think about. You have your future."

"What future? I have none now. I grow weary of this life. Always in hiding. I cannot walk outside for fear of death. Poor Jorge yearns to play in a park. He wants to run and jump and play with a ball. He wants to be a boy. Yet we are perpetually trapped in eight hundred square feet twenty-four hours a day for fear of being taken and beaten and…whatever else. And now these criminals and thugs are threatening the happiness you have finally found. I cannot do this anymore. I will not."

Laila's heart seized up. She had already lost Trees tonight, maybe for good. She could not lose her sister, too. "Valeria, do not—"

"Put myself at risk?" She scoffed. "For too long, I let you risk yourself for Jorge's benefit…and mine. I may be the older sister, but you are so much braver than me. Seemingly so undaunted. You never give up. You never stop fighting for those you love. And I have failed you in every way."

How could she say such things? "No."

"Yes. The night I escaped with that affluent doctor's daughter with EM Security's help? I wanted to come for you so badly and take you with me. But I knew if I was caught wandering the compound, I would be questioned and taken straight to Emilo. If that happened, I worried I would never have another chance to escape. I was pregnant. I worried it would not be long before Emilo knew, too. Then he would kill me."

For having his child. That made no sense, but Emilo had been an abusive bastard. Maybe he had never wanted a son or daughter.

But if that was true, why had he hunted them down in St. Louis? To kill Valeria for the "sin" of leaving him?

"I do not understand."

"I left you behind, and I never should have. I should have risked myself to take you with me that night. I could have spared you a year and a half of utter abuse and misery. But I was too afraid of what would happen to me and my baby…" Valeria started crying, and Laila heard the genuine remorse in her voice. "I am so sorry, *hermana.*"

That confession had obviously weighed heavily on her sister, and Laila hated to hear her tear herself apart over making the obvious—and correct—choice. "I understand. I support your choice. Nothing is more important to me than you and Jorge. Do not get involved in this mess, except maybe to demand that EM Security help me find Trees."

After all, his point about having no backup, no equipment, and no help was true.

"No, it is time I do more. The root of all our problems is Geraldo. I will deal with him—once and for all."

Laila reeled back in horror. "You cannot."

"I must. He will not hurt me. He will never hurt me. I have the one thing he wants most in this world. Jorge."

"You cannot sacrifice your son to that monster. He will—"

"Never," Valeria said firmly, like a vow. "But perhaps I can negotiate with him since I have leverage, and I refuse to let you risk yourself again. I will call EM Security and work something out."

If Montilla would stop hunting them, maybe they could have a life? "But what if Geraldo will not negotiate?"

"He will." Her sister sounded smug.

Laila didn't understand, but her first priority was Trees. Valeria and Jorge having a cartel-free future was critical. Laila wanted that for them. But if these violent bastards took Trees from this earth, she would have no tomorrows.

"And what of Victor?"

Valeria scoffed. "Ramos is nothing but ass-licking pond scum. Emilo was right about very little, but he was right about that. He is more dangerous than smart, and I think I know a way to ensure that he gets exactly what is coming to him."

Laila blinked. This was her sister? Valeria almost always allowed her to plan and execute whatever needed to be done. "I do not understand."

"I know. And...there are things I should have explained much sooner, but I was embarrassed. If you had known, however, I might have saved you some heartache and trouble. Another grave mistake I will have to live with. I hope you can forgive me someday."

"Valeria—"

"Give me an hour. I will see what I can work out. See if you can locate Victor. And take care of yourself, *hermana*. I will be in touch."

"I cannot wait an hour to start saving Trees." She had already wasted too much time as it was.

At least locating Victor would give her something to do. She could find out if he had taken Trees and plead for her beloved's life. She would offer Victor whatever he wanted for Trees's safe return.

"Would he truly want you putting yourself in danger for him? No. The man who confessed to me that he loves you would give his life to spare yours. Please honor him. I will be in touch soon."

Then Valeria hung up. Immediately, Laila went to work, trying her best to plot how she could both keep her promise and save the man she loved.

CHAPTER Ten

As Laila left the bathroom, she found Matt in the hall. He'd been assigned to guard her?

"Did you think someone would take me captive while I was in the bathroom?" She sent him a quelling glance. "There are no windows."

"We thought you might be plotting something behind our backs. From what I hear, you're good at that."

She ignored the flush stealing up her cheeks and brazened her way past him. "I was talking to my sister."

"That doesn't mean you're not plotting something."

Laila didn't dignify that with a reply, mostly because he wasn't wrong.

When she made her way back to the breakfast bar, Matt still trailing, she was surprised to see Kimber waiting for her, holding the baby. Her temporary sentry sent her a flinty warning glance, then made his way to the cluster of operatives, now huddled over the dining room table, deep in discussion.

Kimber smiled and cooed down at her baby. "I have something useful for you. Play along."

She didn't have to act to stare at the baby like she was adorable. "I am listening."

"I don't know how the guys know this—something about online chatter from sources—but Montilla has Trees."

Laila's heart leapt into her throat, clogging it until she couldn't breathe. It was good to know who had Trees...but bad that the powerful drug lord, not the easily manipulated Victor, had taken him. "They are sure?"

"They seem to be." Kimber brushed a thumb along her baby's cheek, then hazarded a glance up at Laila. "I know you haven't always had good experiences with EM Security. My brothers told me your story and some of the hardships you've endured. But I swear, they're the best. And if they're this sure of something, it's almost one-hundred-percent true."

Almost true didn't make it fact, but Laila had to concede it was possible they had sources she didn't and knew things she couldn't. She just had to figure out how best to use the knowledge. "Thank you so much."

"I owe you a hundred times more. Tell me if there's anything else I can do."

Laila's panic urged her to take this woman up on her offer, but Kimber wasn't the person most qualified to rescue Trees, and she had a bigger responsibility. "Stay with your children and be safe. I will figure this out. I promised Trees that if he ever needed rescuing, I would not act alone and I would not risk myself."

The woman's gaze slid down to her infant daughter, then she nodded. "I think that's wise. My brothers want Trees back, too. They're hardheaded, but they *will* hear logic. I'm sure you can all work together."

Laila hoped so. "Thank you."

"When this is all over, I would love to do something to truly thank you for helping to facilitate my rescue."

"That is not necessary, but I would enjoy more of your company."

Kimber smiled and squeezed her hand. "Same. Stay safe. I hope you have Trees back soon."

With that, Deke's wife returned to her husband's side. They departed together, Deke letting the others know that Jack Cole would be arriving soon to lend a hand—and his tactical smarts.

Even if he arrived in two minutes, that would be two minutes too late to start plotting a scheme. Somehow, she had to figure out what Montilla wanted—other than Jorge—and give it to him in exchange for Trees.

Wouldn't the leader of the cartel want the head of the man who had humiliated him by stealing his car? Serving Victor on a platter to Montilla might not be enough to sway him, but she had to try.

She opened her phone and pondered the best way to find Victor without giving away her ploy, her location, or her dilemma when an unfamiliar icon labeled LOCATE ME jumped out at her. Someone had installed it on her device without her knowledge. How? The only person who had had access to her phone was Trees.

Hope surged.

Despite her suddenly shaking fingers, Laila couldn't press the icon fast enough. She held her breath as she waited, eyes glued to the screen. A map appeared, slowly piecing together. Lafayette and surrounding areas filled her screen. In the center was a little blue dot, traveling southeast. A red line showed her every location that device had been since last night—starting with Trees's place.

She gasped. That had to be his phone. Had she actually found him? Her gaze bounced up to the men, mouth agape.

Matt, who was still watching her, was by her side in a handful of steps. "What is it?"

"I know where Trees is."

Surprise crossed his face, but before he could say anything, Hunter swore soundly across the room. Laila looked up to find him with his phone pressed to his ear.

"Are you fucking serious?" the elder Edgington brother roared.

"What is happening?" She worried it was bad news about Trees.

"He's talking to Kane. Your sister demanded a meeting. Hunter promised her one once this crisis is over, but she insists on seeing him now, and I'm guessing she didn't wait for anyone to give her permission before she left her safe house. Then again, she's paying the bills…"

Valeria was coming here? What the hell was she doing, risking herself and Jorge?

Logan gestured to Matt with a sharp jerk of his head. The cowboy nodded, then slipped out the back door. Laila's mind whirled. Amid the mental chaos, she tried to devise a plan, discarding possibilities and nailing down more viable options while following Trees's still-moving blue dot. A plot began to take shape.

Minutes later, Matt entered again and stepped aside. Valeria appeared, holding a sleepy Jorge. Kane stood right behind them, on alert, gun in hand.

"Were you followed?" Hunter barked to Kane.

The man with the mustache shook his head. "Hardly anyone on the streets at this hour."

Hunter and his brothers visibly relaxed as they locked the door.

Valeria ignored them, searching her surroundings. When Laila met her gaze, her sister gave her an imitation of a smile. To fool everyone else? It wasn't fooling her.

They met in the middle of the room, hugging as if they hadn't seen each other in weeks, rather than yesterday. Still, with everything that had happened, that heart-to-heart in the apartment seemed like a lifetime ago.

Laila drank in her sister's familiar comfort, then kissed sleeping Jorge's head. "What are you doing here?"

"Making sure you finally get a chance to be happy. What have I missed?"

In low tones, she filled Valeria in, aware of the men and their perceptive gazes. As she and her sister put their heads together, Laila outlined her working plan. Granted, it had one giant hole. "But if Montilla will not be satisfied with an exchange of Trees for Victor, I have no other leverage…except myself."

Without that, the man she loved would die. She couldn't bring herself to say the words aloud. Terror threatened to shred her composure. She was doing her best to compartmentalize.

"But you do." Valeria grabbed her hand and led her toward the cluster of plotting men. "Come with me. Tell them your plan. I will fill in details as needed."

The group fell silent as they approached. Hunter turned to them, looking at Valeria as if she'd lost her mind. "You shouldn't have come."

"My sister needs me."

"We had you in a secure location. And you risked compromising it because you wanted to give Laila a hug?" He pinned her with a glare. "If you have another problem, we'll absolutely address it, but—"

"I do not."

"Then with all due respect, you're making our jobs a lot harder. We need to keep you and your son locked down so we can focus on rescuing our operative."

Valeria raised a brow. "Will all due respect, if we all work together, we can accomplish what none of us alone are able to, which is not only Trees's rescue but to stop Montilla once and for all."

That made Hunter pause. Not that anyone here was naive enough to believe that ending the drug lord would stop the cartel. But it would make Valeria safe, enable Jorge to have a real future, and free the man she loved.

"We're listening," Logan said.

"I know where to find Trees." Laila showed them the blue dot on her screen, now approaching the airport. That was both good and bad. Good because it seemed they meant to keep Trees alive long enough for a flight, which gave her and EM Security time. Bad because they likely meant to take him someplace where it would be much harder to extract him. "Any chance we could reach him before the plane takes off?"

Hunter didn't reply, simply fired off a text and waited for a reply with toe-tapping impatience.

"I doubt they're flying commercial," drawled the younger Edgington. "If they're going private, that means they're on their own schedule, so no. Fuck!"

Though Laila had been half expecting that answer, it still crushed her. "Can anyone else stop them? The police?"

"If they go in, sirens blaring, there's a good chance Montilla's thugs get spooked and Trees doesn't survive. The only teammate who could get there fast enough is Zy, but he can't take on three of Montilla's thugs without assistance and backup. He'd either become a captive or a casualty, too."

Hunter's phone dinged. "Okay, Dad reached out to his friend at the airport. The air-traffic control tower said there's a private plane due to take off in twenty minutes."

"Can the tower delay the flight?" Laila asked.

"I doubt it," Hunter answered regretfully. "They've already been pre-cleared and they're about to pull away from the gate. But Dad did say they've filed a flight plan to an airstrip northeast of Mexico City."

"Geraldo has a residence near there," her sister supplied. "He also has an operation in the mountains to the east."

Laila turned to Valeria. How did she know that? From Emilo? Had her late husband shared such things with her?

"So it's a safe bet that Montilla will have Trees taken to one of those locations," Hunter said.

Yes, but how would they know which one? "We cannot wait for Trees's blue dot to settle in a spot before we act."

"No, and they'll dump the phone well before they reach their destination. Did you two have an idea how to shut Montilla down permanently?"

Valeria turned to her. "Tell them."

Laila took a deep breath. "I will write Victor and say that I know he has captured Trees and that I am willing to exchange myself for him."

Logan scowled. "Why? Victor doesn't have Trees."

"I know, but he needs only to *think* I believe he does. He is furious with me for betraying him to Montilla. Trust me, he will not pass up an opportunity to hurt me in the name of revenge. If we lure him to a location, you can capture him. We will then offer him to Montilla in exchange for Trees."

The three brothers who owned EM Security frowned in unison, but Hunter spoke for them. "And if you're talking about taking out Montilla for good, I assume you're saying we need to capture him, too? What if Victor isn't a strong enough lure for him to agree to a meet?"

Exactly where Laila had been hung up.

"I will take care of that," Valeria answered. "It is me and my son he ultimately wants."

Laila turned to her sister in horror. "You cannot!"

"Oh, I have no intention of staying with Montilla or letting him infect Jorge, but he will jump at the chance to meet my little boy. Take my word on that."

The grandson he'd never met. Perhaps that was true. Except... "There is a rumor Montilla is in a coma, one Trees put him in when he shot the old man during Kimber's rescue."

"Can you verify that?" Muñoz chimed in.

Laila gnawed on her lip, thinking through possibilities. "I can try."

"Good, because I doubt Montilla's men would hop countries to grab Trees if *el jefe* himself hadn't okayed the op."

"My thoughts, too." Hunter nodded.

"Same," Logan tossed in. "Not unless he had a second-in-command with a lot of power."

At once, everyone turned to Valeria. Even Laila had no idea what her sister knew. They had rarely talked about life trapped under a drug lord's thumb, as if they had both wanted to forget their dark pasts.

Valeria nodded, surprising Laila again. "Federico Chavez. He's ambitious, smart, and cruel. I have seen him do unspeakable things to gain favor and get ahead. Before I left, he was well on his way to becoming Geraldo's right hand."

"Which means he will probably want to take over as boss some-day," Hunter surmised. "And your son is a threat to him."

"Very much."

That got Laila's thoughts turning again. "Is it possible Federico would pretend to spy for the enemy, then sell them out to his boss at the last minute?"

"Without blinking."

It was just a hunch, but… "Victor had an informant on the inside of Montilla's organization. He clearly knew things, could influence the boss, and had power of his own. Could it be—"

"Federico is the only one Geraldo trusts that much." Valeria shrugged. "Or that was the case before I escaped."

That was probably the case now. In a den of criminals and cutthroats, trust like that wasn't won over night. "I think I have spoken to him. And I think he will talk to me again. If I am right, this may be the last piece of the puzzle we need." Laila turned to her sister. "You want no part of Tierra Caliente's future? You do not wish to run the cartel or have Jorge raised to take over?"

She clutched Jorge to her chest. "Never. It is why I ran from both Montilla men."

Laila palmed her nephew's head. "Good. Then I think we have a plan."

Hunter narrowed those uncanny blue eyes on her. "You're going to trade Victor to Montilla, then trade Montilla's position to Federico in exchange for the promise that you, Valeria, and Jorge walk free from the cartel. Am I right?"

She lifted her chin. "Do you have a better idea?"

"No." Then he smiled her way, and she saw respect spread across his face. "Trees said you were crafty. That's an understatement. You're a hell of a tactician. I wish I would have listened sooner."

She stopped bristling. "Thank you."

"Can you get in touch with Victor now? And his informant?"

"I think so."

"Then set everything up. Logan is bomb with maps. He'll help you find the best locations to draw them to. If this plan unfolds the way it should, you and your family will finally be free."

And if it didn't, they would all be dead.

When Hunter turned away, Laila grabbed his sleeve. "What about Trees?"

"I'm not leaving without him, I promise."

"Thank you." His vow made Laila breathe easier, but she had demands of her own. "I am coming with you to make sure."

He didn't even hesitate. "No."

"Yes. This affects my family, and Trees is my man. You cannot stop me."

"If word gets out that we took clients on a mission and one of you dies, our business is over. For good."

"Then you are fired as bodyguards and hired to take us to the cartel," Valeria said.

"If we refuse?" Hunter raised a brow.

Laila shrugged. "We could hire others. Or I could act alone."

The room fell silent. Everyone knew she wasn't making empty threats.

"I am coming, too," Valeria insisted, shocking Laila. "For too long, my sister shielded me and my son from danger. But we are family." Valeria took her hand. "Rise or fall, we do it together."

"Fuck," Hunter sighed out. "Please let me talk you out of this. Give me your contacts and I'll—"

"No," Laila insisted. "They know me, and they will speak to me. I do not wish to waste time on a pointless argument. Are we in agreement? Or do I take my contacts and my leverage and find my own way to rescue Trees?"

Hunter looked to Logan and Joaquin, each of whom gave a grudging nod, then he held out his hand. "Deal. You contact everyone, and I'll get the men locked and loaded."

Laila shook his hand, eager to start finding Trees. "Deal."

Mexico

Twenty hours later, Laila trembled anxiously, her head full of what-ifs, as she waited for Geraldo Montilla to show. She prayed she could hold herself together and keep everyone safe for the next hour. Everything would likely be over by then.

After that, she would either be in Trees's arms…or mourning the loss of a man she could never replace in her heart.

Beside her, Valeria was rattled but holding herself together. Jorge, though listless, was unusually quiet, as if he sensed the tension in the air. Around them, most of EM Security, along with Jack Cole, Deke Trenton, Trevor Forsythe, and Ghost, guarded the abandoned hospital they had chosen as their meet point. Kane and Zy had Victor Ramos, whom EM had captured three hours ago, under wraps nearby. Thankfully, that part of her plan had gone off perfectly.

It had been poetic justice to watch Victor swagger in, assuming he would take advantage of her foolish belief that he had abducted Trees and trap her. The look on his face when he realized she had duped him instead was priceless. With his minions subdued and his wrists shackled, Laila had relished slapping his face as hard as she could. She'd wanted to do far more, but they needed him alive—for now. She'd contented herself with her stinging palm, the pain a happy reminder that, if all went right, Victor would soon join his brother, Hector, in hell.

Her elation was dimmed by the fact that Trees's blue tracking dot had been extinguished shortly before the flight that had taken him out of the country left. It had not flashed on since. She didn't want to think about the implications of that.

"Are you ready?" Valeria reached for her hand.

Laila nodded. "As I will ever be. You know Montilla and his thugs may barge in, guns blazing."

"Not with Jorge here. He will never put the boy at risk."

Not for the first time, Laila wondered why her sister was so sure of that. Maybe he realized he was surrounded by sharks like Federico and wanted his heir to be family? Perhaps, but would the drug lord still be alive and able to run his business by the time Jorge matured into a man capable of running a massive criminal organization...if he ever did? Then again, Valeria had been proven right when Montilla had snapped at the chance to meet Jorge, along with taking Victor captive, in exchange for Trees's life.

Beside Laila, Matt hovered protectively. Someone must have spoken into the comm device in his ear because he stiffened. "Roger that." Then he cupped her elbow. "Montilla and his entourage are on their way in."

"Is Trees with them?"

Matt paused, then shrugged. "One of their vehicles is a van. That's all we know."

Which could mean anything. Laila tried not to think the worst. But if she could double-cross, maneuver, deceive, and trick people to save Trees, she knew Montilla was capable of doing the same for his own ends. After all, he hadn't survived nearly three decades as the head of this cartel without being crafty. She had barely lived.

The realization made her uneasy. She swallowed back a bundle of nerves.

Minutes ticked by like hours until a couple of armed thugs appeared, glaring menacingly at EM Security, who also dripped weapons. One wrong move or one hot-headed maverick, and they could all be dead. Laila hated that her sister and Jorge were here, but there had been no dissuading Valeria.

The next man to enter the expansive, dilapidated reception area swaggered in, wearing a white shirt that accentuated his sun-roughened face. He had thick black brows over piercing dark eyes without a soul. He was younger than Laila had imagined and attractive in a sinister way. He was definitely dangerous. She resisted the urge to shudder.

"That's Federico," Valeria murmured just above a whisper.

Laila made a mental note to give him a wide berth.

Then an older man filed into the room next, leaning on a cane as if it was more a bother than a necessity. He was average height, average build, dressed like a college professor, minus the tweed jacket, in a crisp dress shirt, a bold blue tie, and a gray vest. He wore a simple wristwatch and had a piercing gaze.

Geraldo Montilla. He had aged since the last time Laila had seen him, but he still had a commanding air.

When he set eyes on Valeria, he stopped. Stared. His face changed. Softened? Then he clapped his eyes on Jorge. His stoic expression almost melted into something she couldn't fathom on a man like him.

It seemed tender.

The old man swallowed. "Is that—"

"Yes," her sister snapped.

There was an undercurrent between them she didn't understand.

"Can I hold him?" The old man's voice sounded both shaky and scratchy.

When Valeria hesitated, Laila shook her head. They had a plan. They needed to stick to it. "Not yet. Where is Trees? I want proof of life."

Montilla's gaze fell on her and his dark eyes turned cold. "There is the bitch who helped steal my car. Why should I let you live?"

Laila's fear swelled. Her heartbeat surged. "Because I am also the one who made this meeting with your grandson possible. Now where is Trees?"

The drug lord sent Valeria a surprised glance, then motioned to one of his thugs. "Bring him."

Laila held her breath as the armed man filed out the door, taking another with him. Silence ensued, and time seemed to stretch into infinity as she waited. Finally, the door scraped open again and the armed goons dragged Trees in.

He was alive! But Laila's relief was quickly tempered by the sight of him. She lifted a trembling hand to her mouth in shock.

Trees had a black eye nearly swollen shut, a busted lip, and a mottled contusion flaring at his temple. He stumbled in between the two guards, looking exhausted or disoriented. No, drugged. He'd been pumped full of something to keep him contained and he looked barely awake and upright. One shoulder hung awkwardly, as if it had been dislocated. He had cuts and bruises all up his muscled arms. His knuckles were torn and bloody. Somewhere along the way, he'd fought —hard.

When their eyes met, he suddenly jerked up and scowled. "Laila, you shouldn't be here."

She didn't argue. He was wrong, but now wasn't the time.

Instead, she turned to Hunter. By their previous agreement, he would do the talking from here. After all, Montilla was an old-school chauvinist. He wouldn't take kindly to negotiating with her or her sister.

As Hunter approached, Montilla sized him up. "Mr. Edgington, I presume?"

Hunter nodded. "We've brought Victor Ramos. He's nearby with guards, awaiting my instructions. After you've visited with your grandson, we'll bring him to you. Then we will have fulfilled the terms of our agreement and you will return Mr. Scott."

"Of course," the old man returned smoothly. "I was promised fifteen minutes with Jorge first." He turned to his armed guards. "Take Mr. Scott to the morgue in the basement until then. He will be unable to escape, and if he tries to shoot me again or Mr. Edgington reneges… well, he will already be in a morgue."

Laila stiffened, and she whirled to Hunter. "If we cannot see him, they may continue to torture him."

Hunter hesitated, then turned to Montilla. "I'm sending one of mine with one of yours to ensure Mr. Scott's continued health."

The old man shrugged as if he didn't care, then motioned to one of his thugs, who grabbed Trees by his awkwardly dangling arm and tugged.

The agony that crossed Trees's face made everything inside Laila twist with hate and rage.

Hunter also looked pissed off as he gestured to Matt. "Follow them."

The cowboy nodded, and the three of them disappeared down a set of stairs on the far side of the room, into the darkness beyond the handful of portable lights EM Security had rigged for this meeting.

Then Montilla snapped his fingers. An armed goon produced a folding chair. The drug lord ambled to it and sat, then turned his attention to Valeria, his stare drilling into her. "Bring the boy to me."

Her sister held Jorge tighter. "I did not say you could hold him. I said you could meet him."

"He is my flesh and blood. I would never hurt him."

"Merely kill his mother," Valeria shot back.

"I can concede a child this young requires a mother. You will not be harmed. You have my word."

"Forgive me if your word means very little to me."

Montilla's expression turned to thunder. "Bring me my son!"

Laila reared back. His son? The old man wasn't senile. Had he actually fathered Jorge?

At her side, Valeria's spine went even straighter. "After what you did to Emilo, the last person he needs as a father is you."

Laila gaped at her sister. Jorge was truly Geraldo's son?

"What did I do? I gave Emilo every advantage," the old man growled. "Ungrateful, inept prick."

Valeria scowled. "You indulged and corrupted him. He was a sniveling boy, playing at men's cartel games. You turned him into a criminal, even as you undermined his every move. You ensured he could not lead without your permission, then you constantly told him that nothing he did was good enough."

Fury twisted the old man's face. "He was not fit to follow in my footsteps. His mother was weak, which she passed on to Emilo and his sister, Clara. Good riddance to them both. They were foolish enough to let their emotions overwhelm them. And they were both stupid enough to let themselves be killed by Pierce Walker. They got what they deserved. But this boy will be different. He belongs to me."

Valeria clung to Jorge tighter. "He is mine. I gave birth to him."

"I say now he is *mine*." Montilla stood, rising to his full height. Suddenly, he looked a lot less injured and a lot more vital. "Once upon a time, you begged me to fuck you. Because you wanted a real man.

Because you knew where the power in the cartel truly lay. This boy is my price."

Valeria scoffed. "I only fucked you so my sister and I would be protected. I never expected to get pregnant."

Laila blinked at her sister. Had she offered herself to Geraldo Montilla to buy their safety?

Montilla looked amused. "I did. That was my goal. Or will you try to convince me that Jorge is my son's offspring?"

"He could be," Valeria hedged.

"If that was so, you would not have run from my son in fear when you realized you were pregnant. But you fled because you feared he would be suspicious. And you knew he would have killed you for the truth. So you escaped with Colonel Edgington and his sons, leaving your younger sister without any help, ally, or hope for the future." He tsked. "Not very sisterly of you."

Valeria sent her the briefest glance filled with shame and apology, then she glared at Montilla. "I left so you could not corrupt or abuse my child. The world did not need another Emilo."

As much as Laila felt shocked and betrayed by all her sister's secrets, she couldn't argue with Valeria's conclusion. Laila had found ways of coping with life under the thumb of Victor and Hector Ramos in her brother-in-law's compound. As a baby, Jorge would have been utterly vulnerable.

Montilla stalked closer to Valeria. "Give me my son."

At Hunter's signal, every operative he'd brought raised their weapon and pointed it at the drug lord. "We are not the police or the DEA. We aren't here to threaten your business, but you made a simple fucking agreement: fifteen minutes with Jorge and Victor Ramos's lousy ass in exchange for my operative. You've got five seconds to comply or I'll blow your fucking head off."

Montilla stared him down, looking simultaneously amused and annoyed. "Do you really believe you can compel me to do anything? For every gun you have trained on me, I have one pointed at each of your men. Would you like to see your brothers die? Mr. Scott in the basement? Everyone else who relies on you for a paycheck? And I assure you, once they are gone, your clients will suffer most. Valeria is young enough to breed again several times if I desire. And Laila will make a more than acceptable whore for my men."

Terror clawed through her. After knowing the pleasure of Trees's touch, she couldn't imagine enduring sexual violence and abuse again. But how could she stop what seemed like an inevitable slaughter?

One thing she had learned over her years of captivity was that no one expected her to be a fighter or capable of foiling the plans of dangerous men. She'd use that to her advantage.

Clandestinely, she looked around the room for some way to hide Jorge and her sister while she reached Trees. She glanced over her shoulder at Hunter Edgington. He had a scheme in mind. She saw it on his face. Laila wished she knew what.

To Montilla's right, Federico—who hadn't said a word during this exchange—assessed the situation. What did he have up his sleeve?

"I'm serious. You have five seconds to lower your weapons," Hunter warned the drug lord.

"Or what?" He scoffed. "You will shoot me? We will return fire. Is that really safe with a child in the room? Did they not teach you Navy SEALs better?"

"If you're itching to get it on, let the women and Jorge leave."

If Montilla agreed, they would kill everyone, including Trees. And did Hunter really think that, once the drug lord had succeeded, he would allow her and Valeria to take Jorge and walk free?

She had to contrive some plan—fast.

The old man smiled. "Your forthright earnestness amuses me."

His condescending attitude clearly rubbed Hunter the wrong way. "Five."

"Counting, are we? Do you think that will change anything?"

"Four."

Laila watched Logan grip his weapon tighter before he shuffled her behind him. Joaquin did the same with Valeria.

"Give me the boy, stop this ridiculous counting, and no one has to die."

"Three. Drop your weapons and live up to your negotiations or you won't live until sunrise."

"Fuck you." Montilla charged them.

Logan blocked his path. Joaquin shoved him back and cocked his gun in the old man's face. Laila tugged on her sister's arm, easing her and Jorge back a few covert steps from the fray.

"No, fuck you," Hunter spit. "Two, asshole. After one, you're dead."

"You wish."

The elder Edgington gestured to his operatives, who went on high alert. "One. Last chance."

Federico stepped closer to his boss and murmured in his ear, "Do not back down. We must show these *vaqueros* and *gringos* who is in charge."

Montilla nodded, raising dark eyes full of contempt at Hunter. "Kill them and take the boy!"

Laila didn't waste a second. She pulled on her sister's arm, using her body to shield Jorge from the hail of gunfire that suddenly erupted around them. As much as she feared for the lives of everyone at EM Security, she had to ensure her family stayed safe and free Trees before it was too late.

Jorge began wailing. Valeria did her best to cover his mouth so the boy didn't give away their position as Laila hustled them through the chaos to find someplace safe to hide.

She headed toward the shadowy corners of the room and spotted an opening that led to a long corridor. At the end, a strip of moonlight filtered under the door. "Run. Find Kane and Zy. Tell them to start driving you far away now."

Valeria gripped her hand tightly. "I will not leave you."

Laila gave her a shove. "For Jorge, you must. Or he will be raised by a monster."

"Come with me," Valeria entreated. "I left you before. I do not want to do it again."

"I am choosing to stay because I need Trees. I do not want to live without him." When Valeria opened her mouth to argue, Laila shook her head. "No. Stay in the shadows and go!"

Her sister hesitated, then kissed her cheek. "God be with you. Please be safe."

"You, too."

"I hope my secret does not make you angry. I love you."

Valeria wasn't one for soft words. Neither was Laila. Life had been too hard on them both. But she also knew life was too short to hold a grudge against her only sister. "I love you, too."

Her sister slipped out the door, clutching Jorge. Laila watched until it shut, then eased back to the end of the hall, closer to the ugliness of combat.

Someone killed the lights. Now only the silvery light of the moon shone through the busted-out windows. Gunfire rang through the cavernous room. Shouts of rage and grunts of pain filled the air as the battle raged.

If she was going to rescue Trees, Matt would need backup. She must find a gun.

Laila dropped to the dirty tile, crawling into the fray on her elbows and knees, staying as low as possible to avoid the flying bullets. By the dim light, she caught sight of a man, one of Montilla's, sprawled lifeless two feet in front of her. She scrambled to reach him, patting him down quickly to find his weapon.

Seconds later, it was in her grasp, warm and wet with something slick and coppery. Blood. She shuddered and wiped the weapon clean on her pants, shoved it in her waistband, then turned in the direction Montilla's men had taken Trees.

As she crawled for the exit, she ran into Hunter Edgington. She recognized his boots.

He glanced to see who was at his feet. "Get the lights back on. Some fucker turned them off."

"How?"

"There's a switch." He aimed and fired at some combatant she couldn't see. "I can't do it myself."

But... "Montilla will only kill you faster."

"You think I don't have backup? An ace in the hole?"

She hadn't considered that, but hadn't he and his brothers been doing missions like this their whole adult lives? Yes, and if the lights would keep them alive so they could help her rescue Trees, rather than her having to brave the dark to the morgue alone, she would do what she could. "On it."

It took some effort, but she found her way to one of the light boxes the Oracle team had brought in and fumbled under the weak beam of moonlight. Suddenly, her fingers encountered the switch and she flipped it on. Light flooded the room, startling Montilla and his goons.

Emboldened, she ran to another light and flipped it on, too, this one blinding Montilla and Federico with a bright beam directly in their eyes.

Both cursed. She looked around and saw a few corpses strewn on the ground. Thankfully none belonged to anyone from EM or Oracle.

Crouching and ducking, she made her way across the room, dodging bullets until she was a handful of feet from the stairs that led to the basement.

Then cruel fingers in her hair yanked her up by the tender strands.

"Where are you going, little sister?" Montilla rasped in her ear as he wrested the gun from her waistband and tossed it to the floor.

Her heartbeat surged with fear. "What do you want?"

"My son. Where is he?"

"I-I do not know," she lied.

"You waste my time. Tell me now or I will blow your brains out." He lifted the gun to her temple.

She tried to hold in her scream, but it escaped as a whimper. Terror shook her from head to toe. She had no illusions that Montilla would end her. She meant nothing to him. Nor did taking a life.

If this was how she died, trying to protect those she loved, then she would gladly perish, but she would leave behind one gaping regret— that she had broken her promise to Trees yet still hadn't saved him. She could only hope that EM Security prevailed and that they would rescue the man she loved so he could have a long, hopefully happy life.

"I will not tell you." She raised her chin in defiance.

"Shame. You will look far less pretty with your brains splattered across the floor."

He cocked the gun. The sound reverberated in her ear. Her breathing turned ragged, and she closed her eyes, praying for a miracle. But she would not beg this monster for her life.

Suddenly, she heard a splat, felt a gush of hot liquid spray across her face. Her breath caught. Had she been hit? Was she bleeding? Why didn't she feel pain?

Montilla's grip on her hair loosened, then his body began to fall away. Laila turned—and saw his wide, lifeless eyes, along with a small bullet hole in between. The back of his head had been blown open and his brains littered the floor.

She screamed.

"Get her!" she heard someone roar in a heavily accented voice.

Laila took off running, ducking long enough to grab the gun Montilla had tossed, and made her way toward the basement stairs.

One of Montilla's thugs charged after her. She heard his pounding footsteps above her harsh breathing and turned to find him barreling down on her. She looked around for help and saw some wounded among the EM Security operatives. Others she didn't see at all, like Hunter. She prayed they were still alive.

Logan charged across the giant, empty room to help her, but he would reach her too late. Her pursuer was already taking shots at her. One bullet whizzed past her ear.

To her right, she ducked down an unexplored hallway. It was still and shadowy. Maybe too dark for Montilla's murderous underling to see her? Perhaps, but the encroaching blackness terrified her.

As she darted down the corridor, it closed in, threatening to suffocate her. She started to panic. Her breaths got louder, and she still heard his pursuing footfalls. Her thoughts tumbled and whirled. How could she sneak past her assailant to reach the basement stairs?

As possibilities rolled through her head, Laila tripped and stumbled. Her shoulder crashed into a door that gave way and slammed against the opposite wall. Moonlight shined through the lone rectangular window here, enough for her to see she'd cornered herself in a closet.

The door swung shut again. Panic clawed at her as she looked for an escape. The shelves lining the walls were empty. Maybe she could climb them, break the glass, and shimmy through the small window above. But then she would be forced to run around the hospital perimeter, find a door to enter, and locate the stairs to the basement— precious minutes in which EM Security might be overrun by Montilla's thugs and Trees might die. But if she ran back out of the closet, her assailant would catch her.

The window it was.

Laila tested the sturdiness of the shelves, then started climbing—only to be stopped by a sign to the right in big red letters. A small, square opening sat beneath.

The laundry chute. It should take her down a level, into the basement, right? But would she fall to her death?

Behind her, the door crashed against the wall again. Knowing she had no time to waste, Laila yanked the narrow panel open and crawled into the chute. It was a tight squeeze. Darkness overtook her again. She closed her eyes and tried to ignore her fear.

Then she was falling, down, down. Laila bit her lip to keep from screaming. Would she break a leg when she landed or simply plummet to her death?

Gravity finally hurled her out of the chute. She tumbled feet first onto the cold concrete floor with a thump, rolling to her hands and knees. But she was unharmed.

Laila stood and fought a fresh wave of impending terror. The dark down here was absolute. She held up a hand in front of her face. She couldn't see a thing.

Her heart gonged furiously against her chest. She panted hard and fast but struggled for air. Panic surged, threatening to strangle her. She tried to tell herself she was fine. Her pursuer—and nearly anyone of any size—would struggle to fit in that chute. He hadn't followed her down. She was free to find Trees and rescue him.

But hysteria froze her in place.

Laila shook from head to toe, her eyes wide and alert, despite the complete blackness. Every sense was on hyperalert, cataloging the cool air on her skin drifting from the chute to the sound of something scurrying—a rodent?—a few feet on her right.

Against her will, a whimper escaped. Memories of sleeping in the narrow, uncomfortable bed in Emilo's underground compound rushed back. At first, she had appreciated the fact that sunlight never cut her sleep short. Then came that horrible night. The scraping noise of metal on metal. The footsteps. The echo of her own voice asking who was there…and the chilling silence.

Then she'd been held down, her screams muffled by a sweaty hand before a strong, cruel hand shoved her nightgown up and a man slid between her legs.

Laila shoved the rest of the memory away. That was then. Now she had to save Trees. Victor and Hector weren't here to rape her, and she would be damned if she was anyone's victim again. Everything she'd been through had only made her stronger, and Trees had done so much to save her physically and emotionally. She refused to let him down.

Slowly, she rose, feeling her way through the inky room until she came across something square and metal, about waist high. A washing machine? She groped her way from that one to another, then several more, all in a row.

Finally, her fingers encountered a wall, then an opening. Laila edged into what she suspected was a hallway. She desperately wanted to reach for the phone in her pocket and use the light to guide her through the blackness. But she didn't dare alert Montilla's guard.

She simply had to be brave.

Laila fumbled along the wall, tiptoeing and listening for noises. The sounds of the battle upstairs grew fainter and fainter as she made her way past other doors, none of which were the morgue, she supposed, because she didn't hear Matt or Montilla's lackey.

Finally, she reached the end of that wall and found herself in the intersection of two corridors. The pounding of something against metal—a fist?—resounded down the empty space almost directly ahead.

Then she heard a voice she'd know anywhere. "Get me the fuck out of here!"

Trees! He was still alive. Still fighting.

"Shut up, freak," an accented voice spit at him with contempt, sounding even closer.

"You shut up. He's not a freak," Matt defended.

"I would love to fight you, tear you limb from limb, *vaquero*. If *el jefe* gives me the go-ahead…"

"You're all talk." Matt sounded annoyed.

Laila crept closer, still shaking and fighting the urge to curl up into a fetal-position ball, rock back and forth, and beg someone to turn the light on. But she would brazen her way through this and rescue Trees, even if it took all her will.

"I can hear your fucking voices. Let me the hell out!"

Trees was alone, probably in the dark, too. Was he afraid of what would happen if EM Security lost the battle? Did he even know it was going on? In this floor, in a separate wing, she could hear none of the commotion above.

"One more word, and I will come in there and kill you myself."

"You fucking try," Trees sneered. "You don't have the brains or the balls."

"*Pinche pendejo,*" Montilla's man spit. "I will fuck you up."

Suddenly, a little light flickered on at the end of the hall. Laila glimpsed the hazy outline of a dark-haired man facing the door, gun in hand. She heard the scrape of metal, then the thug yanked on the door.

Matt, weapon in hand, clamped down on his shoulder. "You're not touching him."

"No, I am going to kill him. Back off."

Matt surged into the small circle of light and shoved the man. The light dropped between their feet as the sounds of curses and flying fists filled the hallway.

They were distracted. This chance would not come again.

Laila swallowed back more fear and rooted along the wall toward the morgue.

As Matt and the drug thug tangled toward a corner, they kicked the light. Beams spun crazily on the sagging ceiling as Laila crept closer, now mere feet from the door.

Before she reached it, it wrenched open. Trees busted out. Scattered beams lit his face in stark relief. He breathed hard and growled, looking like a blunt-force instrument of vengeance.

Then he turned to Matt and Montilla's goon. They were both armed. Trees wasn't.

He needed her help.

Before she could give him her gun, Matt scuffled back into the circle of light and hit the criminal over the head with the butt of his gun. Montilla's lackey wilted, seeming to melt toward the concrete floor.

They were safe—for the moment.

"Trees!" she called out.

His head snapped up. His stare fastened on her. "Laila, what are you—"

"No time. We must go." She fumbled with the gun in her waistband, then handed it to him before bending to grab the firearm off the body near Matt's feet. "There is a shoot-out upstairs. I sneaked my sister and my nephew outside, but everyone else—"

"Why didn't I hear it?" Matt demanded, picking up the flashlight and shining it down the hall, almost in her face.

"Too far away. But I am worried. If they lose..."

"We're all dead. Let's go." Trees took her hand, alert and battle ready as they charged toward the stairs. "You stayed behind to fight?"

At the chiding note in his voice, she shook her head. "I stayed behind to find you."

"In the dark?" he asked softly as they reached the end of a long corridor, past what had once been an industrial elevator, and headed up. "You must have been terrified."

"I was more afraid of not finding you." She squeezed his hand, meeting his stare in shadow.

Trees squeezed her hand in return, then looked over her head to Matt. "You have to help me with this shoulder."

"Your arm isn't broken?"

"No."

Matt still hesitated. "I shouldn't do this, and putting it back in place is going to hurt like hell."

"I'll only be half as effective in getting us out alive if you don't."

"Roger that." Matt nodded, then handed her the flashlight. "Get on the floor."

Trees didn't hesitate to get supine.

Matt took hold of Trees's wrist and winced. "Laila, kiss him. Don't let him pull away."

"Now?"

"I'm going to scream, honey. He's trying to muffle the sound. Come here." Trees held his good arm open to her.

She fell to her knees, then fitted herself against him and looked down into his face. "I thought I had lost you."

"Shh." He kissed her forehead. "I'm here, but clearly this shit isn't over."

She might still lose him.

Laila surged forward, pressing her lips to his battered ones gently, aware of Matt raising Trees's limp arm as he pumped it in small, sharp circles.

Trees stiffened and roared into their kiss, pressing against her lips so hard she swore hers would bruise, but she didn't pull away until Matt stepped back.

Breathing hard, Trees groaned and got to his feet, rolling his shoulder experimentally. He gave Matt a thumbs-up. "Thanks."

The cowboy nodded. "Let's go."

"As soon as I get Laila someplace safe."

"By then, it will be too late," she argued, ensuring the safety on the gun was off. "I can help."

"The hell you will, woman."

"She's not a fragile doll, man. And we don't have time to find the fucking way out of here or to argue."

Trees swore heartily but grabbed her hand and climbed the stairs. "Stay behind me."

"I will." Unless he needed help. Until it no longer made sense.

Her heart pounded as they ascended and reached the main area at the front of the hospital. Everything and everyone had fallen quiet. Were they all dead?

Then Logan appeared, looking relieved as hell. He pressed a finger to his lips, then tipped his head toward the middle of the room.

"You want to negotiate or you want me to blow your brains out?" Hunter growled.

Federico's face was twisted with anger and dark with defeat. "Tell me what you want."

"All shooting stops. Now."

"Fine—if you and your operatives get your business out of my cartel." Montilla's successor spit at Hunter's feet. "And do not come back."

"As long as you agree to leave Valeria, Laila, and Jorge alone for good. No coming after them, no stalking, no threatening, no—"

"They were Montilla's concerns, and he is dead. That makes me boss now. Those women are not my whores, the kid is not my son, and I am not a foolish, sentimental old man. If they swear to stay far away from all things related to the business, I will not bother them."

"We want money," Laila called out. "For our years of suffering."

Trees cursed under his breath. "You're playing with fire..."

"I am making sure my sister is secure." She tried to untangle her fingers from his and face down Federico.

Trees was having none of that, protecting her with his own body as he led her to the new drug lord.

"How much?" Federico sneered.

"Five million." The amount was a pittance to an operation like Tierra Caliente but everything to her family. "Cash."

Federico didn't even blink. "If you and your sister agree to relinquish any right to future profits, yes."

"We will." Gladly. She wanted no part of that life. Valeria would agree.

"And everyone walks out of here alive. We all go our separate ways without another shot being fired or another punch being thrown?" Hunter pressed. "Without any vendettas being issued."

"Agreed...in exchange for the other concession you promised. I want Victor Ramos."

Of course he did. Victor had been trying to undermine the senior Montilla and the Tierra Caliente hierarchy since Emilo died, not merely because he'd hated the old man. He'd wanted the power for himself. Naturally, the new management of the organization wouldn't stand for that. They would want Victor snuffed out at all costs.

He deserved it.

"Done," Laila answered.

Hunter jerked his stare in her direction.

She raised a brow back at him. "What use do you have for him? Did you think to turn him over to your American justice system where justice is almost never served? Where he could too easily use his money and pull strings to walk free so he can continue to torment me?"

Hunter hesitated, then glanced at Logan and Joaquin. When they both nodded, he scowled. "Fine. You and all your boys disarm. Let us get our wounded out. You can do the same. We'll be back with Victor."

Federico nodded, then met her stare. "I can have the cash brought here as well. Then I expect never to see you, your sister, or your nephew ever again."

"Nothing would make us happier."

The new boss and his men left their weapons with Deke Trenton and Jack Cole, who stood over a dusty reception counter against one wall. Federico snapped at some of his grunts to carry out their dead, including Montilla, who, despite his threats and demands, had never once held his son.

Good. That man's tainted blood already ran in her nephew's veins. Jorge didn't need the stench of his touch, too. Laila didn't know what Valeria would tell her son someday about his father. She hoped by then her sister had found a good man who would be a positive male role model for the boy so he never succumbed to the evil half of his genes.

At her side, Trees took her in his arms, his gaze watchful as Matt helped an injured Trevor, who had been shot in the shoulder. Joaquin offered a hand to Ghost, who cursed and clutched his middle like he had some bruised ribs.

"Is that the extent of our injuries?" Trees asked Hunter.

"Yeah. One-Mile saved our asses. I called him on his honeymoon in Maui and flew his ass out here, and... Speak of the devil."

Walker strode through what had once been the front door, sniper rifle in hand, and headed straight for her. "You all right, Laila?"

She nodded, realizing what had happened. "You shot Montilla?"

"When he had the gun to your head, yes."

Trees looked taken aback—and horribly pissed off—at the news. "The asshole had a gun to your head?"

Laila squeezed his hand. "I am fine. Thank you, Señor Walker. I owe you a giant debt."

"You don't. You helped me escape your brother-in-law's compound last fall. Without you, I would have died and rotted in that place. As far as I'm concerned, the score is even."

Trees stuck out his hand. "Thanks. If anything had happened to her…"

"I get it. Being in love and having something to lose? It's terrifying." One-Mile shook his hand. "I'm, um…sorry I accused you of being EM Security's mole."

"I didn't love it, but it was the logical conclusion. Next time, maybe confront me to my face?"

"Sure. And I'll give you the benefit of the doubt first."

"That would be great." Trees smiled.

"Trees!"

Laila looked up to find Zy entering the big space and, with Kane's help, dragging Victor inside. Valeria trailed behind them, holding Jorge close.

"Hey, buddy." Trees smiled.

"You good, man? You look like shit."

"Aww, you're just being nice."

"What are friends for?" Zy teased as he stopped with Victor in the middle of the room.

Her former rapist and tormentor still had venom in his eyes, but he also had the good sense to look afraid. She didn't feel an ounce of pity for him. Perhaps someone better would be looking into their heart to find forgiveness. Laila couldn't lie. She was just looking forward to his death.

"This is your fault, *puta*," he snarled.

"Shut the fuck up." Trees barreled toward him.

Laila held him back, loving that he wanted to protect her. But confronting Victor was something she needed to do herself. "No, it is yours. You chose to violate me as a child, over and over, using me for your sick pleasure. But you made me stronger. You made me a fighter. And because of that, you made me the instrument of your demise."

"Are you going to shoot me yourself? Is that your little revenge?" He sneered. "I doubt you have the stomach."

Laila realized she could do it now. She had a gun. No one would stop her. Federico might be put out that he didn't get to torture Victor before ending him, but ultimately the new drug lord wanted this piece of trash dead.

Still, killing Victor quickly would be too easy and merciful for him. And she refused to waste more time and attention on this scum. Besides, she wasn't violent. Trees had shown her a path to happiness. Why taint her soul with vengeance when she could take his hand and embrace her future?

"You are right. So I will simply say good-bye—my way." She stepped closer.

"Laila…" Trees warned.

"*Hermana!*" Valeria gasped.

She sent them both soft, reassuring glances. Then she released Trees's comforting grip and faced Victor. Her smile turned cutting. And she spit in his face.

He blanched, his eyes shooting fire as he lunged for her. Zy and Kane held him back, each with an unyielding grip on one of his arms.

"Pipe down, motherfucker," Zy growled, then turned to her. "Got more for him?"

"He deserves it. Go on," Trees encouraged, pointing a gun in his face. "And if he tries anything…"

Of course her beloved would shoot him. Trees was protective, and he hated this bastard. But it was more. He wanted her to close this chapter of her life and not regret walking away without getting whatever justice she could.

"Just one thing." Because she knew that whatever Federico had planned for Victor would be far more horrific and painful than anything she could dream up.

Laila braced herself on Victor's arms. He trembled with rage. She ignored him completely—until she used all her might to drive her knee into his balls.

He groaned and doubled over, falling to his knees.

Laila stood over him. "You are a pedophile and a rapist and a piece of shit. You deserve everything coming to you."

Behind him, she caught sight of Federico's men returning. A new arrival in a suit hovered outside, looking very official and carrying a briefcase. The rest rushed in, heading straight for Victor with cuffs, old-school tools, and evil smiles.

"Mr. Ramos, what a pleasure to see you already on your knees." Federico grabbed Victor by the hair and yanked his head back cruelly. "It is the perfect position for you."

Then he motioned to two of his men, who took Zy's and Kane's places and dragged a struggling Victor across the room. They cuffed one arm to a decorative bracket under the counter. The other they restrained to the nearby door handle. When they were done, one thug whipped out a pair of pliers.

The man's awful grin sent shudders down Laila's spine—and left her no doubt that Victor wouldn't leave here alive. "Give me your tongue."

Federico motioned her and Valeria outside. They followed, as did Trees, watching as Chavez took the briefcase from the suit's hands and handed it to Laila. "The money for you ladies." He sent her an amused glance. "It is good to be the hero, yes?"

The words echoed exactly those she had exchanged with Montilla's informant. "It *was* you I texted with."

He nodded. "It is also good to keep your own best interests in mind."

Those words rolled around in Laila's head until she realized what he meant. "You told me where to find Kimber because you wanted Montilla weakened for your own purposes."

"She did not belong there, and your lover nearly did the job for me when he shot the old man. But Montilla came out of his coma last week, forcing me to regroup. You and your sister's perfectly timed message gave me exactly what I needed to wrest control for good. It is fortunate, indeed, that both of you want nothing to do with the organization."

Or he would have killed them without a second thought. She suppressed a shiver. "Nothing at all."

"Ever," Valeria chimed in, clutching Jorge tight. "Neither will my son."

"Excellent. This concludes our business, then. Mr. Edgington." He nodded at Hunter, who exited the hospital and headed straight for them, Logan and Joaquin in tow. "You and your men have been admirable adversaries. I hope this is where we part ways?"

Hunter scowled. "I fucking hate what you do for a living, but it's not my job or my crusade to put you down, especially since, if I did, another you would only spring up tomorrow."

"It is wise to know the battles you cannot win. I wish you safe travels," he murmured, as if he was a gracious host, not a criminal boss.

Before he could return inside, Laila grabbed Chavez's arm. "I want to know how Ramos will die."

The man smiled. "Bloodthirsty, huh? If I did not have a wife I loved with all my heart, you would be a very interesting woman to tame."

Trees pulled her back, against his big, protective body. "She's going to be *my* wife."

"And you will ensure she stays out of my business?"

"Damn straight."

"Good man." Federico turned his attention back to her. "My men will end Victor Ramos and make it as torturous as possible. I am not sure quite how. You are welcome to stay and watch."

In a way, his offer was tempting. A part of her wanted to see Victor's awful end. But her heart had other ideas. That part of her didn't want to spend another moment in the past or fixated on violence. She'd rather look forward, embrace happiness, and start her future. Now that her family was safe and their tomorrows were secure, it was time.

"No. I have a life to live." With the man she loved.

"A wise choice. I wish you all health and happiness. Goodbye." Chavez nodded their way one last time, then sauntered back into the abandoned hospital just as Victor's screams began to tear through the night.

Laila ignored them and kissed her sister's cheek, then laid a soft kiss on her nephew's forehead before handing her the briefcase. "For you."

Valeria shook her head, then settled the money back in Laila's grip. "Keep it. I took much more from Emilo before I left, and you deserve every penny."

"You're sure?"

"Positive. Perhaps you and Trees could use it to start your married life?"

Laila frowned. "Are you going somewhere?"

"Back to St. Louis, I think. It felt like home to me. I enjoyed the seasons. I liked my neighborhood. I made friends. It is a place to start."

Laila frowned. After fighting so hard for her family, they wouldn't be staying together after all? "But…"

"You thought I would remain in Louisiana? Follow wherever you went?" Valeria shook her head. "You do not need me anymore. And I must stand on my own two feet. I will raise my son and, hopefully, find a good man someday. In the meantime, I think I will go to beauty school. That sounds…nice."

Laila took her sister's hand. "I will miss you and Jorge, but I want you to be happy."

"For the first time ever, I will. You have taught me so much about being brave." Valeria squeezed her fingers. "I can move forward now. I love you."

Then she turned away and murmured something to Kane, who escorted her to the van, opened the door, and sealed her inside.

Trees led her away from the others, under the moonlight and away from the sounds of Victor's pain. Then he took her face in his hands. "You okay, little one?"

She turned to him, visually tracing every cut, scrape, bruise, and scab. "Are you? We should get you to a doctor."

"When we get stateside. But I'm fine. No, I'm great. I have you, so I have everything." He settled a kiss on her forehead. "You scared me in there."

"I was terrified of losing you."

He shook his head. "You can't lose me, honey. From the first moment I saw you, I was yours. Nothing's changed."

Her face softened as her heart melted. "When I met you, I did not believe there was such a thing as a good man. But God blessed me with the best when He sent you to rescue me. I am sorry for all I've put you through. But I swear I am yours forever. I want to marry you, Forest Scott."

Thrill crossed his face, followed by a frown of regret. "I wanted to propose to you the right way. I wanted to put you in a pretty dress, take you to dinner, then get down on one knee with a sparkling ring and find the perfect words."

She set the briefcase at her feet and clutched his arms. "I do not need any of those things. I only need you. I love you."

"I love you, too, honey. Let me take you home now so we can start our forever."

CHAPTER
Eleven

June
Four months later

T he day dawned perfect. Trees opened his eyes, vowing this was the last time he'd ever wake up in his bed alone.

Today, Laila would finally become his wife.

She'd spent last night at a cozy bed-and-breakfast doing "girl things" with Valeria, Kimber, and Tessa—who had recently returned from her honeymoon—along with Brea Walker and the bosses' wives, Kata, Tara, and Bailey. Laila had called around eleven last night, seeming very carefree and something he thought he would never hear his bride-to-be sound like—giggly.

Apparently, all the wives had started dishing their best marital advice, some of which had been hysterical. Then Alyssa Traverson had stopped in with a decadent dessert from her restaurant, Bonheur. Delaney Murphy tagged along because she'd needed a break from the testosterone overload at her house, where she and her husband were raising their boys—ages four, two, and nine months. Then she'd announced that the baby she was expecting was another boy. Amid the hearty congratulations and good-natured teasing, Delaney had laughed and swore she felt blessed.

If Trees had his way, he and Laila would have a big family. He'd already made plans to expand the house—and none too soon. They hadn't told anyone except Valeria, Zy, and Tessa, but Laila was eleven weeks pregnant. Finally, the morning sickness was nearly over. Second trimester hormones had arrived early, and Laila was hungry for him all. The. Time.

Trees was the happiest bastard on the planet.

After a quick roll through his morning routine, he woke Zy on the futon in his home office. Barney loped into the house after his morning kibble and licked Kane awake on the sofa, who came up sputtering.

Holding in his laughter was impossible.

"Bastard," Kane grumbled, but he was smiling as he petted the big dog.

Then Trees stood at the opening of his guest room and stared at the two people whose presence here surprised him most—his two brothers, Nash and Wade.

Trees hadn't seen them in over a dozen years. When he'd left home, Nash had been a gawky fourteen, just beginning to grow hair in interesting places and sprout up. Wade had been a rambunctious twelve, still more interested in any sport with a ball than contact with a girl. Now they were grown-ass men—and about his height. It was a novel experience to walk into the room and not be the tallest dude there.

But while last night's bachelor party of music, whiskey, poker, and horribly inappropriate jokes had been great, it was the deepening relationships—the roots—that made Trees happiest of all. He had family now. Real family, defined not only by blood but by loyalty, respect, and honor. That, along with Laila's love, had mended the hole he'd carried in his heart since leaving home at eighteen. Not only were he and Zy closer than ever, but his circle was expanding. Kane was rapidly becoming both a friend he enjoyed and a peer he relied on. And having the contact with his biological brothers he firmly believed would go beyond this weekend was the cherry on top. And that wasn't all...

"Up and at 'em, boys," he called to his brothers.

They both jackknifed out of bed in their boxers, looking sleep-deprived and hung over.

"Holy fuck." Nash gave a bleary-eyed glance at the first stirrings of sunrise out the window. "What time is it?"

"Oh-dark-thirty." Wade winced. "My goddamn head..."

Trees just grinned. "What time did you boys finally turn in?"

They looked at each other, then Nash shook his head. "No comment. But we'll try to keep the bitching to a minimum since it's your big day."

"Much appreciated." Trees winked. "So who spent the night with the stripper?"

Everyone had pitched in to send him female entertainment. Trees hadn't been interested in the blonde with fake assets. His very single brothers, on the other hand...

They exchanged another glance. "No comment."

He held in a laugh. If they'd tag-teamed her, he didn't want to know. "You're picking up the folks at noon?"

"We'll be at the church no later than twelve thirty," Nash promised. "Kellyanne and Wren flew in last night, too, so we'll bring them along."

Trees was really looking forward to seeing two of his sisters. In fact, his whole family had been thrilled when he'd reached out with the news of his engagement. And so welcoming. Though his other three sisters—Audrey, Lydia, and Daisy—were unable to attend the wedding due to jobs or family obligations, they had sent their well wishes and love.

When his parents had arrived, their reunion had thankfully been more sweet than bitter. They were in a different phase of life now and had apologized for their shortcomings decades ago. Their words and assurances—along with Laila's devotion—had gone a long way to assuring him that he was wanted and loved. Forgiving his parents had been easy. Becoming a family again had been even easier. And his parents absolutely adored Laila.

His whole life was coming together. Now the day just had to hurry up so the most incredible, brave, clever, beautiful woman he knew would finally be his wife.

A text alerted him that he had company at the outer perimeter of his security. He pressed a few buttons to let Matt in, then met him at the door.

"Hey." Trees stuck out his hand. "Welcome back."

Matt shook it, pulled him in for a bro hug, then handed him a box of donuts. "Whew. I wasn't sure I'd make it back to town in one piece."

"Since when is a tech conference dangerous? Something go down in New Orleans?"

"Not like you're thinking, but every time the client turned his back, his just-turned-forty-and-so-fucking-horny wife jumped me. Dodging her wasn't fun."

Trees laughed. "Used your evasive maneuvers, huh?"

"I had to. Jesus, the number of times she grabbed my junk in the car…" He sighed. "I need to get laid. I've batted a huge zero in this town since I rolled in."

Mostly because he hadn't had time to troll the bars, Trees suspected. Matt was a good-looking SOB. The quiet cowboy thing would get a lot of female attention—as soon as he wasn't working all the damn time. "Well, weddings are a target-rich environment, my friend. You never know." Then he realized exactly who Matt needed to meet. "Remind me to introduce you to Madison."

"The girl Tessa offered to introduce me to after she turned me down?" Matt didn't look thrilled.

"Madison is cute and really sweet."

"No, thanks. I'm not up for a pity date, man."

Trees thought Matt was missing out, but he just shrugged. "Suit yourself."

All the men congregated in the kitchen. The remnants of last night's cigar-and-booze fest had been cleared away. They all chowed down on coffee and donuts and some bacon that Kane and Zy nuked. His brothers opted for java with an ibuprofen chaser. Then after showers all around, they were off to the church, tuxedos in protective bags.

Two hours before the ceremony, Trees was ready and pacing the floor impatiently, Laila's simple wedding band jingling in his pocket, burning a hole.

Trees texted her. `Let's get married now.`

She sent back a laughing-crying emoji. `No, my love. Two o'clock. I am still getting ready.`

`You're beautiful as you are. I just want you to be mine.`

`Very soon.` She sent him a heart and a kiss emoji, then followed with another text. `Then tonight, you are mine.`

Amen to that.

Since returning from Mexico and finally getting free of the cartel, Laila had blossomed. Sure, she'd missed her sister when Valeria had decided to take Jorge and return to St. Louis. But that had prompted Laila to come out of her shell and make friends, first with Tessa, then with some of the other wives.

She had also taken in the briefcase of money Federico Chavez had handed her and funded causes like drug rehab centers, women's shelters, and counseling for cartel victims. The only funds she had used for herself were for college, which she would start after the baby was born. Laila wasn't sure exactly what she wanted to do with her degree, except help children who had been the victims of assholes like the Ramos brothers.

Trees thanked God every day that Laila's personal nightmare was over. Sure, he'd put Hector six feet under while helping Zy and Tessa rescue Hallie from her abductors—and thankfully the little girl didn't remember anything. But Victor had been another matter.

A few days after leaving Victor to Chavez's dubious mercy, his corpse had turned up, horribly mutilated. Laila had breathed a sigh of relief. News reports had expressed horror about the brutal torture Victor Ramos had endured, but Trees considered it karma. Laila hadn't been able to look at the pictures, but Trees had, and he was still convinced that, despite Victor having all the dangling parts of his body severed before death, that he'd still had gotten off easier. After all, Victor had suffered for mere days. Laila had endured six long years.

His phone buzzed again. I love you. Laila sent more heart emojis.

I love you, too. He wasn't much for emojis, but he sent a heart back, along with an eggplant, a honey pot, and water droplets. Their wedding night was coming up, after all.

She sent another laughing-crying emoji.

Trees checked his watch again and almost groaned. Fuck, it was taking forever to marry this woman.

Finally Nash and Wade showed up at the church with his parents and sisters. He was not only grateful to see his family but damn glad to have something to take his mind off his impatience.

"Hey, Mom and Dad. Wow, Kellyanne and Wren, you've both grown up." He opened the door wide for them, marveling. Wren had been little more than a baby last time he'd seen her. "Thanks for coming early."

"Do we need to talk you off a ledge?" Kellyanne teased.

"No. I just… This needs to hurry up."

His mother laughed, her eyes seemingly brighter now that her hair had gone silvery. "We're so thrilled for you, son. And you look so handsome in your tuxedo."

He had worn a monkey suit a handful of times in his life, and rental shops always had fits when he walked in, but he'd had to admit he'd cleaned up pretty well. "Thanks."

His dad hugged him, then clapped his shoulder. "You ready for marriage and all it comes with?"

"I am. Laila and I are beyond excited." He'd tell them they were about to be grandparents again later. He already knew they'd be thrilled.

"Lots of compromising..." his dad said so cheerfully, he obviously loved married life.

"I'm learning that. Laila has already seen fit to redecorate the house to make it 'homier.'" Trees grudgingly admitted he loved everything about it. Barney especially appreciated sleeping indoors more, the upgrade in his food, and the extra love. She was going to make an amazing mother.

"Seriously, you look so happy." Kellyanne kissed his cheek.

"Congratulations." Wren did the same.

He hugged them all, then his family filed out and took their seats.

Time flew in a blur of activity then. Everyone was busy, except his brothers, who slumped in the corner and tried to sleep off their hangovers. The reverend came in, and they shook hands. Then Zy took Laila's ring and slipped it into his pocket before they all headed to the altar.

Finally, Laila was almost his.

The little white church was full of flowers and cheer as music started. Hallie and Jorge toddled down the aisle together, dressed so cutely their guests oohed and laughed. Tessa's daughter threw pink rose petals, smiled like the ham she was, dancing to the altar. Jorge followed in his little tux, ring pillow in hand, looking deer-in-the-headlights as he headed to the front, where Kata and Tara Edgington waited for them both with pieces of candy and high-fives.

Once the children were settled in the front row, Kimber walked down the aisle in a delicate V-neck dress in a shade somewhere between pink and beige. Tessa glided to the front of the church, dressed similarly, except her gown was draped across one shoulder, leaving the other bare. A glance at his best friend told Trees that Zy only had eyes for his wife, and their love for each other was palpable. Finally, Valeria made her way to the altar in a strapless dress of the same color, holding a bouquet of soft summer flowers—and finally looking at peace.

Then the music changed again. Everyone rose. Trees held his breath, his heart chugging wildly.

The most beautiful bride ever walked toward him, a vision in dark curls, white lace, and a smile of radiant joy. She beamed with love. He could feel it in the way she looked at him as she approached, one graceful step at a time, never taking her eyes off his.

God, he felt so humbled, his devotion for his bride so thick it almost choked him.

Finally, Laila stood before him, fitting her hands into his, trusting him with her body, her heart, and the rest of her life.

In front of their friends and family, he vowed to love, honor, and cherish her, forsaking all others for the rest of his life. Trees didn't think that would be hard. He was already doing it happily.

Laila spoke the same words in return, tearing up as she bound her future to his.

They exchanged rings. He was gratified that Laila's fit her finger perfectly, and he was touched to find her hand shaking as she slid the titanium band onto his finger while swearing she would love him until the end of time.

Then finally, the minister told Trees to kiss his bride.

"About damn time," he murmured for her ears alone.

Through her happy tears, she smiled, and Trees swore he'd do whatever he could to put that smile of pure joy on her face every day.

Their lips clung. He breathed her in as he soaked in the moment—his first as her husband. The rightness of that hit him in the heart, and in some ways, Trees felt as if he was just starting his life.

Then he took her hand and ushered her back down the aisle. He'd love to keep running straight to their tricked-out honeymoon suite he'd booked at a posh hotel in Baton Rouge before they left for a week at a cabin on the lake where he'd spent summers as a kid. She wanted to know more about his childhood while he taught her to fish. He was dying to show her all about cuffs, blindfolds, and clamps while he reminded her how to scream.

First, they had to make it through the reception.

After an amazing toast from Zy that made everyone both laugh and cry, Valeria followed with a moving speech about her sister's tenacity in the face of adversity and the strength of Trees's love for her against all odds. There was clapping, crying, and hugs all around.

Dancing followed, first Trees leading his gorgeous wife onto the floor for a slow love song. He held her and kissed her and thanked God again for bringing Laila into his life and making it so much better.

At the end, he took her lips again to the sound of their guests clapping. "Can we leave now?"

She sent him a chiding grin. "We have not even cut our cake."

"I can live without cake. I don't think I can live without you, wife."

Her smile glowed with love. "I cannot live without you, either, husband. But you must be patient because I am not skipping our cake."

They ceded the dance floor to their guests. Brea and Pierce Walker slipped in to congratulate them with hugs. The birth of their son, Ryker, three weeks ago, had been joyous but exhausting. Brea was still recovering—and having new-mom jitters about leaving their son for long, even with her dad and stepmom.

Trees shook hands with the sniper.

Pierce's answering smile was genuine. "How's it feel to be married?"

"Amazing."

"It is." He took his wife's hand and kissed her fingers. "Congratulations, man. I'm happy for you."

They hadn't always seen eye-to-eye, but over the last couple of months…they were getting there. Trees would forever owe the man for saving Laila's life. "You, too. Hope you're enjoying fatherhood."

"I am. It's a lot, but…wow. It's a love you can't even comprehend. You'll see someday."

Sooner than someday, but Trees kept that to himself for now.

"Look." Laila pointed across the room discreetly to the familiar guy not actually wearing his cowboy hat today.

Despite Matt's insistence otherwise, he had approached Madison, who was dressed in a flattering pastel purple dress. The cowboy was flirting hardcore and showing off those dimples. She didn't look immune.

"Good for them." He grinned.

"Fingers crossed," Laila whispered as the two made it onto the dance floor, where Matt spun Madison into his arms and held tight. "They are both good people who deserve to be happy."

"I don't think they need luck." Even across the room, he could feel their chemistry.

Tessa sidled up to them then. "You're seeing this, right?"

Trees smiled. "Yes, ma'am."

"I tried to tell him."

"Me, too. But I think he's on board now."

"I think you're right," she drawled, then laughed and kissed Zy like a newlywed should.

The deejay called him and Laila up to the front to cut their cake. The photographer took a billion pictures, and Trees nearly lost his mind with impatience, but his wife slid a bite of the sweet dessert onto his tongue, and he groaned as the flavor exploded in his mouth. He did the same to her, then they heeded the clinking of forks against glasses and kissed.

"Speech. Speech. Speech!" the crowd chanted.

Reluctantly, he pulled away from Laila's lips and wrapped his arm around her as Zy brought him the mic. "Thank you, everyone, for coming today to celebrate my wedding to the most amazing woman, the one God put on this planet just for me. Probably because she's the only one who can put up with me."

Their guests laughed, and Laila shook her head, mouthing, *I love you.*

Trees pressed a peck to her lips again. If he took the kiss any deeper, he would only get lost in her sweetness, so he pulled back. "When people ask where we first met, I say an alley. When they ask where we first fell in love, I admit it's an RV. Our courtship wasn't glamorous, and nothing has been easy. But there's no one I want to do life with other than you, Laila Scott. I love you, now and always."

Guests aahed and wiped their tears while he sent Laila a questioning glance. Did she want to share their baby news with everyone else yet?

She gave him a little shake of her head. It was their special secret, just for them...just for a bit longer.

He nodded in agreement, then they sealed their love and their special day with a kiss that convinced him all over again that they belonged together forever.

Epilogue

July
10 p.m.
Three years later

Matt Montgomery cursed as he stared out the window at the pouring rain. He'd lived here for three years and there were still things he didn't understand about this goddamn state. Like swamps everywhere, hungry gators, and a community who spoke a version of French that sounded nothing like the language he'd learned in high school. As if that wasn't head-scratching enough, now he had to contend with a summer rain that lasted for days and felt like a hot, sticky blanket.

Why did he still live here? Right, because he liked the people and the Southern hospitality. He loved his job.

And you keep hoping she'll *come home…*

With a curse, he turned away and paced the house he'd been renting since deciding not to return to Wyoming. He had no business thinking of Madison Archer. Or rather, Madison Archer-Pershing. It had been three years since Trees and Laila's wedding, when he'd spent that absolutely mind-blowing weekend in a hotel suite, sharing champagne, cheese fries, laughs, and great sex with her. Now, she was very much married to some bigwig senator's son. She'd moved out of the bayou and moved up to the world of wealth and influence—two things he could never give her.

That realization was the big turd on top of a giant shit sundae.

His phone buzzed and he pulled it from his pocket, praying it was work. He could use a little adrenaline and action to take his mind off Madison and spice up his night.

Instead, it was a text message from Casey, his latest friend-with-benefits. As usual, she didn't beat around the bush.

`Rain turns me on. Let's fuck.`

Normally, he would. In fact, since news of Madison's engagement to Senator Winston Pershing's grandson, Todd, had splashed across newscasts and social media, Matt hadn't turned many offers down. A hookup at a bar here and a sexy neighbor sleepover there? Why not? A blind date? A flight attendant? A random hookup at a grocery store? Check, check, and check. Hell, even a former client, a gym pal's little sister, and an ex's best friend. He'd totally been game. When he'd met Casey at a community food festival and they'd gotten to talking about mutual acquaintances, she'd pointed out he'd already fucked two of her friends. They'd apparently left with smiles, and she wanted some of that for herself. At the time, it had seemed perfect.

Two weeks later, he wasn't interested anymore.

Why not? Dude, she isn't coming back. Move the fuck on.

Good advice, especially since he was pretty sure he'd soon be hearing about Madison having kids with that stuffy blue blood. God, he was a stupid ass, because the thought of her in bed with the entitled prick made Matt homicidal. He really should get laid.

He just didn't want to, not by Casey. Not by anyone else he could think of.

Just Madison.

How the fuck had she ruined him in forty-eight hours?

Matt sighed, grabbed a beer, downed half of it, then headed back to the window. She was out there, somewhere. Probably at some pompous, ten-thousand-dollar-a-plate fundraiser, rubbing elbows with people who would look down on him for making a living by his gun.

Fuck them. And fuck her. Whether he wanted to or not, he was going to fuck Casey tonight.

Retrieving his phone, he started to tap out a response when he suddenly heard a tap at his window that startled the hell out of him. He reared back, then saw a face on the other side of the glass. Ball cap, sunglasses, baggy T-shirt plastered to a slight frame. No distinguishing features or tattoos. At first glance, it looked like a teenage boy. But the face had a softness... Smooth, fair skin, gracefully arched brows, and a delicately sloped jaw.

Why the fuck would the kid be out in the pouring rain after ten o'clock at night? Hell, why would he avoid the covered porch, rather than knock on the front door?

The kid wouldn't...unless there was trouble.

Matt unlocked the window and raised it a fraction, aware of his gun a mere split second from his grasp.

"Yeah?"

"Matt?"

That voice. Not a boy at all. Definitely a woman.

One he knew.

No, that was impossible. It couldn't be... But a second glance had him rethinking his assessment.

Holy shit.

His heart slammed against his chest. "Madison?"

She gave him a shaky nod, then looked behind her as if she expected the bogeyman to jump her. "Yes. I'm sorry to barge in—"

"You're not." If she was here, if she was hiding in his bushes and disguising herself as she approached his house late at night in the rain, there was something terribly wrong. "What's going on?"

"I-I need help, and I didn't know anyone else I could trust." She swallowed, and he saw the abject terror on her face. "My husband is trying to kill me."

The End

Ready to continue your Wicked & Devoted journey? Get the lowdown on all the pent-up sizzle when Matt and Madison reunite after three long years!

WICKED AS SECRETS
Matt and Madison, Part One
Wicked & Devoted, Book 7
By Shayla Black

(will be available in eBook, print, and audio)

Coming April 11, 2023!

Want to know first about new releases, excerpts, covers, and freebies? Join my VIP newsletter at ShaylaBlack.com!

Interested in signed Shayla Black print books, cool bookish merch, or early access to Shayla's latest eBooks? Visit the Shayla Store at Shayla-Black.com.

Thank you for reading Wicked and Forever! If you enjoyed this book, please review and/or recommend it to your reader friends. That means the world to me!

WICKED AS SECRETS
Matt and Madison, Part One
Wicked & Devoted, Book 7
By Shayla Black
(will be available in eBook, print, and audio)

Coming April 11, 2023!

The exciting continuation of the Wicked & Devoted series, Wicked as Secrets (Matt and Madison, part one), available April 11, 2023.

If you missed the beginning of the suspenseful, addictive Wicked & Devoted series, catch up with the sexiest bad boy meets good girl story, Wicked as Sin!

WICKED AS SIN
One-Mile & Brea, Part One
Wicked & Devoted, Book 1
By Shayla Black
NOW AVAILABLE!
(eBook, Print, and audio)

She begged him to rescue his enemy from death. In exchange, he demanded her body...

Pierce "One-Mile" Walker has always kept his heart under wraps and his head behind his sniper's scope. Nothing about buttoned-up Brea Bell should appeal to him. But after a single glance at the pretty preacher's daughter, he doesn't care that his past is less than shiny, that he gets paid to end lives...or that she's his teammate's woman. He'll do whatever it takes to steal her heart.

Brea has always been a dutiful daughter and a good girl...until she meets the dangerous warrior. He's everything she shouldn't want, especially after her best friend introduces her to his fellow operative as his girlfriend—to protect her from Pierce. But he's a forbidden temptation she's finding impossible to resist.

Then fate strikes, forcing Brea to beg Pierce to help solve a crisis. But his skills come at a price. When her innocent flirtations run headlong into his obsession, they cross the line into a passion so fiery she can't say no. Soon, his past rears its head and a vendetta calls his name in a mission gone horribly wrong. Will he survive to fight his way back to the woman who claimed his soul?

EXCERPT

Sunday, January 11
Sunset, Louisiana

Finally, he had her cornered. He intended to tear down every last damn obstacle between him and Brea Bell.

Right now.

For months, she'd succumbed to fears, buried her head in the sand, even lied. He'd tried to be understanding and patient. He'd made mistakes, but damn it, he'd put her first, given her space, been the good guy.

Fuck that. Now that he'd fought his way here, she would see the real him.

One-Mile Walker slammed the door of his Jeep and turned all his focus on the modest white cottage with its vintage blue door. As he marched up the long concrete driveway, his heart pounded. He had a nasty idea how Brea's father would respond when he explained why he'd come. The man would slam the door in his face; no maybe about that. After all, he was the bad boy from a broken home who had defiled Reverend Bell's perfect daughter with unholy glee.

But One-Mile refused to let Brea go again. He'd make her father listen…somehow. Since punching the guy in the face was out of the question, he'd have to quell his brute-force instinct to fight dirty and instead employ polish, tact, and charm—all the qualities he possessed zero of.

Fuck. This was going to be a shit show.

Still, One-Mile refused to give up. He'd known uphill battles his whole life. What was one more?

Through the house's front window, he spotted the soft doe eyes that had haunted him since last summer. Though Brea was talking to an elderly couple, the moment she saw him approach her porch, her pretty eyes went wide with shock.

Determination gripped One-Mile and squeezed his chest. By damned, she was going to listen, too.

He wasn't leaving without making her his.

As he mounted the first step toward her door, his cell phone rang. He would have ignored it if it hadn't been for two critical facts: His job often entailed saving the world as the people knew it, and this particular chime he only heard when one of the men he respected most in this fucked-up world needed him during the grimmest of emergencies.

Of all the lousy timing…

He yanked the device from his pocket. "Walker here. Colonel?"

"Yeah."

Colonel Caleb Edgington was a retired, highly decorated military officer and a tough son of a bitch. One thing he wasn't prone to was drama, so that single foreboding syllable told One-Mile that whatever had prompted this call was dire.

He didn't bother with small talk, even though it had been months since they'd spoken, and he wondered how the man was enjoying both his fifties and his new wife, but they'd catch up later. Now, they had no time to waste.

"What can I do for you?" Since he owed Caleb a million times over, whatever the man needed, One-Mile would make happen.

Caleb's sons might be his bosses these days…but as far as One-Mile was concerned, the jury was still out on that trio. Speaking of which, why wasn't Caleb calling those badasses?

One-Mile could only think of one answer. It was hardly comforting.

"Or should I just ask who I need to kill?"

A soft, feminine gasp sent his gaze jerking up to Brea, who now stood in the doorway, her rosy bow of a mouth gaping open in a perfect little *O*. She'd heard that. *Goddamn it to hell.* Yeah, she knew perfectly well what he was. But he'd managed to shock her repeatedly over the last six months.

"I'm not sure yet." Caleb sounded cautious in his ear. "I'm going to text you an address. Can you meet me there in fifteen minutes?"

For months, he'd been anticipating this exact moment with Brea. "Any chance it can wait an hour?"

"No. Every moment is critical."

Since Caleb would never say such things lightly, One-Mile didn't see that he had an option. "On my way."

He ended the call and pocketed the phone as he climbed onto the porch and gave Brea his full attention. He had so little time with her, but he'd damn sure get his point across before he went.

She stepped outside and shut the door behind her, swallowing nervously as she cast a furtive glance over her shoulder, through the big picture window. Was she hoping her father didn't see them?

"Pierce." Her whisper sounded closer to a hiss. "What are you doing here?"

He hated when anyone else used his given name, but Brea could call him whatever the hell she wanted as long as she let him in her life.

He peered down at her, considering how to answer. He'd had grand plans to lay his cards out on the table and do whatever he had to —talk, coax, hustle, schmooze—until she and her father came around to his way of thinking. Now he only had time to cut to the chase. "You know what I want, pretty girl. I'm here for you. And when I come back, I won't take no for an answer."

Don't forget to grab the gripping conclusion of this unforgettable couple…

WICKED EVER AFTER
One-Mile and Brea, Part Two
Wicked & Devoted, Book 2
By Shayla Black
NOW AVAILABLE!
(eBook, Print, and audio)

The good girl is keeping a secret? He'll seduce it out of her until she begs to be his.

WICKED & DEVOTED WORLD

Thank you for joining me in the Wicked & Devoted world. If you didn't know, this cast of characters started in my Wicked Lovers world, continued into my Devoted Lovers series, and have collided here. During Trees and Laila's journey, you've read about some other characters and you might be wondering if I've told their story. Or if I will tell their story in the future. Below is a guide in case you'd like to read more from this cast, listed in order of release:

WICKED LOVERS

Wicked Ties

Jack Cole and Morgan O'Malley

She didn't know what she wanted until he made her beg for it…

Decadent

Deke Trenton (and Kimber Edgington)

The boss' innocent daughter. A forbidden favor he can't refuse…

Delicious

Luc Traverson (and Alyssa Devereaux)

He can't control his desire…and that's just the way she wants it.

Surrender to Me

Hunter Edgington (and Katalina Muñoz)

A secret fantasy. An uncontrollable obsession. A forever love?

Belong to Me

Logan Edgington (and Tara Jacobs)

He's got everything under control until he falls for his first love…again.

Wicked All the Way

Caleb Edgington (and Carlotta Muñoz Buckley)

Could their second chance be their first real love?

Mine to Hold

Tyler Murphy (and Delaney Catalano)

His best friend's ex. A night he can't forget. A secret that could destroy them both.

Ours to Love

Javier and Xander Santiago (and London McLane)

Two estranged brothers. A virgin with a past. A danger that could destroy them all.

Theirs to Cherish

Mitchell Thorpe and Sean Mackenzie (and Callie Ward)

A woman on the run falls for two enemies who both refuse to let her go…

His to Take

Joaquin Muñoz (and Bailey Benson)

Giving in to her dark stranger might be the most delicious danger of all…

Falling in Deeper

Stone Sutter (and Lily "Sweet Pea" Taylor)

Will her terrifying past threaten their passionate future?

DEVOTED LOVERS

Devoted to Pleasure

Cutter Bryant (and Shealyn West)

A bodyguard should never fall for his client…but she's too tempting to refuse.

Devoted to Love

Josiah Grant (and Magnolia West)

He was sent to guard her body…but he's determined to steal her heart.

WICKED & DEVOTED

Wicked as Sin / Wicked Ever After – Pierce "One-Mile" Walker (and Brea Bell)

He's dangerous. She's off-limits. After one taste, nothing will stop him from making her his.

Wicked as Lies / Wicked and True – Chase "Zyron" Garrett (and Tessa Lawrence)

Wicked as Seduction / Wicked and Forever – Forest "Trees" Scott (and Laila Torres)

He'll protect her…even if he has to take her captive to save her.

As the Wicked & Devoted world continues to collide and explode, you'll see more titles with other characters you know and love. Now that Montilla has been defeated, stay tuned for the kick-off of a new adventure with Matt, as well as books about Kane, Trevor, Ghost, and others!

I have so much in store for you on this wild **Wicked & Devoted** ride!

Hugs and Happy Reading!

Shayla

ABOUT SHAYLA BLACK

LET'S GET TO KNOW EACH OTHER!

Shayla Black is the *New York Times* and *USA Today* bestselling author of more than eighty contemporary, erotic, paranormal, and historical romances. Her books have sold millions of copies and been published in a dozen languages.

As an only child, Shayla occupied herself by daydreaming, much to the chagrin of her teachers. In college, she found her love for reading and started pursuing a publishing career. Though she graduated with a degree in Marketing/Advertising and embarked on a stint in corporate America, her heart was with her stories and characters, so she left her pantyhose and power suits behind.

Shayla currently lives in North Texas with her wonderfully supportive husband, her daughter, and two spoiled tabbies. In her "free" time, she enjoys reality TV, gaming, and listening to an eclectic blend of music.

TELL ME MORE ABOUT YOU.

Connect with me via the links below. You can also become one of my Facebook Book Beauties and enjoy live, interactive #WineWednesday video chats full of fun, book chatter, and more! See you soon!

Website: http://shaylablack.com
VIP Reader Newsletter: http://shayla.link/nwsltr
Shayla Store: https://www.shaylablack.com/bookstore/

Facebook Book Beauties Chat Group: http://shayla.link/FBChat

facebook.com/ShaylaBlackAuthor
instagram.com/shaylablack
tiktok.com/@shayla_black
twitter.com/ShaylaBlackAuth
bookbub.com/authors/shayla-black
pinterest.com/shaylablacksb

OTHER BOOKS BY SHAYLA BLACK

CONTEMPORARY ROMANCE
WICKED & DEVOTED
Romantic Suspense

Wicked as Sin (One-Mile & Brea, part 1)

Wicked Ever After (One-Mile & Brea, part 2)

Wicked as Lies (Zyron & Tessa, part 1)

Wicked and True (Zyron & Tessa, part 2)

Wicked as Seduction (Trees & Laila, part 1)

Wicked and Forever (Trees & Laila, part 2)

Coming Soon:

Wicked as Secrets (Matt & Madison, part 1) (April 11, 2023)

REED FAMILY RECKONING
Angsty, emotional contemporary romance
SIBLINGS

More Than Want You (Maxon & Keeley)

More Than Need You (Griff & Britta)

More Than Love You (Harlow & Noah)

BASTARDS

More Than Crave You (Evan & Nia)

More Than Tempt You (Bethany & Clint)

Coming Soon:

More Than Desire You (Xavian & ??) (November 1, 2022)

FRIENDS

More Than Dare You (Trace & Masey)

More Than Hate You (Sebastian & Sloan)

1001 DARK NIGHTS

More Than Pleasure You (Stephen & Skye)

More Than Protect You (Tanner & Amanda)

More Than Possess You (A Hope Series crossover) (Echo & Hayes)

FORBIDDEN CONFESSIONS (Sexy Shorts)

Sexy Bedtime Stories

FIRST TIME

Seducing the Innocent (Kayla & Oliver)

Seducing the Bride (Perrie & Hayden)

Seducing the Stranger (Calla & Quint)

Seducing the Enemy (Whitney & Jett)

PROTECTORS

Seduced by the Bodyguard (Sophie & Rand)

Seduced by the Spy (Vanessa & Rush)

Seduced by the Assassin (Havana & Ransom)

Seduced by the Mafia Boss (Kristi & Ridge)

FILTHY RICH BOSSES

Tempted by the Billionaire (Savannah & Chad)

Coming Soon:

Tempted by the Executives (January 24, 2023)

THE WICKED LOVERS (Complete Series)

Steamy Romantic Suspense

Wicked Ties (Morgan & Jack)

Decadent (Kimber & Deke)

Delicious (Alyssa & Luc)

Surrender to Me (Kata & Hunter)

Belong to Me (Tara & Logan)

Wicked to Love (Emberlin & Brandon)

Mine to Hold (Delaney & Tyler)

Wicked All the Way (Carlotta & Caleb)

Ours to Love (London, Javier, & Xander)

Wicked All Night (Rachel & Decker)

Forever Wicked (Gia & Jason)

Theirs to Cherish (Callie, Thorpe, & Sean)

His to Take (Bailey & Joaquin)

Pure Wicked (Bristol & Jesse)

Wicked for You (Mystery & Axel)

Falling in Deeper (Lily & Stone

Dirty Wicked (Sasha & Nick)

A Very Wicked Christmas (Morgan & Jack)

Holding on Tighter (Jolie & Heath)

THE DEVOTED LOVERS (Complete Series)

Steamy Romantic Suspense

Devoted to Pleasure (Shealyn & Cutter)

Devoted to Wicked (Karis & Cage)

Devoted to Love (Magnolia & Josiah)

THE UNBROKEN SERIES

(co-authored with Jenna Jacob)

Raine Falling Saga (Complete)

The Broken (Prequel)

The Betrayal

The Break

The Brink

The Bond

Heavenly Rising Saga

The Choice

The Chase

Coming Soon:

The Commitment (August 2, 2022)

THE PERFECT GENTLEMEN (Complete Series)

(co-authored with Lexi Blake)

Steamy Romantic Suspense

Scandal Never Sleeps

Seduction in Session

Big Easy Temptation

Smoke and Sin

At the Pleasure of the President

MASTERS OF MÉNAGE (Complete Series)

(co-authored with Lexi Blake)

Steamy Contemporary Romance

Their Virgin Captive

Their Virgin's Secret

Their Virgin Concubine

Their Virgin Princess

Their Virgin Hostage

Their Virgin Secretary

Their Virgin Mistress

STANDALONE TITLES

Naughty Little Secret

Watch Me

Dirty & Dangerous

Her Fantasy Men

A Perfect Match

THE HOPE SERIES (Complete Series)

Steamy Contemporary Romance

Misadventures of a Backup Bride (Ella & Carson)

Misadventures with My Ex (Eryn & West)

More Than Possess You (Echo & Hayes) (A Reed Family Reckoning crossover)

SEXY CAPERS (COMPLETE SERIES)

Bound and Determined (Kerry & Rafael)

Strip Search (Nicola & Mark)

Arresting Desire (Lucia & Jon)

HISTORICAL ROMANCE

STANDALONES

The Lady and the Dragon

One Wicked Night

STRICTLY SERIES (COMPLETE DUET)

Victorian Historical Romance

Strictly Seduction (Madeline & Brock)

Strictly Forbidden (Kira & Gavin)

BROTHERS IN ARMS (COMPLETE TRILOGY)

Medieval Historical Romance

His Lady Bride (Gwenyth & Aric)

His Stolen Bride (Averyl & Drake)

His Rebel Bride (Maeve & Kieran)

BOXSETS/COLLECTIONS

Wicked and Worshipped (One-Mile and Brea duet)

Wicked and Forbidden (Zyron and Tessa duet)

More Than Promises (Reed Family Reckoning: Siblings)

Forbidden Confessions: First Time

Forbidden Confessions: Protectors

First Glance (A trio of series starters)

The Strictly Duet (Victorian historical romance)

Made in the USA
Las Vegas, NV
19 May 2022

49103078R00154